Twenty-five-year-old Abby McDonald grew up in Sussex, England, and studied Politics, Philosophy and Economics at Oxford University. She began writing at college, becoming music editor of *The Oxford Student* and completing her first novel. She has since worked as a music journalist and entertainment critic, interviewing acts as diverse as LeAnn Rimes, The Kings of Leon, and Marilyn Manson. Her writing has appeared in the *NME, Plan B* magazine, *CosmoGirl!*, and a variety of websites and blogs.

THE LIBERATION OF ALICE LOVE

Alice Love keeps her life running in perfect order. But then her bank card is declined. Someone has emptied her bank account, spending her savings on glamorous holidays and a to-die-for wardrobe, leaving Alice with thousands of pounds' worth of debt. When, to clear her name, she enlists the help of dashing fraud investigator Nathan, she discovers that her thief is closer to home than she imagined. Following the clues from London to Rome and LA, Alice edges into a world where rules are made to be broken. Perhaps her alter ego's extravagant lifestyle is the one Alice should have been leading all along . . . But how far will Alice go to find the truth? And whose life, exactly, is she fighting for?

ABBY McDONALD

THE LIBERATION
OF ALICE LOVE

Complete and Unabridged

CHARNWOOD
Leicester

First published in Great Britain in 2010 by
Arrow Books
The Random House Group Limited
London

First Charnwood Edition
published 2011
by arrangement with
The Random House Group Limited
London

British Library CIP Data

McDonald, Abby.
    The liberation of Alice Love.
    1. Identity theft- -Fiction.
    2. Large type books.
    I. Title
    823.9'2–dc22

    ISBN 978–1–44480–580–2

Published by
F. A. Thorpe (Publishing)
Anstey, Leicestershire

Set by Words & Graphics Ltd.
Anstey, Leicestershire
Printed and bound in Great Britain by
T. J. International Ltd., Padstow, Cornwall

This book is printed on acid-free paper

Dedication

To my family, and the friends who have acted as support, cheerleaders, and critique partners: Elisabeth Donnelly, Veronique Watt, and Narmada Thiranagama. Thanks to Dom Passantino for the email fwd that set this in motion. And finally, thanks to my mother, Ann, for everything.

Acknowledgements

Thanks first, as always, to my agents, Alice Lutyens and Jonny Geller. To Gillian Holmes, Ruth Waldram, and the rest of the fabulous team at Arrow. Huge appreciation to Emma Rose for all her early support, and many thanks to Danny Harrison at CPP Group and Dr Tim Holmes from the School of Social Sciences at Bangor University for their expert advice on identity theft.

1

It began with a vibrator. A smooth, stainless-steel, jewel-encrusted vibrator that — according to the ribbon-trimmed user manual — cost over seven hundred pounds. Even Alice, who valued her orgasms as much as the next woman, had to wonder what delirious pleasures it could possibly deliver to justify that kind of expense.

'Yes, is that customer service?' She blinked awake, almost surprised by the sound of a real human voice. With the soothing hold music, and afternoon sunlight spilling through the attic windows, Alice had been lulled into a daze, tracing the embossed script on the heavy cream box, back and forth, back and forth. She sat up. 'There's been some kind of mistake,' she explained. 'One of your . . . products was delivered today, but I didn't order — No, I don't . . . *Je ne parle pas* . . . *Anglais? Parlez-vous Anglais?'*

The bored-sounding French voice on the other end of the line gave way to another surge of Schubert. Alice let out a long sigh of defeat.

It had arrived that morning: the inconspicuous brown box addressed to her from a company in Paris. Already late, Alice had stuffed it into her bag with a handful of other post; now the box's luxurious contents sat in the middle of her antique desk, utterly out of place surrounded by stacks of contracts and her mug of camomile tea.

It was a mystery.

'What's that?' A familiar head appeared around her open door, blond hair falling in a floppy fringe over warm blue eyes.

Alice jumped. Sweeping the box into a drawer, she quickly leaped up. 'Rupert!' Her voice was strangled with embarrassment. 'Oh, nothing, just . . . a mix-up. What are you doing here?'

'I've got some things to sign, thought I'd come down in person. Besides,' Rupert added, moving closer to kiss her on both cheeks, 'I think I'm due another Lunch.'

They shared a rueful smile. Vivienne's Lunches were notorious. Whenever one of her clients had been going through a dry spell — and might otherwise start questioning the wisdom of their illustrious agent — Alice's boss would whisk them out for a three-hour session of compliments, champagne, and star-studded visions of international acting success. Alice had seen them wander back to the office a hundred times, dazed and delirious with future promise, their faith completely restored.

'Arbutus?'

'No, L'Escargot,' he replied gloomily, naming an even more expensive restaurant. Alice tried not to wince. Things must really be slow.

'Well, good luck,' she offered. Few clients bothered to acknowledge her, let alone brave the perilous winding staircase to say hello, but Rupert had always been the nice one. Too nice. His promising string of period drama parts had slowed to a trickle, and personally, Alice thought his gallant enthusiasm was the problem. The

2

ones who made it as leading men came equipped with brash arrogance, not boyish good looks and a sweet devotion to their wives.

'If you want, your tax declaration is around somewhere,' she suggested, not wanting him to have ventured up there for nothing. She began to click through her files on screen. 'Are you all right waiting?' She glanced up. 'Do you want tea, or something?'

'Oh, I'm fine.' Rupert moved aside a stack of books and took a seat on the battered leather couch. 'The girl at reception is getting me a coffee. She's, ah, very eager to help.'

'I'm sure she is.' Alice murmured. Fresh from drama school, the new assistant, Saskia, was especially accommodating to clients. The attractive, male ones, that was. 'Ah, got it! Let me just print you a — ' The words died on her lips as the computer let out a strangled bleep. Suddenly, her screen began to blur into a sequence of binary code and hieroglyphics.

'No, no!' Alice cried, but it was no use: her mouse was frozen, her keyboard, dead.

'What's wrong?' Rupert hurried to look over her shoulder as Alice stared at the angry-looking symbols. 'Oh. That doesn't look good.'

'No, it doesn't.' She swallowed, not wanting to think about all the client data in peril. 'I wonder if it's just me, or . . . ' An angry cry echoed up from downstairs. ' . . . not.'

She found everyone crammed into the reception area, arguing loudly. Vivienne refused to let the Grayson Wells Agency inhabit anything as ordinary as an office block; instead, Alice worked in a narrow, three-storey town house on a cobbled Soho backstreet. The agents operated out of low-ceilinged nooks, visitors were greeted by a chequer-floored lobby, and Vivienne herself held court from the second-floor drawing room, complete with damask wallpaper and a Georgian-style chaise longue. After years spent wilting under strip lighting in a grey cubicle at a corporate firm in the City, Alice adored her attic hideaway. She could play Radio Three, grow pansies in the window box, and never be bothered by the daily dramas of the other staff.

Well, usually.

Ducking to avoid the low lintel, Alice edged into the room. Vivienne was fluttering her hands as if she was having a fainting fit, the agents were milling about in panic, and Saskia was proclaiming her innocence in between dramatic gasps of dismay. Yes, it was business as usual at Grayson Wells.

'What's happening?' Alice asked. 'Are everyone's computers — '

'Fucked.' Tyrell answered shortly, folding his arms across a spotless white shirt. A new agent from the States, he sauntered around in designer tailoring and box-fresh Converse sneakers, wooing prospective clients with talk about taking their careers to the next level, touching bases, and leveraging their brand potential. 'I'm waiting on an email — '

'My client needs his contracts and — '

'My Black Berry's down and I can't function — '

Alice manoeuvred to the front of the room. 'I

know this is a stupid question,' she said, 'but has anyone called the technician yet?'

There was silence.

'And I'm guessing everyone's turned their computers off at the mains,' she added, 'so this thing can't do any more damage?'

There was a lurch of motion as Anthony, the ageing literary agent, dived towards the power socket, knocking his glasses askew in his rush to yank the plug out. 'There!' He held it triumphantly aloft, the flickering desk lamp reflecting on his bald spot.

'Well done.' Alice patted his dandruff-speckled shoulder. 'Now, what actually happened?'

All eyes turned towards Saskia, standing beside the reception computer in a ruffle-necked blouse and pencil skirt.

'I didn't know it would do that!' she protested immediately, blue eyes wide with innocence under flame-red ringlets. 'I was just downloading a file. For research!'

'Downloading?' Vivienne finally spoke up. Her face was pale as always beneath a severe dyed-black bob; petite figure swathed in a voluminous black pashmina and trailing ropes of pearls.

'A film.' Saskia's voice faltered, as if she realised the gravity of the situation for the first time. 'No Hope ... and Then Death. It's Russian.'

Of course it was.

Alice was about to escape them all and wait for the cavalry of the IT call-out man when she was gripped by a terrible fear. 'You did back up the database, though, didn't you Saskia? Every night, like we talked about?'

Saskia flushed.

Alice closed her eyes for a second. 'When was the last time?' She looked at the girl, pleading. 'Last week? Tell me you backed up before the weekend, at least.'

Saskia bit her lip. 'There were just so many new things to learn. I was meaning to ask someone . . . '

Alice gulped, as the full extent of the damage finally became clear. Months of records, lost!

'Well, what's done is done.' Vivienne clapped her hands together, suddenly roused from her fluster. As Alice watched, Vivienne's gaze slid over the incompetent receptionist, ruined system, and room full of disgruntled staff as if they didn't exist. 'Ah, Rupert.' She brightened. 'Wonderful timing. How about that lunch?'

'Now?' Alice couldn't help but question.

'Of course, dear. Nothing I can do now! You can deal with it, I'm sure. You always do.' Pulling a black cape off the coat stand and tossing it over her shoulders, Vivienne sailed past. Rupert sent Alice an apologetic look, but — like everyone — was powerless in Vivienne's clutches. 'I'll be back later . . . ' Vivienne looked around. ' . . . Perhaps.' Then she was gone, in a cloud of avoidance and heavy Chanel perfume.

* * *

Alice spent the rest of the morning patiently hoisting boxes out of storage. As the company

6

lawyer, she knew it wasn't exactly in her job description to do anything other than construct dense, watertight contracts for Vivienne (and find imaginative ways to pick apart the dense, watertight contracts of everyone else), but Alice had realised soon after joining the agency that details were not Vivienne's strong point. No, too often, it was left to Alice to wrangle things into some semblance of order, but she didn't mind. She'd always been the one to corral things into their place, be they her hopelessly impractical father, wayward friends, or a room full of old client records. There was a certain satisfaction to it, she found: a quiet moment of calm carved out of the ongoing chaos.

With the sleeves of her pale silk blouse rolled up, and a particularly rousing Prokofiev piano sonata playing, Alice had almost finished restoring order when her mobile rang. She scooped it from the depths of her handbag, smiling when she saw the caller ID.

'Let me guess, the dragon lady has gone?' Alice shoved a box out of the way and sank down on to her threadbare rug.

'Just left for a meeting. Can't you hear the Hallelujah Chorus?' Ella laughed. 'Or should it be that song from *The Wizard of Oz*? 'Ding Dong! The Witch is Dead'!' She hummed happily. 'So, sneak out and meet me for a late lunch? I've got a couple of hours, at least.'

Alice sighed. 'I don't think so. I have to wait for the IT guy.'

'But you have the darling Saskia for that stuff. Come on,' Ella wheedled, 'help me enjoy my precious freedom. We could go to that Italian place, the one with the cream cakes.'

'Well . . . ' Alice wavered.

'And didn't you say you need an outfit for Flora's anniversary?' Ella reminded her. 'We could do both. There, efficient enough for you?'

Alice grinned. 'OK, OK. Meet you in twenty minutes?'

'Done!'

★   ★   ★

They ate virtuous salads to balance out the indulgencies of dessert, squeezed into a corner of the tiny restaurant, with the waiters yelling orders over their head — and flirting shamelessly at every opportunity.

'That kid was in love with you,' Alice teased, as they emerged into the sunshine. 'How many water refills did you need?'

'He was just trying to stare down my top, little pervert,' Ella grinned. 'But I scored with the guy at the till, see?' She tried to pass a handful of complimentary truffles, but Alice waved them away, groaning.

'How can you manage any more? That cake was enough to feed four, at least!'

'Lightweight.' Ella popped a chocolate into her mouth. 'It's in my genes, I think. My mum's family were Italian, way back,' she mused, 'so I inherited the ability to eat my body weight in pasta. I would have preferred to look like Sophia Loren, though.'

Alice laughed. 'I know, the exotic genes passed

me by too. My dad practically came out of the womb in tweed and Wellington boots. And my mother . . . ' she paused, suddenly remembering the flash of red lipstick, the hair set in perfect curls, even to go to the village post office. 'She was American. *Is*, I guess.' A group of teenage shoppers pushed between them, laughing, so Alice waited before continuing. 'But Dad and Jasmine, they're practically poster children for the joys of rural life right now. He spent twenty minutes on the phone the other day, telling me about his plans for the greenhouse.'

'Are they coming up for Flora's party?'

'I'm not sure.' Alice sighed at the mention of her wisp of a stepsister.

Ella looked over. 'Aww, I'm sorry I can't be there for back-up. Save you from the sight of them swooning all over each other.'

'It's fine. Or, at least, it will be, when I figure out what on earth to wear,' Alice linked her arm through Ella's. 'You know how much I hate shopping.'

'Then you're lucky it's my specialist subject.' said Ella, steering her into a shop.

Ella wasn't exaggerating. Somehow, she'd been blessed with the skills Alice sorely lacked, and under her watchful eye, outfits were assembled as if they'd been pulled from the pages of a glossy magazine. She never wore anything daring herself, Alice noticed, but there was always a statement necklace or pair of swooping earrings that lifted Ella's conservative wardrobe and mid-length brown hair to something fashion-worthy. Alice flicked through the style pages, yet somehow never quite managed to translate those spurious commandments that tribal (or futuristic, or biker chic) were 'in' to her own neutral wardrobe.

'So how is Flora?' Ella asked, as Alice tugged at the hem of a sundress in yet another clothes shop dressing room. 'Still deep in wedded bliss?'

'I think so. We haven't talked for a while.'

Ella shook her head. 'I can't believe she's married. God, I can't believe *anyone's* married. Or buying property.' She gave Alice a good-natured nudge.

'I'm only thinking about buying,' Alice protested. 'And just because some of us feel it's time to start acting grown-up . . . '

'Don't!' Ella put a hand to her forehead, feigning a swoon. 'You're all the same. Thirty comes looming on the horizon, and suddenly, it's all mortgages and ISAs and panicking because you haven't signed your unborn children up for kindergarten yet.'

They were silent for a moment, Alice staring at her reflection. Thirty. God, she had been trying not to think about that, but Ella was right. There was nothing like the big three zero hanging over them to make every choice seem so much more . . . urgent. She had always thought she'd be settled by now, with a partner and a home and a solid, fulfilling career. If Alice were entirely honest, it was the reason she'd spent the last five years scrupulously saving for her deposit, as that birthday hurried ever closer. She needed something to show for her life, after all.

'What's wrong?'

Alice looked up to find Ella watching her. She shrugged, reaching for a belt to try with the dress. 'Oh, nothing. I'm just wondering what to do about work.' Pausing for a moment, Alice finally admitted what had been itching in the back of her mind for months now. 'I've been feeling sort of . . . restless.'

'The dull monotony, you mean?' Ella adjusted the belt, then added a silk scarf at Alice's neck so that she looked like she'd strolled out of *La Dolce Vita*. 'I still don't see why you don't make the switch to agenting. After all, you can manage all the contract stuff already, and you must know exactly what to do from watching Vivienne. And what *not* to do,' she added with a grin.

'I don't know . . . I've talked about it a few times with Vi, but she's not convinced. Besides, agents need to be, ruthless. Hustlers, you know?'

'Alice Love can be a hustler!' Ella protested. Alice fixed her with a dubious look. 'OK, so maybe you're not slick and insincere like that Tyrell guy, but that should be a good thing. What was it he said to me that time? He'd enjoyed *connecting* with me. Ugh.' She shuddered. 'I'm not a bloody power socket!'

Alice laughed. 'No, it's fine. I'm OK doing what I am right now. Besides, I could always see about moving to a bigger agency, doing contracts at one of the corporate places.'

'You mean processing twice the paperwork for half the satisfaction?'

'But three times the money.'

Ella tutted. 'There's more to life than cold hard cash, my dear.'

Alice tutted right back. 'Tell that to my bank.' She looked at her reflection again, trying to see past the black bra-straps peeping over the neckline, and her boring French pleat. 'All right,' she decided, realising her lunch hour was dangerously close to being over, 'this is the one.'

She quickly changed back into her work clothes, Ella waiting with her at the counter while the saleswoman packed her purchases in tissue paper and a crisp paper bag. 'What about you — anything thrilling planned for the weekend?'

'Hmmm . . . there's always yoga.' Ella met Alice's eye for a moment, and they both laughed.

They'd met in the polished exercise space of a local gym, suffering through the strenuous contortions of a beginner's class. By the time the goateed instructor decided to turn the heat up another five degrees 'to really let you sweat it out', Ella and Alice had suffered enough. They made their escape when he went to change the CD, dashing from the room to the strains of Peruvian panpipes.

'And . . . ' Ella looked hesitant, 'I might have a date.'

'Ella! You didn't say.'

Ella blushed. 'I know, a rare and momentous event. It's a set-up, though, so bound to end in disaster,' she sighed. 'A friend of a friend of Julie's, at the office.'

'Ah, the wonderful Julie.' Alice had heard plenty of stories about Ella's colleague's need to fix up everyone in sight. 'What do you think, will you — ' She stopped mid-sentence. The

12

sales-woman was waiting with an impatient expression.

'It's been declined.' She dropped Alice's card on the counter with a sneer.

Alice frowned. 'That's impossible, I just . . . Never mind, use this one.' She found her wallet again and passed her back-up credit card.

'Anything wrong?' Ella asked.

'No, it's fine.' Alice shook her head, while the woman ran up the sale again, this time keeping a suspicious eye on them, as if they were about to bolt. 'Probably just a mix-up with my bank. They've cancelled that card three times this year. Last time, they said they sent me the wrong colour, can you believe? Like it makes a difference.'

'Ugh,' Ella agreed. 'Mine's not too bad, if you need to switch. Except I have to spend about an hour on hold every time I want to reach an actual human being!'

★ ★ ★

It wasn't quite an hour, but after being shuffled between three different departments that afternoon — all of them with a tenuous understanding of the words 'I didn't order this' — Alice finally gave up on the mystery of the jewel-encrusted vibrator. As far as she could tell, she hadn't been billed for it, so wrapping the box in a fresh layer of packing paper, she printed up the return address and reached to add it to her stack of post. There had been a moment when she'd wavered, looking curiously at the dull gleam of

13

the metal and its strange curves, full of promise. Now, turning the box over in her hands, she wondered, could it really be worth so much?

Alice smiled to herself. It was unlikely. For all their aesthetic appeal, toys like this were for people who preferred the accessories to real sex; the performance, rather than the act. Alice had never been one to bind herself up in uncomfortable lingerie, or fuss over dripping candles. No, she preferred a little more honesty in life. Tossing the package aside, she turned back to her stack of paperwork.

And that, as far as she was concerned, was the end of it.

2

After the trials at the office that week, Alice would have relished a weekend of relaxation; instead, she found herself hovering awkwardly in the corner of her stepsister's vast walled garden in Hampstead, clutching a glass of Pimm's and worrying about her lipstick smudging.

'Canapé?'

Alice blinked at a silver tray of elaborate appetisers, all coloured a vivid shade of pink to match the party theme. 'No, thank you.'

She shook her head politely, watching as the waitress circulated amongst the crowd of guests who were scattered across the immaculate lawn. Although there had been no mention of dress code, there was obviously a memo Alice hadn't received. Her blue silk sundress may have looked the perfect garden party choice, but every other woman was draped in shades of palest cream and caramel, an array of blousy tops and layered gold jewellery that made her feel as stiff as a shop mannequin amongst the lounging, honey-hued guests.

'There you are!'

Alice turned towards the huge, stuccoed house as Flora, in a floaty print dress, emerged out of the French doors onto the patio. She surveyed the garden in delight. 'Isn't it lovely?'

'Lovely,' Alice echoed faintly. And it was. From the white, canopied awnings to the

15

spotless tables, overflowing with pink cupcakes and even pinker flower arrangements, the garden was beautiful, a testament to what a husband with a private equity fortune could achieve. Even the sky was a cloudless blue, the sun warm on her bare shoulders. Alice took a slice of cucumber from her drink and nibbled. It, at least, wasn't pink.

'Have you met everyone yet?' Flora linked her arm through Alice's and led her onto the lawn. She had turned twenty-four just a few months before, but with her wispy, petite frame and expression of perpetual bemusement, she still looked exactly like the child who had gazed absently at Alice across the table at Christmas and bank holidays for the last ten years. 'I don't even know half the people here,' she confided, waving at different groups as they passed, 'but Stefan has all these clients, and their wives, and friends . . .'

'And accountants, and car dealers,' Alice finished, smiling. Despite the joking, she found her brother-in-law a solid, sturdy relief from her family's vague chaos. She'd had her reservations when they met, three years ago. Flora had been toying with watercolours at art school when she literally tumbled into Stefan's lap at Glyndebourne. At first, Alice had wondered what a laid-back, thirty-year-old Swedish financier could possibly want with her dreamy, childlike stepsister, but somehow, it worked. Stefan adored Flora, Flora basked in his adoration, and within months, they were walking down the rose-petal-strewn aisle.

16

'Are Dad and Jasmine coming up?' Alice looked around for a familiar face, but found none.

Flora shook her head, fine blonde hair fluttering out in the breeze. 'No, I called this morning, but Mum's deep in a new sculpture and I don't think Dad's come out of his workshop in two days. You can tell Mum's not going anywhere — it took her five minutes just to remember where he was!'

Alice nodded, well used to their eccentricities.

'Here we are!' Flora led Alice to a group of tanned, tawny-haired women. 'Everyone, this is my sister, Alice.' There were coos of welcome, and she began the loop of air-kisses as each woman was presented in turn. 'Alice, meet Mimi, and Sascha, and Ginny . . . '

★　★　★

Half an hour later, Alice was beginning to notice a theme. 'Is there anyone here . . . younger?' she asked casually, finding Flora by the dessert table. 'I mean, everybody is around my age, aren't they? Or older.'

'Nathalia is twenty-three.' Flora pointed out a doe-eyed model in what Alice could only assume were next season's hot, draped peg-leg trousers. 'With Jonty. He and Stefan used to race yachts together round the Mediterranean.'

'Mmm.' Alice murmured tactfully. Jonty may well be a very nice man, but he was also pushing fifty. 'What about your art-school friends? Or people from back home.'

17

Flora gave a small shrug. She picked at frosting on her tiny cake, earlier enthusiasm fading. 'It's been hard to keep up with people.' Her voice was soft. 'They were weird enough about Stefan, but then when we bought the house, and I got the deal with my paintings . . .' she trailed off, looking so mournful, Alice felt guilty. She often felt guilty around Flora.

'Well, everyone here seems nice!' she exclaimed brightly. 'And if they weren't happy for your success, then they can't have been good friends to begin with.'

'That's what Stefan says. When Zara sold her first print, we all had the best celebration. But when things started happening with me . . .'

'It's all right.' Alice glanced around, wishing she hadn't brought it up. 'Oh, look, there's Julian! He said he'd be dropping by. Probably to scope out your catering. You know he's always sizing up the competition.'

She steered Flora firmly across the garden, chatting about the divine profiteroles in an effort to raise her party spirits again. She couldn't blame her for the moping, but she had some sympathy for those art-school friends too. Flora's paintings were pedestrian, to say the least: endless dreamy watercolours of flowers and pastoral scenes that Ella had once described as 'not so much art, as a visual sleeping pill'. None the less, Stefan had somehow used his business contacts to wrangle a deal with a publisher, and now Flora was officially the twelfth most-sold artist in the country; her prints (and coasters, and calendars, and wipe-clean placemats)

18

snapped up in gift shops from Scarborough to the Isle of Wight. Alice could see how that might sting her old classmates, struggling in their run-down bedsits, with night jobs waitressing to get by.

'Happy anniversary!' Julian strode over to meet them, sweeping Flora into a bear hug. He was casual as ever in his weekend uniform of corduroy trousers and a crumpled shirt; after ten years of friendship, Alice would have been shocked to see him in a tie. 'You outdid yourself this time, Flor, everything looks great.'

Flora brightened. She looked around at the pink wonderland with a faint smile. 'It's all Stefan — he found the best party planner through a client. He did Sienna too.'

'And who did you use for the food?'

'See,' Alice laughed. 'I told you!'

'Told her what?' Julian stole a pastry from Alice's plate, looking back and forth between them. He had oversize, almost dramatic features: a large nose, deep-set eyes, wide cheek-bones. Caught still for a moment, they didn't seem to add up, until he made a gesture or expression, and then they slipped together perfectly.

'Just you and your obsession.' Alice slapped his hand away lightly. 'One of these days, you're actually going to have to open that restaurant, instead of just talking about it all the time.'

Julian gave a sheepish shrug. 'When I get my ducks in a row. Anyway, I have to dash now, I just wanted to say congrats and all.'

'Oh,' Flora pouted, 'can't you stay longer? There's going to be croquet, and the cake.'

'Sorry. Yasmin's flight gets in at five. I have to be there to pick her up.'

'But — '

'I'll save you a slice,' Alice interrupted, before Flora could guilt-trip him into staying. 'We still on for lunch tomorrow?'

'Definitely.' Julian shot one last look at the dessert table. 'Yasmin will probably still be crashed out with jet lag, so I'll meet you at the pub around one?'

'Perfect.'

★　★　★

By the time the sunlight faded to a rosy dusk, the Pimm's was flowing freely, and laughter was loud in the candle-lit garden. Alice made her excuses to Mimi (and Ginny, and Sascha), slipping towards the house for a few moments of calm. She'd offered her advice on a breach-of-contract suit Ginny had mentioned, and inadvertently found herself holding a legal advice session for the next hour: advising on nanny disputes, fiddling accountants, and shoddy workmanship on those vital conservatories.

'Leaving already?' Stefan called to her from the patio. He and Flora were tucked together on an antique love-swing, her hair even blonder against the blue of his shirt. Their children were going to look angelic, Alice could say that for sure.

'Just taking a breather.' She wandered closer. 'Don't tell me you've been locked up in your study all this time?'

'On a call, with Hong Kong,' Flora answered for him, slightly petulant.

'Shame on you,' Alice teased. 'Workaholic.'

'Don't remind this one.' Stefan gave Flora's tiny shoulders a squeeze, grinning. 'She still hasn't forgiven me for the wedding.'

'You took a call,' Flora protested. 'Two hundred guests, a lorry-load of imported roses, and when I appear at the end of the aisle, you're off in the vestry arguing over returns!'

Stefan gave an exaggerated sigh, hanging his head. 'See, she won't let me forget it.'

Alice looked at Flora, tucked snugly in the crook of his arm. 'Don't hold it over him for ever,' she agreed a little wistfully.

'Oh, I will. How else do you think I got everything pink?'

Alice watched Flora's face glow. The tender intimacy between Flora and Stefan was still touching to see. Alice herself had only fleeting memories of experiencing that kind of love, years ago, and when the months stretched out alone, Alice even wondered if she'd ever really known it at all. So at rare family events or holidays she watched them as if she were an anthropologist, studying for proof of a foreign tribe. The light glances, the reassuring touch — the completeness of their world together was beautiful, and almost baffling to her. To share that much with somebody; to need someone the way Flora so clearly did . . . Alice could hardly imagine it.

'Do you need anything from inside?' she asked, automatically checking the drinks and thinning dessert table. 'I could bring some things out, if you need.'

'No, no, you're a guest,' Stefan insisted, wrapping his arms carefully around Flora. 'Just enjoy yourself.'

Alice left them curled together on the swing and made her way into the cool of the house, relaxing as the chatter of the party receded behind her.

'They're that way.'

She looked up. A man in a loose linen suit was coming down the hallway towards her. Alice thought she recognised him from outside; perhaps they had even been introduced in that first whirl of greetings. 'I'm sorry?'

'The bathrooms,' he explained, his voice edged with an American accent. He made a show of looking around before leaning in, conspiratorially. 'I've got to warn you, it's kind of a trek. You take a left past the stairs, and then a right . . . ' He sketched out his route in the air before correcting himself with mock seriousness. 'No, I tell a lie: it's another left, at the strange ceramic statue. A horse, I think?'

'Unicorn,' Alice said with a smile.

The man raised his eyebrows. 'I stand corrected. And the little bronze figurines in the hallway . . . ?'

'Dolphins.'

'Really? Huh. I would have guessed mutant slugs myself.'

Alice couldn't help but laugh. Flora's décor had always been eclectic, to say the least.

'You need a map?' The man lingered in the

hallway with her, making a show of patting down his pockets. Up close, he was square-jawed and sturdy, with leather braces edging out from under his linen jacket, like something from a Prohibition-era movie. He made a change from the rest of Stefan's sharp-suited guests, Alice noted, relieved she wasn't the only one out of place. 'I think I've got a napkin here somewhere . . .'

'That's all right, I know my way around,' Alice assured him, and then, in case he thought she was snooping, added, 'I'm Flora's sister.'

'Really?' He glanced at her in surprise.

Alice bristled, just imagining the comparison that was going on in his mind. It was always the same whenever people heard that they were related. Blonde and ethereal, she wasn't. But the man simply gave her a teasing grin. 'You don't seem to have inherited her love for all things pink.'

Alice relaxed. 'We're stepsisters,' she explained, 'The pink is definitely in her genes.'

'I guess that settles the nature versus nurture debate,' he laughed.

'Someone should alert the media,' Alice agreed.

There was a pause, one of those natural conversational spaces Alice knew signalled the time for a polite retreat, but this man was such a welcome, friendly break from the forced conversation that she lingered.

He stuck out a hand. 'Nathan Forrest.'

'Alice,' she shook it firmly, 'Alice Love.'

'Good to meet you.'

'So ... how do you know Stefan?' Nathan didn't strike Alice as the hedge fund type, but perhaps there was a Rolex lurking under those sleeves, and home was a mansion in Holland Park.

He hesitated. 'It's actually kind of an embarrassing story.'

'Really?' Now it was Alice's turn to raise an eyebrow. 'You have to tell me, with a build-up like that.' When he made a face, she added, 'You should have just lied, said you met through work or something.'

'We did, kind of,' Nathan explained, leaning back against the wall. 'It was one of those corporate parties, a couple of years ago. I was trying to impress a potential client, this Russian oil guy, and for some reason, he was determined to set me up with his daughter.'

'Lucky you.'

'Nothing lucky about it,' Nathan shook his head at the memory. 'She was eighteen, and way more interested in flirting with the bartender than hanging out with me. So the party goes on, I notice the kid's gone, and when I go looking, I find her stumbling out of a supply closet with not just the one guy, but a bus boy too!'

'Ouch!' Alice watched him, charmed by the note of self-deprecation in his voice.

'Wait, it gets better. The guys make a hasty exit, leaving me to try and get her dress zipped — when who should show up?'

'Daddy dearest?'

'Yup.' Nathan grimaced at the memory. 'I was this close to getting 'disappeared' to Siberia by his hulking bodyguards, when Stefan appears from nowhere with a bottle of twenty-year-old Scotch. We manage to get the man so drunk, he doesn't even remember, come morning.'

'That's Stefan,' Alice said, laughing. 'You can always rely on him in a crisis.'

'The man should join the UN,' Nathan agreed. 'What about you?' he asked, tilting his head slightly as he looked at her. 'Are you an artist like Flora?'

'Oh, no. I'm a lawyer. I never really had the creative spark.'

'No? Some lawyers are the most creative bastards I know, at least when it comes to their billing,' Nathan grinned.

'I wish. I just stick to contracts,' Alice explained. 'I like the order of them, the structure. Everything has to be precise, or the whole thing falls apart.' She stopped, realising how boring she must sound, but Nathan was nodding.

'It's all in the details. Still, aren't you tempted to slip some small print in sometimes?' he asked. 'You know, 'I the undersigned do pledge my soul to Satan . . . ' '

Alice widened her eyes in mock outrage. 'Mr Forrest! Are you implying I'm ever less than scrupulously professional?'

'I wouldn't dream of it, Ms Love.' Nathan dipped his head in polite contrition. 'I'm sure you're the model of good business and decorum.'

They laughed.

'It has crossed my mind sometimes,' Alice

confided. 'Not to bargain their souls away — my boss takes care of that — but to slip something in. Move a decimal point, maybe, just to see if anyone notices. Most of the time, I wonder if I'm the only one reading the things.'

'A whole decimal point? You rebel, you.'

'That's me,' Alice agreed wryly. 'I'm living life on the edge.'

There was another pause, but this time, Alice thought she'd better not linger. 'I should . . . ' She pointed vaguely further into the house.

'Oh, sure.' Nathan gave an easy smile. 'I'll send out a search party if you don't make it back in, what, an hour?'

'Right.' Alice smiled. 'I'll see you out there, I'm sure.'

She turned, but had only taken a few steps down the hall when he called, 'Wait, Alice.'

She looked back. He was framed by the evening light streaming through the far door.

'I was thinking . . . ' He seemed to be assessing her. Then he reached some decision, and asked, 'Do you want to get out of here?'

Alice stared, taken aback.

Coming closer, Nathan said mischievously, 'I'm pretty much ready to leave, so I thought, maybe you'd like to come.'

'Come where?' Alice was still confused.

He shrugged. 'Dinner, drinks . . . I know a great hotel in Paris, if you're in the mood for a trip.'

'Paris?'

'Sure, cute little place, in the fifth *arrondissement*,' Nathan played along. 'We could stare meaningfully at art, and have blazing fights in restaurants.'

'Over red wine and macaroons?'

'I'm more a *pain au chocolat* man myself, but sure, whatever you want.' He smiled, skin crinkling warmly at the edge of his eyes. For a moment, Alice let herself be amused. 'Wait, you're serious?'

'I never lie about pastries.'

'I mean, Paris?'

Nathan just nodded, utterly at ease. 'Why not?' He began to hum an old Cole Porter song, 'I Love Paris.'

Alice wanted to dismiss it as an outlandish joke, but he was still watching her, something new in his eyes. A note of challenge.

The proposition suddenly became clearer.

'I — I don't even know you,' she said slowly, surprised to feel a faint thrill.

'What's to know?' Nathan waited, casual. As if he did this all the time. 'It's, what, a two-hour trip on Eurostar? Plenty of time. I'll start at the beginning, if you want: the toilet-training years. Or we can skip ahead, to first grade. Miss Kellan, if I remember right . . . '

Alice smiled, despite herself. 'That's OK,' she stopped him. 'I get the picture.'

'So what's the hold-up?' Nathan began to back away, beckoning. 'We should say our goodbyes before your sister starts that croquet game. She was saying something about pink sashes for team uniforms . . . '

Alice's mouth dropped open as she finally realised the truth: for all his joking and easy

27

charm, this man really meant them to leave for some foreign triste.

Together. Now.

She felt herself blush, aware of his presence in an entirely different way. The smile that had been so casual took on new meaning; the friendly banter between them was now loaded and reckless. Alice was suddenly self-conscious in a way she hadn't felt in a long while; a delicious sense of possibility shivering down her spine. For a brief, tantalising moment, she imagined it just as he suggested: the charming little hotel, the romantic restaurant, strolling arm in arm down the Champs-Elysées . . .

But just soon enough, her brain snapped back to life.

'I can't,' Alice said, flustered. 'I mean, you're a complete stranger!' Her voice came out louder than she'd intended, ringing with disapproval.

Straight away Nathan gave a shrug.' Hey, no problem. It was only a thought.'

Alice didn't know what to say. She thought she should feel offended, but this wasn't a drunk, lurching pass, this was . . . polite. Almost daring. 'Well . . . thank you?' She managed at last.

His lips twitched with amusement. 'You're welcome.'

'Enjoy, um, the rest of your evening.'

She backed away, and then turned, wandering down the hallway in a daze. After making a couple of blind turns, Alice found herself in the kitchen, drifting in the middle of a sea of polished granite counter-tops.

Do you want to get out of here?

His words repeated, full of promise. A cute little hotel in Paris . . . ? She found herself blushing at the idea. She wasn't the most spontaneous person, even Alice would admit that, but taking off with a complete stranger to, what, have rampant sex at some undisclosed location? No, it was ridiculous, not to mention irresponsible and quite possibly dangerous too, she told herself sternly. He clearly didn't know her at all.

Alice absently reached for a tray of those cupcakes and bit into the fluffy topping.

Completely ridiculous.

3

Monday arrived too soon, and by the time Alice was settled at her desk, surveying the stack of work awaiting her, it felt as if she'd never left. The blue skies that had blazed all weekend were gone, and now her windows rattled with a dull grey drizzle; summer, it seemed, was still a long way away. She delayed the inevitable for a while: watering her plants, setting her radio to one of Chopin's particularly mournful waltzes, but soon there was no avoiding it. Alice braced herself, and reached for the first contract in the pile.

A chat window from Ella appeared on-screen: '*Remind me never to go on a blind date. EVER.*'

'*Bad?*' Alice typed, gladly turning away from her inbox.

'*He was writing a graphic novel. About a time-travelling gnome.*'

Alice spluttered on her camomile tea. '*This I've got to hear.*'

Ella's reply came straight away. '*Tonight? I scored tickets to the Liberty Reigns premiere — our client has product placement in every bloody scene.*'

'*Ooh, I wanted to see that, but Tyrell snatched our client freebies.*'

'*Leicester Square @ 7?*'

'*See you then!*'

Alice had barely finished typing when she heard footsteps on the stairs. She minimised the

30

window and quickly reached for the nearest papers guiltily.

'Hiya!' Saskia burst in with an armful of post. Alice relaxed.

'Morning.' She gave her a smile, reaching to take the mail.

Saskia dumped it on the nearest surface instead, sending a neat stack scattering to the floor. 'Whoops! Let me help you with — '

'No!' Alice yelped, as she reached towards a painstakingly sorted pile of contracts. 'I mean, it's fine. I have it all under control.'

'OK.' Saskia gave her a saccharine smile. 'Oh, I need the administrator passwords. Vi wants me to do some resetting stuff.'

Alice paused. What kind of havoc could she wreak with those? 'If you're sure . . . ' She found the master list in her top drawer and reluctantly scribbled down the codes. 'Be careful with them,' she warned. 'They can access all our payroll details.'

Saskia rolled her eyes. 'Of course!' She turned to go. 'Oh, there were some messages for you.'

'Really?' Alice straightened.

'Just a couple of clients. About tax stuff?' Saskia shrugged. 'I can email them up.'

'Oh,' Alice sat back again. 'Thanks.'

As Saskia bounded back down the stairs, Alice felt a small pang of disappointment. It was foolish, she knew, but she'd spent Sunday hoping that Nathan would call. It would be easy enough for him to get her number and although she'd been thrown by his proposition, Alice couldn't help but feel that thrill of possibility. It had been so long since she'd met anyone interesting, let alone someone who seemed to like her too — enough to invite her on a scandalous weekend abroad, at least. Alice idly toyed with her pen as she remembered his expression, and the flash of interest in his eyes. Perhaps he would invite her to dinner, or drinks . . .

Alice stopped herself. What was she even thinking? She didn't waste time pining over men; she'd learned that lesson years ago. If they were interested, they would do something about it, and if they didn't . . . Well, then they clearly didn't care enough to waste her time wondering over them. It was simple, far simpler than any books or magazines or even her friends would admit. Believing otherwise, she knew, would only leave her feeling an ache every night; absence like a physical form in the empty bed beside her.

Alice turned the music a little louder, and went back to work.

★   ★   ★

She had almost untangled the mess of an option clause a producer had tried to slip through when her business line lit up. Alice reached for it absently, still scribbling in the margins when she heard her stepsister gush, 'Sweetie, hi!'

'Flora?' she stopped, surprised. 'Is everything OK?'

'Hmm? Oh, I'm fine.' Her voice was light. 'How are you?'

'I'm . . . good.' Alice frowned. She and Flora usually kept up with brief, infrequent emails, and she had only seen her a couple of days ago. 'It was a lovely party, really beautiful.'

'Thanks!' Flora exclaimed. 'It was pretty, wasn't it? Ginny asked for the decorator's number, and oh, those éclairs! You were right about them,' she giggled. 'I found the tray of uneaten ones and couldn't help myself. I think I ate at least five!'

'Oh dear,' Alice murmured.

'It was awful,' Flora continued merrily. 'I woke up feeling like such a pig. But Sascha sent me over details of a great detox. You consult with a nutritionist, and get rid of all processed sugars and carbs.'

'That's . . . nice.'

'Stefan's working round the clock again!' Flora chirped. 'But he's promised me a holiday soon, somewhere with sparkling white beaches and no phone lines at all.'

'Mm-hm.' Alice's gaze drifted back to her desk. Now, if she could just change the section on intellectual property rights . . .

'The Caribbean, maybe, or somewhere in South America. I don't know about hurricanes, but Nathan talked about this little place — '

'Nathan?' Alice snapped back to the conversation. 'What did he say? I mean,' she forced herself to sound more casual, 'we chatted for a while, I think. He's the American, isn't he?'

Flora wasn't fooled. She let out a squeal of excitement. 'Ooh! Do you like him? Do you want me to fix you up? I could put a dinner party together, or talk to him for you, or — '

'No!' Alice yelped. She had a sudden flash of

Flora running around, gossiping to Stefan, or worse still, Nathan. Her stomach lurched. 'I mean it, Flora,' she said quickly. 'We only talked for a minute, you're getting carried away.'

'But — '

'No,' Alice said sternly. 'Promise me?'

'Promise,' Flora muttered. 'But we should still have dinner, the two of us. Or lunch sometime. Or drinks!'

'That sounds nice,' Alice replied slowly. 'Why don't you email me over the date? I'm on my way out for lunch now, but I'll let you know.'

'OK!' Flora sounded far too excited. 'Will do!'

Hanging up, Alice pulled on her jacket and hurried down the stairs, as if leaving right away would make her excuse to Flora less of a lie. The Grayson Wells office was tucked away just off Carnaby Street, and as Alice fell into step with the rest of the tourists and midday shoppers, she tried to shake off a slight sense of unease at Flora's sudden avalanche of invitations.

The two of them had never been close. The year her father met Jasmine, Alice left for university, and having spent her adolescence making sure he surfaced from his current historical obsession long enough to eat and occasionally sleep, it was a relief to hand responsibility to someone else. That is, until it became clear that the wafting, temperamental artist and her wide-eyed thirteen-year-old had as tenuous a grasp on domesticity as he did. But by then, Alice was a safe hundred miles away from their ramshackle cottage, and returned only occasionally after that, to check Jasmine hadn't burned the house down with her incense, or that her father wasn't wasting away on a diet of wild nettle soup and organic oatcakes.

No, Alice thought, as she reached Pret and swiftly assessed the chilled cabinets; Flora had always remained something of a stranger to her, a needy, emotional girl who would burst into tears during *EastEnders* and sit, watching birds in the garden with curious concentration. Now, the space between them was something more than their age difference, but Alice was content with their usual rhythm of warm detachment. After all, they had never conspired together against their parents, whispered secrets, or fought angrily the way other siblings did; there was no shared childhood or fierce intimacy to bind them together now they were grown.

Except now Flora was reaching out, clearly hopeful, and Alice didn't know why.

It wasn't until she reached the head of the lunchtime queue to pay for her salad that she remembered the problem with her debit card.

'Sorry, sorry . . . ' Fumbling hopelessly for change, she resorted to grabbing at crisps and useless snack bars to meet the credit card minimum. The crowd behind her shifted impatiently while she went through the routine of swipe and scribble, already resigning herself to another afternoon on hold. But to her surprise, back at the office, her call was answered almost immediately, by a bored-sounding Scottish woman called Laura.

'If you could give me the sixteen-digit number, sort code and expiry, please,' Laura rattled off in a blank monotone. Alice recited the details obediently, cocking her head to trap the phone against her shoulder as she peeled off the lid of her salad and carefully drizzled a tiny amount of dressing over the leaves.

'If you'll just bear with me . . . '

There was a light tap at the door, and Saskia poked her head around. 'I've got some papers,' she whispered loudly. Alice waved her in.

'Miss Love?'

'Yes, sorry,' Alice turned back to the phone.

'Can you confirm your mother's maiden name?'

'Scott,' she scribbled her signature on Saskia's pages in quick succession, 'her maiden name was Scott, and my postcode is N1 OHD.' Putting her hand over the phone, she asked Saskia, 'Take those too, by the door? I need another five copies of each.'

Saskia nodded, retreating just as Laura seemed to make some kind of breakthrough. 'Ah, I see,' she said, the monotone rising ever so slightly. 'For your convenience, it's now our policy to cancel cards after dispatching a replacement. You need to switch to the new one.'

Alice sighed. 'But I haven't got the new one yet.' She stabbed at a slice of cucumber in frustration.

'But it says here it was dispatched last month, on the twenty-fifth.'

'Well, I never got it.' Sinking lower in her seat, Alice wondered why so many hugely inconvenient things were done in the name of her convenience: Tube maintenance at weekends,

36

self-service check-out aisles . . .

'That's funny, it says here the new card has been active for two weeks.'

Alice sat up with a jolt. 'What?'

'I'm going to have to transfer you to an agent in our fraud unit,' Laura trilled.

'No, wait,' Alice tried to stop her. 'What do you mean, 'active'?'

'Please hold.'

While a panpipe version of one of Boyzone's greatest hits played, Alice flipped to the back page of her organiser and used the details there to log on to her bank website, anxiety building with every passing second. She didn't normally access it at work, suspicious that the network wasn't as secure as the tech people liked to believe, but this was an emergency. As her account slowly loaded, she tried to remember the last time she'd seen a statement. Not for at least a week, and she hardly ever checked the balance at the ATM . . .

Her balance flashed up on screen. Two thousand, six hundred and seventy pounds overdrawn.

Overdrawn!

'This is Ahmed in fraud prevention, can I help you? Hello?'

Alice struggled to find words. On the screen in front of her was a litany of spending that had drained her current account beyond empty before the month was even half-way through. A hundred and twenty-two pounds in Liberty's? Over two hundred pounds in the Apple Store? The last time Alice had visited Selfridges, it was to spend twelve pounds on a Clinique mascara, but according to her statement, somebody had charged sixty-odd pounds for lingerie there only two days ago. Suddenly, that luxurious vibrator began to make a lot more sense.

'Hello?'

Alice finally broke out of her shock, and, taking a deep breath, began to speak. 'Hi,' she swallowed, still fixated on that tiny negative sign next to her balance. 'I think we've got a problem . . . '

* * *

'Shred everything!' Ella declared that evening, the minute Alice explained what had happened. 'They have gangs out there now, fishing through the bins for all your old statements and stuff, it's awful.' She plucked two glasses of wine from a passing waiter and steered them through the throngs milling around in the cinema lobby.

Outside, Alice could hear faint cries from the fans lining the red carpet, waving their banners with glee, but inside, there was a different kind of chaos as the industry insiders made their rounds, whipping through the crowd, and calling out to old acquaintances across the room.

Ella located a free sofa in the corner and gracefully sprawled onto the overstuffed cushions. 'I'm serious. Get one of those machines from an office supply place and just destroy everything.'

'I will.' Alice sunk down beside her. 'At least they only got access to that one account.' She tried to look on the bright side. 'I checked my savings and credit card — they're all fine.'

'Thank goodness.' Ella reached up absently to tug free light brown tendrils of hair catching in her gold filigree earrings. 'Well, here's to catching the bastards.'

'Amen.' They clinked glasses. Alice tried to relax, soaking up the bustle of excitement as the room began to fill. Premieres and launch parties were a perk of the job — when the other agents didn't snatch up the invites, that was — but Alice didn't just love them for the star-spotting. A-listers tended to lose their impact after prolonged exposure; noticing a screen god pick his teeth, or that doyenne of British cinema forget to wash her hands in the ladies' tended to drain their mystery. No, Alice liked to watch everyone else: the people who were clearly revelling in the achievement of all their dreams. The writers, the directors, the debut performers still breathless from their big break — there was something wonderful about playing her part in that, however small.

'Any sign of the man himself yet?' Ella scanned the room, excited.

'Chris Carmel?' Alice looked for the broad shoulders and blond, chiselled looks of the latest Hollywood god. 'I thought he was gay now?'

'No! Really? God, soon there won't be anyone left to fantasise about during mediocre sex.'

Alice laughed for what felt like the first time all day. 'Never mind. There's always George. Or Brad, Or Jake, or Clive . . . '

'Ah, the trusty back-ups. Ooh, what's this?'

Ella reached for the glossy estate agent's folder spilling out of Alice's bag. 'Looking at flats? Don't tell me you're finally going to take the plunge.'

'I think so,' Alice replied. 'I can't be like Julian, and put things off for ever. Besides, I've got the deposit lined up, and my landlord is being a pain again. He sent me a note, warning me about noise after you came over for dinner last week. Apparently, the sound of our heels on the floor kept him up past ten.'

'What?' Ella exclaimed. 'We were watching *Empire Records*, not doing the bloody flamenco!'

Alice shrugged. 'I suppose he's got super-human hearing. I'm on probation now.'

'Bastard.' Ella flipped through the brochure. 'So let me guess, you're dreaming of your perfect little bijou flat, with bay windows and a balcony?'

'Not quite.' The estate agent had pointed her towards a new development in a gated area set back from Stoke Newington High Street.

Ella frowned at the photos. 'This? It's kind of soulless. I pictured you somewhere with, I don't know, character.'

'Character costs,' Alice told her, wistfully. The red brick exterior and the white, boxy rooms may not look impressive, but on a single income, she was lucky to find anything reasonable at all. 'This place is a solid investment.'

'If you say . . . ' Ella put the brochure aside. 'I'm sure it's great in person.' She looked around, 'Come on, let's make a dash for the loos before this thing starts. I heard it goes on for hours.'

★ ★ ★

They took turns manoeuvring in the tiny lavatories, freshening their lipstick while the other stall remained locked and suspiciously silent — save the odd shuffle and sniffing noise.

'Lily Larton,' Ella said, the moment they left the room. She tapped her nose meaningfully. 'I heard they dragged her out of rehab to do the promo circuit for this.'

'How do you even know this stuff?'

'Never underestimate the PR people. We have eyes everywhere!' Ella gave a mysterious look. They took up position on the edge of the room. 'So how was the party? Did Flora smother you with fairy cakes and bonbons?'

Alice felt herself blush.

'Aha!' Ella exclaimed. 'You have gossip!'

'It's nothing,' Alice protested, self-conscious. 'I just . . . There was a man,' she admitted. 'And he sort of . . . propositioned me.'

'Alice! Was he hot?'

Alice exhaled, remembering Nathan and their curious conversation. 'Yes. Kind of . . . rugged. And charming too. But what was I supposed to do?' she protested. 'Leave with a complete stranger? I'd probably have wound up dead in an alleyway somewhere.'

'Or enjoying a hot, sweaty marathon of mind-blowing sex.'

Alice rolled her eyes. 'Right. Because that

41

happens. Anyway, there's no point, he hasn't called.'

'Uh, you could have given him a chance — '

'Ella! You know that's just not me.'

'Well, maybe it should be.'

Alice was just about to launch a defence of staying safe and well, without her limbs hacked off, when they were interrupted by a high-pitched voice cutting through the noise of the crowd.

'Alice! Sweetie!'

Heads turned to watch the angular woman sashay towards them, dropping air kisses on both of Alice's cheeks. 'Look at you!' the woman cried, eyes bright beneath a black, blunt-cut fringe. 'It's been for ever!'

'Since last month, you mean,' Alice laughed. She turned to Ella. 'I forget, have you met Cassie?'

'I'm Alice's oldest friend.' Cassie thrust a hand at Ella to shake. Wide-legged pinstripe trousers hung off her narrow frame, a simple white vest highlighting her perfect collarbones. 'We skipped together in the playground, would you believe?'

'Great to meet you.' Ella barely had time to reply, before Cassie turned back to Alice.

'He's here, isn't he?'

'He' was the all-consuming ex. Alice frowned 'I'm not sure — '

'God, I knew I shouldn't have come. But Tony said, I need to do the red carpet. You know I've got a callback next week for the new Andrew Davies thing? Corsets and crinolines, down in the depths of Dorset for a month.' Cassie shifted, radiating nervous energy. 'God, I'm dying for a smoke. I don't suppose . . . ? But no, you never touched the things. Smart girl.' Cassie glanced around the room, eyes widening as she spotted someone, 'Shit, Devorah!'

Grabbing Alice's arm, she ducked behind her. As Cassie was at least three inches taller and twice as noticeable, Alice doubted it would be an effective evasion.

'What's going on?' Ella looked over with clear amusement.

Cassie sighed, peeking out from behind Alice's neat plait. 'She hasn't forgiven me for spilling gin on her Givenchy loaner at the BAFTAs.'

'Drama.' Ella raised her eyebrows at Alice.

She shifted, uncomfortable. 'Can I move yet?'

'No!' Cassie yelped. 'She's looking right at us.'

'No,' Alice corrected gently, peeling Cassie off her. 'She's stalking Chris Carmel, like every other single woman here tonight.'

'And half the taken ones too,' Ella pipped up. 'And every gay man between here and Brighton.'

'Ooh, she's looking away. See you soon? Call me!' With another flutter of kisses, Cassie disappeared into the crowd.

'Wow,' Ella said faintly, watching her go. 'Was she always like this?'

'Mm-hm,' Alice agreed. Technically, the 'oldest friend' routine was a somewhat rose-tinted view of the past. They'd been at primary school together, yes, but while Cassie ruled the Year Five cliques from her prized seat under the apple tree, Alice had been staying in at lunch, reading in the book corner. It wasn't until later, when

43

Alice started at Grayson Wells, that their paths had crossed again.

'See, this is what I'm talking about.' Ella turned back to Alice. 'You need some more excitement in your life. I mean, you have Vivienne, and Flora, and Cassie there buzzing around with all their drama, but what about you?'

Alice made a noise of protest. 'I have plenty of excitement. Hello, banking fraud!'

Ella rolled her eyes. 'Spending hours on the phone to some call-centre drone is not excitement. I'm serious, Alice, you spend all your time making their lives run smoothly, and what do you get?'

'So you're saying I'm a doormat?' Alice folded her arms. She knew Ella meant well, but she couldn't help feeling a touch defensive.

'No, that's not it.' Ella must have realised Alice was offended, because her tone became soothing. 'It would be different if you were, if you just lay back and let them trample all over you. But you're brilliant, and capable — you swoop in and set their whole lives straight.'

Alice shrugged. 'So?'

'So . . . oh, I don't know.' Ella sighed. 'I'm sorry, I didn't mean to be a bitch. I just never see you be selfish, that's all.'

'I thought that was a good thing,' Alice replied. Selfish women wreaked havoc, they caused pain. They left. 'I just don't see what good it would do me to burst into tears the whole time, and throw tantrums the way Flora does.'

'You'd be surprised,' Ella told her with a wry expression. 'Men love high-maintenance women.'

'Where did you read that?' Alice snorted. '*Cosmo*?'

'*Glamour*, actually. And I'm right. It makes them feel like they're in some kind of *film noir*. You know, caught up in a *femme fatale*'s plot.'

'That's ridiculous.'

Ella exhaled. 'You're probably right. But not about the drama. You need to go crazy sometimes.'

'Sure.' Alice felt a smile tug the edge of her lips. 'I'll walk around my flat with heels on past 9 p.m. Rebellious enough for you?'

'It's a start.'

4

Alice tried not to think about what Ella had said, but as she spent the next week on hold with her bank, fielding overwrought emails from Cassie about the precise meaning of 'good to see you' in a note from The Ex, and avoiding Flora's increasingly insistent demands for lunch — 'or drinks, or dinner, or maybe even shopping?' — she couldn't help but remember the instructions to be more of a drama queen. Dramatic, Alice would never be, but perhaps there was something to be said for putting herself first, and using her brisk efficiency to further her own career for now, instead of treading water, organising everyone else.

Delivering a stack of contracts to Vivienne one afternoon, Alice decided to take the plunge. Again.

'Do you have a moment?' she asked, as Vivienne carelessly scrawled her signature over every page, not even glancing at the dense print. The drawing room was dim, with lace curtains shrouding the windows, Vivienne hunched behind her desk like a gothic Miss Havisham.

She looked up, dark eyes lined with a swipe of black liner behind the tiny quizzing glasses she donned for all her contract signing. 'Of course, darling, what do you need?'

'Well, I was hoping we could talk again about me agenting.'

Alice took a seat in one of the faux Louis XV chairs, strangely nervous. She was out of her comfort zone here, asking for something she couldn't back up with charts and figures. She'd negotiated pay-rises every year and expanded her benefits package, but this was new, uncertain territory. Balancing her organiser on her knees, she flipped to the page she'd prepared with bulleted talking points.

'I know I brought it up earlier in the year,' she began with a purposeful tone, 'but I've been thinking more about it, and I think now would be a good time to start transitioning away from the strictly legal side of things.'

Even though Alice had picked her words carefully to avoid any mention of 'change', 'leaving' or 'difference', Vivienne laid down her fountain pen and sat back, assessing Alice with one of those swift gazes. 'What's brought this on? I thought things were running so smoothly.' Her tone held a note of surprise. 'You've been doing such great work here. I swear, we'd be lost without you keeping track of those things. You're my most valuable asset.'

That was what was so seductive about Vivienne's compliments: they were undoubtedly sincere — just deployed at moments to suit her best.

'We'd find someone to replace me, there's no problem there,' Alice tried to sidestep her argument. 'And it's not as if I'd be leaving. I just think . . . ' She tried to think of the best way to put it without sounding ungrateful. After all, Vivienne had only hired her in the beginning as a favour to her father, who had been deep in a biography for her (on 'the Byron of botanicals', as Vivienne billed it). Without that first break, Alice would still be buried in one of those chrome and glass towers in the City. Or, more likely, unemployed from the last round of banking redundancies. But that favour couldn't last her for ever. Taking a short breath, Alice said firmly, 'I'd like more of a challenge, and I think my skills would work for the clients.'

Vivienne gave her an indulgent look. 'I hear you, Alice, I do, but we have been through this before. Agenting requires a certain flair. Some cut-throat instinct.' Rising from her seat, she circled the desk and settled into the chair beside Alice, smiling at her fondly. 'You've no idea what kind of stress and pressure we're under. I've got to be out, doing deals, sniffing out the best roles all the time, never a moment to relax!'

Now was probably not the time to remind Vivienne about the two-hour block on calls she'd had that morning, because she simply had to take a nap for her poor headache.

'You're a wonderful lawyer,' Vivienne continued, patting her hand, 'but really, don't you think you're suited best . . . behind the scenes?'

The words sat between them, undoubtedly true.

'Anthony isn't particularly cut-throat,' Alice tried. 'And his clients are happy.'

'Yes, but he's got a reputation to fall back on.' Vivienne waved her objection away with a flutter of her hand. 'Nowadays, it's about people like Tyrell who can really close the deal. Did you know he's signed three clients away from their old agencies this month?'

'No,' Alice admitted quietly, 'I didn't.' Poaching was another thing she couldn't abide: tempting successful stars to abandon their old agents, dangling promises of better parts, bigger deals. Loyalty should count for something.

'You see?' Vivienne seized on her obvious reluctance. 'You just don't have what it takes — and there's nothing wrong with that. Your contract work here is stellar!'

Alice steeled herself, making one last attempt. 'But I really think I could bring a fresh perspective on some problems.' She glanced down at her notes. 'Take Rupert, for example. He's not booked a job for months now, and I think the issue is, he's not suited to the leading-man roles we keep sending him for. If we just tried something new, maybe for a supporting part, the best friend, or the — '

Vivienne cut her off. 'Darling, you don't need to worry. Rupert got a callback for the lead in the new BBC costume drama just the other day. You see,' she gave a knowing look, 'that's another thing you need for agenting: the ability to hold the course even through tough times. Sometimes our clients can toil for years unnoticed, before getting that big break. It wouldn't do to just sell them short because you lose faith, now, would it?'

Alice exhaled, her earlier resolve fading. 'I suppose not . . . '

She should have picked her moment better: when Vivienne was full of post-spa languor, or celebrating a particularly large commission cheque. Instead, she'd found her in a lucid moment, when nothing slipped past without a fight. Defeat was inevitable.

Alice closed her organiser. 'Well, thanks for talking with me.' She managed a smile, but her disappointment must have shown because Vivienne flew into sympathetic mode. 'Oh, sweetie, don't feel bad. You know I'm only looking out for your best interests, you've been with me so long. Now, how about we take the afternoon and do tea at The Wolseley? It's been ages since we caught up, just the two of us.'

'I can't,' Alice began, 'I have a pile of work and — '

'Never mind that!' Vivienne was already up, checking her lipstick in one of the gilt-edged mirrors and reaching for her pashmina. 'Work will wait. We need some time to unwind!' She left the room in her usual swirl of expensive fabrics and perfume, and Alice, resigned to at least another six months of checking termination clauses, had no choice but to follow. At least rejection by Vivienne came catered with *petits fours* and champagne.

★ ★ ★

'The problem is, she has a point.' Alice curled up with her phone later that afternoon, slightly woozy from the Veuve Clicquot Vivienne had insisted on buying. Contracts were probably best left alone in this state.

'Excuses, excuses,' Ella replied in a singsong

voice. Alice could hear her munching on some crisps. 'I won't play devil's advocate for you.'

'I'm not making excuses!' Alice insisted. 'It's not as if I'm toiling away, unappreciated. I'm successful, and well-paid.'

'And bored out of your mind.'

'I have independence,' Alice continued. 'And even if I tried to make it as an agent somewhere else, then I'd be starting from scratch as a trainee. I'm too old to move backwards like that, if I want to buy a place of my own. It's too much of a risk.'

Ella sighed. 'There's really nothing I can say, is there? You're set on being safe and dull and stable for the rest of your life.'

'Yes.' Alice was defiant. 'You don't understand. I don't have the luxury of wafting around like Cassie and Flora. They assume someone's going to be there to pick up the pieces, but I can't do that. I'm on my own, so why ruin everything on some foolish whim?'

The more Alice thought about it, the more she convinced herself this was for the best. Embarking on a radical career change at her age? It was ludicrous. Better by far that she focus on taking the next sensible steps she'd always planned: buying a flat of her own. So, as the next days drifted past in a blur of subclauses and residual payment exemptions, Alice swallowed her disappointment and turned her attentions instead to estate-agent brochures and home-décor magazines, dreaming of the one thing that would make her steady wage worthwhile. A home all of her own.

'Miss Love?'

'Yes, hi.' Alice bobbed up from the row of scratchy blue seats. After two long afternoons there filing paperwork about her stolen card, she felt like the bank was a second home to her now, full of familiar leaflet stands, and a row of tired assistants behind the glass partition. This time, however, she was actually there by choice, not necessity.

A greying man stuck out his hand, coughing slightly. 'Mr Weatherton. I'll be your advisor. If you'll just come back here . . . '

Alice shook his damp palm and trotted after him, clutching her neat binder of statements and payroll records. She was starting to feel excited about venturing onto the property ladder. Scared, yes — after all, it was only her entire life savings she was putting on the line — but confident too. This was what adults did, wasn't it? Put down roots; made a home. And finally, she'd be able to pick the colour of her paint and the style of her curtains without some onerous landlord watching her every move.

Mr Weatherton ushered her into a cluttered office and gestured for her to sit. 'Now, you're thinking about loan options?' He peered at some papers.

'A mortgage, yes. Your HomePlus variable package.' Alice pulled out the thick wedge of application forms.

Mr Weatherton looked up, frowning. 'I'm sorry, I, uh, think we have our wires crossed. I thought you wanted to talk about extending your overdraft, or some kind of loan arrangement.'

'No . . . ' Alice shook her head slowly. 'It's a mortgage I need. See, I've already filled in most of the application.' She passed him the papers, marked in pencil just to be on the safe side. 'I just need you to complete the rest. Do you need a minute to find the right file?' she asked, watching him flip through the folder.

Mr Weatherton looked awkward. 'There seems to have been some misunderstanding. I'm not sure who you've spoken to, but we have very clear borrower guidelines, and, ah given the recent change in your credit rating, and lack of funds with the bank . . . ' He cleared his throat. 'Well, I'm afraid you just don't qualify.'

Alice looked at him, speechless.

'See, it states quite clearly in the literature that all agreement is based on your reliability as a borrower.' He helpfully slid her application back to her, as Alice scanned her own leaflets, trying to follow what he was saying. 'Our credit checks show the, ah, worrying state of your current finances, so the best you can hope for is a high-rate loan.' Mr Weatherton glanced down at his file. 'Also, I see here that you've emptied your savings account with us. Miss Love, I shouldn't need to tell you that you'll have to show some proof of your ability to pay a deposit before we can even begin to work out a mortgage agreement. It's all laid out in the subclauses . . . '

Alice stopped listening. All she could hear was her blood thundering loudly in her ears, and those few, terrible words.

It took her an eternity to remember how to breathe, and another few moments until she could manage to speak.

'What do you mean, emptied my savings account?'

5

Mr Weatherton broke off his lecture on fiscal responsibility and stared at her, surprised. 'The Super-Saver account you have with us. The contents were transferred out two days ago.'

Alice shook her head, almost in a daze. This couldn't be happening.

'I never transferred anything,' she stumbled, her voice no louder than a whisper. 'There — there was over thirty thousand pounds in that account!'

He stared at her. The expression on Alice's face must have been vivid enough to convince him, because suddenly, Mr Weatherton gulped.

'You're . . . sure?' Their eyes met, a mirror of panic.

'Oh, yes.' Alice nodded faintly. 'It was my deposit, for the flat . . . ' She trailed off, helpless.

There was silence.

'Wait here,' he ordered, lurching to his feet. Alice managed to obey him for all of five seconds before leaping up herself, following him across the branch floor.

'It's gone?' she exclaimed, voice picking up volume now. Mr Weatherton had seized control of somebody's computer and was frantically clicking through the files. Alice felt dizzy. She gripped hold of the partition wall for support. 'It was in my account and someone just . . . took it? Don't you have security?' she demanded. 'What about all those questions I have to answer just to talk about my balance?'

'Please, Miss Love, if you could just stay calm and wait in my office!' Mr Weatherton didn't look particularly calm himself. In fact, a strange vein was bulging on the left side of his forehead.

'But I don't understand!' Alice repeated, louder. She was vaguely aware she sounded hysterical, but she was beyond caring. 'Shouldn't you have some kind of alert set up? Especially after my card fraud! How can someone access my account and take *that much* money without you knowing?'

The amount flashed into her head, and Alice felt sick all over again. Oh God. She let out a whimper.

'Please, Miss Love, if you could just wait in my office?' Mr Weatherton hurriedly summoned a pimply assistant and had him guide Alice back, away from the now nervous-looking customers. She followed him to the small room, numb. She hadn't checked her account the past few days, but why would she? Nobody logs on every night to make sure someone hasn't stolen a vast amount of money; besides, the only problem she'd had was with a misplaced card and PIN, and that was over now, Ahmed at the call centre had reassured her. So how was this even possible?

'Can I, uh, get you anything?' The boy hovered awkwardly, and even though Alice shook her head, he reappeared a few moments later with a paper cup of cold water.

She took it silently.

Thirty-two thousand pounds. *Thirty-two thousand pounds.* The words spun around in her head so often, they began to lose all meaning. This wasn't a shopping spree of lingerie, or a shiny new iPod bought using her card. Alice didn't even know how to picture that kind of money. It was nothing but numbers to her, black print on her savings account statement, but to whoever took it . . . That was money to them now. Real money.

She wasn't sure how long she sat there, but eventually Mr Weatherton returned. Alice looked at him dully as he took a seat, and nervously set about reshuffling his papers.

'Well?' she asked, her earlier outrage fading to a chilled resignation. 'Do you know what happened, Mr — '

'Call me Rodney.' He pulled at his tie, a sheen of sweat now coating his forehead.

'Rodney,' she repeated quietly. Apparently they were now bonded by disaster. There was another pause.

'It, ah, appears that the money was transferred by telephone.' Rodney's disapproving demeanour was now gone, the expression in his eyes defeated. It was hardly reassuring, Alice noted, as if from outside herself. 'You — I mean, the caller identified themselves as you. They cleared all the usual security checks,' he added quickly, as if that somehow made it less of a monumental failing.

'But . . . ' Alice tried to re-engage her brain. 'where did the money go? You must have some record of that, at least. Can't you just, cancel the transaction?'

Rodney exhaled. 'They asked for priority handling, for convenience. The transfer cleared this morning.'

Alice stared. It took them for ever to process a simple cheque deposit, but that kind of money could disappear overnight?

'So, what . . . ? I mean, what happens now?'

Rodney exhaled a shaky breath. 'Well, ah, we'll be contacting the recipient branch, to follow up. But it was a numbered account, in the Caribbean — '

'The Caribbean!' Alice yelped. 'And that didn't flag any warnings?'

Rodney quivered. 'I suppose the assistant thought it was payment for a flat. So many developers are based overseas these days . . . '

Alice opened her mouth, but Rodney pressed on. 'I understand, you must be feeling stressed, but please, Miss Love, do try to stay calm.' He pulled out a pocket pack of tissues and began to mop his face. Alice couldn't believe this.

'But . . . What . . . ?' She grappled to find sense again. 'Is that it? I mean, you can get it back, can't you?'

'I . . . we'll have to investigate. But it's not just your savings, your credit score has plummeted,' he explained. 'For it to fall so quickly, you would have had to have defaulted payments on other cards or loans in the last few months.'

She shook her head. This wasn't happening. 'I have one credit card.' Alice fumbled with her purse, laying the small square of plastic out on the desk to prove it. 'And I'm never late with payment. Never!' She looked at Rodney pleadingly,

'You believe me, don't you? This isn't me!'

He looked back, helpless. 'I can't . . . I mean, there will be an investigation, and I'm sure . . . But, I can't say anything right now. It's out of my hands.'

'Then who do I talk to?' Alice demanded, horrified to hear her voice break. She sucked in a breath and tried to stay composed. 'Just give me their names, and numbers, and I'll call. I need to sort this!'

'Someone from head office will be contacting you.' Rodney swallowed. 'We'll see what we can do.'

★ ★ ★

His words taunted her for the rest of the day. Her savings were gone, just vanished into nothing, but she still couldn't quite process the truth. Alice half-expected an apologetic call, explaining that it had just been a clerical error; some terrible mix-up, but none came. By the time she arrived on Julian's doorstep that evening, her scattered panic had given way to a sharp kind of terror.

'What am I going to do?'

He barely had time to usher her into the narrow hallway before Alice found herself retelling the entire sorry mess, words tumbling out of her mouth as if saying them out loud would somehow make it all less absurd. But it didn't. 'They say the account is protected against this kind of thing. I don't understand, how could it happen?'

59

She forced herself to take a breath, staring blankly at Julian under the bright spotlights. Usually, she found his sparse, minimalist flat a refuge, but now, it just seemed to mock her with a neatness and order that were far, far from her reach. 'The bank won't get a handle on this for days, and he was saying all these things about credit scores and defaults, and — ' She broke down, finally surrendering to the tears that had been building since she heard the awful news.

'Shhh, hey, Aly, it'll be OK.' Julian enveloped her in a hug. His grey sweater was soft against her face as he gently stroked her hair.

'I'm sorry.' She pulled away, embarrassed. She never broke down like this. 'It's just, it's been going round in my head all afternoon. I don't know what to do.'

Julian held out a handkerchief. 'To start with, blow.'

Alice took it. She always teased him about them, using the monogrammed cloths instead of hygienic tissues, but now there was something comforting about the cool fabric against her face. She sniffled loudly.

'It'll be OK, I promise.' Julian steered her towards the kitchen, already warm and steaming with some delicious buttery smell. Alice sank down at the table, while he put the kettle on and began assembling cups and milk. 'The bank has to have some kind of insurance policy, you'll get the money back.'

'And the rest of it?' Alice felt utterly useless.

Julian gave her a reassuring hug. 'I'll get a copy of your report, we'll find out exactly what's been going on. Now, how about some tea? And I'm trying a new carrot cake, with nutmeg and cardamom. You can be my guinea pig.'

Alice nodded limply, watching him move around her in a comforting bustle of activity. He was right. There was nothing else she could do right now but drown her sorrows in hot, sweet tea. But even that went against Alice's every instinct, and as her body gave in to the wave of exhaustion sweeping through her, her mind was already searching for some kind of solution.

She needed a plan.

★ ★ ★

Julian set about using his accountancy contacts to fast-track a copy of her credit report, while Alice began poring over every fraud guide she could find. Work the next day was a blur, nothing but a vague memory of phone calls and conversations she forgot the minute she put the phone down, but the moment Vivienne waltzed off to dinner, she dashed home; meeting Julian at her flat to assemble all the paperwork she would need for her claims.

'Bank statements, credit card bills, utilities . . . ' Alice laid out the papers on her coffee table, next to the bottle of wine and homemade chocolate torte Julian had brought as comfort food. 'What am I missing?'

'Just this.' Julian came back into her sitting room, bearing a corkscrew and a thick sheaf of pages from her printer. 'Miss Alice Love's credit report, fresh off the press.'

'Pass me that.' She reached up. Julian held out the wine-opener. 'No, the other one.'

'Not so fast.' He collapsed heavily on the sofa. 'I should look first, find out what we're dealing with. Some of the statements I see at work are all over the place.'

'Fill me with confidence, why don't you?' Alice took a large slice of cake, but her stomach was twisted too tightly with nerves. She picked at it, anxious. 'Well? The bank said there had to be something going on for my score to have slipped so low.'

Mr Weatherton had been flustered, yes, but on that he was certain. With a rating like hers, she'd be lucky to get even a tiny overdraft, let alone a hundred-thousand-pound mortgage. Somebody had already taken out a loan in her name, and nobody had known the difference. Alice felt another surge of terror. There could be thousands more pounds of debt out there.

'Hmmmm ... ' Julian frowned, flipping through the pages.

'Is that a good 'hmm' or a bad 'hmm'?' Alice watched him carefully, but the seconds ticked by without any further comment. 'Please, Jules, I'm dying here!'

He looked up. 'Don't panic,' he started, voice cautious.

She panicked.

'What? What does that mean?' Alice snatched the list from his hands. The very long list. She held her breath as she scanned the details. Names of banks and credit card companies jumped out at her: not just major ones, but firms with names like 'Creditloans4u' and 'Badcredit-plus'. There were loans and credit cards and unauthorised overdrafts stretching back almost two months.

'How much is it?' She gazed at the dense print, aghast. All of this, in her name!

'We'll start contacting the companies right away,' Julian told her in a low, soothing voice. 'And inform them what's happened. The sooner we get the process going, the better.'

'But how much is it?' The numbers were blurring in front of her eyes.

Julian sighed. 'As far as I can tell, around sixty thousand pounds. So far.'

Alice felt her mouth drop open.

'I . . . You can't . . . I don't . . . '

'Like I said, we'll straighten this out,' Julian told her, a reassuring hand on her arm. Alice struggled to listen, blood pounding in her ears. 'I'll find someone at my firm, or maybe Stefan knows something. But you should be prepared for it to take a while.'

Alice could only whimper. 'I think I need that corkscrew now.'

★ ★ ★

'You know, I'm surprised they haven't started chasing you yet,' Julian said thoughtfully, after Alice had numbed her panic with two glasses of wine, and they'd broken down the worst of the fraud. 'Although, it's all pretty recent. Most of these have missed only one or two payments.'

She shivered. 'I still can't believe I didn't know it was happening.'

Of everything, Alice wondered if her ignorance was the worst. All this time, she'd taken these ordinary things for granted: she opened a bank account, she paid her bills, she filed away her statements every month in the big black file marked 'banking'. But now it turned out it wasn't safe or secure at all. The most boring parts of her life were wide open for anyone to just stroll in and . . . take it.

Everything.

Julian looked at his phone, restless. 'We should probably wrap this up. Yasmin will be over at my flat soon, with the first of her stuff.'

Alice stopped. 'She's moving in?' Her problems faded, just for a moment, as she looked at Julian in surprise. 'When did this happen? I mean,' she recovered, 'congratulations. You didn't say.'

Julian seemed flustered. He ran one hand over the crown of his head, from his neck to his forehead, flattening his hair in an awkward clump. 'It wasn't exactly planned. We were talking, and she said how she never saw me, and I said something about her living on the other side of the city, and then the next thing I knew . . . ' He gave a small shrug. 'It'll be good, I think. Got to try it sometime, right?'

'Of course. I'm sure it'll be great for you.' Now it was Alice's turn to be reassuring. 'And you'll finally have someone to cook for!'

Julian made a face. 'Not exactly. Yasmin doesn't really do butter, or oil . . . ' he paused,

' . . . Fats of any kind, really.'

'Oh.' Yasmin had been with Julian for close to six months now, but was still rather an enigma to Alice. She did something terribly important involving foreign buy-outs at an investment bank, and was forever slipping away from drinks or dinner with her BlackBerry to cajole somebody about sell rates in honeyed tones. Alice liked her, in the vaguely pleasant way she liked most of Julian's girlfriends. Anything more was a wasted effort. But anti-butter? That didn't bode well.

'Thanks for the help, anyway.' Alice set aside the papers, and showed him to the door. 'I really appreciate it.'

'It's nothing.' Julian pulled her into another hug. 'I just hate that some bastard would do this to you. You'll call if you need anything else?'

Alice nodded.

'Hang in there.'

She closed the door behind him and slowly sank back against the hard frame. That was something she hadn't even begun to contemplate, what with the panic and terror and rush to discover the true extent of the damage. But now that those were out in the open, the question wrapped itself around her brain.

Who had done this to her?

Rodney and Julian said that it had to be criminal gangs, taking advantage of her perfect credit rating and large savings account, but Alice couldn't understand it. Intercepting her mail, forging her signature . . . Even if they'd been hunting through her rubbish for months and hacking all her online accounts, it was all unnervingly personal. The things they would have had to know about her to carry on, undetected, all this time: her date of birth and contact details were only the start of it. To even access a report of her current account by phone, Alice had often had to list her mother's maiden name, random security words, town of birth, or the name of her first pet (a sadly short-lived hamster called Snuggles). How could someone know those things?

A sudden sharp knock on her door broke through Alice's reverie. She peered through the peep-hole to see her landlord waiting in the hallway, his arms folded and a scowl on his wrinkled face.

She braced herself and opened the door. 'Mr Bloch,' Alice tried to sound warm and friendly, 'how are you?'

He glared back, unmoved. 'I came to give you this.' He thrust a single sheet of paper into her hand. 'I'm a reasonable man, so I'm giving you three days. That should be plenty of time to get your things out.'

Alice stared at him in confusion. 'What do you mean?' She glanced at the typed letter, 'I don't under — '

She stopped, her words catching in her throat as the letters curled innocuously across the page and arranged themselves into meaning.

'*Notice to evict.*'

'No.' Alice looked up at him in panic. 'You can't.'

'Oh yes I can.' Mr Bloch puffed out his chest.

'You're four days late with this month's rent.'

'But I told you the standing order wouldn't go in this month,' Alice protested. 'I explained about what happened with my bank!'

'And I was understanding.' He pursed his lips. 'I let you have a whole extra day to pay by cheque. But it bounced.'

Alice's heart fell. 'Next week — the bank said it would have my current account refunded by Wednesday, at the latest!'

Mr Bloch was unmoved. 'Your tenancy agreement clearly states, all rent must be paid on time. And since you were already on probation, you've left me with no choice.'

'Please, I — '

'I'll be round to inspect the property before you leave.' He shot a suspicious look past her. 'I expect everything to be accounted for.'

Alice watched him march back down the stairs, her mind already buzzing with panic. What was she going to do? There were still two weeks until her next payday, and she barely had enough for day-to-day living, not a temporary rental, or the security deposits on a new lease. And where could she go? Staying with Ella or Cassie was one thing, but what about her belongings — a whole flat full of books and furniture and . . .

With a sinking heart, Alice realised there was only one place she could go now. A place of chaos, disorder and distraction.

She was going home.

6

Alice woke with an ache in her back and the sound of breaking china echoing through the Sussex cottage. She yawned, bleary-eyed. The muscle pain was from lifting boxes all weekend, and sleeping in the tiny single bed in her childhood room, but the china? She could only imagine.

There was another crash.

Alice reluctantly went to investigate, her feet bare on the dusty floorboards. She'd brought up only a haphazard suitcase of things from the van, so she took a blanket from the hall cupboard to wrap herself up against the draught that always drifted through the house. It was a charming home, with wooden beams, an open fireplace, and an abundance of small nooks perfect for a small child to hide away with her latest book. As a girl, she'd loved it, but now all Alice could see were the patches of damp creeping in the corners, and the original features crumbling into disrepair. And the clutter. Oh, the clutter. Between her father's ever-expanding collection of second-hand books (hunted down at every charity shop, church rummage sale and car-boot sale in a twenty-mile radius), and Jasmine's hoarding for future art projects, every room and shelf in the place was loaded down with random knick-knacks. Her bedroom, still papered with fading floral print, now housed three vast oak bookshelves, a broken set of mirrors, and a collection of chipped shepherdess figurines in various states of repose. Alice had dreamed of porcelain sheep all night long.

By the time she reached the kitchen, there had been several more crashes. She paused cautiously in the doorway and peered in. Her stepmother was standing in the middle of the room, her petite frame swathed in a bright sarong, her greying curls caught back from her face as she happily hurled china at the far wall.

'Oh, hello, sweetie. I didn't know you were up.' Jasmine paused to greet her, a green vase in her hands. Alice watched it smash on the stone-paved floor, exploding in a burst of fragments. 'Put something on your feet,' Jasmine warned, reaching for a large bowl. 'Your father got a nasty shard of glass in his foot last week.'

'All right,' Alice answered faintly.

'There's some quinoa if you're hungry!' Jasmine called helpfully, now picking through the rubble for shards of particular interest. 'And I made a gluten-free pasta bake the other day.'

'I think I'll go into the village,' Alice decided, finding a lone apple in the corner of the fridge. 'Is Dad in the garden?'

'I think so.' Jasmine glanced up with an absent frown. For a moment, she looked identical to Flora, with the same expression of pale confusion.

'It's OK,' Alice reassured her, 'I'm sure I'll find him somewhere out there.'

★ ★ ★

After waiting twenty minutes for the hot water to get going, Alice showered and pulled on some jeans and a jumper, assembling a matching pair of wellies from the mud-splattered jumble in the porch. It was a clear, sunny day, and as she ventured out into the overgrown back garden, she had to admit that being stuck in the middle of the countryside had some advantages: the house backed onto open fields, and the patchwork of grass and crooked hedges stretched in front of her, wide and windswept.

She headed towards the dilapidated shed, tucked away behind flowerbeds and an overgrown vegetable patch. 'Hello?' Alice tapped at the peeling doorframe and peered in. As usual, her father was in his old rocking chair, surrounded by an avalanche of research notes and unfinished manuscripts. The sunlight dappled his thin face, grey hair sticking out in tufts as he pored over one of his red and black spiral-bound notebooks.

'Pumpkin!' He blinked in surprise from behind large, grandpa-style spectacles, as if he'd forgotten she was even visiting. 'Everything all right?'

'Good enough.' She slipped inside, careful not to disturb the mess. 'Jasmine is tearing the place apart again.'

Her father smiled slightly. 'Ah, yes, she said something about a new mosaic for her studio.'

'That would explain the china.' Alice looked around. The last time she'd been down, the room had been full of American revolutionary War paraphernalia, but now, the muskets were being edged out by new curiosities. Small model hot-air balloons spilled from the narrow windowledge, and blueprints trailed over the wide desk. 'Starting a new project?' she asked. Now that Alice thought about it, her father was looking different: his threadbare jumpers had been replaced with a shirt and blue scarf, tied at his neck like a cravat, and there was a sense of energy and purpose about him that always meant he'd found some new fascination.

'Maybe, maybe . . . early days yet.' He tapped one finger to his lips and winked.

She smiled. 'I'm just going into the village to stock up. Did you want anything?'

'Hmm . . . maybe some twine, and pepper-mint creams?'

Alice raised her eyebrows.

'The Montgolfiers were big believers in peppermint creams,' her father explained. 'Look out the good sort, would you? They should have some at Bishops.'

'Peppermints and string, coming up.'

★ ★ ★

Alice decided to walk the half-mile into the village, and set out along the winding lane with one of Jasmine's tie-dyed cloth bags over her shoulder and a long list in her pocket. She was relieved her father's Civil War period was over; for months, she'd been half-expecting a call from Jasmine to say he'd accidentally shot himself in the leg with one of those antique muskets. Not that hot-air balloons were much better. God knew what damage he could do if he took it on himself actually to build one . . .

Her father had always been an eccentric. The question 'And what do your parents do?' would bring a different answer every year. He wasn't an academic, or a writer, or anything so easily defined. No, Alice considered him more of an enthusiast. From eighteenth-century botanists, to alchemy in the ancient Ottoman Empire, he would become gripped with a new passion, immersing himself completely in the subject for months, sometimes years. Once mastered, he would give a series of lectures, or write a book, or even — in one case — oversee the planting of a thirty-acre garden in the style of renegade gardener, William Robinson. Then a new topic would catch his interest, and he would be off again.

She had to be grateful for his commitment to his subjects, Alice supposed, otherwise she would never have been born. Because her father didn't simply research the topic, no, he seemed to take on the lifestyle and characteristics of his subjects as well. Hence her mother (a glamorous American breezing through London) was wooed by the dashing man quoting Byron and Keats as if he were one of the Romantic Poets himself, and not just knee-deep in old texts. By the time he tired of poetry and switched his allegiance to exploring sewage systems of the early industrial age, Natasha Scott already had a ring on her finger, a child on the way, and a ramshackle cottage to call home.

Alice often wondered how, faced with such a

72

bait and switch of her dramatic, romance-filled dreams, her mother lasted even the eleven fractured years she did before abandoning her husband and child to the leaking pipes, overgrown garden and lack of local cocktail bars. If she was truly honest about it, her mother's leaving was something of a relief. By then, Alice had witnessed enough dress rehearsals to know — and fear — the more permanent version was on its way, so when her mother finally packed up every designer dress and expensive, unworn shoe, and disappeared for good, Alice told herself it was better this way. At least there was no more of Natasha dragging her to London for days on end, or disappearing for summers at somebody's house in Cannes, or Morocco, leaving Alice, uncertain, to await her return.

★ ★ ★

Alice bought a loaf of bread, still warm from the bakery, and sat on the war memorial bench, tearing chunks off to share with the sparrows that nested nearby. The village had changed little in the last ten years: home to three pubs, an organic farm collective, and a revolving parade of antiques/children's clothes/crystal jewellery boutiques. She must have sat in this exact spot a hundred times as a girl, waiting for her father to finish browsing old curios in the antiques shop, and later, as a bored teenager trapped by the sporadic bus timetable and lack of any actual place to go.

And here she was again, with all her worldly

possessions stored in the back of the garage as if she'd never left. Alice watched the birds fluttering at her feet and thought bleakly how quickly everything had changed. Homeless, broke — in a single week her life had been turned upside down, and she was still reeling, trying to understand how it could have happened. Was there something she should have done differently?

Her phone lit up, and Alice reached for it, glad of the distraction from her own self-doubt.

'How are you holding up?' The phone suddenly went silent, and there was a muffled rustling noise. 'Sorry,' Ella said breathlessly. 'I've been stuffing these envelopes all day. Two hundred gift packs have to be ready by the launch.'

'No trainees around?' Alice relaxed, just a little.

'I wish. Apparently you can't make them work weekends if you're not even paying them.'

'Wimps.'

'So, are you OK?' Ella sounded concerned. 'Any news yet from the bank? I can't believe they're being so incompetent.'

Alice sighed. 'Nope, nothing yet. The account the money went to is protected with all kinds of anonymity. But they're pulling CCTV tapes, seeing if they can match anyone to the cash withdrawls. I should know soon.'

'Aww, sweetie,' Ella was sympathetic. 'So what are you going to do? You know I'd have you stay here, but I leave for Rome tomorrow for the launch and my landlord's been threatening to repaint.'

'No, it's fine,' Alice assured her. 'I'm taking a couple of days off work to get things sorted down here, and then Cassie's back from filming. I'll stay with her.' She let out a long breath. 'And then, who knows? Maybe the bank will get its act together.'

'I'm sure it will. But you're holding up?' Ella checked. 'Surely they can't find you liable for any of this.'

'No,' Alice agreed, moving her feet out of the way as a woman walked past with a pushchair and two resistant toddlers. 'At least not the bank: this is their mistake. Thirty two thousand pounds worth of mistake.'

Ella sucked in her breath. 'I still can't believe it. I mean, what would you do with that kind of cash?'

'Buy a flat?' Alice said drily.

Ella laughed. 'Ever the sensible one.'

'So, Rome . . . ' Alice stretched out, her back still aching from those boxes. 'That should be fun.'

'Sure.' Ella's tone was wry. 'Four days in an industrial exhibition centre, trying to convince people that the pseudoscience crap in our face cream is better than everyone else's. No, it should be OK. At least I'll get to drool over the sexy CEO again. I swear, Aly, he belongs on a Mills & Boon cover.'

Alice giggled. 'I'm guessing it's too late to be his captive virgin bride.'

'Hmm, maybe by about twelve years!'

They laughed.

'Anyway, I better get back to this,' Ella sighed.

'The blaggers of the beauty world need their freebies. Speaking of which, how about I pick you up some goody-bags?'

'Ooh, that would be lovely.' Alice slowly got to her feet again. The street was busier now, with people out shopping before everything closed for lunch. Ah, village opening hours. 'Call me when you get back. We'll have cupcakes at that place in Soho.'

'It's a plan.'

★ ★ ★

Alice tried to view the next few days at home as an unexpected break: taking walks out in the forest, and snuggling in the sitting room with a book, but relaxation was impossible with her financial nightmare looming over her head. Back in London, her life was tangled in the worst kind of mess: one completely out of her control. How long had this been going on? What other kind of damage had the thief done? The questions chilled her. She wasn't irresponsible, or careless with her affairs. She didn't use default passwords and leave her papers lying around, but still, somebody had managed to infiltrate her life, rifling through her personal details the same way a burglar would shuffle through drawers. Only a simple burglary would be over and done with by now, not stretching out with such terrible uncertainty.

She gave up on idle activities and turned her attention to the dusty floors instead; cleaning in a focused whirl of energy. She needed a distraction. Jasmine was as bad as her father when it came to single-mindedness. She practically lived in the studio they'd built onto the far end of the house. It was a wonder Flora had managed to fend for herself at all, but knowing how things magically worked out in her stepsister's favour, Alice thought that small birds and woodland creatures had probably fed and clothed her all those years.

★ ★ ★

'You don't have to do that.' Her father appeared, just as Alice was on her hands and knees, scrubbing the kitchen floor. Jasmine had disappeared, leaving a mess of pottery remains to sweep up — on top of the regular layer of grime.

'It's fine,' Alice insisted, wringing out her cloth in the paint-splattered bucket. 'It needs doing anyway.' She looked up to find him gazing hopefully at the fridge. 'There's bread, and bacon. If you want, I can make you a sandwich.'

'Oh, no,' her father shook his head, and pushed his glasses up with a determined gesture. 'I can manage.'

Alice endured only two minutes of his faffing — clattering the pan, hunting for a knife, staring uselessly around for the butter — before taking over. Swiftly putting the bacon on to grill, she sliced the bread and made him a cup of tea while he waited.

'Thanks, pumpkin.' He watched her from the table. 'It's good to have you home. We haven't seen you in a while.'

Alice concentrated on buttering. 'It's been pretty busy, with work, and the move.' She caught herself, and sighed. 'Well, it was.'

'Don't you worry,' he smiled at her absently. 'I'm sure it'll all turn out fine in the end.'

It was the same comforting reassurance Julian and Ella had been giving her all week, but her father's tone was so laid-back that Alice felt a flutter of irritation. He never did understand what it took to live in the real world. 'It's not going to 'turn out' fine.' She tried to keep her reply measured. 'I'm going to have to spend weeks straightening it out, and even then, I might still find it hard to get any kind of credit card, or new mortgage.'

Her father nodded, but it didn't seem like her words had any impact. 'Ebb and flow, Alice.'

Alice tried not to slam the plates down and give Jasmine any more material for her mosaic. He always did this. Any problem, every success — it was all just ebb and flow. Ebb and fucking flow.

'Have you seen Flora?' he asked, oblivious to her annoyance. 'Jas was saying she'd love to spend more time with you.'

'Mmhm,' Alice murmured noncommittally, flipping bacon onto the plates and adding a squelch of ketchup from the almost empty bottle. Another thing to add to the shopping list. 'I went to her party, just the other week, remember?'

'Ah, that's it.' He nodded as she set his food down in front of him. 'I saw the photos. Lovely.'

'You couldn't make it?' Alice asked, a little

arch. He didn't wait or make room for her before starting to eat, so she pulled up a chair herself, clearing a stack of old newspapers she still needed to put in the recycling bin.

Her father looked puzzled for a moment. 'No . . . what was it? Oh, yes,' he brightened, 'I was waiting for a delivery. Those old models — did you see them? Mint condition, perfect working order. Such a find.' He beamed, a smudge of ketchup on his chin, and Alice couldn't help but feel a tug of affection.

'You'll have to show me,' she told him, getting up to find him a napkin. He hadn't always been this scattered. While her mother had seemed to find parenting an unwelcome distraction, her father had filled the gaps: propping Alice on his knee as he jotted notes in those journals, watching over her as she laboriously practised her handwriting, and reading to her every night (even if it was from *A History of Slavic Warfare*, rather than her favourite ballet stories). It was only after Natasha left that he began inching away from reality, year by year, until by the time Alice was eighteen, she was the only one in that house with any grasp of what it took to function — to stack the bills on his desk by due date, and make sure they weren't out of laundry detergent, and forge signatures on her class trip forms.

Yes, he had earned his reclusive habits, Alice reminded herself, watching as he hummed under his breath and scanned the nearest (three-day-old) newspaper, oblivious to the dirty plate he'd discarded and the stack of unread post. And she couldn't say the same about the other absence in her life.

★ ★ ★

Alice's cleaning frenzy had extended through the living room, front hall, and up the back stairs by the time she got the call from Rodney at the bank asking her to come in and look at CCTV footage. She barely paused to strip off her rubber gloves before dashing to catch the next train; her nerves growing as the countryside sped by, until by the time she pushed through the familiar smudged glass doors, she was breathless with anticipation. Finally, she would put a face to the crime.

'Hi, Rodney.' Alice managed a smile for him, but despite the camaraderie they'd previously struck up, he seemed stiff.

'Miss Love, how are you?' Rodney was in the same off-white shirt he'd been wearing last time. She could tell it was the same because of the scribble of biro still creeping across the front pocket.

'Fine, thanks.' Did this formality mean it was bad news?

He ushered her into the small room and tried to turn his computer screen so she could see it across the desk. 'Now, this is footage from our Islington branch. We have a transaction on your current account that day that you've disputed, at around 2.30 p.m.'

'I would have been at work,' Alice said quickly.

Rodney nodded in his noncommittal way, cueing up the footage.

The clip began to play, in a jerky, stop-motion stream: a typical afternoon in the bank. The camera was angled on the wall over the door, showing people's backs as they walked to the row of tellers, waited by the ATM, and hovered, hoping to catch an advisor's eye. At two twenty-nine, a woman walked in. Rodney paused.

'Hmm,' he murmured. Alice could see why. Shoulder-length brown hair worn in a French pleat, pale blouse, grey trousers. It looked like her. But it wasn't.

'Keep playing,' she told him, and with a sharp look in her direction, he did.

The woman went straight to the far teller and passed some papers through the division.

'Our records show that you — I mean, the woman — withdrew four hundred pounds, using a passport and the bank card as identification.' Rodney's tone was decidedly icy at this point. Alice realised with a sinking heart that he really believed it was her.

'Keep playing,' she said again, impatient. Just one look, that was all she wanted — one look at the person who was causing her this grief.

Money withdrawn, the woman turned to leave, facing towards camera for the first time. Alice leaned closer to the screen. The woman's head was bent as she rummaged in her bag, but as she neared the door, she looked up.

Alice froze.

'Well?' Rodney paused it again, squinting at

81

the blurred image while Alice stared in disbelief. 'Hmm,' he said again, but this time, his tone was softer. 'That's her.' He turned to Alice expectantly. 'Anything familiar?'

But Alice couldn't say a word. She blinked at the face, trying to take it in. It didn't make any sense, but there it was in front of her: the truth. The reason for her nightmare.

'Miss Love?' Rodney pressed. 'Do you know her?'

Dumbly, Alice nodded. But that wasn't right either, not really, not if that video was anything to go by. Because despite everything, she couldn't have known her at all.

It was Ella.

7

The woman Alice knew as Ella Nicholls didn't exist.

There were no bank accounts or identification registered in her name; her flat was empty, paid month-to-month in cash, and when Alice turned up at her PR firm, she found nothing but blank stares and a confused middle-aged woman in accounts named Ellen Nicholas. Ella was gone, and Alice was left with nothing but chaos and confusion in her place.

'Personally, I didn't like her when I met her,' Cassie offered, looking up from where she was sprawled on her sofa, engrossed in her laptop. It was late, and she was draped in a black silk kimono over designer lingerie, her lips painted with a perfect scarlet pout. 'There was just something not quite right. I could tell when we met. Oh, can you be careful with my Diptyque in there?'

Alice obeyed, respectfully leaving the row of half-burned candles in place as she went to lay out her neat row of Simple skincare products in the bathroom. There. She was almost unpacked — if by unpacked, she meant arranging the basic suitcase of possessions she'd brought back up to London with her. The rest of her life remained in boxes down in Sussex awaiting her return. Alice looked across the hall at the three-metre-square study that was her new abode and sighed. It was a good thing she'd always been a believer in capsule wardrobes.

'More vino?' Cassie waved the bottle at her, as Alice drifted listlessly into the living area. 'Go on,' she urged. 'Practically the only reason I'm letting you stay is so I don't feel pathetic and useless drinking alone.'

'When you put it like that . . . ' Alice took a refilled glass and sat down on one of the retro Eames-style seats. The flat was a warehouse conversion in the heart of Shoreditch, but the architects had some interesting ideas about interiors: as well as the unfinished walls and steel pillars strewn about the space, the bedroom and bathroom boasted frosted-glass-brick walls. She'd been here only a day, but already Alice was resigning herself to the blurry sight of Cassie's naked — and undoubtedly perfect — body drifting around behind closed doors.

'But what about you, sweetie?' Cassie fixed Alice with a concerned look. 'How are you holding up?'

'I'm . . . still trying to process it, to be honest.'

'Of course you are,' Cassie yawned. Even that small movement was a spectacle, Alice noticed: the arch of her back, the pale wrist lifted to cover her mouth. Cassie had never believed in being off-duty. 'It must be such a shock, to have trusted a con artist.'

Alice tugged her cardigan sleeves down over her hands. 'I don't know if you could call her that . . . '

'Really?' Cassie seemed dubious. 'She preyed on your vulnerabilities, wheedled her way into your life, and then took everything. Sounds like a con artist to me.'

'But I couldn't have known,' Alice said quietly, almost to herself. 'Julian agrees, she had everyone fooled.'

Fooled was the right word. She couldn't even begin to understand what had happened, but the one thing she did know too well was the slow flush of shame that descended whenever she was reminded of her naïvety. It was one thing to be defrauded by professional criminals — some nameless band of mastermind thieves — but her own friend?

'So have the police been able to make any progress,' Cassie asked, 'now that they know who it is?'

'No, nothing.' When she looked up, Cassie was staring at her expectantly. 'She's gone,' Alice explained dully. 'I mean, really vanished. Her flat was packed up, and the references she gave her landlord are disconnected numbers now.' The speed and thoroughness with which Ella had erased herself was chilling. A whole life disappeared, within days.

Alice curled deeper into her chair. 'I told them the names of some people we'd seen out,' she continued. ' 'Work friends', Ella called them, but they all said the same thing: they'd met her at a party, or launch, and believed what she told them.'

'See,' Cassie gave her a comforting smile, 'you weren't the only one.'

'I was the only one she ripped off, to the tune of about a hundred thousand pounds.' Alice exhaled. It still hurt to say it, to even think it, but she couldn't escape from the truth: Ella — whoever she really was — had been lying all along. Everything she'd ever said, and all those anecdotes she'd dropped so casually into conversation — 'My family was Italian, way back,' and, 'My first boyfriend had an awful little goatee,' and, 'I want to go and open a little bakery one day' — had all been untruths, spun out in the bigger fiction of their friendship.

And Alice had believed them all.

'She took my passport,' Alice added, forlorn. 'My birth certificate too. I checked my 'important papers' file once I found out . . . once I found it was her. I suppose that's how she got all my bank details.'

'You labelled the box 'Important Papers'?' Cassie raised one perfect eyebrow.

Alice flushed. 'No, of course not.'

But it had been a special file, an elegant grey folder she'd bought especially to store all those vital pieces of information; not just passport, and bank codes, but her National Insurance card, rental agreement . . . She hadn't wanted to risk losing anything, but in the end, she'd offered up her entire identity, gift-wrapped with a smart cream ribbon.

'You know, I read last week about a woman who had her identity stolen.' Cassie's forehead creased in a frown. 'The thief didn't just run up huge debts, she got a criminal record too — just gave the other person's details every time she got caught. The poor victim couldn't get a job, and kept getting arrested. She lost her house, and ended up on the streets. I think she's still trying to clear her name! Not that it will happen to you,' she added hurriedly, finally noticing Alice's distress. 'And see? There's a silver lining. It could have been so much worse!'

★ ★ ★

That was little consolation. Despite her friend's 'glass half-full' encouragement, Alice couldn't see past the wreckage of what Ella had taken: her flat, her savings, her trust. Once she'd made the obligatory explanations to friends, family and the police, Alice called into work sick, and retreated to her tiny makeshift bedroom at Cassie's to despair. Slipping deeper into a melancholy haze, she couldn't stop herself from worrying over those few, awful questions.

Why had Ella done this to her? How could she have been so blind?

'Snap out of it, sweetie. You're acting like you've been dumped,' Cassie remarked on the fifth morning, when Alice emerged, bleary-eyed, to make some tea. She rummaged in the cabinets. Fuck herbal, soothing blends. She wanted the hard stuff. Earl Grey. 'You've been moping around like this Ella girl broke your heart!'

'Maybe she did.' Alice answered quietly. Cassie's mouth dropped. 'Not like that,' Alice stopped her. 'I just meant . . . she lied, she cheated — behind my back, for months. I trusted her, and then . . . ' She swallowed, feeling the betrayal rise again; hot tears in the corners of her

87

eyes. 'I didn't know. I didn't see any of it.'

Maybe it would be better if she had. If she'd felt even an inkling of suspicion when it came to the other woman, then perhaps Alice wouldn't be gripped with such despair. Even if she'd pushed it aside, she could tell herself now, 'Oh, I knew it all along.' She'd be kicking herself, of course, but at least then it would be frustration and anger clenching at her heart, and not such helpless misery.

'Want to come to Shoreditch House tonight?' Cassie asked, outlining her eyes in smoky grey liner to match the strange draped silk jumpsuit that clung to every bone. She peered in her professional make-up mirror. 'I'm meeting some girls for drinks later, and then maybe a club.' She didn't wait for a response before adding, 'This guy is launching a new night. He worked with Dakota on the last movie, so I'm thinking there's a chance he could show up. He would, right? I mean, it's a friend thing, so it wouldn't look too weird if I was there, just casual, like I didn't even know he was in town.' She paused to ruffle her fringe.

'No, thanks.' Alice shook her head slowly. 'I'm not going anywhere right now.'

'Huh.' Cassie took in Alice's unwashed hair, pasty face and utter misery. 'Well, can I borrow those black pumps of yours? I'm going to try out this deconstructed dress, and I don't have any shoes dull enough to work with it.'

'Sure, Cassie.' Alice exhaled, already exhausted. 'You can borrow my boring shoes.'

When Cassie had waltzed off to a meeting,

Alice shuffled to her room and slipped back beneath her covers, into the cocoon of warmth she'd imprinted there after days of solid wallowing. Her flatmate couldn't understand why Alice was taking this so hard, she knew. To Cassie, betrayal was cause for anger, internet stalking, and vicious calls to every mutual friend they had, not this empty sense of purposelessness that had seeped through Alice's system. But no matter how much Alice knew, on an abstract, intellectual level, that she should be rising above this — shaking it off, and striding with her day planner in hand to set her life to rights again — she just couldn't find the magical switch that would turn such sharp hurt into some purpose or direction.

She had taken it all for granted. Everything Ella had ever said — their coffee mornings, and idle email; the after-work drinks, and in-jokes — Alice had believed it all unquestioningly. And now, picking apart every casual conversation, she felt ill. Had Ella planned it from the very start? Would any of the weary professionals in that yoga class have done, or did she target Alice as an easy mark, trusting enough to fall for the act? Alice had been running through the questions ever since she saw that familiar face on the CCTV film, but she was no closer to answers. Ella's performance had been flawless, and Alice had played her own part perfectly.

The dupe.

★　★　★

She'd been staring at the same patch of exposed brick for over two hours when the buzzer went, loud and insistent. Reluctantly, Alice hauled herself up and slouched over to the intercom.

'Alice? Sweetie, are you there?'

'Flora,' she groaned. Of course. Any minute, her father and Jasmine would appear, to tell her to buck up and pull herself together (and not to worry, anyone would have made the same mistake). She buzzed her up.

'I've been calling for days!' Flora greeted her at the door in another of her floaty gauze dresses, a scarf drifting from her hair and bangles jangling on both tiny wrists. She turned, calling down the stairs. 'We're up here!'

A moment later, two deliverymen emerged from the stairwell, weighed down under huge boxes of produce. As they heaved their goods past her into the flat, Alice caught a glimpse of piles of fresh fruit and vegetables — enough to feed an entire family. Flora beamed at her. 'I was just out at the farmers' market, so I picked up some things for you too!'

'Really, you shouldn't . . . ' Alice protested, eyeing the organic artisan loaves and crisp folds of butcher's paper. 'I don't need — '

'I wanted to.' Flora pulled a few notes from her embroidered purse to tip the men on their way out. 'Thanks so much!' she trilled after them, closing the door with a firm click. Looking back at Alice, her perky grin wavered. 'You remembered our lunch date, right?'

'Um . . . ' She was barefoot, in takeaway-stained tracksuit bottoms beneath her dressing gown. Did it look like she was ever venturing outside again?

'Alice!' Flora looked hurt. 'I left you a message.'

'Thanks, but I don't feel up to it.' Alice's voice was slow and thick, and even standing up felt like a huge effort. She pulled her ratty old dressing gown more tightly around her and yawned. 'Maybe next week?'

'You need to get out and about. It'll make you feel better, I promise.' Flora looked her up and down. 'Why don't you just jump in the shower?'

Alice shook her head. 'I said no. It's sweet of you to want to help, but . . . ' she sighed. There was nothing to be done. Ella was gone.

Flora's eyes widened. Alice knew from experience that it would be only seconds before her lip began to tremble, and a lone, tragic tear would roll down her cheek. 'Look,' Alice added quickly, trying to pre-empt the guilt trip, 'I'll call you when I'm feeling better. Maybe we could do that spa thing you wanted.'

'No.'

Alice blinked.

'You've been hiding out here for days.' Flora folded her arms, looking at Alice with surprising determination. 'I bet you've got a million messages on that phone of yours, and Stefan says that solicitor has been trying to get in touch.'

'I'll get to it.' Alice shifted uneasily on the spot, defensive now.

'Oh, really?' Moving quickly to where Alice's phone lay, discarded, on the couch, Flora dialled her voicemail and switched to speakerphone.

91

'Alice, sweetie, it's me, Flora — '

'Ms Love, this is Peter at Capital One — '

'Hi, I'm calling about your outstanding balance — '

'Aly! It's Flora, call me!'

'Alice, this is Rodney, down at the bank. You haven't been returning my calls — '

There were a dozen more. One by one, Flora clicked through the messages.

'I said I'd get to it!' Alice protested. 'I've had a lot to deal with.'

'Right! And the first step to dealing is actually leaving the flat.' Flora tucked an arm through hers and steered her towards the bathroom. It occurred to Alice that if Flora was steering her anywhere at all, she must be in one sorry state.

'Come on,' Flora beamed at her, 'you get in the tub and have a nice, invigorating shower. I know I always feel tons better after a scrub!'

Alice exhaled. Because foaming bath oil made everything right with the world. But Flora didn't seem to be budging; she was bustling around the black-tiled room, assembling a towel and various fortifying, gloss-promoting products. And it had been a while since Alice had been near hot water . . .

With a sigh of defeat, she reached for the l'Occitane.

⋆   ⋆   ⋆

'There now, isn't that better?' Flora pulled Alice gently out of the taxi and towards a paved square full of cafés and lunching office workers. Flora

92

had taken her down to Spitalfields for some reason; sleek office buildings looming above them and purposeful, efficient people at every turn.

'Why couldn't we have just stayed near Cassie's?' Alice mooched behind her, 'There's a diner down the road. I wouldn't even have had to dress.'

'Because I picked the restaurant especially.' Flora trotted ahead, suspiciously eager. 'And you know I'm gluten-, wheat-, and soya-free now for my detox!'

'Silly me, I forgot.'

Alice knew she sounded ungrateful — after all, Flora was doing her best to help — but as they crossed the square, it felt like every smiling face she passed was a personal insult. They were out enjoying their happy, solvent lives, full of purpose and direction, and friends who didn't lie to them for months before disappearing with their entire life savings, and — Alice now remembered — their favourite blue cardigan they'd lent them just the other week.

'Here we are,' Flora trilled, pushing Alice ahead of her as they neared a corner café, the tables outside adorned with neat white table-cloths that fluttered in the breeze. A waitress waltzed past bearing a delicious-looking sand-wich, and Alice felt the first stirrings of an appetite.

She softened. 'You're right. This looks lovely,' she apologised, giving Flora a weak smile. 'I'm sorry for being such a bitch.'

'It's OK. You deserve to, after everything . . . '

Flora trailed off, looking past Alice. 'Oh, good, he's already here.'

'He?' Alice turned, just in time to see a very familiar man look up from his table and wave.

Nathan.

8

Alice's stomach performed a strange ballet as she watched Nathan unfold himself and saunter towards them, looking disarmingly dishevelled in a rumpled shirt and dark jeans.

'No . . . ' she whipped her head back round and fixed Flora with a desperate look.

'Yes!' Flora exclaimed, oblivious. 'Nathan Forrest. You know, from my party?'

'You set this up?' Alice gulped. 'But . . . I . . . '

She glanced down in the vain hope that her wrinkled top had somehow steamed itself flat, or better yet, transformed itself into something stylish and flattering. But no, she was wearing old jeans and Birkenstock sandals, her hair limp and wet in a ponytail.

Before she had time even to sneak on a coat of lipstick, Nathan reached them, drawing Flora into an enthusiastic hug. 'Flora, great to see you again. And you too, Alice. Although, not the best circumstances,' he added ruefuly.

'Mm-hm.' Alice tried to collect herself. That was an understatement. Of all the occasions Flora could have picked for her matchmaking, she had to do it now — when Alice resembled nothing so much as a faded carbon copy of herself: pale and forlorn? 'Thank you,' she managed, meeting his eyes. 'It's been . . . an interesting few weeks.'

Flora gave an innocent look. 'Oh, do you two

know each other? I wasn't sure if you had a chance to meet at the party.'

'Sure, Alice and I go way back,' Nathan replied easily. 'I was actually admiring one of your statues at the time. A unicorn, right?'

Flora lit up. 'Sirius! I ordered him especially, from the Netherlands.'

'You'll have to give me the number,' Nathan suggested, a grin tugging at the edge of his lips. 'I can see something like that in my hallway. A centaur, maybe, or even — '

Alice let out a strangled cough. They both looked over.

'Oh, I didn't even say!' Flora exclaimed. 'Nathan's a financial investigator, so he's going to help you out with the whole Ella mess. Isn't that perfect?'

'Perfect,' Alice echoed faintly, sneaking a glance while Flora chatted excitedly about the serendipity of their situation. Had he volunteered to help, she wondered, or been roped into this meeting with Flora's limitless enthusiasm — and a dose of emotional blackmail?

' . . . So of course when Stefan said you loved to chase fraud people around, I knew you'd be able to help . . . '

Nathan caught Alice's eye and smiled — a friendly look, not the loaded glances they'd shared last time.

Not that she expected loaded anythings, Alice reminded herself. She may have thought of him since the party, but as far as she knew, she might not have even crossed his mind.

' . . . so he'll get the whole Ella thing

straightened out,' Flora finished brightly. 'Stefan says he's the best in the business.'

Nathan chuckled. 'He's exaggerating. But sure, whatever I can do to help.'

'See? It's perfect!' Flora exclaimed again, looking back and forth between them. 'I'll just leave you two to get started with everything then.'

Alice stopped. 'You're not staying? But I thought — '

'Sorry,' Flora shrugged, already backing away, 'but I have appointments all afternoon, and then work to do. Ring me after, and let me know how it all goes.' With another meaningful look between the two of them, she spun round and all but skipped away.

'So . . . ' Nathan turned to Alice, seemingly unconcerned by the obvious set-up. Either that, or he was too polite to make an issue of it. 'I don't know about you, but I'm starving. How about we get some food, and then you start at the beginning?'

Alice nodded wordlessly, following him back to his table as she cursed her stepsister for what had to be the most ill-timed matchmaking attempt in the history of the world.

At least she'd had that shower.

* * *

They ordered cool drinks and an array of food. Nathan rolled up his sleeves and leaned back, relaxing in the sun, but Alice could find no such ease. She sat stiffly, wondering what he must be

97

thinking. She longed to be back in bed, wallowing in peace, instead of facing an attractive man, with dark circles under her eyes and the barest grasp of poise.

'You shouldn't have teased her like that about the statue.' Alice tried to sound friendly. 'She'll probably order you five of them.'

'Teasing? No, I'm deadly serious,' Nathan informed her, absolutely straight-faced. 'I think it's just what I need to jazz the place up: a row of angels, maybe, beckoning in guests.'

Alice fixed him with a disbelieving stare. He laughed. 'OK, OK,' Nathan held his hands up in surrender, 'we'll say no more of ceramics.'

He took a gulp from his beer. 'So, where do you want to start? Stefan gave me the highlights, but there's a lot I still need to find out.'

'You don't have to help.' Alice said, awkward. 'I know Flora can be . . . persuasive, but if you're busy . . .'

'It's no problem,' Nathan insisted. 'I'm usually stuck trailing tax cases and wayward CEOs, so identity theft should be a fun break.'

'I'm glad,' Alice replied drily.

He laughed. 'Aw, come on . . . You've just got to get into the spirit of it, that's all. I was wading through safe-deposit receipts when Stefan called. This is like a vacation compared.'

Something about his ease began to grate at Alice. Did he treat everything as a joke? 'It's nice my nightmare is appealing to you.'

'Right, sorry.' He stopped, pausing for the waitress to deliver their food. When the plates were laid out, he adjusted his expression from delight to appropriate concern. 'Why don't you start at the beginning?'

Nathan managed to keep the solemn look while Alice ran through the whole sorry tale of cheating and betrayal. Then, the corners of his lips tugged up again, as if he couldn't help it.

'You know what this means, don't you?' He leaned forward on his elbows, eyes bright.

Alice was almost used to that flush of shame, but this time, it was worse. Nathan didn't know that she was usually the picture of responsibility; he must think her such an idiot. She picked at her salad, blushing. 'That I'm stupid and trusting, I know.'

'No — that she's *good*!'

'Good, right.' Alice nodded along. She should have ordered something alcoholic; wine, perhaps, or even whisky. Anything to numb the embarrassment of having blindly trusted Ella for so long.

'No, think about it,' Nathan urged. 'She spent that long pretending to be your friend, and her story never slipped — not once? That takes something special. I mean, months of work, flawless preparation, and nobody had a clue?' He shook his head with clear admiration. 'The woman's a professional.'

'I'll let her know she has a fan,' Alice remarked wryly. 'She'd like that.' Then she caught herself. 'At least, the Ella I knew would have liked that. But I suppose all of that was fake.' She took a long sip of her drink, still not used to referring to Ella in the past tense — or thinking of her as anyone but Ella.

'I wouldn't say that for sure . . . ' Nathan paused thoughtfully, applying a liberal coating of ketchup to his burger. 'Playing a long con like that, criminals typically keep a lot of the details true, saves them from having to learn too many lies, or getting tripped up over the easy stuff. It was months she had you going, right?'

'Five months.' Alice confirmed. 'But it felt longer. We all . . . ' She trailed off, feeling foolish, but Nathan was waiting, so she pressed on. 'Everyone who met her, they agree: it was like we'd known her for years.'

He nodded. 'There are ways to do that. Tricks, to build a sense of camaraderie, and make you feel you've been friends for ever.'

'Wonderful.' Alice let out a long breath. Another manipulation to add to the charade. 'I suppose I won't get any real answers until you track her down. How does that work, anyway? The police have done nothing but send me paperwork.'

Nathan gave a sympathetic grin. 'They do seem to be big on ticking all the right boxes. But, finding someone — anyone — is a piece of cake. You track their card transactions, log any passport activity — even hotels or car rental places need ID of some kind.'

Alice felt reassured for the first time. 'So you can find her?'

Nathan hesitated.

Her confidence slipped. 'What?' she asked, confused. 'You said, it's a piece of cake. And you never lie about pastry,' she added, recalling their banter at the party.

'Usually, yes. But I've run all my usual checks already, and, well, there's nothing.'

'Nothing?' Alice sank back in her seat.

'Which is incredible,' Nathan told her. 'I mean, people have tried to disappear as a game, and they're caught like that.' He snapped his fingers. 'But Ella was using a false identity, so she just slipped into a new one the minute she was done. There's no trace of where she went, or when; not even a log-in to her email account to trace.'

'She was planning for this.' Alice realized. 'All along, she had her exit strategy mapped out.'

Nathan nodded, finishing a mouthful. 'I'll look some more, see if she didn't slip up somewhere, but I don't want you getting your hopes up. Best-case scenario, I find your money through my banking contacts, or even just prove she's enough of a professional that the banks have to refund you.'

Alice slowly absorbed his words. 'You mean, they might not?'

Nathan looked at her sympathetically. 'Never underestimate what fucking assholes they can be. Sorry, language,' he added. 'Now you're her friend; they'll try and claim it's your fault — that you were negligent with your details somehow. It gets them off the hook. You've got to love the small print.'

Of course.

Alice exhaled, stabbing at her lettuce. 'Bastards,' she muttered, but even that was lacklustre. All her emotion had long since been drained away.

'Stefan said he's got a solicitor on the case, so I'm sure he'll fix things eventually,' he encouraged her. 'But from what I've heard, it's not so much the identity theft that causes the stress, as trying to untangle everything afterward.'

There was silence for a moment, filled by the chatter around them. Alice should be one of those brisk women, she knew: back at work, with purpose and direction, but somehow that drive eluded her. She was still deep in wallow. When she glanced up, she found Nathan watching her, thoughtful.

'What?' she asked self-consciously. It was a miracle, at least, that Flora had got her washed and dressed for the meeting, but Alice was still painfully aware of her lank, bedraggled appearance.

'It's nothing,' Nathan paused. 'I just . . . wonder what made her become friends with you. They usually don't,' he explained. 'Not close friendships, anyway. It's more dangerous that way — more chance of them being caught out in one of their lies.'

It was just another question in a long list of things that didn't make sense to Alice. 'So she could get access to all my information, I suppose. I wasn't a complete idiot. I was cautious, at first. We met at cafés or bars, and I don't think I had her over to the flat for about a month or so.' When Ella invited her out for drinks after a long, tiring week, Alice had suggested that they stay in instead. Ella had brought pizza, Alice rented *Before Sunrise*, and they'd spent the evening musing over the naïve hopefulness of first loves. Of course, now that she looked back on the casual evening, Alice had to wonder if Ella was snooping through her cupboards every time she left the room.

'Maybe,' Nathan nodded. 'It would tell us how she got away with being so lowtech. Most identity thefts are internet hacking jobs, it's why I don't get involved. Nothing but code, and passkeys, and there's nothing fun in that.' He caught himself, and coughed. 'Fun for me, I mean. Anyway, it doesn't look like she hacked any of your passwords, for a start.'

'She wouldn't need to, would she — not once she had my helpful list of codes and PINs. I locked it away!' Alice added quickly, noting the disbelieving look on his face. 'I had a small safe in the back of my wardrobe.'

'Let me guess, the combination was your birthday.' The sceptical expression remained.

Alice bristled slightly. 'No. My mother's — which nobody would ever know,' she defended herself quickly.

'Unless they spent months secretly compiling a list of every significant number combination in your life,' Nathan finished, his tone sympathetic.

They ate their food in silence, but Alice barely tasted a thing. If Nathan — who didn't seem the modest type — was doubtful about the chances of finding Ella, then what hope had she for answers?

'Can I get you a cab?' Nathan asked chivalrously, when everything was cleared away.

103

'I have to stick around here for a meeting, but — '

'No, thank you. I'm staying nearby.' Taxis were an unnecessary luxury right then, given Alice's limited funds. None the less, she took out her purse. 'Let me,' she said, reaching for the bill. 'It's the least I can do. You've already spent all this time — '

'It's nothing.' Nathan swiped it out from under her hand and took a few notes from his wallet. He gave another of those boyish grins. 'I can deduct it. Business expenses.'

'Oh, well, thanks.' Alice got to her feet, wishing she could feel as relaxed as Nathan seemed. They hadn't mentioned what happened at the party, and now, at this late stage, it seemed almost impolite. Besides, what would she say: 'Remember that time you invited me to Paris?' That was surely the way to create a casual, professional relationship. Alice wondered if he'd be just as unconcerned now if they actually had spent the weekend in a passionate embrace. Some people's ease she envied.

They left the restaurant, strolling slowly past an urban garden area with grasses and a waterfall; cool in the shadow of the towering buildings overhead. Nathan paused, reaching in his pocket for a business card. He found a pen, and scribbled another phone number on the back.

'If you could make copies of everything, and send it my way, that would be a start.'

Alice gave a short laugh. 'That makes, what, four now? The solicitor, the police, the bank . . . '

'I'll buy shares in Xerox,' Nathan chuckled. 'And think if there's anything Ella said that could be a clue,' he added, 'even the smallest details are good for the hunt.'

'You like the thrill of the chase,' Alice realised, strangely disappointed.

'No, I like the catching.' Nathan shot back with a grin.

Alice studied him, intrigued. 'How did you even get into this? Tracking down missing millions, I mean.' It came out sounding only a little dramatic, but Alice knew that her deposit must be insignificant compared with cases he usually took: Stefan and his kind were not men who usually fretted over a stray thirty thousand.

Nathan took a seat on one of the wrought-iron benches beside the garden, and shrugged. 'My dad was a cop — just a regular patrol, nothing fancy — but he would always complain how they were running around after every street punk in the city, while the real criminals were off on their yachts somewhere. So I set up to do the job for him. I get to pick and choose my clients, only take the most interesting cases . . . '

'Like fraud and deception,' Alice finished. 'But doesn't it frustrate you — all the unanswered questions and dead ends? I've only known about Ella for a week, but already I feel like I'm going mad, trying to understand what she did.'

'I'm not so attached,' Nathan pointed out. 'But the great thing about what I do is, the data never lies. The answers are always there. You've just got to know where to look.'

'My data lied!' Alice objected. 'Look at all the

105

damage Ella did, because people believed my details.'

Nathan paused, looking at her sideways for a moment as if he was itching to disagree. Alice wondered why he was even bothering to show restraint, and made a gesture as if to say 'go on'.

'With you, it wasn't so much the facts that were wrong, it was the context. What happened — what she bought, and claimed, and where the money went — that's all fact. Undeniable. Someone took X amount of money from Y ATM on some specific date. Now, whether or not that was you, it doesn't really figure. Someone did.'

'I suppose,' Alice agreed, reluctant. Her chances of finding Ella seemed slimmer by the day; Nathan might be her only hope left.

'I'd better be going now.' Nathan got up, extending his hand with mock formality. 'Good seeing you again, Ms Love.'

She shook it. 'You too.'

'And remind Flora to call about those statues.'

Alice watched him walk away, wondering for a moment how different things would be now if she'd said yes; if she'd gone to Paris with him on that whim. Would it have become something real and thrilling, or just faded away — a brief spark swiftly extinguished by the reality of his snoring, and her need for an ergonomic pillow? He seemed so unaffected by her now.

She'd done the right thing, Alice decided, slipping into the crowd and making her way slowly back towards Cassie's. She wasn't designed for foolish spontaneity any more than she was meant for this listless wallowing she'd been caught up in recently. Enough of mourning Ella's betrayals, Alice decided firmly. She was gone.

It was time to pull her life back together.

9

Moving on, however, proved something of a challenge for Alice when there were still credit agents harassing her daily, and the bank to contend with. As Nathan predicted, it only took the words 'known to the victim' for them to abandon their helpful reassurances and become a cold, unsympathetic foe. To read their official rejection of her claims made it sound as if she was some kind of financial harlot, wantonly waving her PIN number around for anyone to see, and practically forcing her security answers on any new acquaintance. Alice half expected to find her file marked 'asking for it' in some secret internal memo.

The debt collectors weren't quite so polite.

'No, you're not listening,' she tried again, as the man on the other end of the line at Cash4U began another ominous rant about the dire consequences that would entail if she didn't make an immediate payment. It was first thing in the morning, and she hadn't even climbed out of bed before her mobile rang. 'I've been a victim of identity fraud. There will be no payments while the police investigate.'

She had learned the speech by heart. Stefan had recommended it, to keep her from getting frustrated or overemotional — as he had kindly put it. He was right. Even now, on what must be her twentieth call, Alice found herself faltering at the grim threat in the man's voice.

'If you keep defaulting on your loan, we'll have to resort to more drastic action. We have your address on file, Alice.'

She shivered, giving brief thanks that she didn't live there any more. Then she realised she was going to have to get in touch with her old landlord, to warn him that bailiffs might soon be showing up on the new tenant's doorstep.

'We'll be applying for copies of the loan contract,' Alice pressed on. 'My legal representative will be in touch. It really wasn't me,' she added.

The man was unimpressed. 'All our debtors go through multiple anti-fraud checks.'

'I know,' Alice apologised. 'I'm sorry.'

'Sorry won't get you anywhere. If you think you can just weasel out of — '

Alice gulped. 'I appreciate your patience and understanding,' she parroted quickly. 'Goodbye!'

She sat a moment, the phone still gripped tightly in her hands. She was going to need a new number if this kept up, or maybe even a sparkling new identity of her own. But they couldn't touch her, she reminded herself. The paperwork would take a while, but everything would be all right in the end.

She had to believe that.

★   ★   ★

When Alice finally emerged from her makeshift bedroom, she found Cassie exercising in the living room. 'You're up?' she said with an

109

expression of wide-eyed astonishment.

'Surprise,' Alice replied, crossing to the kitchen area. Thanks to Flora, at least the cupboards were well stocked; Cassie seemed to subsist on a curious diet of soya yoghurts and sushi. 'I have to get back to work before Vivienne loses her mind.' And she lost her job.

Selecting a small brioche loaf from Flora's bounty, Alice cut a few slices and opened a glossy jar of strawberry jam, adorned with a sheet of red polka-dot paper and a matching ribbon. Adding a handful of fresh apricots to her plate, she slid onto a stool by the breakfast bar and began to eat. God, that was good.

Cassie stretched, rolling over on her yoga mat. 'I knew you'd snap out of it eventually.'

That wasn't quite the case, but Alice preferred to focus on her breakfast rather than explain all the ways her heart was still broken. 'What are you up to this week?' she changed the subject. 'Any more auditions?'

Cassie shrugged, twisting her legs into an elaborate pretzel shape as if she were double-jointed. Her hair was tied back in a messy ponytail, spilling down over a thin white tank top that concealed absolutely nothing. She stretched up and backwards, dipping almost to the floor. 'Later, maybe. I have some lunches . . . '

It always amazed Alice how much of Cassie's career revolved around these lunches — with producers, casting agents, and directors. Never mind show-reels, screen tests, or the little she actually ate; jobs seemed to materialise as if by magic in those back booths at exclusive eateries or on the terrace at the latest chic bar.

Perhaps that was what they needed to try with Rupert to revitalise his semi-stalled career: just send him on an intensive lunching tour, and soon every dashing young hero role would be his.

'Anything good coming up?' she asked.

Cassie shrugged. 'There's a support part in the next Keira film . . . ' She pulled one perfectly trim ankle behind her head. Alice averted her gaze.

'That sounds wonderf — '

A strange man had wandered into the living area, wrapped in Alice's cream dressing gown. An expanse of tanned thigh was visible beneath the lace trim, riding perilously high.

'Oh, this is Vitolio.' Cassie looked up. 'From that club night?'

'Ah, hi, Vitolio,' Alice ventured.

He gave her a casual nod, strolling over to the coffee machine as if there was nothing untoward about lounging around in her broderie anglaise. And maybe to him, there wasn't.

'So, the audition?' Alice stumbled, trying to act normal. A little warning would have been nice.

'Hmm, oh, yes.' Cassie was distracted by the newcomer too, raking her eyes over his body as he made the coffee. He reached up to a cupboard for a mug, and the robe rose even higher.

Oh.

Alice made a mental note to buy a new dressing gown.

'I'd better get going!' she exclaimed brightly, leaping up. Quickly tucking her breakfast into a couple of paper napkins, Alice found her bag and keys and bolted towards the door.

'Mm-hm,' Cassie murmured, her head still tilted sideways in admiration. 'Maybe call first? Before you come home, I mean.'

Alice stared at her, blank.

'You know,' Cassie broke into a dazzlingly seductive smile as Vitolio wandered back towards her with the coffee, 'to check.'

'Right.' Alice answered quietly, leaving before they could give her a visual demonstration of whatever it was she was supposed to check for. Privacy was out of her price-range, she reminded herself, hurrying downstairs as certain, interesting noises began to emerge from the flat. Privacy, and untampered with, clean laundry.

★　★　★

The office, as expected, was in a state of vague chaos. Alice entered the chequer-floored lobby to find Fed-Ex boxes and post piled high in every corner, florists' bouquets wilting gently on the side table, and a collection of mugs in various states of mouldering decay.

'Saskia?' she called, slipping off her jacket, and slipping into her familiar organisation mode. To tell the truth, it felt something of a relief to have some mess other than her own life to focus on. 'Saskia, where are you?'

'Hello?' Saskia wandered out of the back room, an open bottle of nail varnish in her hand

and three purple fingertips. She stopped dead at the sight of Alice. 'Oh. I thought you'd be off another week.'

'I made a speedy recovery.' Alice began flipping through the nearest stack of post. 'What's been happening? Some of these arrived days ago.'

'Vivienne's been on holiday.' Saskia replied, as if that were an answer. Absently blowing on one hand, she blinked at Alice. 'She decided to take a break at her Suffolk cottage.'

'Right.' Alice gave her a cool smile. 'But that doesn't explain why this place looks like a student bedsit. Hasn't the cleaner been?'

Saskia looked blank. 'I don't know. Was she supposed to?'

'He,' Alice corrected, sweeping the mugs up and walking briskly through the office. Although it was past ten, several of the agents were missing, and every nook had a look of unkempt abandonment. And as for those who were there . . . Well, Alice spotted one episode of *The Office*, two chat windows and a decidedly unsafe-for-work screensaver as she breezed through to the tiny kitchen. 'The agency number is in your file, so why don't you give them a call and find out what's happened?'

'OK.' Saskia bobbed her head reluctantly.

'And in the meantime, you should do a quick tidy-up,' Alice added, ignoring the expression of distaste that came over the assistant's face. 'We can't have clients seeing the place like this. Cleaning supplies are in the bottom cupboard!'

She left Saskia gingerly pulling on a rubber

glove, and returned to crisis management duties out front. The post was swiftly distributed to appropriate agents, a stern peek over their shoulders dealt with the extra-curricular web activities, and as for the blinking answer machine . . . Vivienne could face that delight on her return. Alice was just wading through the last stack of faxes when the bell above the front door chimed, and a tall, handsome man sauntered in.

'Hi there.' He fixed her with a dashing smile. His voice was arched with public school vowels and blue eyes were sparkling beneath the careless flop of his blond hair. Propping an elbow on the front of the reception desk, he casually surveyed the room. 'Nick Savage. I have a meeting with Tyrell.'

Alice gave him an absent smile. 'I think he's been out,' she answered carefully, holding her finger in place in the middle of the pages. 'But I'll have someone check for you.'

'Great.' He flashed a grin at her again, running one hand through that artful fringe. 'And if I could get a coffee? Soya no-fat latte with extra vanilla.'

Alice paused at the arrogance in his tone, but he had already turned away, to check his reflection in the polished prints of screen greats that hung on every wall.

Charming.

Alice found Saskia leaning against a dirty counter, painting the remainder of her finger-nails. 'I need you to run out to Starbucks,' Alice told her, trying not to notice the stack of mugs waiting, untouched in the sink. She'd better find that agency number . . .

'I'm sorry, but that's not really my job.' Saskia had the nerve to smile at her with faux sincerity. 'I need to stay in the office, for the phones. You understand.'

Alice took a deep breath. 'It's not for me, it's for a client. And regardless of your job, the clients always come first.'

'Nick's here?' Immediately, Saskia brightened. Putting down the tiny bottle, she blew frantically on her nails. 'Is my hair OK?'

Alice managed not to roll her eyes. 'Yes, Saskia, your hair is just fine.'

'Fab!' Saskia quickly sashayed out towards reception, but Alice lingered in the back, taking a detour by the agency board. Vivienne kept large charts of client activity, for the agents to keep track of each other's bookings — and to inspire what she liked to term 'the natural hunger of professionals'. In other words, competition. Scanning the various notes, Alice was surprised to see that this Nick Savage was already a client — and booked solid with auditions and meetings. Rupert, on the other hand, had a lone pencilled comment reading 'Brit-flick walk-on? (director — *Sex Lives of the Potato Men*).'

Alice felt the first stirring of unease. Had Vivienne found a replacement to fill Rupert's dashing breeches?

Out by the front desk, she found Saskia and Nick engaged in a time-old ritual of fluttering eyelashes and dazzling smiles.

' . . . Just a small place, to get away.' Nick was still leaning against the desk, eyes drifting down to appreciate the flash of cleavage in Saskia's hastily unbuttoned blouse. 'It's so beautiful down there, I always find it so inspiring.'

'Mmm,' Saskia breathed, gazing at him with rapt adoration. 'I just love Dorset. I always think of Thomas Hardy, and what an influence the wild landscape had on his passions.'

Alice watched them from the doorway, amused. Any minute now, Saskia would be quoting old A-level essays about extended metaphors, and Nick would break into a monologue.

'Ah, Hardy,' Nick nodded, switching from 'rogueish charm' to 'serious artiste' in a moment. At least he had range. 'I starred as Jude at the Playhouse up at Oxford last year. What was it he said about destiny?' There was a pause, and a furrowed brow. 'He might battle with his evil star — '

Oh God, not this. Alice cleared her throat. 'Saskia, that coffee?'

She looked over, resentful, but Nick quickly spoke up. 'Oh, there's no need. I'm fine.'

Of course he was.

Alice was about to exile Saskia back to the kitchen and save herself a re-enactment of the novelist's collected works when the door chimed again, and Tyrell sauntered in.

'Nick, you savage beast, you!' A complex ritual of fist-bumping and back-slapping ensued. 'Hope you weren't waiting too long. Had a crazy meeting over at Working Title.' Tyrell tapped a finger to his nose and pointed at Nick. 'Got some things coming up, perfect for you, but it's all still hush-hush.'

'No problem,' Nick laughed, still nonchalant. 'They've been taking care of me here.'

'Of course we have!' Tyrell pounded him on the shoulder. 'Our Alice is a gem.' Sending a wink over his shoulder at her, he steered Nick towards the door. 'Now, let's get down to business.'

Alice watched them go with a shiver of distaste: a matching pair of designer suits and oversized egos. Oh, it was petty of her, she knew, to fault them for their infinite ambition when she was the one left filing papers — again — but Alice also knew without any doubt at all that each of them would happily stab the other in the back and trample all over his bleeding body to get ahead. Like some other people . . .

As she gathered up her papers and retreated to her attic, Alice wondered again how she could have been so wrong about Ella. Of all her friends, she would never have expected her to be the one to let her down. Cassie, in an episode of single-minded selfishness, perhaps; Flora, out of thoughtlessness, but Ella? And to do it in such a heartless, manipulative fashion? Alice could never have imagined. Even Julian — who had spent long evenings with both of them — was shocked by her duplicity. But of course that was the point. It wasn't out of character because Ella had never had a character to begin with — or rather, it was all character: carefully constructed, artfully performed. The perfect friend.

Alice had tried to move on and put the whole matter out of her mind, but as she slowly settled back into her office — dusting down surfaces, watering the poor, neglected window box, and deleting the twenty-odd threatening phone messages from debt collection agencies — she couldn't shake that deep sadness that came over her whenever she thought of Ella. There wasn't a single detail of their time together she could look to as genuine, or a moment that meant anything at all.

Not a single detail.

Alice paused mid-polish, the cloth wavering in her hand. *The data never lies*, Nathan had said. He'd rhapsodised about the power of simple facts and figures, as if they were cryptic clues to be deciphered. He was tracking the money itself, forwards through the trail of transfers and bank accounts Ella had to use to withdraw it from Alice's account, but what about the other data?

Quickly, she put down her cloth and crossed to her desk, finding the ever-expanding file of statements and letters from banks and the solicitor. Pulling one at random, Alice perched in her chair and pored over it again.

03 APRIL. SELFRIDGES. LINGERIE 783–21. 56.99
04 APRIL. PRET A MANGER. CHKN SLD 4.99
08 APRIL. LNDN TRNSPT OYSTER 15.00

She'd checked through all this before, several times, but then she'd only been looking to see if it was her making the transaction or not. She'd registered the items, of course, but she'd been

118

more concerned with the dates, times, and totals: cross-referencing with her own schedule to discount or add it to the list of fraudulent payments. Now, those same printed lines took on new meaning.

03 APRIL. SELFRIDGES. LINGERIE 783–21. 56.99

The data never lied. On a Wednesday afternoon, Ella had been in Selfridges, buying lingerie. They'd met for dinner that evening too, Alice's own diary told her; Ella had said she'd been in the centre of town for a product presentation, and told a story about Jeanette, the flamboyant Italian accounts manager, who wore transparent blouses over a shocking-pink bra, and reduced the men in the meeting to drooling idiots.

LINGERIE 783–21. 56.99

Pulling her keyboard closer, Alice quickly tapped in the product code and clicked through to an online catalogue. The underwear appeared on the page. It was a matching set of silky briefs and a bra, embroidered with delicate whorls of lace. Shocking pink. Italian-made.

Alice stared at the screen for a long time. A new feeling was slowly creeping through her, replacing the helplessness and frustration she'd been trapped in for so long.

Power.

Ella's story had been lies — just another in the litany of untruths — but now, for the first time,

119

Alice knew the truth. It wasn't much, just the passing of a random weekday afternoon, but it was something. It was fact. And she had more of them: two months worth of statements, to be precise, spilling over with irrefutable, undeniable details about Ella, and how she'd spent her time — and Alice's money. Looking at the bulging file with new eyes, Alice was filled with a curious kind of excitement. She may not know anything for certain about her former friend, but Alice could know this much.

She pulled the file closer, and began to read.

10

Alice hadn't spent her entire adult life as an organised, purposeful woman for nothing; soon, she was focused on her new project with the same single-minded thoroughness and matching stationery that she applied to all her goals in life. Carefully compiling a chronology of ATM withdrawals and debit charges in a new leather-bound calendar, Alice spent the next days poring over bank statements to reconstruct her former friend's movements. The secret life of Ella Nicholls wouldn't remain secret for long.

'You want it like that, hmm? How about . . . there?'

Alice paused with her key in the lock. They were still home.

'Vitolio!' A squeal rang out through the flat, followed by several thuds, and then some moaning.

She had to give them credit for stamina, at least. Alice had left at eight that morning, chased out by the grunts and moans from Cassie's room. Now it was past noon, and her hopes of a lazy Sunday on the sofa with the paper were clearly a distant dream.

Alice peered inside. She supposed she could go into town to loiter in Waterstone's, or another identical branch of Starbucks, but she'd already spent the morning in a local coffee house, drinking her body weight in herbal teas while a chic hipster type hovered over her shoulder, willing her to leave. Her attempt to unwind with a novel hadn't lasted long either: now she was itching to collect another batch of bank statements to double-check for clues.

The main living area seemed to be clear, so Alice darted to her room, ignoring the noises down the hall. She was hunting through her folder when her phone rang. Alice let the ringtone play for a while, hoping it would alert Cassie and Vitolio to her presence. But no: they continued unabated.

She eventually picked up, putting one hand to her ear to block out the noises. Whoever had converted the warehouse had failed on sound-proofing, that was clear.

'Hi, Flora.'

'Hey!' Flora exclaimed with her usual high-pitched enthusiasm. 'Where are you right now?'

'At the flat.' Alice perched on the very edge of her bed. The single, fold-out bed, with approximately two feet of space on every side.

'Fab! Want to grab some lunch? I have to go check on an exhibition space in Notting Hill, but I could pick you up on the way.'

Alice paused, reluctant to give up her vision of a restful weekend. Alone. 'I did have plans . . . ' she semi-lied.

'Oh.' Flora's voice fell, but she quickly recovered. 'That's no problem. We could catch up for drinks later this week. Make it a girly night out? Oooh, we could go to a day spa, and get facials and manicures and everything.'

'Perhaps?' Alice felt her guilt return. These exchanges with Flora were growing more frequent, but still they kept to the same familiar pattern. Flora longed for close bonding, Alice resisted, and guilt — or surrender — soon followed. Usually both. 'I've been so busy with straightening everything out. I'll call you,' she promised.

'OK,' Flora agreed immediately, as always. 'See you later!'

Alice hung up, and returned to her file. She'd made quick work of cataloguing Ella's presence, managing to plot out her daily movements in a calendar to compare with Ella's stories. Still, there were large gaps still taunting her, whole weeks where there were no ATM withdrawals or debit charges, or just anonymous transactions marked only by number sequences or a business name. It was those that Alice was focused on deciphering next. Who knew what revealing information lay behind a fifty-two-pound payment to 'R. Jenkins Services', or a hundred-and-six-pound charge at '32 Westbourne Gardens'?

Suddenly, there was a loud slamming noise. Alice emerged from her room to see the outline of two fleshy bodies pressed up against the glass brick wall of Cassie's room, writhing with particularly forceful passion. Wonderful.

She reached for her phone again, averting her eyes. 'Hi, Flora? It turns out I can make lunch after all.'

'Oh, fantastic! I won't be long at the gallery, I promise. And then, maybe we could go shopping . . . ' As Flora exclaimed her unbound enthusiasm, Alice's gaze drifted back to her file. Westbourne Gardens? That was near Notting Hill, wasn't it? Well, at least she could multitask.

'That's great, Flora,' she interrupted. 'Pick me up in half an hour?'

★ ★ ★

Even though the sky threatened cold drizzle at any moment, Alice waited out on the front kerb rather than linger in the flat a moment more. None the less, she thought she could hear the faint echo of moans through the windows above — or maybe they were just haunted echoes in her imagination. Either way, her relief at escaping was tempered somewhat when Flora arrived not in a taxi, but behind the wheel of a sporty silver convertible. Alice gulped. Flora had finally passed her driving test last year on what must have been her seventh try, but even so, she suspected it had more to do with the torrent of tears Flora unleashed after failing her three-point (or, in that case, seven-point) turn, rather than any real driving ability.

'Don't mind all this stuff,' Flora greeted her cheerfully, reaching over to clear some picture boards from the passenger seat. A bouncy pop hit was playing on the radio, and a jewelled diamanté bunny rabbit dangled from the rear-view mirror. Alice clambered in, looking around to find what looked like a career's worth of work piled in the back of the tiny car: a mass of pastel landscapes, dreamy garden scenes, and delicate still-life prints, miniature copies of

Flora's vast canvas creations.

'I have to consult with the curator before we install the real paintings,' Flora explained, yanking the gear-stick into position. Alice noticed with trepidation that it was a manual transmission. She lunged for her seat-belt. 'Stefan says I need to make sure he's not planning to hang them wrong. Last time I had a show, the gallery put *Serene Imagination* right next to *Soothing Daydream*, would you believe?'

Alice chose not to answer that. 'You have a show coming up? That's wonderful. Is it for new work?' She took a firm grip on the door handle as they whipped into a flow of speeding traffic.

'No, it's a retrospective. Five years on, and all that.' Flora turned to smile at Alice; they drifted across the road.

'Flora!' Alice yelped.

'Whoops!' She dragged the steering wheel back into place. 'Um, can you check the map for a sec? I don't want to get distracted.'

'No, that would be bad.' Alice quickly turned down the volume on the stereo and dug the crumpled pages from the glove compartment. 'Why don't you have sat-nav? I would have thought Stefan would be the first to get it installed.'

'Oh, he did, but it was so confusing.' Flora furrowed her pale brow at the memory. 'That woman just kept talking at me in that stern voice, and I couldn't figure out the settings. I don't drive much,' she added, as if to reassure Alice. It had quite the opposite effect.

'Turn left up ahead,' she told her quickly.

Flora cut blindly into the next lane of traffic; there was a loud blare of horns, and a muffled angry yell from the car next to them. Flora hummed softly, oblivious.

'So, tell me how it's going.' She shot a quick look at Alice. 'Have you spent much time with Nathan? Is he . . . helping?' She was clearly expecting gossip, but Alice had none to give.

'I haven't really heard from him,' she shrugged, trying to seem nonchalant. 'We talked about the case during lunch, and then I sent over the papers he wanted. He said he'd be in touch if anything turned up.'

'Oh,' Flora's face fell. 'I thought, maybe — '

'You thought wrong,' Alice cut her off. 'He's being nice, helping like this, but it's just business. Really.'

'Awww,' Flora pouted. 'I was sure there was something going on there.'

Alice laughed, as if Nathan's casual professionalism wasn't a disappointment to her too. 'Anyway, I'm getting myself back together.' She picked a thread from her linen trousers. 'Work is a distraction, I suppose, and the solicitor's doing his best with the bank. Living with Cassie is . . . challenging.'

'I don't know why you don't just move in with us,' Flora said. 'Stefan's travelling so much, and we've got tons of room.' She gave Alice a hopeful look.

'Flora, brake!'

There was a screech, and they came to a halt inches from a zebra crossing. A very full zebra crossing. Alice gasped for breath.

'So, what do you think?' Flora wasn't about to let the idea go. The minute the trail of pushchairs had passed, she revved the engine and squealed away.

Alice quickly shook her head. 'It's sweet of you to offer, but I'm fine where I am. Really. You guys are doing enough for me already with the solicitor.'

'Are you sure? Because — '

'I'm good! Everything will be fine, eventually.'

If she kept repeating it, perhaps it would become true.

'You're such a star,' Flora said as they sped through an amber light. 'I would still be a total wreck.'

Alice exhaled softly. 'What's done is done. There's no changing any of it.'

'Ugh, it still makes me so mad to think she did that to you.' Flora scowled, her delicate features suddenly fearsome; then she brightened. 'Oooh, I love this song!' and reached to turn the radio up, happy once more.

Alice eased her grip on the car a little, trying to relax as they wound their way through the busy Central London streets. There was a method to Flora's reckless driving style, she was beginning to see: Flora simply had perfect faith in the ability of every other driver on the road to see her coming and work around her to avoid all major incidents. So they sailed over intersections with barely a second glance, lurched dangerously between thirty and three miles an hour, and finally parallel parked in a tiny space without any hesitation — to the annoyance of the car carefully lining itself up to reverse in.

'There!' Flora turned the engine off and paused to apply a slick of Vaseline to her lips, while the wronged driver made obscene hand gestures through his windows at them. She looked at Alice expectantly. 'All set?'

'Mm-hm.' But Alice waited until he'd driven off before daring to climb out of the car and help Flora unload the prints.

They were parked just off the top of Portobello Road, with a procession of antiques shops and designer bakeries winding down the hill. It was still cloudy out, but optimistic shoppers were strolling around in flimsy summer dresses and oversized shades, clearly expecting more from British summer than the weather deigned to deliver.

'Have you got a cardigan?' she reminded Flora, as they crossed the road to a gleaming, stucco-fronted gallery. 'You'll catch a chill like that.'

Flora looked over her armful of cardboard with a sheepish expression. Alice pulled a spare pashmina out of her handbag and draped it over Flora's shoulders. 'Honestly, it's a wonder you haven't been struck down with pneumonia by now.'

Flora laughed. 'Like Jane, in *Pride and Prejudice*.' She sighed happily at the thought while Alice held open the gallery door and then followed her in. Trust Flora to view a deadly virus with such rose-tinted romanticism. *Pride and Prejudice* — the classic, Colin Firth BBC serial, of course — had become an institution in their household from the moment Flora and Jasmine arrived. Every Christmas, it was mandated that after the family meal, they would all gather around the tree, pass out presents, and settle in for six hours of Flora swooning over breeches and Regency banter. Alice could recite Darcy's 'In vain have I struggled . . . ' speech from memory, such was the ardent devotion those first merry notes of the theme tune inspired.

'Flora, sweetheart!' A jovial man approached, landing air-kisses on the both of them with practised ease. 'And this must be your sister. Great to meet you, Alice, was it? Gregory Kirk.'

'Nice to meet you.' Alice shook his hand, deftly juggling her load. He had a Greek or Cypriot look to him, with tanned skin, dark curly hair, and a voice that boomed out in the empty gallery.

'Thank God you could drop by and lend your expert eye to all of this.' Gregory ushered them deeper into the pristine white space. 'Helena here has been getting in a terrible muddle over the hanging.'

Helena there didn't look particularly muddled. In fact, the tall, tawny woman with the clipboard was the picture of efficiency, black-rimmed spectacles low on her nose and a crisp white sundress showing not a smudge or sweat-mark. 'Flora, so good to see you again.' She greeted her with a broad smile. 'I'm just thrilled about the show, aren't you?'

'I've brought copies of everything,' Flora said eagerly, 'so we can see how things work with different arrangements.'

'Lovely,' Helena agreed, taking in the large piles of prints Alice and Flora were bearing. 'Well, we'd better get to it.'

'So,' beamed Flora, 'did you want to start with my *Rosebud* period, or *Reflections on a Garden Path*?'

★　★　★

Alice wandered the gallery a while, taking in the current exhibition: a stark, modern series of abstract paintings, full of angry slashes and exclamatory dots. Flora was still happily chatting away to Gregory about the need to put the lilac pastels next to the pond sketches, so Alice slipped outside, and found Helena smoking on the front kerb. She was sucking in the cigarette with barely disguised relief, exhaling in a long, elegant plume.

'Have you worked here long?' Alice asked, leaning against the front window.

Helena nodded, hair falling in a flat, shiny sheet. 'I'm the manager.' She flicked ash onto the pavement.

'It's a great space.'

Helena inclined her head slightly. 'Thank you. We have a reputation for showing some of the most provocative, challenging artists around.' Her gaze drifted back through the open door, and Alice was certain she saw her lip lift in the smallest sneer.

'Well, Flora's show should be a big draw.' Alice felt curiously defensive. 'She's very popular.'

'Yes,' Helena agreed, looking amused. 'She is, isn't she? Gregory just loves her little prints.'

Alice narrowed her eyes, but before she could say anything, Flora came breezing out. 'All done!' she declared. Helena's features rearranged themselves into pleasant enthusiasm.

'Fab!' she cooed, kissing Flora farewell. 'I can't wait.'

'Me neither,' Flora agreed happily. 'Looking back at some of those old paintings, I can't believe how far I've come.'

Alice, who had seen everything from Flora's earliest watercolour smudges, had to agree. Her work may not be as provocative or challenging as Helena desired, but it had a certain quintessential charm — if you enjoyed *Meditations on a Wheelbarrow*, that was.

★ ★ ★

After a lunch of Iberian charcuterie and artisan breads (since it was apparently impossible to find a plain ham sandwich within a mile-wide radius of Westbourne Grove), Alice and Flora strolled back to the car. The day was finally warming, with hints of sun glinting between the wash of grey clouds; Alice shrugged off her cardigan and rolled up the sleeves of her printed silk blouse, enjoying the brief flashes of warmth on her face.

'Do you mind if we take a detour?' she suggested, as Flora searched her handbag for the keys. 'I need to drop by . . . ' Alice consulted the printed address, 'Westbourne Gardens.'

'Sure,' Flora agreed, 'just as soon as I find

131

. . . aha!' She triumphantly held the pink beaded keychain aloft. 'What's there?'

'I don't know yet.' Alice climbed in. 'I'm trying to track down some of these payments.'

'From Ella?' Flora paused. 'I thought Stefan's people were handling all that.'

'They are,' Alice agreed quickly, should Flora think she was ungrateful. 'And they've been great. Thank you, again.'

'Oh, it's nothing,' Flora insisted.

'It isn't,' Alice corrected, thinking of the hours of work — and wages — the solicitor and Stefan were contributing to her care. 'But I appreciate it all.'

'So, this place?' Flora prompted, pulling away from the kerb. Alice wondered whether that had been a crunch of metal she heard as they drove off.

'What? Oh, right. I'm trying to piece together Ella's movements, from all her fraud,' she explained. 'There was a payment to a business with this address, so — '

'So you're going to investigate?' Flora's eyes widened. 'Like Nancy Drew!'

Alice laughed. 'If Nancy Drew had a debit card and online banking.'

'Cool.' Flora was obviously thinking of haunted mansions and mysterious jade shipments, but when they parked outside the address, they found only an innocuous stucco-fronted house. 'Do we go in?' Flora peered up at it.

'Why not?'

Despite her determination to fill in all the

missing blanks in her purple leather calendar, Alice wavered for a moment as they stood on the doorstep, wondering what kind of nefarious business the bright exterior could conceal. She was assuming that Ella hadn't been mixed up in anything terrible — more terrible than fraud, theft and deception, of course — but that was only based on the persona she thought she'd known. Who knew what underground crime she was a part of? Gangs, or drugs, or —

Flora reached out and rang the buzzer. 'What?' she protested, noting Alice's expression. 'I thought you wanted to know.'

The door clicked.

Inside, the hallway was cool and airy, with pale cream walls and a bleached wooden floor. Framed photos of Italian villas and market scenes were arranged in clusters on the wall, and a side table was elegantly set with fresh-cut lilies. Alice let out a small breath of relief. Drug dealers probably didn't go for fresh-cut lilies.

'Helloo?' Flora went ahead, further down the hallway. 'Is anyone here?'

Alice hurried after her, coming to a stop by the calm grey kitchen. Set across the whole back of the house, it put even Flora's to shame, with three different stoves, and stone-hued granite work-counters stretching far down the room.

'Can I help you?' A woman emerged from the pantry, dishcloth in hands. Middle-aged, with cropped brown hair and a warm, make-up-free face, she looked at them expectantly — but not, noticed Alice, as if it were out of the ordinary for strangers to be wandering through her house.

'We want to sign up, for your . . . services,' Flora announced, turning to give Alice a non-too-subtle wink.

Alice quickly stepped forwards. She had planned another dull explanation of rogue charges and debit fraud, but now she found herself trying to look innocently interested. Perhaps a less obvious tactic would yield more information. 'I, ah, heard about this place from a friend, and thought I would come by and see it for myself.' She tried to sound as vague — yet knowledgeable — as possible.

The woman relaxed. 'Of course! Which class were you wanting?' She walked forwards, reaching for a haphazard folder on the near counter, stuffed with stained pages and loose sheets of paper. 'I have a pastry series just finishing, and meat preparation next week . . . '

'Cooking classes?' Alice couldn't stop herself exclaiming. Ella had gone through the effort of defrauding her for sauté skills?

The woman stopped. 'I don't understand.' She looked back and forth between them. 'I thought you — '

'This is such a cute kitchen!' Flora interrupted quickly. She smiled at the woman disarmingly. 'I love the rustic influences,' she cooed. 'Is that a Falcon range?'

'Yes,' she paused, distracted. Flora quickly peppered her with questions about design themes, and the darling little side bowls, while Alice tried to think. So Ella had been taking classes here now, but somehow, that still wasn't enough. When Flora had finished her spiel about earth-tone accents, Alice adopted a regretful expression.

'I'm trying to remember what class my friend took with you. She was raving about it so much, I'd love to try it out myself.'

Beside her, Flora's eyes widened. 'Good one!' she mouthed, giving Alice a thumbs up. So much for subterfuge.

Luckily, the exchange went unnoticed. 'I can check,' the woman offered, flicking back in her organiser. 'What's her name?'

'Alice,' Alice said quietly. 'Alice Love.'

'You're friends with Alice?' Immediately, the woman brightened. 'Oh, that's great! How is she? Feeling better, I hope.' She looked concerned. 'It's such a shame about that stomach bug. She had to miss our final session. Everyone sends her their best,' she added, beaming.

Alice blinked at the outpouring of enthusiasm. 'Ah, thanks. I'll . . . pass that along.'

'So, she was signed up to Tartes and Tatins,' the woman consulted her book, 'which ran for four weeks. I don't have another starting for another few months, but our Italian country cooking class begins next week? What did you say your name was?'

Alice paused. 'Ella,' she said suddenly, beginning to back away. The name felt foreign on her lips. 'Ella Nicholls. But I'll just take your details for now, and then call later?'

'Of course!' the woman smiled. 'Here, take some leaflets. And give my love to Alice!'

As they climbed the stairs to Cassie's flat later that afternoon, Alice was still puzzling over her discovery. 'I don't understand why she would choose that, out of everything she could buy.'

Flora shrugged. 'Maybe she wanted to eat cakes.'

'So why not pay a hundred pounds at a patisserie?' Alice argued. 'Classes are . . . different.' They weren't something you just picked out from a shelf: they took planning, and commitment, and a process. She tried to picture Ella, joking with the other students over a counter of sugar and spices; showing up every week with a new anecdote. Did she tell those people the same stories she'd told Alice? Was she the same character for them, or someone completely different?

There was a thought. Alice felt a slight chill at the idea of Ella play-acting another role, this time as 'Alice'. But before she could let it settle, she opened the front door.

'Oh!' Flora squealed.

In front of them, Cassie and Vitolio were twisted in a decidedly athletic embrace on the living-room floor — naked, sweaty, and enthusiastically thrusting at each other. Alice tilted her head, mesmerised. Could *that* really go *there* . . . ?

'Mghmm!' Flora made another noise, and Alice automatically reached to cover her eyes.

'Sorry!' she called, backing away, and taking Flora with her. Cassie flashed her an absent smile, and then turned back to Vitolio.

'Oh, yeah!' she cried, voice rising, 'that's it! Aughhhh!'

The moans echoed after them down the staircase.

'So . . . ' Alice cleared her throat as they emerged into daylight again. Flora was still wide-eyed with her thousand-yard stare.

'Was that . . . was that a . . . pomegranate?' she whispered, looking over at Alice.

'Yes,' Alice answered faintly.

'Oh!'

11

During the next week, Alice did her best to work around Cassie and Vitolio's passionate encounters. She was a guest, she reminded herself frequently, and a little inconvenience was the price she paid for staying there rent-free. But, due to the open-plan living space, poor sound-proofing and Cassie's apparent penchant for sex on non-traditional surfaces — floors, walls, the granite-topped breakfast bar — avoiding the amorous couple became a substantial challenge. Alice tried instigating a dorm-like 'hair scrunchy on the door handle' policy, a text early-warning system, and even a 'quick glance before entering any room' strategy, but when she arrived home from work one evening to find Cassie spread-eagled and blindfolded on the couch, with Vitolio wielding a large green dildo above her, it was clear that the situation had become untenable.

Given that her savings were still being held hostage by the bank, her credit rating would cause even a daytime TV ad loans company to pause, and Julian was otherwise engaged picking out new linens with Yasmin, Alice had no alternative but to accept Flora's offer of a place to stay. She moved her things out that same day, as soon as Cassie's S&M-lite session came to its natural — and loud — conclusion.

'It's not that bad,' Alice said into her phone, the day after her move. By her calculations, this made three in under a month, although her stock of possessions seemed to be dwindling while every accommodation improved. At this rate, she'd be living out of a single suitcase in a castle somewhere by the end of summer.

Julian's laugh was comforting even through the mobile speaker. 'I thought you said you would throttle her if you spent more than two days in her company?'

'I did?' Alice reached into the huge stainless-steel fridge and paused over the selection of three different types of bottled water. 'When?'

'Years ago.'

'Well, I was wrong. Stefan's away on business again, but I've hardly seen her so far. She's spent most of the day out in her studio, working.'

Evian it was. Alice unscrewed the top and took a cool gulp, wandering to where the French doors were thrown open, filling the kitchen with a gentle breeze and the faint scent of roses. She stopped, gazing at the expanse of neat lawn and mature trees: an idyllic summer scene enclosed behind the tall, crumbling walls. 'What am I even saying? I'm ridiculously lucky to be staying here. With everything Ella put me through, I could be out on the streets by now.'

'Have they made any progress?' Julian asked. 'I mean, do we even know her real name yet?'

'No,' Alice answered slowly. 'She's still a Jane Doe, as far as the police are concerned.' She paused, wondering whether to divulge her own work, but said instead, 'I have another meeting with the investigator later, so perhaps he's found something new.'

'Probably best to leave it to them, now you're moving on.' Julian sounded relieved. 'I was getting worried, all that time you spent wallowing over it.'

'Mm,' Alice murmured. This was why she hadn't told anyone about her private investigations, not even revealing to Flora the true extent of her project. She was supposed to be forgetting about everything, and just letting the professionals get on with their work, but instead, she was becoming even more determined to discover everything she could about Ella's double life. The things she knew now may be minor details — nothing more than Ella's love of American TV drama box-sets, her strange adventures in Italian cooking, her bra size — but they were true. And the truth, to Alice, could not be overestimated.

She pressed the cold water bottle against her throat, savouring the icy sting against the sweltering heat. To her disappointment, her stack of statements had finally been exhausted. Ella must have been using other stolen or fraudulent cards and accounts, because her trail was far from complete.

'So are we still on for the film later?' she asked. 'My meeting won't run long, so I can be at the South Bank by six.'

'Uh, that's actually why I called.' Julian paused. 'I can't make it, I'm afraid.'

'What? Julian Hargreaves missing out on a

Hitchcock showing?' Alice joked. 'What happened — a death in the family?'

Julian laughed. 'No, sorry. Yasmin has a company dinner she needs me for.'

'Oh, well, have fun.' Alice bit her lip. She hadn't seen him for at least two weeks, now that she thought about it; their long-standing lunches and film nights falling aside with Alice's upheaval. 'Maybe we could do a pub lunch this weekend? What was the place we found in London Fields?'

'The Drooping Whistle?' Julian chuckled.

'That was it. Dirtiest pub name ever. How about Saturday?'

'Sure, I'll check with Yasmin. I think she's free.'

'Great. I'll see you both then.'

Snapping her phone shut, Alice took her drink and wandered back through the house to freshen up before her meeting with Nathan.

When she arrived, Alice had braced herself for a bedroom with a cacophony of printed wallpaper or waterfalls of embroidered lace, but instead, she'd been pleasantly surprised by the large, airy space. There may have been rosebud upholstery on the window seat and floating muslin draped from the canopied double bed, but the look was simple and fresh, rather than Flora's typical cluttered chintz. She'd even hung Alice's favourite of her paintings over the mantel: a washed sunset scene that captured the light beautifully.

Crossing to the antique wardrobe, Alice quickly dressed. This time, she wouldn't be

141

caught off-guard in a wrinkled blouse and damp ponytail; she'd already blow-dried her hair into sleek submission, and hung out her navy shirt-dress in preparation. There. She knew that making such an effort was foolish, given that Nathan seemed to have forgotten he'd ever flirted with her, but for some reason, it felt like a matter of pride to Alice to seem efficient and put together at the very least.

Tripping lightly back down the sweeping staircase past a procession of Flora's artwork and beaming family pictures, Alice paused by the front hall. Should she let Flora know she was leaving? Cassie had taken it for granted Alice would come and go as she pleased, but somehow, being installed in the pristine guest suite felt different, as if Flora was a proper hostess rather than a friend. Which was almost more complicated, Alice realised, given that they were family, and should be even more casual around each other. Deciding to err on the side of politeness, she quickly made her way down the winding, polished hallway and tapped lightly on Flora's studio door.

'Come in!'

Alice cautiously entered. Stefan had spent a vast amount of money knocking through several walls to create the perfect artistic environment for Flora; now a long, L-shaped sunroom stretched almost the length of the house, with huge sash windows flooding the room in light. Stacks of fresh canvases leaned against one wall, a paint-stained table was covered with pots of colour and pastels, and a set of comfy couches were arranged in the far corner, surrounded with vases of lilacs. It was there that Flora was curled up, sketching.

'I was just heading out . . . ' Alice gestured awkwardly.

Flora looked up, immediately flipping her sketchbook closed. 'Oh, OK. Have fun. Will you be back for supper?'

Alice paused. 'Ah, I think . . . Yes,' she corrected herself, seeing Flora's hopeful expression. She looked very small and delicate, tucked in amongst the huge cushions. Alice softened. 'Did you want us to eat together?'

'That would be fun,' Flora replied. 'There's stuff in the fridge, but we could order a takeaway. Chinese, Indian . . . Whatever you want.'

Alice took a step back. 'Don't go to any trouble, really.'

'Oh, no, it isn't. I usually just order in when Stefan's away. He does all the cooking,' she added, her voice becoming slightly wistful.

'Well, then fine. Takeaway,' Alice agreed. 'Your pick.'

'I'll see you later then!' Flora smiled, but she didn't resume her sketching. Instead, she watched Alice. 'You look nice.'

'Oh, thanks.' Alice glanced down, pleased, but still self-conscious about her effort. 'What are you working on?'

Flora looked embarrassed. 'It's nothing. Just . . . I'm trying out a new project. It's completely different from anything I've done before,' she added quickly, 'so, I'm kind of nervous.'

143

'Don't be,' Alice reassured her. 'I'm sure it'll be great.'

'I don't know . . . ' Flora sighed expressively. 'It's much more challenging. But I've been wanting to push myself, as an artist, you know? Really try something different, new.'

Alice was surprised. She would have wagered that Flora would keep churning out her dreamy lakeside scenes and pretty still-life paintings for years. 'What's the subject?'

Flora took a breath, as if to brace herself. 'Kittens!'

'Kittens?' Alice repeated. Feeling Flora's gaze on her, she did her best to keep a straight face. 'That's . . . lovely!'

'I know, right?' Flora broke out into a smile, relieved. 'I've been doing preliminary sketches, trying to get used to the anatomy, and movement, but it's such a change.' She held out her pad, and Alice had no choice but to come closer and make appreciative noises over the rough sketches of balls of furry delight in various poses. 'See, I've been working from these photos of Ginny's new kittens. Here's Snowball playing with yarn, and Tinkerbell sleeping, and Princess Fluffy . . . Doesn't she look so cute, with her little paws!'

'Very cute,' Alice agreed. 'Look, I'd better get going . . . '

'Oh, of course!' Flora gave her a sunny grin. 'You really like them?'

'I do,' Alice nodded, backing away.

★ ★ ★

Leaving Flora to her kittens, Alice took the Tube across town. She was meeting Nathan at his own office this time, in Bloomsbury, and as she made her way down escalators and through the grey, cavernous tunnels beneath London, she couldn't help but think of her stepsister with a faint twinge of envy. The kitten project would undoubtedly be a huge success: earning Flora adoration and more substantial sums that Stefan would wisely invest on her behalf — further cushioning her in the perfect world of comfort, satisfaction, and zero responsibility that she'd inhabited ever since she was a child. The world seemed to bend itself around Flora in a way it never had for Alice: curving gently to protect her from harsh realities, while the rest of them struggled and ached and slammed against rejection and indifference at every turn.

She loved Flora, of course she did — and trying to hold a grudge against her was like holding a grudge against those adorable kittens — but Alice wondered sometimes what would happen to her if this favoured existence ever crumbled. Flora folded like tissue paper when her favourite pink pastel broke, so how would she ever cope if, say, Stefan wasn't around to wrap her in a warm cocoon of cotton wool? But of course, that would never happen, Alice reminded herself, pushing through the press of sweaty bodies in time to make her stop. Or, if it did, another man would ride up, eager to play Prince Charming. There were probably half a dozen likely prospects already: art collectors or investment bankers, who already gazed wistfully at Flora across crowded rooms.

Alice pulled her card from her handbag and briskly swiped through the turnstiles, checking her A to Z to orientate herself before setting off down the street. Comparing herself to Flora had always been a futile task, she knew, but still, Alice felt a small pang remembering those looks of adoration. She doubted anyone had ever gazed at her like that. She just wasn't the sort.

★ ★ ★

Nathan's office wasn't quite what Alice expected. Or rather, it looked exactly how a serious financial professional would choose to present himself — and that was the odd thing. She didn't know him at all, but Alice hadn't thought he was the kind of man to pick dark wood panelling, sombre leather furniture, and a wall full of important framed certificates and photos at the golf course/cigar club/yacht club.

'Alice, good to see you.' Nathan's voice was easy as he ushered her into the room. 'You found the office OK?'

'Yes, fine, thanks.' He was dressed smarter than she'd seen before, in navy trousers and a crisp white shirt, but as Alice followed him in, she caught sight of his jacket flung over the back of an executive chair; carelessly crumpled. For some reason, she found it reassuring.

'Take a seat. I'd offer you a coffee, but the machine and I are having something of a disagreement.' He took some papers from the top of a filing cabinet. 'Well, all-out war, to be honest. Many good beans lost in pursuit of a fine grind, but I'll beat the damn thing into submission eventually.'

'It's OK, I'm all right without.' Alice took a seat and glanced at his antique desk, curious. It was clear, except for a cluster of small, shiny gadgets: an array of hi-tech toys in gleaming monochrome that she couldn't even begin to identify. For some reason, this didn't square with her memory of him either, old-fashioned in that linen suit at the garden party.

But, of course, those were only her idle thoughts, Alice reminded herself, feeling self-conscious for even remembering. She didn't really know him at all.

Alice pulled out her notebook and brandished her pen, trying to snap back into a more business-like mode. 'What's the news?'

Nathan slid into his chair and looked at her, amused. 'Straight to the point, huh?'

Alice stopped. 'Well, you did arrange the meeting . . . ' she trailed off, embarrassed by her eagerness. Since she'd exhausted every lead her bank statement had provided, she'd been waiting on any new break that could push her profiling along. A withdrawal, a lone payment: anything that would give her a new flash of insight into Ella's life.

'No, you're absolutely right.' Nathan pulled the papers closer. 'I'm due in Soho at six, and my date . . . well, she's not the most forgiving woman, if you know what I mean.'

Alice smiled along, even as she felt a small twinge of disappointment. Date. Interesting. Not

147

that he would have one — Alice assumed he was the kind of man who was never unaccompanied — but that he would slip it into the conversation like that; a clear sign that this was to be a professional relationship only.

'There's not much to report, I'm afraid.' Nathan flipped through the papers to illustrate this. 'I managed to track the transfer as far as a German bank, but they're not exactly falling over themselves to help me out. As usual. Don't worry,' he reassured her. 'There are always some sticking points along the trail, but we'll make it eventually. I just have to pile the pressure on.'

Alice nodded.

'For now, we've got this to be dealing with.' Nathan selected a few pages from the bottom of the pile and slid them across the desk. 'I thought I'd go a little deeper with the loan companies, just a hunch. They were almost as forthcoming as the Germans,' he added. 'Anyway, I managed to find the account she was using for all the larger transactions. She opened it at another bank, under your name, to keep it off your radar completely. Chances are, you'd have noticed if your balance suddenly grew by forty, fifty grand.'

'I would hope.' Alice took the pages, and then looked at the figures, confused. 'Wait. It says the account's been open for months. Why haven't I known about it?'

He settled back. 'There are ways. My best guess, she probably used your birth certificate to open the account in person, then intercepted the mail with all the initial 'welcome' correspondence. Once she had the PIN, she would have

148

just signed you up for paperless statements.'

Simple.

Alice scanned the long list of print. 'Let me guess, another overdraft I'm liable for?'

'Actually, no.' Nathan frowned slightly. 'There was an overdraft facility set up, but she never used it. I'd say it was her everyday account, for expenses, and moving money around while the bigger loans were processed. She probably didn't want to draw attention to herself before the time was right. She cleared it out before she ran, though.'

'Of course.' Alice wouldn't have expected anything different. Ella was thorough. 'Is this all the paperwork?' she asked, the fresh pages crisp in her hands.

'Uh, no.' Nathan seemed surprised. 'I have a ton of it.'

He was probably expecting sighs or more resignation, but the prospect of new payments filled Alice with excitement. This was her missing link, the clue to Ella's everyday life. 'I'd like copies,' she said, trying to hide her enthusiasm. 'Every statement, if I can, and the credit card bills too. For my records,' she added.

'Sure.' Nathan didn't seem concerned. Crossing to a cabinet, he flipped through, pulling out folders. 'Take these, for a start — it's the bank account transactions, and a couple of the cards. I can have copies of the rest delivered on Monday.'

'Perfect.' It was all she could do not to start flicking through the pages right there. A thick wedge of data, just waiting to be untangled? She couldn't wait. She pulled back her chair. 'Was there anything else?'

Nathan made a woeful expression. 'You're leaving me already?'

'Well, you did say you had plans . . . '

'So I did.' Nathan bounced out of his seat. 'Sorry I don't have any better news for you.'

'Oh, this is plenty.' Alice happily clutched the file. 'I'll let you get on with, well, whatever adventure you have planned.' Her eyes drifted to the photos behind him: the energetic, sunkissed snapshots, no doubt featuring the kings of international finance.

'Skiing in Val-d'Isère last year.' Nathan followed her gaze. 'And that was a scuba trip in the Caymans, courtesy of a client.'

Alice raised an eyebrow. 'You do get around.'

He chuckled, following her towards the door. 'Let me guess, it makes me look like — what do you Brits call it? — a right wanker?'

'I didn't say that,' Alice demurred.

'You didn't have to.' He seemed unconcerned. 'What can I say? It puts my clients at ease. I'm not exactly the most . . . traditional choice for this line of work. They're used to good old boys; you know — pinstripes and Oxbridge. So, I do what I can to make them feel at home around here, until they hire me, that is. After that, it doesn't really matter, as long as I deliver.'

'And you do that?'

He flashed her a grin, tinted with more than a touch of arrogance. 'Always.'

Alice looked around again, pleased that she'd been right about the staid veneer of their surroundings. Her instincts had taken something of a hit these past months; it was good to know that they were still worth something. 'Right, I'll let you get on with . . . your evening.' She edged away, eager to get to work.

'Don't give up just yet,' Nathan said, obviously misinterpreting her mood. 'I'm not so easily beaten. My coffee-maker will agree to that. I'll find you that money.'

Alice sent him a quick smile as she stepped out into the hallway. 'I'm sure you will.'

* * *

Since she had a few hours to spare before dinner with Flora, Alice wasted no time delving into that thick new file of data. She would work through it more methodically later, complete with calendar and charts for cross-referencing dates and times, but for now, she simply took the first vague transaction listing from Ella's debit card. Ten pounds at BodyFirst Fitness? Perfect.

The gym turned out to be a bright, glass-fronted space filled with shiny machines and even shinier exercise devotees in a range of lurid-coloured workout gear. The eighties, apparently, were back. Approaching the front desk, Alice glanced around at the stream of people clutching towels and water bottles. She and Ella had always joked about their slothful approach to health, and how their bodies would probably go into cardiac shock should they ever get a dose of endorphins, but perhaps Ella had been a secret step-aerobics addict all along.

'Hi, I was wondering if you could help me.'

Alice smiled brightly at the woman on duty. Her hair was scraped back in a bouncy blonde ponytail, and she was wearing a pink Lycra vest and shorts over an impossibly sculpted body. 'I was recently a victim of identity fraud, and I need to confirm a payment made here.'

The woman looked blank.

'Do you have records of your debit payments,' Alice tried, 'so I can see what she bought?' For all Alice knew, Ella might have popped in to buy a towel, or some branded shower slippers. It was a small detail, but all she had were small details — painstakingly built into the bigger picture.

'I'm sorry,' the woman told her, looking anything but. 'Mandy', her name-tag read. 'Our client information is confidential.'

'Yes, but she stole my details,' Alice explained. 'So technically, I'm her.'

Mandy blinked. 'But you're not.'

'Not exactly,' Alice tried another smile, 'Look, can't you just check for me? It was one payment, on the third of — '

'It's against policy.' Pursing her lips, Mandy looked around. 'Now, is there anything else I can help you with? A membership application, or class schedule?'

'No.' Alice shook her head. 'Are you sure you couldn't help, just this once? It's a payment for ten pounds — '

'I'm sorry.' Mandy gave another bland unapologetic smile. 'Company rules.'

Alice sighed. 'Thank you for your time.' She walked away, disappointed. Policy, regulations — somehow, they didn't seem to matter so much when it was Ella wreaking her havoc, but when it came to a legitimate request . . .

She reached the doors, but turned back to look at the desk one more time. Mandy was gathering up her things, lecturing a young, friendly looking man. His white T-shirt was slashed almost to his navel, and his blond hair was sculpted into a magnificent quiff. Alice waited, loitering by a notice board. She could try again, with this new boy, but would his answer be any different?

Mandy disappeared into one of the exercise studios, and Alice felt a sudden rush of adrenalin. Before she could change her mind, she walked swiftly back to the desk.

'Hi!' Alice greeted the boy brightly. 'I was wondering if you could help me out?'

'Sure,' he smiled back. 'What do you need?'

'Well, I have this payment on my card here,' she began, her pulse beginning to race despite the fact that technically, it was all true. 'I'm trying to remember what it was for, but I'm just getting a blank.' Alice smiled again, casual. 'My accountant is such a stickler for details. Can you track it down at all?'

'Absolutely!' The boy took her card and began tapping at his keyboard. 'Alice Love . . . '

'That's me!' Alice agreed quickly. She took a breath, trying to calm down. She wasn't lying — much — but pretending to be Ella (pretending to be Alice) filled her with a strange sort of nerves, as if she could be discovered at any moment. And if Mandy returned, she would be.

'Here you go . . . ' The boy peered at the screen. 'It was for the Ballet Workout class.'

'Of course it was!' Alice exclaimed. She made suitably 'silly me' expressions. 'Can you print that out? For my accountant, I mean.'

He nodded, and Alice waited nervously as the printer clicked on, and the paper began to feed. It felt agonisingly slow, and she forced herself not to look round. 'Did you want the rest of them, too?'

'What?' Alice jolted at his voice.

'The rest of your membership details.' He looked at her curiously. 'It's on another card, but they're all in the same record.'

'Yes!' Alice said quickly. 'All of it. That would be great.'

The paper fed through with infinite slowness, until Alice was certain she would be discovered. It wasn't much of a crime, of course, but if they cared enough about client confidentiality to stonewall her polite request, then who knew what trouble she'd get into for lying and impersonation — even if the person she was impersonating was technically herself?

At last, the final page printed, and Alice practically snatched them from his outstretched hand. 'Sorry,' she added quickly, 'I'm running late.'

'So you won't be making it this evening — for Street Jazz? Damon has a great routine planned.'

'Tonight?' Alice paused. 'No, but I'll . . . catch up later.' She flashed another smile, already backing away. 'Thanks so much for your help!'

Tripping down the front steps, Alice clutched the membership listing triumphantly. Cooking classes, Ballet Workout ... The more she discovered, the more of a mystery Ella revealed herself to be.

12

Although Alice didn't venture into a class that evening, she returned two days later, packing her exercise outfit in her bag, along with contracts, and detouring to the gym after work. The membership record showed that Ella had paid upfront for six months, so the perky girl on the front desk was more than happy to replace Alice's 'lost' membership card and provide their latest schedule.

'It's down the hall, Studio B.'

'Great, I'll just . . . ' Alice gestured awkwardly to the changing rooms, still half expecting the fearsome Mandy to come storming out of aerobics class and catch her in the lie. But the gym was busy with after-work crowds, and nobody gave Alice a second glance. She swiped in with her shiny new card, laced up her trainers and took her place, unnoticed, at the back of the dance class that Ella had been attending for months.

'And one, and two, and kick, hands, lunge!'

She was terrible, of course. The rest of the class seemed to have arrived straight from their day jobs as professional West End dancers, and picked up the routine in an instant, effortlessly moving from step-swivel-bounce to glide-glide-leap while Alice stumbled over simple steps and flailed her arms around in confusion, sweating at the pace. But for some reason, she persevered, and by the end of the hour, she could perform those last eight beats of the routine in perfect time with the others — an achievement that filled her with an unexpected elation, which more than made up for the ache in her thighs.

Alice hadn't danced since she was a child, leaping and twirling around the village hall, under the tutelage of Miss Dee, the ample-bosomed ballet instructor. As Alice leaned over the mirror in the changing room after class, unpinning her hair, she was struck with a sudden memory of her mother, brushing out the stiff residue of hairspray after one of Alice's end-of-term shows. Natasha had loved dressing Alice up in those outfits. Not that regulation leotard and pale pink wrapover cardigan — no, these were elaborate costumes the mothers of the group would slave for weeks over. Or, in Natasha's case, commission from Betty O'Neill, the seamstress up the road. King Midas's urchin helper in glittering gold sequins; the Sugar Plum Fairy's assistant, with lilac tulle. She would pin Alice's hair up in elaborate plaits, carefully painting her pale face with a slash of liquid liner and a cherubs-bow smile, while Alice sat patiently, running over her steps in her head for fear she would trip, and disappoint everyone.

'Could I just use that plug?'

Alice slipped back into the warm changing room, filled with chatter and the whir of styling appliances. 'Oh, sorry.' She moved aside, making room for a dark-haired woman wielding a blow dryer.

'You were in the Jazz class just now, right?' The

157

woman expertly divided her fringe into sections and began winding one around her circular brush. 'Damon's brutal, but you pick it up.'

Brutal — that was about right. Alice's limbs ached, but there was a lightness there too, unfamiliar after so many years of sitting up at a desk. Alice smiled, pulling her bag from the small locker. 'I don't know . . . I was just trying it out.'

'Stick with it,' the woman insisted, over the roar of her dryer. She had thin, wire-rimmed glasses, and a smattering of freckles over her nose. 'I swear, a month ago, I couldn't even touch my toes. I'm Nadia, by the way.'

Alice paused. 'Ella.' Her reply was a beat too late, but Nadia didn't seem to notice the hesitation. 'Ella Nicholls,' she said again, with more confidence.

Nadia smiled back, starting on another section of hair. 'See you next time, Ella!'

'Maybe.'

Alice slowly made her way back to the lobby. She'd only meant to try the class once, to understand what Ella had been doing, but perhaps she would come back next week, or try out the Ballet Workout class Ella had also attended. There was no photo on her gym ID, and if she kept going by a different name, then there would be no awkward conversations about the real Alice Love — or whose card, exactly, the membership had been paid with.

Nobody need know who she really was.

★ ★ ★

'Ginger beer?'

'Yes, thanks.' Alice held out her glass tumbler for Flora to pour. 'And here, you take the salad.'

It was the end of the week, and they were sitting out on the back patio, eating dinner in the late slants of evening sun. After all her recent upheaval, Alice was surprised how quickly she'd settled into a domestic kind of routine with her stepsister: getting a lift into the city with Stefan every morning when he was home, then making it back in time for supper with Flora. Stefan worked late almost every night, so after she was finished with work (and her new dance classes, and whichever detour Ella's bank statement prompted that day), she and her stepsister would take their meal out into the tranquillity of the lush garden and sit in the shade of the awning together to read, sketch, and even, occasionally, to talk.

'How are the kittens coming along?' Alice took a forkful of pasta, settling back in her wrought-iron garden chair.

'I don't know . . . ' Flora sipped her drink, the ice cubes clinking gently in the tall glass. 'I'm getting the anatomy just fine, it's the movement that's being evil. No matter what pose I try to draw, they always end up looking static, like they're frozen in place.'

'You could do a still series,' Alice suggested. '*Kittens at Rest.*' She kicked off her court shoes, wriggling her bare toes in the sun. July had barely started, but already, it was warm until dusk.

Flora gave a smile, but she seemed downcast.

'At this rate, I'll have to. I just wanted to have something wonderful for the exhibition next month. To show everyone how far I've come.'

Alice gave her a sympathetic look. 'You'll get it, eventually. Remember how long it took you to master the view from the kitchen window?' Dishes had piled high that Father's Day weekend, as Flora monopolised the room for her project.

'I suppose . . . ' Flora toyed with her bread for a moment, then fixed an upbeat grin on her face. 'What about you — how was work? Any scandal and intrigue?'

'Today?' Alice had to think for a second. She'd sat in that office for eight hours, but her memory was completely blank. 'Nothing new. Contracts, more contracts . . . '

To tell the truth, her work had drifted even further into the background since Nathan had revealed news of Ella's secret bank account. The fresh documents had been exactly what she'd hoped. While the data from her own statements had been sporadic at best — just occasional online or phone purchases Ella had kept under the radar — she obviously hadn't been so worried about the second account. Using it as a base to receive the fraudulent loans and make minimal payments on her bogus credit cards, Ella had spent freely and frequently, much to Alice's delight. The journal of Ella's real movements soon swelled, until Alice could pinpoint her location and real activities on almost every day of the last few months.

'Rupert got a callback,' Alice finally offered,

160

wanting to add something to the conversation that didn't involve fraud and deception.

'Oh?'

'A new costume drama film,' Alice related, through a mouthful of marinated artichoke. She swallowed. 'An adaptation of some biography, an inventor in Victorian England. They're down to just a few now, so I think he's got a real chance.'

'That's great.' Flora beamed. 'We should invite him to dinner sometime. I met his wife once, what's her name . . . ?'

'Keisha.'

'That's it. She was lovely. We could all have drinks, or a barbecue.'

'I don't know . . . ' Alice was reluctant. 'I always think about inviting them to things, but it can get rather messy, socialising with clients.' Especially the way Vivienne operated. Alice never knew when a calm, dependable client relationship would explode in tantrums — on either side.

'Oh.' Flora shrugged, unconcerned. 'Whatever you think. We should still do the barbecue idea, though; Stefan loves firing up that thing.'

'Sounds good to me.'

They drifted into companionable silence for the rest of the evening; Flora tackling the intricacies of kittens at play, while Alice slowly worked her way through a new book, until Flora screwed up another page and tossed it to the ground.

'No luck?'

Flora shook her head.

'Maybe you just need a break,' Alice

suggested. 'Try again tomorrow, when you've had some time to refresh.' Ten solid hours of kitten sketching would certainly wear on anyone's nerves.

'I suppose . . . ' Flora looked around, restless. 'What are you reading?'

Alice held up the cover.

'Ooh, I know him. Stefan just finished one, he has the sequel, I think.' Flora tilted her head slightly, 'I didn't know you liked crime novels.'

'I don't, usually. But, I thought I'd give it a try. It's quite good,' Alice admitted. She'd noticed the purchase on Ella's statement, and ordered it online, along with a handful of albums and DVDs from the list. Research.

'Can I borrow it, when you're done?'

'Of course. But I'm warning you now, it's rather grisly.'

Flora screwed up her face. 'How grisly?'

'Blood, guts, the usual. Oh, and there's a scene where they find a dismembered body — '

Flora shuddered. 'That's enough!'

Alice laughed. Flora had long ago declared she would only read books with happy endings, and, as far as Alice knew, she had kept to the resolution. 'I think you're best sticking with Mills & Boon,' she advised, just as the phone began to ring inside.

'I'll go,' Flora bounced up. 'Leave you to your dismemberment.'

Alice marked her place with a paper napkin and stretched. The sun had set behind the garden walls now, and a cluster of midges was dancing out of range of the anti-insect lamps stationed around them. It felt odd to be relaxing out of doors on a weeknight, when she was usually working late, or watching the TV at home, but she supposed there was no 'usual' in her life any more. Her old routine had been pulled apart, and although it had been only a couple of months since those first fraudulent transactions had shaken her world, Alice felt as though her life was divided into two unrelated parts: before the discovery, and after.

'Oh.'

Alice looked round at the sound of Flora's sigh. 'What's wrong?'

'Stefan's caught up with a business dinner.' Flora's voice was plaintive. She hovered in the doorway, suddenly looking forlorn. 'He won't be back for ages.'

'That's a shame,' Alice answered absently. 'Wait, what time is it?'

'Half nine?'

'Oh crap!' Alice struggled to her feet, reaching for her shoes and cardigan. 'I'm supposed to meet Cassie at ten.'

'Something fun?'

'A birthday thing, across town. This actress we both know.' Alice wasn't entirely enthused, but she hadn't seen Cassie since fleeing her sex-capades, and Cassie was certainly one to take offence.

'Oh.' This time, Flora's voice quavered a little. 'Well, have fun.'

Alice paused. Flora had wrapped her arms around herself, and was drifting absently around the patio. Alone.

163

'Say 'hi' to Cassie for me,' Flora added.

Alice sighed. 'Do you want to come with me?'

Flora brightened. 'Really?'

'Sure. Why not?'

Flora darted over, giving Alice a fierce little hug. 'Ooh, this is going to be so much fun! What are you wearing? I could maybe wear my pink dress, the floaty one, but not if you were going to be in something red. We don't want to clash!'

★   ★   ★

By the time they arrived, Alice was running almost an unheard of hour late. Flora had fluttered around for a good thirty minutes, selecting and rejecting an array of seemingly identical print skirts, before insisting on 'jazzing up' Alice's navy shift dress with armfuls of intricate gold bangles. She seemed to think they were in one of those chick flicks she loved so much, drinking white wine and dancing around to songs on the radio, so it was as much as Alice could manage to bundle her into a taxi and direct them across town before she began singing into a hairbrush to the *Pretty Woman* soundtrack.

'Alice, where have you been?' Cassie accosted them in the front lobby of the club, waving her membership card at the sleek, black-clad staff behind the desk and signing them in with a careless scrawl. 'Oh, hi, Flora,' she greeted her briefly, before turning back to scold Alice. 'I've been waiting for you for ever!'

Alice doubted that. Cassie was constantly

164

behind, if she ever made an appearance at all; it was Alice who felt flustered if she wasn't five minutes ahead of schedule, and made a point of calling if she would be even a little late. But not tonight. 'I'm sure you survived somehow.' Alice kissed her on the cheeks and followed her to the lift. 'Isn't Flavia dancing on the tables yet?'

'Almost.' Cassie squeezed in the tiny space with them and selected the top floor. 'Lexi and Noel are here too, in from Berlin, and Petros is in town as well — you remember him, right?' She didn't wait for a reply. 'He said he ran into Dakota the other night at a show, he was with some hipster bitch: perfect hair, but no boobs, Petros said.' Cassie glanced down, as if to check her own chest was suitably perky, encased in a sheer black blouse tucked into wide trousers. Alice sent Flora an amused look. Two minutes before a mention of The Ex? The sad thing was, that wasn't even a record.

'Anyway,' Cassie eyed her reflection in the shiny lift interior, smoothing down her already glossy hair as they came to a halt, 'come say 'hi' to everyone and start drinking. You're way behind.'

'Everyone' turned out to be lounging on the far side of the slim, roof-top pool, balancing cocktails precariously on padded recliners as they laughed and chatted and otherwise eyed the rest of the fashionable crowd. Cassie led them over, carefully picking her way across the damp tiles and throwing a wave and a careless smile to people as she went.

'Look,' Flora hissed, jerking her head at the

man who was, for some inexplicable reason, swimming laps after dark in tight-fitting white trunks.

'Modest,' Alice laughed, before they were swept up in enthusiastic greetings.

'Darling!' Flavia, teetering on thick wedge sandals, pressed a glass of wine into Alice's hand. Her curves were barely constrained by a skin-tight red dress stretched over a lacy black bra. 'Mwah, mwah. You look fabulous!'

'Happy Birthday.' Alice hugged her affectionately. A six-foot, Brazilian ex-model with wild, curly hair, Flavia could get away with acting like an Ab Fab character; a cigarette dangling from her left hand and lips smeared with red. 'You don't look any older, I promise.'

'Oh, hush,' Flavia giggled. 'I'm booked in for Botox tomorrow morning.'

Alice gasped. 'No!'

'Yes!' Tossing back her hair, Flavia struck a pose; one hip jutted out and her breasts thrust forwards. 'You think I'm letting anything sag? Darling, this ass is all I have in the world!'

'A toast!' Vitolio cried out. Alice had hardly recognised him fully clothed. 'To Flavia's fantastic arse!'

'Hear, hear!'

With a group as extroverted as Flavia and her friends, Alice wasn't required to do anything more than sip her champagne and appreciate their ever-more outrageous stories. She and Flora settled back on the loungers, and for the next hour, bore witness to the increasingly drunken antics of European cool-hunters, South

166

American fashion designers and, of course, the London creative élite. But by the time the fifth bottle of champagne arrived at their table, and Cassie once again began to describe the perilous working conditions in Poland, Alice was beginning to feel restless.

Unfolding herself, she slipped her shoes back on and turned to nudge Flora. 'Do you want anything from the bar?'

'Maybe some water?' Flora suggested. A chivalrous member of their group had draped his jacket over her as protection from the faint chill, and she was curled up, happily watching the crowd with a dreamy expression on her face.

'I'll be right back.'

Carefully navigating her way around the pool, Alice slipped inside. The bar was loud with laughter and noise, packed with ultra-stylish young things in bright print romper suits, leggings, and skinny jeans. Some kind of product launch was going on, with dark bottles of whisky stacked in precarious pyramids along the back wall, and flat screens set up at strategic angles playing advertisements on mute. Thanks to the issues of *heat* Saskia left piling up around the office, Alice recognised at least three minor reality television 'stars' and a clutch of former boyband pin-ups as she made her way to the bar and ordered two mineral waters.

'That's not getting into the spirit of things.'

Alice looked back from the clique of D-listers. A man wearing a designer suit was standing next to her. 'The spirit, get it? Because of the whisky?'

Alice groaned. 'That's a terrible pun.'

'I know,' he admitted, reaching up with one hand to tousle his already artful mess of choppy blond hair. 'What's worse is I've been waiting all night to use it.'

She laughed, despite herself, just as the barman delivered her drinks. She rummaged in her purse for change.

'I've got this,' he stopped her, sliding a note to the barman.

'Thank you,' Alice said politely. Ordinarily, she would have left it at that and returned to her group, but she'd been restless for a while. 'What would you have done if I'd ordered champagne?' she asked him.

'Gone and hit on the girl drinking cranberry juice,' he replied, nodding further down the bar.

Alice laughed. 'You're honest, at least.'

'An underrated virtue,' he flashed a smile. 'I'm Johan.'

Alice took his outstretched hand. 'I'm . . . ' She paused, the words dissolving in her mouth. She could tell him anything, she realised suddenly: any name, any story. Why would he doubt her? She could create whatever fiction she desired. Alice felt a spark of power rush through her. For one night, she could be the successful agent, or jet-setting actress, or nationally bestselling artist. Anything.

But just as quickly, she swallowed back the temptation. What was she thinking? 'I have to get back,' she said, nodding in the direction of the pool. 'But, thank you for the drinks.'

Johan shrugged. 'No problem.' His eyes drifted past her, already seeking out his next target. 'Enjoy the rest of your night.'

Alice hurried back outside. Flora was boxed into a corner, Cassie's sleazy designer friend leaning ever closer, so Alice deftly inserted herself between them. 'Here you go.' She brightly passed Flora the water, turning away from the man and pushing back a few steps so he was forced to retreat.

'Thanks,' Flora whispered gratefully. 'He started insisting I come by his studio for some private fittings!'

'Lovely.' Alice took a sip and looked around. The lone swimmer had long since abandoned the pool, but the water looked even more appealing now in the dark: glowing an ethereal turquoise as it rippled and shifted in the breeze.

'Are you doing OK?' Alice checked with Flora. 'They can be a little overwhelming, I know.' Her own years with Vivienne and Cassie had inured her somewhat to the adventures of her more high-maintenance acquaintances. Flora, how-ever, looked pale, and faintly exhausted.

'No, I'm great!' she insisted. 'Everyone's so interesting, and well-travelled. It's wonderful.'

'But you'll let me know if . . . ' She trailed off, catching a glimpse of a new arrival emerging from the lift. 'Oh, no.'

'What?' Flora followed her gaze.

'The Ex.'

He was strolling out onto the roof, a messy cravat knotted at his neck and an arm draped around a rake-thin girl. Petros had been crude but correct in his description, Alice noted: her hair was a long, sweeping mess of blonde curls,

169

but her torso was completely flat. Alice looked quickly over at Cassie. Perched in Vitolio's lap, laughing loudly, it seemed as if she hadn't noticed him yet, but Alice detected a wild, determined look in her eyes. She knew exactly what was happening.

Alice sighed. The last time they'd had a run-in with Dakota in person, Cassie had spent the rest of the night downing tequila shots and weeping in the women's toilets. Alice practically had to carry her back to the Tube; passing tissues as she bawled all the way home, hiccuping over how they were meant to be together, and how it didn't matter what a bastard he seemed, because they had so much history. Alice had heard it all too many times.

'Do you want to get going?' she asked Flora, suddenly determined. Just because Cassie ran like clockwork, it didn't mean Alice had to play her part this time too. They were surrounded by people who could hold Cassie's hair back as she retched, and murmur sympathetic encouragement that she would only ignore.

'Sure, if you want to.' Flora sounded reluctant, but she reached for her handbag.

'Good,' Alice exhaled. Cassie was already gulping from the nearest bottle of wine, but this time, at least, Alice wouldn't have to suffer through the carnage. Quickly, they said their goodbyes and headed back towards the lifts. But Cassie chased after her.

'Wait, Alice.' Cassie grabbed her arm. 'You're not going, are you? You can't!'

'I know, hon.' Alice carefully detached herself.

'But Flora has a terrible headache, I need to get her home.' She was surprised at just how easily the lie fell from her lips.

Cassie stared at her, uncomprehending. 'But, He's here!'

'And you'll be fine,' Alice patted her reassuringly. 'You've got Vitolio now, remember? You've moved on.'

'I know, but — '

'It was lovely to see you.' Alice followed Flora into the lift. Although she usually would have stayed, comforting Cassie until dawn, tonight she was unmoved. Pressing the lift button, she sent Cassie a supportive smile through the closing doors. 'Take care!'

13

With the London weather providing a rare stretch of hot, sunny days, Alice watched as the Grayson Wells Agency slipped into a leisurely holiday pace. Half the agents disappeared on their official vacations, while the other half lolled around the office, returning from three-hour lunches with faint sunburn and half-empty bottles of Pimm's.

Alice enjoyed no such break. After all her time spent untangling Ella's movements, her backlog of paperwork had grown to unprecedented proportions, until even Vivienne remarked that contracts seemed to be moving remarkably slowly.

Guilty, Alice pledged to put her extracurricular interests aside, and focus on her real job, but the debt-collecting agencies clearly didn't pause for warmer weather. Despite every effort of Stefan's solicitor, they were back, pursuing their monies with renewed threats.

'I'm sorry, but I — ' Alice tried to get a word in, but the man on the other end of her line that morning wouldn't let up.

'If you don't pay up now, this will go to court.' His voice was loud and menacing. 'Do you really want criminal charges? Because that's what'll happen, I'm warning you. We'll send the bailiffs in too.'

Despite the sweltering heat, Alice shivered.

'My solicitor has been in touch,' she tried again, when at last he paused presumably for breath. 'He's sent the relevant papers, and police reports. You need to stop harassing me like this.'

'The payment is due now,' he repeated, as if she hadn't said a word. 'We'll take you to court, and start criminal proceedings.'

Alice hung up.

They were all the same. It didn't matter what she said, or what papers were sent, they just kept calling. Alice had changed her mobile number and moved several times; this was the only place they could reach her, but still, she couldn't screen every call.

'These just got sent over.' Saskia heaved into the room and dropped a new pile of papers into her overflowing inbox. 'Vivienne says they need to be double-checked and messengered out by the end of the day.' She pushed strands of red hair from her face, flushed and sweaty in the heat.

'Mm-hm.' Alice looked up from her computer. As if she needed any additional work. Fanning herself with a file, she remembered to add, 'Thank you. Who's is it?'

'Nick Savage.' Saskia beamed.

'I'll have them back downstairs this afternoon.'

When she'd departed, and Alice had dispatched another three overdue contracts in swift succession, she settled in to see what role their new golden boy had won himself now. Flipping through the contract, she finally found the details: the lead role in an upcoming BBC drama, playing an enigmatic yet dashing

Victorian inventor. Alice paused. That was the role Rupert had been called back for, the one Vivienne had declared would be his return to form. They'd said the part was as good as his, Alice remembered. In fact, the last time Rupert had dropped by the office, he'd told her with no small relief that it would save his career — and had shown her Keisha's ultrasound pictures. But now it was Nick who was signed on, for (and at this, Alice had to stare hard at the small print) a good twenty per cent less than scale. He might as well be working for free.

She shouldn't interfere, it wasn't her place, but Alice couldn't stop herself from hurrying down the staircase and knocking firmly on Vivienne's door.

'Come in!' The cry was impatient, which never boded well. Alice wavered for a moment, wondering if she should pick a better time.

No.

'I was just looking at Nick's latest contract,' she began, striding into the room. Vivienne had the curtains drawn, all the windows thrown wide, and was reclining on her chaise longue with a damp towel draped over her face. Alice stopped. 'Are you feeling all right?'

Vivienne made a wafting gesture. 'What is it, Alice?'

Clearing her throat, Alice asked, 'This contract, for *The Magnificent Mappin Brothers* . . . I just wanted to check with you.'

'Yes?' she sighed, lifting the towel as if it weighed ten pounds.

'Nick's pay . . . ' Alice hesitated, 'it's less than

174

I'd expect. For a project like this, I mean.'

Vivienne gave her a dismissive wave. 'Oh, no, that's all arranged.' She began to recline again, but Alice took a few steps forward.

'I don't understand. Why isn't he being paid the full amount? And how did he end up with the contract at all? I didn't see him down for any of the auditions, and I thought that Rupert . . . ' she hesitated, 'I thought Rupert had won the role.'

'Nothing was in writing. You know how quickly these things change.' Vivienne gave Alice a patronising smile. 'And Nick taking reduced pay is all part of the plan. He's been getting plenty of interest, but no actual offers so far. So, we thought this would kick-start things.'

'What do you mean?' Alice didn't understand. Of course, they negotiated pay all the time, but union rates were the bare minimum; a client never worked for less.

Vivienne sighed, as if it was a vast burden to have to explain these things. 'My sources said that the production wants to keep costs low, so I suggested the deal with Nick. He's fine living off his trust fund for now, so this way, everybody wins.'

Vivienne lay back on the couch and closed her eyes, clearly finished. But Alice didn't move. Did Vivienne think her completely naive? She knew that cutting a few thousand in performer fees would make barely a dent in even the most frugal of costume drama budgets.

'So what have you planned for Rupert?' She found herself asking, trying not to sound accusatory. 'Now that this hasn't worked out.'

Vivienne didn't move. 'I'm sure we'll find something.'

'You mean like you've being doing so far?' This time, Alice couldn't keep the note of challenge from her voice. Ever since Nick sauntered into the agency, Vivienne's already minimal interest in Rupert's career had dwindled to nothing. 'He hasn't worked in what, three months?'

At this, Vivienne slowly opened her eyes. 'Which is all part of our long-term strategy for him.' Sitting up, she fixed Alice with a steely gaze. 'We've talked it through, and he's on board with my plans. This part just wasn't the right step for him.'

'But it was right for Nick.'

'Exactly.' Vivienne's smile was thin. 'Now, was that all?'

Alice swallowed. Vivienne had a vicious temper, which could be unleashed at any moment, but in all her years working at the agency, it had never been aimed at Alice. Now, she could tell, the warning signs were there.

'Alice?' Vivienne waited, her expression dangerously calm.

There was silence.

'No, that's all,' Alice answered quietly.

'Are you sure?' There was an arch of an eyebrow.

'Yes.' Alice felt a small tremor of disappointment as she backed away. 'The contract's fine, I'll leave it here on your desk.'

'Good.'

Alice felt Vivienne's eyes follow her as she retreated, carefully closing the door on her way out.

She'd failed.

Alice could tell herself she was simply picking her battles, and choosing her timing, but as she stood in the middle of her cluttered office, a knot of frustration swelled; sharp and angry in her chest. To Vivienne, it may be just a job, and some strategic client manoeuvring, but to Rupert, Alice knew this part meant everything. They were letting him down, and she was complicit now.

Her intercom buzzed.

'Alice?' Vivienne's voice rang out. 'Saskia's not feeling too well in this heat. I need you to cover her desk for the afternoon.'

Alice didn't move towards the phone. This was her punishment, it was clear, for questioning Vivienne's great wisdom. But how was Vivienne to know she was up here, waiting to be summoned? She could have already left for lunch. She could be anywhere.

'Alice?'

Ignoring Vivienne's cries, Alice reached for her handbag, and her thick, ordered file of Ella's activities. Quietly, she crept out of her office and tiptoed down the staircase, edging silently past Vivienne's office. There was no sound from behind the closed door, so Alice hurried down another flight and straight out of the building, emerging onto the pavement with new determination. She may not be able to achieve much at the agency, but she had other work to do.

★ ★ ★

Two Tube changes, one bus, and a ten-minute walk later, Alice found herself standing outside a nondescript, red-brick building in Battersea. She pondered her next move. Discovering this place had been her hardest challenge yet; she'd had to cross-reference Oyster top-ups and cash with-drawals across three different credit cards before discovering a curious pattern. Every Tuesday and Thursday, for two whole months, Ella had come to this area. She'd bought a handful of glossy magazines, a pint of milk and some HobNobs and then came . . . here. At least, Alice assumed it was here, because between 10 a.m. and 5 p.m. on those days, there were never any charges — a complete credit blackout. Aside from one: a lone transaction of fifty pounds charged to CDM Services on that first Tuesday.

At this address.

Studying the building, Alice wondered what this new development signified. She'd been prepared to find another exotic class, or a bespoke designer service, but there was no hint at what lay behind the grimy exterior. The windows were barred, and covered inside by grey blinds, and the door was made of some type of reinforced steel; a video-phone and single buzzer in the entryway. Alice swallowed, suddenly nervous. This was a long way from the chic Soho streets and buzzing central London bars she'd thought Ella had inhabited. Was this finally the darker side to the fraud she'd been dreading to find?

178

Alice was wondering how to navigate the security system — and if she should even try — when the door opened from the inside. A grey-haired woman emerged, manoeuvring a wheeled shopper. Alice darted forwards, catching the door before it closed.

'Thanks.' The woman thought her gesture was kindness, not self-interest, and gave Alice an absent smile before heading towards the bus stop.

Alice steeled herself, and stepped inside.

Out of the dim entrance hall, she found a surprisingly bright space: open, like the waiting room in a doctor's surgery or dentist. She felt disorientated. There was a front reception desk cluttered with leaflets and charity boxes, posters tacked to a notice board and a row of yellow plastic chairs between two potted plants; a box of toys spilling onto the faded blue carpet.

'Can I help?'

Before Alice could decide where she was, or even what approach to use, a woman appeared from a back room. She was large, dressed in a bright orange kaftan-like dress and sturdy Birkenstocks, her hair lacquered into a bun.

'I, ah . . . ' Alice stumbled, thinking quickly for a vague excuse, but nothing came. To her relief, the phone rang. 'You get that,' she smiled quickly. 'I can wait!'

The woman gave her a sharp once-over, but evidently Alice's sensible office outfit passed some kind of test. 'I won't be a sec.' The woman reached for the phone. 'Safe Haven,' she answered in a soothing voice, turning away

179

slightly. 'What service do you need?'

Safe Haven. Alice glanced quickly around, looking at the posters and leaflets more closely. Refuge. ChildLine. Family Planning. They were women's services, she realised, advertising helplines and legal support for victims of abuse or assault. This must be some kind of shelter.

'Yes, we have someone you can talk to.' The woman spoke warmly into the phone, making a scribbled note in an open file. 'They're trained to help, don't worry. I'll just transfer you now.'

Alice paused, trying to process this unexpected development. What had Ella been doing here? Had she needed help, or been a victim?

No. Alice caught herself before she could get swept up in terrible speculation. The data never lied, and her data told her that Ella's appointments were too regular to be a desperate cry for help. The magazines, the biscuits, the normal hours . . . She must have been working here. But even that explanation baffled Alice; why would Ella do something like that? She'd spent her days helping the poor and defenceless, and then waltzed back home to commit fraud, theft and deception?

Waiting until the woman had dealt with the call, Alice approached the front desk. 'Now, how can I help you?' She gave Alice an encouraging smile.

'I was . . . thinking about volunteering here.' Alice felt a twist of guilt at her latest lie. She'd become used to giving a false name and probing people for information about Ella, but somehow, it seemed even worse to be deceiving this worthy,

180

charitable woman. 'I was wondering if you had any information, about what it entailed?'

'Of course.' The woman's face relaxed. 'Although, I have to warn you, it's a serious commitment. You'll have to go through training, and pay for a criminal check, even to do the most basic admin work.'

A criminal check: that's what that first payment must have been. And, of course, it had come back clean. Alice Love had no record at all.

Alice nodded. 'I understand. I just thought I'd come and find out more.'

'Well, why don't I give you a quick tour? I'm Hazel, by the way.'

'Ella. Nice to meet you.'

The woman led her out of the reception area, down a narrow hallway. The carpet was faded, and posters were peeling from the wall, but it was clean and well kept. 'Through here we have our helpline area.' A bald man was set up at one of the desks, talking on the phone in a low voice. He nodded at them, before continuing the conversation. 'And here we have the classrooms, for workshops and seminars.' Hazel's beaded bracelets rattled as she pointed out the different rooms. Alice glanced through a glass partition. A group of women were sitting on a circle of chairs, copying details from a whiteboard. They looked tired, as if they wished they were anywhere but there. 'Upstairs, there's short-term housing facilities for up to five families,' Hazel continued, 'with shared dormitories and kitchen.'

'For victims of domestic abuse . . . ?' Alice

181

ventured. She felt painfully self-conscious, intruding somewhere she had no right to be.

Hazel nodded. 'That's our primary focus, but we also offer help for rape . . . all kinds of things.'

'Oh.' Alice looked around, unnerved. She'd never been one to sense the atmosphere in buildings — that kind of fluttering had been left to Flora — but there was a definite emptiness hanging in the corridor. She couldn't even begin to imagine what its inhabitants had been through. 'And the volunteers . . . ?' Following Hazel back to reception, Alice began her subtle questioning.

'There's a range of different things.' Edging into the tiny kitchen, Hazel gestured towards the kettle. 'Tea?'

'No, I'm fine. Thanks.'

Hazel flipped the switch on and rinsed a mug in the sink. 'We're always looking for helpline staff,' she told Alice, over the running water. 'Training for that takes a month, to qualify you in basic counselling. But we do need someone in the office, our last volunteer just left us.'

Alice spied her opening. 'Was that Alice?' she asked casually.

Hazel blinked. 'That's right. You know her?'

'Not well,' Alice covered quickly, 'but I heard her mention this place. Did she work here long?'

'No.' Hazel's face tightened. 'She stopped coming about a month ago, really left us in the lurch. Something like this is a commitment,' she added, giving Alice a stern look. 'A lot of people rely on us.'

Alice nodded in agreement. 'I'm sure she didn't mean to,' she found herself saying. 'I heard something about her sister being taken ill. An accident, in Australia.'

'Oh, no.' Hazel softened. 'That's terrible.'

Alice nodded again. Why was she making excuses for Ella, after everything? But for some reason, she didn't want Hazel thinking badly of her. Every week, Ella had trekked out to this miserable corner of the city to do something . . . good. And that was more than Alice had ever done. 'I think everything's all right now,' she added. 'But it must have been a shock, for Alice. Probably why she left without warning.'

'Well, if you see her, send our love.' Hazel poured out the water, adding a tea bag and sugar. 'She was a good worker. Kept to herself, but she was very conscientious. She set up the whole database, and managed everything by herself.'

Alice nodded, even more confused. She was used to people telling her how outgoing Ella had been, or what fun she'd brought to the cooking class or dance group, but this sounded like a different person.

'I should probably leave you to it.' Alice's discomfort finally became too much. 'If I take some leaflets . . . '

'Sure, I'll just find you the info.'

Back in the reception area, Alice hovered while Hazel assembled an information pack. As she waited, a man in a reflective jacket appeared from what Alice presumed was the main office. 'The estimates will be done next week.' He turned to the red-haired woman who had followed him out. 'But we should be set to start work by the end of the month.'

'Wonderful!' She looked genuinely thrilled, giving Hazel a thumbs-up as she showed him out.

'We're extending, into next door,' Hazel explained to Alice, 'We've owned the building a while, but it's been in such a bad state, we haven't had the funds to fix it up.'

'Oh, shame,' Alice murmured, taking the handful of leaflets she offered.

'But we had a great big donation, just a few weeks ago,' Hazel continued chatting. 'So it's back on. There'll be room for more temporary housing, and education facilities. It's amazing what thirty thousand pounds can buy!'

'Thirty thousand?' Alice looked up.

'That's right. Well, thirty-two thousand, really. Isn't it wonderful?' Hazel clasped her hands together, obviously contemplating what good the money could do. 'And it was anonymous too, so we'll never know who to thank.' The phone rang again, so Hazel gave her a bright smile and mouthed 'goodbye' as she answered. Alice forced a smile and backed away, almost tripping on a stray jack-in-the-box toy in her haste to leave.

Thirty-two thousand pounds.

Alice felt a strange bubble of laughter well up in her throat as she stood on the grimy pavement outside, breathing in wafts of exhaust fumes but barely noticing the traffic or bustle around her. Thirty-two thousand pounds.

It was her money.

The miraculous donation, the anonymous gift — it was her money. It had to be. The amount and timing was too exact to be a coincidence; Ella had stolen her entire life savings . . . and donated it to charity.

14

Now that Alice knew her life savings weren't lining the pockets of a criminal mastermind, or being distributed around the luxury shops of the Caribbean, she felt a surprising relief. Ella may have stolen twice that amount again via the credit cards and bad loans she'd accumulated in Alice's name, but that still seemed like paper money. The real funds — the money she'd earned and carefully saved, little by little for years — that money had gone somewhere good, at least, and Ella had herself shown a glimmer of humanity in the process. Alice was even shocked to feel a sense of reassurance. All this time, she'd been shamed, even resentful, thinking she'd trusted someone without an ounce of truth or decency. This new discovery felt like a vindication. Ella's moral compass may be decidedly skewed, but it existed. In fact, the more Alice thought about it, the more it seemed exactly like something Ella *would* do. She had always tried to find change for a *Big Issue* vendor, and talked about volunteering, one day; a spontaneous gift to charity fit what Alice had managed to glean of her character perfectly — particularly if she wasn't actually the one providing the funds.

But now that she knew what Nathan and the solicitor had yet to discover, Alice was faced with a new worry. Should she tell?

'Stefan, can I ask you something?' After mulling the issue for days, Alice made a tentative approach at breakfast. Stefan was back from his latest trip, drinking his coffee in the morning sun.

He lowered his newspaper. 'Of course. What is it you want to know?'

Alice perched on the edge of a wrought-iron patio chair, her hands wrapped around a mug of herbal tea. 'It's about my money. What happens if Ella's spent it all? Say she . . . bought something,' Alice paused, 'could the bank demand the money back — from whoever has it now, I mean?'

Stefan looked thoughtful. 'If the vendor took the money in good faith — that is, they had no reason to suspect it was stolen — then no, I don't think so. The account was insured, so the bank has to pay you regardless.'

Alice exhaled. Even if they traced that money back to Safe Haven, nobody would be demanding it back. She took a long sip of tea, relieved.

'They might take steps to recover it, however,' Stefan continued.

Alice tried not to splutter. 'What do you mean?'

'Well, there's no specific legal basis for them to reclaim the money,' Stefan folded up the business pages, inspired now by the hypothetical wranglings, 'but they would certainly try — appealing to the vendor's sense of duty, et cetera. And, I suppose, it could also fall to you to decide whether you wanted to honour that transaction.'

'Oh,' Alice answered faintly. Safe Haven would insist on returning the money, she knew that for certain. Worthy, charitable organisations did not base their business on lies and fraud. So, the decision would be hers: take her savings back, and ruin their plans to help the desperate victims of abuse, or forfeit her hard-earned security and future. Alice gulped.

'What if you can't track down the money?'

Stefan gave her a reassuring smile. 'Like I said, the account is insured. The bank is doing everything they can to get around it, but don't worry — they'll replace the funds in the end.'

He went back to his newspaper, oblivious to her dilemma. Alice slowly sipped at her tea and took in this new irony. For weeks now, she'd been hoping fervently they would track down her missing money; now, she had to hope just as hard that they wouldn't.

★ ★ ★

Luckily for her — and any impending moral dilemmas — Nathan was distracted by a multi-million-pound CEO embezzlement case, and flew off to Switzerland the very next day. The bank, meanwhile, finally tired of the solicitor's stern letters and photocopied dated affidavits, had conceded that Alice might just have been the innocent party in her theft. They were refunding the contents of her current account, and would, at some nebulous point in the future, be restoring her savings to their former glory — provided that there were no 'major developments' in the case.

Alice rejoiced. The spectre of Safe Haven still loomed, uneasy on her conscience, but for the first time in weeks, she could treat Flora and Stefan to dinner, replace her worn summer raincoat, and even purchase a new dress in the sales. She had never been particularly extravagant, as Ella had commented on several occasions, but Alice's spending habits since the fraud had been positively frugal; suddenly released from her careful budgeting, she had to admit, she went a little wild.

'Did you do something to your hair?' Julian met her at their usual Saturday morning rendezvous at a Primrose Hill deli. It had been a couple of weeks since they'd managed to catch up, Julian's workload, as an accountant, as heavy as Alice's now that the tax season was well underway. He paused by the chiller cabinet, assessing her. 'You look . . . different?'

'Really? Hmm, it's nothing new.' Alice reached past him for a bottle of juice, breezily dismissing his claim despite the fact that everything aside from her hair was, in fact, new. Her sundress was her favourite shade of navy, but it billowed to the floor from a beaded neckline in a goddess-like style, matched with a bright bracelet of thick-cut gemstones borrowed from Flora. Alice felt more elegant and feminine than ever before, thanks to the impulse purchase. She'd seen the item listed on Ella's debit card, but it wasn't until she was in French Connection, looking at the soft folds of fabric, that she'd been tempted to purchase it for herself. They shared a similar complexion, so of course, it suited her perfectly.

'Anyway, I was thinking we could do something else today.'

Julian looked surprised. 'What do you mean? We always picnic, if the weather's good.'

'I know.' Alice followed him down the aisle of fresh-baked breads. 'But there are lots of other things on today. I read about a car-boot art fair on Brick Lane, or there's a festival on at the Southbank.'

'Maybe if we'd planned it.' Julian took a French stick, and added it to his basket of cheese and olives. 'But I told Yasmin where we'd be. She's just checking some things at the office.'

'So text her, say to meet us somewhere else,' Alice protested, but Julian was already pondering the fresh salads, deep in thought. 'Jules?' she prompted.

'Maybe another time, OK?' He shot her a smile, clearly distracted by the choice between niçoise and mozzarella. 'Besides, the weather's glorious. You don't want to be inside, or crammed in some car-park on a day like this.'

'All right,' Alice sighed.

She wandered the deli, trying not to feel frustrated by the regularity of their routine. The problem was, those weeks she spent poring over her bank records hadn't just revealed Ella's spending, but Alice's old patterns too. Her life, according to the dense print of her debit

190

statements, was painfully predictable: her penchant for M&S meal deals, bought at the station on her way home from work twice a week; the lunch trip to Pret, always resulting in a salad and single piece of fruit; the collection of toiletries she'd buy fortnightly in Boots, gradually accruing her meaningless loyalty points. Alice had always liked the reliable structure of her days, but seeing her life laid out in those dull lines of data had shifted something. She wanted to do something new, exciting for a change.

'And get crisps too,' Julian called from the next aisle. 'Those Kettle ones you know I like!'

Perhaps tomorrow.

★ ★ ★

The weather was indeed glorious. Alice and Julian set up their picnic in the civilised shade of their favourite tree, with London stretching below them in a clear, sun-drenched view. A tartan blanket, the newspapers, and a bottle of white wine — it was the leisurely weekend idyll, and as Alice snapped the lids from their array of food containers and spooned the contents onto plastic plates, she tried not to dwell on how many times they'd done this before, but, instead, the loveliness of their surroundings.

'Cheers.' Julian bit hungrily into his cheese-smeared bread, sprawling back on his elbows in contentment.

'Cheers,' Alice echoed. She hitched up her long dress and shifted her legs into the sun. 'So, what's been happening with you? How's it working out, living with Yasmin?'

Julian chewed thoughtfully. 'Interesting . . . '

'Hardly a glowing review,' Alice noted, reaching for the bread. She tore off a hunk and waited patiently for the litany of Julian's minor irritations that would, as always, add up to the end of the relationship. The anti-butter stance would, she predicted, rank high on his scoreboard of domestic disharmony.

But this time, Julian wasn't forthcoming. 'It's an adjustment,' he said, as if trying to convince himself. 'It's been a while since I lived with anyone — except you, of course,' he added. They'd been flatmates for a couple of years when Alice had first moved to London; during which time she hadn't lifted a finger in the kitchen, and had gained at least fifteen pounds of dessert weight.

'That's right.' Alice thought hard. 'Who was it last? That environmental woman, Whitney?'

Julian nodded. 'Whitney . . . that was, God, two years ago. Or was it three?'

'We're getting old.'

'Tell me about it.' He sighed, wistful. 'And I'm even older.'

'By two whole years. That's nothing.'

'I don't know . . . ' Julian rolled onto one side, looking at her across their debris. He tilted his head, giving her a curious half-smile. 'I always thought something would have stuck by now. Someone.'

'Well, Yasmin seems nice enough.' Alice tried to be diplomatic. 'She's very ambitious, and together. And you need someone who can keep you organised,' she added, playfully tossing a strawberry at him.

'Why? I've got you for that.' Julian retaliated with an olive. Alice caught it, and popped it in her mouth triumphantly. 'No, the thing about Yasmin is — '

'There you are!'

They both looked up. The woman herself was approaching, in a crisp emerald sundress with matching sandals. 'I've been trying to call.' Yasmin stood over them, breathless. 'Did you leave your phone off?'

Julian checked. 'Oh, yes, sorry.'

Yasmin rolled her eyes. 'Jules! This park is enormous, you could have been anywhere.'

'Hi, Yasmin,' Alice ventured brightly. She shifted over to make room, clearing some of their food aside. 'How are you?' Leaning in, they exchanged air kisses, while Julian foraged for another wine glass and plate. 'Thank God you came to help us eat all of this,' Alice added, 'I don't know why, but Julian always buys enough food to sustain a small army.'

'He does get carried away,' Yasmin agreed. Carefully arranging her skirt, she accepted the wine and settled back. 'Oh, I need this. They left such a mess at the office, I thought I'd never get away.'

'Well, this is an official stress-free zone,' Alice announced, 'Which is why I'm sticking to the newspaper review sections. Hand them over.' She passed the news pages to Julian in exchange, stretching out lazily to read while Yasmin updated him on various high-finance wranglings.

193

'And how about you, Alice?' Yasmin asked eventually. She was resting one hand on Julian's chest, taking small sips of her wine. 'That awful fraud must still be a nightmare.'

Alice looked up. 'Actually, it's all getting cleared up now.'

'Oh, that's wonderful. Julian said it was taking its toll.'

'I was stressed for a while,' Alice agreed, remembering the early, fraught weeks. 'But Stefan and his people have absorbed most of the chaos.'

'Crap!' Julian exclaimed. 'I was supposed to get back to him, about that squash match.'

'You mean, squash massacre,' Alice laughed.

'Hey! I happen to be rather adept with the racket.'

'Adequate, maybe,' Alice smirked. 'I remember a certain rather painful tennis game . . .'

Julian pointed the baguette at her in mock threat. 'Of which we swore never to speak.'

Yasmin blinked back and forth between them. 'I didn't know you played tennis, sweetie.'

' 'Playing' is an overstatement,' Alice told her. 'Even Flora can beat him.'

'The honour is in the noble attempt,' Julian declared grandly. 'And I still say I let her win.'

'Of course you did,' Alice laughed.

Yasmin turned to Julian, stroking his hair. 'The company has tickets for Wimbledon next week. We could go, if you want.'

'That sounds great,' Julian lit up. 'What do you say, Aly? Come cheer on some other great British failures?'

A look of annoyance flickered across Yasmin's face, so Alice just shrugged. 'I don't know . . . '

Julian frowned. 'You were just saying you wanted to do something different.'

'I'll think about it.'

'Actually, I think I can only get two seats,' Yasmin interrupted. 'So, perhaps not this year.'

Alice met her with an even smile. 'Perhaps not.'

There was a pause, and them Yasmin leaned in to murmur something to Julian. He laughed, kissing her fondly. Alice ate another strawberry. She hadn't realised it, but she'd hardly spent any time alone with Julian and Yasmin before: somehow, they usually met at some distracting event, or with Ella around to act as a convenient buffer. Now, for the first time, she was aware of the small, but noticeable moves Yasmin made to mark her territory.

'Have you got any more business trips coming up?' Alice tried a more friendly tone. 'You're always off to such exciting places.'

'A couple, in the next month.' Yasmin narrowed her eyes, and Alice realised too late that the question may have sounded strategic, as if Alice were checking when she would leave next, so — of course — she could leap on Julian.

'Anywhere nice?' Alice pressed.

Yasmin shrugged. 'Tokyo, and then Paris again.'

Julian looked up. 'Remember the time we went to Paris?' He grinned at Alice, oblivious to Yasmin's displeasure.

'We were backpacking,' Alice explained quickly.

195

'Stayed in a big hostel dorm with a group of rowdy Irish guys.'

'Oh. Fun.' Yasmin's lips pressed together thinly.

'It was!' Julian didn't seem to grasp the tactless nature of discussing foreign travel with another woman, however innocent — and unhygienic — the adventure may have been.

'You should take Jules with you on one of these trips,' Alice tried again to defuse the growing tension. 'A break would be good for him, he's been slaving away.'

'It's not like they're holidays.' Yasmin managed to make Alice's friendly suggestion sound like a slur. 'I'm working non-stop.'

'Right.' Alice exhaled. 'Of course.'

They fell silent again, turning back to the food and newspapers. Alice idled with the magazine section, exasperated. She should stay an hour or so longer, and try to put Yasmin at ease. She might be resistant now, but with more effort, and conversation, Yasmin would surely thaw; it would just take work, that was all.

But the thought of more work was somehow not appealing. 'You know, I think I'm going to make a move.' She smiled, decision suddenly made.

'Really?' Yasmin brightened.

'Yes. Flora wanted us to spend some time together.' Alice began to gather the papers and her share of the food. Just because she was leaving, it was no reason to forsake her lunch.

Julian looked confused. 'I thought you said she was locked away in her studio.'

196

'Exactly.' Alice agreed. 'Which is why she's counting on me for a break.' She pulled her sandals back on and got to her feet, brushing down her dress for stray grass and leaves. Strangely, she wasn't even lying. Flora had been shut away in that studio for most of the week, looking pale and anxious whenever she did emerge. Alice had found a DVD rental listing on Ella's statement that looked just Flora's sort: a rom-com starring Colin Firth, Kate Hudson *and* Sandra Bullock. It was practically the pinnacle of happy endings.

'Can't you stay a little longer?' Julian asked.

'Afraid not. It was lovely to see you again, Yasmin.' She made her farewells warmly, and gave Julian a hug. 'Enjoy the rest of the day!'

Alice strolled away, swinging her bag as she meandered back down the hill. It was a small, simple thing to leave a social function when she first felt the urge, rather than tolerating the situation until it was polite to make her departure, but Alice felt remarkably cheerful as she left Yasmin and Julian to their brie and kisses. The day was hers now, to do with what she pleased. Perhaps she'd even stop for ice cream.

★   ★   ★

'Flora?' Alice arrived back at the house that afternoon, exhausted from a dance class. She'd popped by the gym on an impulse to check their schedule, and found a session about to get underway. Nadia, the girl from before, had been there too, and together they'd laboured in the back row, trying to perfect their jazz hands. 'Flora, are you in?'

There was no reply, so Alice made her way to the studio and poked her head inside. Last time she'd dropped by, the room had been bright and ordered, with canvases neatly stacked along the walls and paints lined up on the big table. Now, there was disarray. Paintings were piled haphazardly, and brushes and bottles were strewn across the floor; open books, and easels upturned. Disconcerted, Alice hovered in the doorway, unsure, but curiosity won out. She took a tentative few steps deeper into the mess.

The kitten project was clearly still stalled. Torn-up sketches littered the floor, and as Alice carefully smoothed out the pages, she found Princess Fluffy toying with a ball of string, or nudging her milk bowl — over and over: watercolour, charcoal, even pen-and-ink drawings; Flora had been locked in that room, working for days, but even though to Alice they looked perfect, full of movement and joy, Flora didn't seem to agree.

Alice wondered for the first time whether Flora's moods were something more than artistic temperament. Or, was this just a natural part of her creative process — one that Alice had simply never been around to witness before?

She backed away, already guilty for intruding, but just as she turned to leave, something caught Alice's eye. A leather portfolio was tucked between the table and a bookshelf, but it had fallen open, showing a flash of dark brushstrokes and deep, violent red. Alice reached for it. They were portraits, crammed carelessly into the folder: some sketched hurriedly, others laboured over in full oil paints — a blur of faces, united in grief, anger and misery. For a moment, Alice didn't understand where they had come from. Then Flora's tiny looping signature became clear on the corners, half buried by a layer of paint.

Alice stared at them. The colours, if she could even call them that, were murky and dull, and the brushstrokes were sharp, etched deep into the canvas and paper in places, as if the artist had hurled them there in fury or pain. But the artist was Flora.

There were dozens of paintings stuffed into the portfolio. Who knew how long she'd been working on them?

'Alice? Is that you?' Flora's voice echoed faintly from the back garden. Alice closed the folder and shoved it back in its hiding place, just as Flora arrived at the open French windows. She was wearing a candy-pink bikini top and a trailing, gypsy-style skirt, with oversized sunglasses pushed up on the top of her head.

'There you are.' She beamed at Alice. 'I heard something, but I wasn't sure if you were back yet.'

'I was just looking at . . . this!' Alice grabbed the nearest piece of paper. ' 'The Nelson-Rhodes Fellowship,' ' she read from the printout, moving away from the portfolio. 'That sounds fun. Are you going to apply?'

Flora shook her head, quickly taking the page from Alice's hand. 'No. It's in Florence, for three whole months.' She folded it several times and tossed it aside, before turning to Alice with a bright smile. 'Anyway, they only take real artists!'

Her eyes drifted past Alice. 'Oh, you've seen the mess then.' She gave an embarrassed grin. 'I was looking for my favourite pencils. Searched everywhere!'

'Any sign of them?' Alice kept studying her, but there was no hint that anything was wrong.

'Not yet, but I'm sure they'll turn up.' Flora shrugged. She linked her arm through Alice's and steered her out into the garden again. 'Do you want some lemonade? I just made a jug. And Stefan brought back these amazing truffles from Brussels. Truffles from Brussels,' she said in a singsong voice. 'Ha!'

'Sounds good to me.' Alice followed, still thrown by her discovery.

'Yay! Oh, and I found the cutest little music box at this antiques shop. It plays 'Twinkle, Twinkle, Little Star' just like one I had when I was younger. You have to see!'

Perhaps she was reading too much into it, Alice told herself, shaking off her unease. The paintings were probably old work from a brief era of teen angst, or just experimentation. Flora was an artist, after all, and who said she couldn't try something other than wild roses and weeping willows from time to time? Watching her stepsister carefully as she poured their drinks, Alice told herself not to be so dramatic.

This was Flora, after all. It was nothing to worry about.

15

Sunday found Alice browsing in the gift shop at the National Gallery, surreptitiously assessing the staff for helpfulness — or, more often, the lack thereof. She'd learned by now that not all assistants had been created equal: some were counting down until the end of their shift, others sighed with impatience when asked to do anything more than blindly ring up an item, and some greeted her requests for information about 'her' billing activities with suspicion and deferral to the manager.

As she watched from a strategic vantage point behind a table of Monet mugs, Alice quickly eliminated several candidates. The young woman with thick eyeliner was glaring at the pair of toddlers stationed nearby, the older, balding man was constantly darting off to rearrange a perilous display of glass snow globes, depicting Rodin's *The Thinker* in a flutter of glittering confetti, but the young man on the far desk with a tousled fringe and suntan marks . . . ?

He looked over, catching Alice's gaze, and gave her a quick, friendly smile before turning back to the register. Perfect.

She waited until the stream of customers had thinned and then made her way over.

'Hi,' Alice began brightly. 'I was wondering if you could help me.' She smiled up at him, tucking her hair behind her ears. She'd let it dry wavy for a change, and she still wasn't quite used to it falling in her face, unconquered by hair grips or the blast of her blow dryer.

The man — boy, really, since he must have still been a teenager — smiled back. 'That's what I'm here for.'

Alice laughed. 'Of course. Right, see, I'm trying to buy my friend a birthday present,' she began, pulling her notebook out of her bag. 'I want to get her some big prints of her favourite paintings, but when I asked, she just jotted down the codes — not the names themselves!'

'That shouldn't be a problem.' The boy seemed happy that her request was so simple, unlike the Dutch tourists in front of Alice, who she'd overheard asking if the Van Gogh prints were available 'in less aggressive colours'. 'Have you got the codes there? I can just search in the system.'

'Wonderful. Thank you so much . . . Charles.' Alice glanced at his name-tag, passing him the list of codes she'd taken from Ella's debit statement. She purchased a large coffee table art book here in March, along with five unidentified postcards. They'd cost only fifty pence each, and the location was clearly marked, so the transaction hadn't ranked highly on her priority list for investigating. Now, however, Alice felt an urge to see which paintings it was that Ella had wanted to take with her.

After tapping away at his computer for a few seconds, Charles made a note next to the final code and passed it back to Alice. 'There you go.'

'You're a lifesaver.'

'Did you need me to find the prints for you?' Charles asked, still eager to help.

'Oh, no, I think I'll just take a browse first. Besides, I've taken up enough of your time.' Alice made a show of looking behind her at the queue. 'Thanks again!'

Alice wandered the tall, echoing corridors of the gallery as if for the first time. She'd visited before, but today was different. She was viewing the world through Ella's eyes, and as she picked a new path through the labyrinth of cavernous halls and small ante-rooms, she wondered, had Ella taken this same route? What had caught her eye? Had she paused, on that very same leather seat one afternoon to rest, or eavesdrop on a passing conversation, or take a moment longer to study one of the paintings?

Checking her map, Alice came to a stop in front of the first of Ella's paintings, as she thought of them. A Velázquez, it showed a naked woman, reclining on a bed with her back to the viewer. A small cupid kneeled nearby, holding up a mirror, and it was in that small square that the woman's face was visible; shadowed, but staring straight out of the frame.

Alice stepped back, studying it. She remembered seeing it before, but now she looked closely, trying to absorb every detail of the scene. The nude was lounging, her skin pale and luminous, yet the longer Alice looked, the more discomforting she found it. There was something strange about the composition and pose that made it almost . . . provocative; the woman's gaze so direct, yet separate from her lazing form,

203

as if she was another person entirely.

Was this what Ella had been drawn to? She'd separated herself too. The woman Alice had seen as Ella was really only what Ella had permitted her to see. She had constructed herself as artfully as this woman had draped her body, arranging limbs in what seemed to be an unstudied pose, but could have been carefully planned all along.

Lost in thought, Alice moved on. She soon found that the other cards Ella had purchased were all variations on the theme: from Titian to Renoir, it seemed she had a taste for provocative scenes that spilled over with fleshy nudes and anxious tension. *The Death of Acteon*, devoured by dogs as Diana looked on, bold; *A Nymph by a Stream*, with her fixed, challenging stare. Alice took in the paintings, fascinated by the life and colour that spilled from every canvas. They were riotous, violent, sexual — glimpses of a world Alice never ventured near. And then . . .

She paused by the last painting, confused. The final code on her list was for a Turner, one of his vast ocean scenes. The sky hung, misty and pale over a dark shoreline, the water cloudy and deep. The painting was flanked by two others, again showing the ocean, and a far horizon. Alice backed away from the canvas and sank to the low, leather seat facing the art.

This was something different.

She could feel it at once, a shiver running lightly down the back of her neck. This meant something different, something more. Not just the style, a world away from the classical nudes, but the ominous shadows lingering in the sky and the way the light glimmered in the distance, a horizon that could never be reached.

Slipping on her headphones, Alice gazed at the vast, empty landscapes as the gallery bustled around her. Her soundtrack for the day was a strange, restrained mix of electronica and slow, languid guitar. The xx, they were called, and of all the music from Ella's purchase history, Alice had taken to this little-known London band the most. There was something seductive in the chords: a slow, wistful melody that wrapped around her, letting the busy activity of her regular life just fall away. Today, as Alice lost herself in the dark hue of the water, and the glinting reflection of sunset on the waves, it seemed to cocoon her in a strange world where nothing existed but the music, and the paintings, and her own, curious thoughts. Alice felt almost as if Ella were sitting there beside her, listening to the same song; watching the paintings in companionable silence before they would adjourn to the tearoom for cake, to chat about Yasmin's jealousy, and Ella's charity work, and how they could stop Nathan from discovering the truth about the money.

But Ella didn't know about that. She didn't know that Alice knew anything at all.

Would she be surprised to know the truth?

★ ★ ★

Alice wasn't sure how long she'd been staring at the paintings when a hand came down on her shoulder, startling her out of the reverie. She whirled around.

'It's only me!'

'Rupert,' Alice caught her breath, pulling off her headphones. 'Sorry, I was miles away.'

'I didn't mean to startle you.' Rupert kissed her on both cheeks. He was wearing a loose pair of corduroy trousers and a faded blue shirt, the sleeves rolled up. 'How have you been? You look well.'

'Do I? Thanks.' She shook her head, trying to bring herself back to the echoing hall and regular life. 'And you? How's Keisha?'

'Eating everything that's not nailed down.' He beamed, clearly proud of his ballooning wife.

'Have you got a due date yet?'

'End of January,' Rupert announced. 'Which means it'll be complaining about lack of proper presents and crap birthday weather.'

Alice laughed. 'I'm sure it'll complain about everything, once it reaches its teens.'

'Don't remind me.' Rupert made a face. 'A teenager! I can't even get my head around a toddler yet, let alone the big, scary ones.'

'You'll be fine, I'm sure.' Alice patted his arm. 'I can see you now, one of those swaddling hammocks slung over your back, and a bottle in your hand.'

Rupert grinned. 'I'm already building a crib. Or, at least, trying to. It's still in pieces on the bedroom floor; I thought I better start early.' He looked around. 'Say, have you got time for a coffee?'

'Sure.' Alice agreed. 'Downstairs?'

'Lead on.'

They ordered thick porcelain mugs of tea, and wedges of cake, settling in the wood-panelled café amongst tourists and a battalion of blue-rinsed pensioners.

'How is everyone at the office?' Rupert asked, spooning sugar into his cup. A few granules fell, and he pressed his finger to the table-top to scoop them up. 'I haven't heard from Vivienne in a while, but I suppose everything's winding down for summer.'

'Mm-hm.' Alice swallowed her mouthful of cake. 'Fairly quiet. Which is a relief, for me anyway.'

'Of course. Toiling away up there in your garret.'

'Garret?' Alice laughed. 'You make it sound like I'm dying of consumption.'

Rupert chuckled. 'Still, I wish the summer wasn't like this — so slow. With the baby coming . . . ' he sighed. 'But that's the actor's lot, I suppose. Predictable, our careers will never be.'

Alice sipped her tea, wondering if she should say anything about Vivienne's newly redirected affections. 'Have you got names picked out?' she asked instead.

Rupert's face brightened. 'Some. We like old-fashioned, solid names.'

'None of this Ariel and Bronx nonsense.' Alice agreed quickly.

'Exactly. I like Lucy or Miles, but Keisha has other ideas.'

'Like what?' She took a sip. It couldn't be that bad, Keisha was a sweetly sensible human resources manager he'd met at a 'Learn Your Own Book-Keeping' seminar — hardly the type to go esoteric on him.

But Rupert made a face. 'Napoleon.'

Alice spluttered. 'Oh, no, that's terrible!'

'I've tried to make her see sense,' Rupert shook his head, resigned. 'At least there's time.'

'Wage a good campaign,' Alice advised, 'or, as a last resort, change the birth certificate. I wish my father had managed to get to it in time.'

'What do you mean?' Rupert looked up.

Alice paused, realising her slip. 'Oh, nothing.' She reached quickly for a nearby brochure. 'Have you taken a look at the summer schedule yet? There are lots of good exhibitions coming up.'

'Come on, you can't say something like that and then not spill the details.'

She bit her lip. 'Alice . . . isn't exactly my name. At least, not my full name.' Rupert leaned forwards, but Alice still hesitated. 'You can't tell, I'm warning you.'

'Scout's honour.'

'And I'm only divulging this in the service of baby-naming, as a cautionary tale,' Alice continued. She wasn't even exaggerating: nobody but her parents — and, Alice supposed, Ella — had ever known the full horror of her birth name. By the time it came to her christening, even her father had seen sense, and ensured that the elderly vicar welcomed plain Alice Love into the world.

Rupert waited. 'Now I'm really intrigued.'

Taking a deep breath, Alice admitted, 'My real name is actually Alicia. Well, Persephone Angelique Alicia Love.' She recited the name like the prison sentence it was.

Rupert blinked. 'Wow. Um . . . ' He coughed. 'Wow.'

Alice nodded slowly. There was a method to the madness, she'd been assured. Her mother had wanted an exceptional name for what would surely be an exceptional child, and matching the goddess of the underworld with a more heavenly name made perfect sense. By modern London standards, it wasn't particularly shocking, but twenty-nine years ago, in their small Sussex village? It was only the memory of his recently departed mother that made Richard tack on the last, simpler name, thus saving little Persephone from a childhood of woe surrounded by Kates, Angelas and Stephanies in the local school.

'So, you see, it may be tempting to bow to every one of Keisha's wishes now, when she's highly strung and emotional, but trust me,' Alice warned Rupert, thinking of her own blushes every time a new teacher pulled out her records, until finally she insisted Persephone Angelique be banished altogether, 'little Napoleon will be cursing you every day of his life if you let her have her way.'

'Right. Yes, well . . . Wow.' Rupert was still recovering. Alice didn't blame him. The name had never fit her, any more than the ribbon-trimmed bonnets that plagued her early years. Her mother had given her what she wanted for herself, a mark of someone extraordinary, and Alice — even the small, wide-eyed child — had never really been that.

'Anyway, enough about me, what about you? Any new projects lined up?' Alice was so eager to change the subject, she realised too late she'd plunged them straight into even more contentious waters.

Rupert shrugged, pushing back his flop of fringe with an absent gesture. 'Nothing to speak of . . . There was a callback a few weeks ago, I told you about it, I think?'

'Mmm . . . ' Alice made a noncommittal noise, busying herself with her cake.

'It doesn't matter, I didn't get it in the end.' Rupert sighed. 'I was so sure too . . . But that's how it goes, I guess. You never know what they're looking for.'

Alice stopped chewing. Vivienne had assured her Rupert knew full well about the switch, but looking at Rupert, so downcast, Alice's conscience returned, with annoying clarity.

'You don't know what happened with the part?' she asked, just to be certain.

Rupert frowned. 'What do you mean?'

Alice paused. Vivienne would kill her if she knew. No, Vivienne would have her checking foreign residual payments for all eternity. But Rupert had signed a contract with Grayson Wells, a small voice reminded her — for them to act in his best interests. And if Vivienne wasn't going to hold up her end of the agreement . . .

Alice felt a surprising flash of determination. Fuck Vivienne.

'They gave the role to Nick Savage. Do you know him?'

Rupert shook his head.

'He's a new signing at Grayson Wells,' she explained carefully. 'He'll be working for less than scale. Vivienne arranged it.' Alice paused, and then, just to be absolutely clear, she said it again. 'Vivienne arranged it all.'

Rupert's eyes widened in recognition. 'But . . . Why would . . . ? I mean, she didn't say . . . '

Alice didn't blame him for his surprise. The client/agent relationship was a tricky one, but it was based on a foundation of blind, unquestioning trust. Your agent told you to grow a moustache and learn a Russian accent? You did it. Your agent said to hold out for another two per cent? You swallowed that panic and obeyed. And if your agent said that there were no jobs going, and that they were doing absolutely everything they could? Well, you believed them.

'Are you sure?' Rupert said it quietly, as if even questioning Vivienne's wisdom were sacrilege.

Alice nodded. Now that she was actually doing this, breaking all the codes of confidentiality, it didn't feel the way she'd thought it would — like a victory. No, it felt like she was trampling the hopes of a good man. She braced herself. 'This guy, Nick, he's the new number-one priority. He's you, but . . . younger, flashier, an utter arsehole.'

'So in other words, the perfect leading man.'

211

Rupert was deflating in front of her very eyes, shrinking back into the upholstery and becoming smaller, paler somehow.

'Look, she shouldn't have been putting you up for those roles in the first place.' Alice leaned forwards. 'You're not cut out to be the dashing hero, and I think you know it.'

'Thanks.' He looked hurt.

'Come on, Rupert, you know what I mean. They're all, what, six three, with chiselled features and muscley thighs?' Alice made a face. 'You've got something different: you have the best comic timing, and there's a . . . quirky charm about you.'

Rupert was still slumped there, as if she were giving him an 'it's not you, it's me' break-up speech, but Alice pressed on. She knew what she was talking about, despite what Vivienne may think. 'I'm telling you, change things around, start going for the side-kick roles: the best friend. It wouldn't be your name getting first billing, but you'd steal every scene.'

He gave her a weak smile. 'Or maybe I should just jack it all in. I've been tutoring to bring some extra money in, and I could teach, perhaps . . . ' Rupert's face took on a tint of despair as he contemplated a future away from stage and screen.

Alice fixed him with a stare. 'You shouldn't give up. This is hard, I know, but it'll just take some work.'

And a new agent. The words hung between them, unspoken.

'I don't know . . . '

Alice sighed. She hated to see him so defeated, but she'd had to tell him. She couldn't have watched him turn up for Lunches, oblivious, until his savings ran out and no new parts materialised. 'Think about it, please. I don't know why she hasn't been putting you forward for these parts all along. It wouldn't have taken anything extra.'

'She said she had a plan.' Rupert protested weakly. 'She didn't want to devalue my image.'

Alice gave a sympathetic sigh. 'I know.' Something in her twisted when she thought of all the decent, paying parts Vivienne must have been passing Rupert over for. They weren't flashy lead roles, of course, but work was work.

'Think about it,' she said again, her voice sounding unnaturally upbeat. 'This could be a good thing. A fresh start!'

Rupert gazed back, clearly unconvinced. 'Thanks,' he sighed quietly. 'Anyway, I better be going . . . '

Alice bobbed up to hug him goodbye, watching as he began to walk away, shoulders slumped and head down. 'Call if you need anything,' she called after him. 'And remember, any name but Napoleon!'

16

Rupert didn't quit the agency. Alice spent the next week in a state of alert, waiting for Vivienne's imperious cry, but no such summons appeared. Whatever change she'd thought her information would spur, Rupert apparently preferred denial, and Alice had to admit, there was a small — and rather guilty — part of her that hoped it would stay that way. Concerns about his future had slowly made way for worries about her own, and what consequences would ensue when he confronted Vivienne. Although Rupert would never reveal where he'd got his information, Vivienne wasn't a fool, and Alice had made her opinions clear; it wouldn't take much to link events and produce a conclusion of disloyalty worthy of reprimand, or worse, dismissal.

'Are you sure you have to go in today?' Flora found Alice in the kitchen one morning at the end of the following week, hunting through her large carry-all for a stray contract she'd taken to finish at home.

'It's Friday, Flora, of course I have to go in.' Alice checked the front pocket again, flustered.

'But I thought maybe you could skive today, and we could go to the spa!'

'What?' Alice looked up. She was about to dismiss the indulgent suggestion, but something made her pause, frowning. 'Flora, are you OK?'

'Sure.' Flora bounced up onto a stool and swung her legs.

'It's just, Stefan's gone for a long weekend again, and I thought it could be fun. A sister bonding thing?' She looked at Alice expectantly.

Alice stifled a sigh, feeling every one of the five years between them. 'I have a job, Flora, I really can't.'

'But — '

'Flora!' Finally locating the contract, Alice scooped up her keys. 'It's a sweet idea,' she added hastily. 'Maybe another time? When I'm not so busy. I really need to go; my old landlord called, and I have to pick up some post before work.'

'OK.' Flora trailed after her as she hurried to the door. 'Will you be back for dinner tonight?'

'I'm not sure,' Alice replied, pausing over her umbrella. The skies were clear, and her bag was full, so . . . No. Not today. 'I'll call when I know.' She gave Flora a quick smile. 'Why don't you do the spa thing with one of your friends? Ginny, or,' she searched her memory, 'Mimi, isn't it? You haven't seen them in a while.' Not waiting for a reply, she scooted down the front steps. 'See you later!'

★ ★ ★

It rained, of course, clouding over and drenching the city with cold sheets of water almost as soon as she reached the bottom of the hill. By the time Alice had dashed from the Tube to the office, her thin ballet flats were wet through and unpleasant

215

rivulets of water had begun a slow trickle down her neck. She flung open the door and hurried into the foyer, shivering.

'Can you not stand there?' Saskia smirked insincerely at Alice over the reception desk. 'I only just tidied, and you're dripping all over the floor.'

Alice narrowed her eyes.

'You should probably go and clean up before anyone arrives,' Saskia added sweetly, from her warm, dry vantage point. 'We can't have clients seeing the place like this!'

Ignoring the request, Alice pulled a stack of damp contracts from her bag and set them down on the desk with a thwack. 'These need to be faxed right away,' she said, matching Saskia's expression with one of equal insincerity. 'Cover letters and details are stapled to the front of every file.'

Saskia picked one up between thumb and forefinger with a grimace. 'I'll see when I can get to it.'

'Right away,' Alice repeated, her friendly tone slipping. 'Before eleven.'

Saskia glared. Alice glared back.

'Fine.' Eventually, Saskia admitted defeat. 'I'll do it now.'

'And then the hand towels in the toilet will need replacing. Since I need to stop dripping on your floors,' Alice added, turning on her heel and stalking up the stairs.

She did what she could with the aid of paper towels and a flannel, but Alice was still decidedly damp and bedraggled when, at last, she settled at her desk and surveyed the thick stack of bills she'd had to collect from her old flat. The landlord had let them mount for weeks before remembering to call, and now she faced bold printed warnings on every envelope for her 'Immediate Attention'. Bracing herself, Alice tore open the first. Six hundred pounds still owing on a store card . . . legal action . . . immediate steps. It didn't say what the money had been used for, but Alice already knew: something unexpected, something fun. She tossed it aside and reached for another. More monies owning, even less time to pay. Another. Another. She made her way through the stack, the catalogue of a life Ella had been living without blame or consequence. And Alice was left to tidy up after, as usual.

As always.

The floor was littered with torn envelopes by the time Alice was almost through. She'd have to sort them all, of course: make copies, and forward them to the solicitor, and file them away neatly along with the rest. She sighed, listlessly flicking through the final stack of hateful letters, with their clear windows and typed addresses. Then she paused.

A postcard.

It was tucked between two plain brown envelopes, a small burst of colour with blue skies and some bustling town square scene. Alice pulled it out, flipping to see the back, and the handwritten message scribbled at an enthusiastic slant.

'I love Italy! The men are divine, and oh, the

gelato — it's even better! See you soon Ella xx.'

Alice stopped, her heart suddenly racing. Ella was contacting her now, after everything? She reread the few lines with disbelief. What could Ella possibly be thinking, giving the police a trail to follow like this? Or was it a game, to gloat over her victory?

Quickly, Alice checked the date. Over two months ago.

Her excitement dropped as quickly as it had risen. That was when Ella was supposedly at that conference in Rome, the exhibition of beauty firms and PR agencies that she had sighed over, as if she really had been facing three days in an airless exhibition centre, plying the latest skincare technology. It was nothing new, after all. She must have just sent it to maintain the facade, to fool Alice a little longer while she made her escape.

Alice turned the card over in her hands, feeling a strange sense of disappointment. It would have been nice to know Ella was doing well somewhere, and that she had thought of Alice — enough to risk detection. She often wondered where the other woman was now, and if she considered Alice with scorn, or affection.

'Alice?' Saskia's voice suddenly sounded through the intercom, bored. 'I can't read any of these cover sheets, the ink's all smudged. You need to come redo them.'

Alice gazed another moment at the idyllic foreign scene before placing the card aside. The rain drummed against her window, and her feet made an unpleasant squelch as she slipped them back into her damp shoes. Yes, she sighed with resignation. This was going to be one of those days, she could just feel it.

★ ★ ★

By lunchtime, she hadn't revised her judgement. Or, at least, by what should have been her lunchtime: it was half-past two, and Alice was so buried under paperwork and 'urgent' letters that she had yet to leave her desk. She'd found half an uneaten cereal bar in the dark crevices of her bag, but that small sustenance aside, she was growing hungrier by the minute, and decidedly irritable.

Her phone rang again, and she snatched it up. The credit companies had evidently outsourced to another, even more aggressive collection agency, which had been calling every twenty minutes since the start of the day. 'I've told you already,' she began, angry, 'the police are dealing with it, and my solicitor has been in touch!'

'Woah, calm down, Aly.' Julian was taken aback.

'Oh, sorry.' She exhaled. 'They've been badgering me all morning. I've had it up to here.'

'Can't you take the phone off the hook?'

'No, I get real calls on this line too.' Alice gazed longingly at a banner advertisement for McDonald's that had appeared on her screen. And she didn't even like McDonald's. She dragged her eyes away. 'So, how are you?'

'I'm great.' Julian sounded relaxed enough, but then, he'd probably eaten more than half a cereal bar in the last eighteen hours. 'And I've got some good news. Yasmin's managed to wangle up those festival tickets, some sponsorship thing with her company.'

'Which tickets?' Alice was confused.

'For the literary festival, next weekend?' Julian reminded her. 'Remember, we were saying how much fun it would be?'

Alice had no such memory, but the idea of spending a full weekend with Julian and Yasmin gave her plenty of pause. 'She got tickets for me too?' Alice managed to keep the surprise out of her voice. Well, most of it.

'Well,' Julian hesitated, 'actually, she could only swing the pair, but there were still some available online, so I got the extra.'

'Julian . . . '

'I know what you're thinking, but we won't be roughing it,' he reassured her quickly, as if tents and sleeping bags were her only concern. 'She booked a hotel nearby, and worked out the train schedule. You won't have to lift a finger to organise anything, won't that be a change?'

Alice sighed. Somehow, the usually intuitive Julian was managing to remain utterly oblivious. 'Have you told Yasmin about inviting me?' she tried.

'Of course.'

'And is it all right with her?'

There was the smallest pause. 'Sure,' Julian insisted. ' 'The more the merrier', she said.'

'Right.' Alice couldn't imagine Yasmin ever saying those words, let alone meaning them. She sighed, more with impatience than bemusement.

'Well, I'm sorry, you should have checked before booking everything. I don't think I should come.'

'What do you mean?'

'I mean, I'll pass on it this time.' Alice checked her cardigan, hung up to dry along the radiator. Still damp. 'But you two should have a great time.'

'I don't understand, I already booked the ticket.' To her surprise, Julian sounded annoyed. 'Come on, Aly, it'll be fun.'

'Thanks, but no.' She said it firmly, wondering where he got it in his head to think of the cosy trip at all. She, him, and Yasmin, playing cards together on the train down? It wasn't the most attractive of invitations, surely he could see.

'What's the problem?' Julian's voice rose a notch. 'I thought you'd like it, I planned everything as a surprise.'

'I thought you said Yasmin planned it all,' Alice pointed out.

'But it was my idea, as a special treat for you. Something fun, after all this stress you've been under.'

'That's sweet.' Alice tried to understand why he was being so belligerent about this. 'But I'm fine, really I am.'

'No, you're not,' Julian informed her.

Alice's eyebrows shot up. 'Oh, really?'

'I've been worried about you,' Julian continued, in an authoritative tone she'd never heard before. 'I can never get hold of you on the phone any more, you're always rushing off to these mysterious classes of yours. It's all right,' he reassured her, voice softer now, 'I understand,

221

this has been a tough couple of months. But I really think you need some time out, to recover.'

'And how, exactly, would tagging along on a couple's weekend help with that?' she retorted.

'What do you mean by that?'

'Oh, come on, Jules,' Alice finally exclaimed. 'You're in an adult relationship. I mean, you're living together, for God's sake. Surely you don't need a chaperone any more, in case you get bored of spending all that time alone with her.' It had been understandable, when they were younger, to go on group trips to dilute the effect of all that togetherness, but by now it was safe to assume that being locked in a hotel room for three days with his partner wasn't the worst fate a man could face.

'What? I don't . . . ' Julian spluttered. 'I mean, I don't know why you're being this way. I try to do one nice thing . . . '

'Without asking me, Jules. You didn't ask. And if you had, I would have told you it was a terrible idea!' Alice knew she was exaggerating some-what; perhaps she wouldn't have come straight out and said it was terrible — then. Now, however, she was hungry, worn out, and in no mood to dance politely around his strange bouts of denial.

'You're having a bad day,' Julian told her, annoyed. 'It's OK, we'll talk about this some other time.'

'Jules, this has nothing to do with — '

'I'll call later, and we'll talk,' he cut her off. 'Bye.'

Alice stared at her handset, confused. He had

hung up. He had patronised her, become illogically angry, and then hung up. Wonderful. She put the phone down with a clatter, only for it to ring again.

'Alice Love? This is Thornhill Collections calling — '

This time, she was the one to slam the phone down. Giving her files a final hungry look of disdain, Alice pulled on her still-damp cardigan and headed for the door. She would need fuel to face the rest of the afternoon, that much was clear.

★　★　★

A thick, toasted panini, a bag of crisps and a delicious slice of gateau later, Alice's blood sugar level may have improved, but her mood certainly hadn't. Was it her, or had the world conspired to send the most inane, tedious paperwork to her desk that day? Staring at subclauses until the print began to blur, Alice wondered if she had time to sneak away for a dance class before returning to the breach once more. It would relax her, at least, to be 'Ella' for an hour, and worry only about footwork and her 'line' rather than the division of residual payments. But would the momentary escape be worth the risk of — ?'

'Alice?' The call buzzed on her intercom, Vivienne's voice faint but determined. 'A word, please.'

Leaving her gym bag untouched in the corner, Alice descended, but not without a small flash of trepidation. It could be anything demanding her attention — a contract issue, or a client query, or even just Vivienne wanting company for an afternoon tea at the Ivy — but just as easily, it could be concerning Rupert, and Alice's oh-so-helpful advice.

'Sit down with me a moment.' Vivienne's tone was even, seated behind her long, bare desk. The curtains were half open, and perfume was thick in the air; Vivienne was draped with one of her velvet shawls, her lips painted a bright red. She gave Alice a warm smile. 'How are you, darling?'

'Fine,' Alice answered carefully, perching on the edge of an elaborate antique chair. Realising her response had been rather guarded, she added, 'I'm done with the ITV papers. Saskia should have sent them out first thing.'

Vivienne smiled. 'Wonderful. I'm glad you're back on form, after . . . ' she cleared her throat tactfully, 'well, it's good to see you back together.'

Alice made an effort to return Vivienne's smile, but watched closely none the less. She'd learned all too well these past months that a placid surface could disguise all manner of ulterior emotions. 'Was there something you wanted me for?' she prompted.

'Yes, yes, there was. I've been thinking about our little conversation last month, about your move to agenting.'

Alice was surprised. Of all the scenarios she'd been anticipating, this certainly hadn't featured. She sat forward, eager. 'Really? Because I'm still interested, if you've reconsidered at all.'

Vivienne nodded slowly, her heavy gold pendant catching the light. 'I have. I'm beginning to think you might be wasted up there, with your skills.'

Alice felt her hopes rise. Suddenly, the stack of contracts awaiting her back in her office didn't seem quite so endless; the dreary routine she'd been despairing, merely temporary . . .

'Yes, I can always accept when I've misjudged someone,' Vivienne continued, her eyes fixed on Alice. 'And you had so many good ideas, particularly about Rupert.'

Alice froze. 'Mmm,' she managed. 'Him, among others.'

'Don't be modest,' Vivienne chided her. 'You've always been so attached to him, and that can be a wonderful asset in a client relationship. So, I've decided that he should be your first client, to work alongside me, of course. You can handle his day-to-day business, and I'll sort of — what do they call it? — grandfather the account. You'll have to keep up your regular work, of course, but I'm sure you'll manage. What do you think?'

There was no hint of malice in Vivienne's gaze, but Alice felt her brief, giddy good humour drift away. 'That's an interesting proposition,' she replied, snapping back to reality. She could see where this was heading, and it certainly wasn't towards the fulfilment of Alice's every professional ambition.

'Interesting?' Vivienne narrowed her eyes a little. 'Darling, I thought that this was what you wanted.'

'Of course it is.' Alice was careful to keep her expression even. 'It sounds like a wonderful opportunity.'

Vivienne waited, clearly expecting more effusive delight, but Alice simply sat back and forced a smile. She hadn't worked under this woman for years not to see when trouble loomed on the horizon, but instead of anxiety, Alice was surprised to feel herself grow angry. If Vivienne knew about Rupert, why couldn't she just come out and say it, instead of artfully constructing this cruel trap?

After a moment's pause, Vivienne recovered. 'You're right, it *would* have been a wonderful opportunity.' She made a regretful face. 'But when I called Rupert to discuss the idea, do you know what he told me?'

'No.'

Vivienne stared harder. 'Are you sure?'

Alice gazed back, unmoved. She'd spent weeks growing accustomed to lying about everything from her name to the precise reason she needed a full, itemised summary of her account history, but still, it was a shock to find just how simple it was for her to fix a confused frown to her face and ask, 'I really don't follow. Did he not like the idea?'

Vivienne seemed thrown. 'We didn't get that far. Dear Rupert has decided to leave the agency!'

'What a shame!' Alice gasped, with suitable levels of disappointment and/or surprise. Inside, she was seething. Vivienne had used her agenting ambitions as what — a ploy to provoke her into some sort of guilty confession? Raise her hopes, just to make the revelation that much more of a blow? For a moment, Alice was tempted to rise up out of her seat and declare it had been her all along, and that Vivienne was welcome to check her own contracts from now on. But, of course, she restrained herself.

'Did he say why?' Alice continued her innocent act. 'Did another agency tempt him away?'

Vivienne shrugged. 'No, he just said it wasn't working out.' She peered at Alice, clearly looking for something in her reaction, but after another pause, she cleared her throat. 'It, ah, happens, you know. Some clients can't make the necessary sacrifices, or see the agent's vision.'

Alice nodded. 'So which other client shall I be working with?' she asked brightly, as if she'd believed every word.

Vivienne looked uneasy. She obviously hadn't thought this far ahead. 'I, ah, haven't yet found a suitable match for you. It's important to pick just the right one, to get you started.'

'Of course,' Alice agreed. 'What about Kieran Bates or Julia Wendall?' She suggested two younger clients, who'd yet to find a footing on the audition circuit.

'Perhaps.' Vivienne's noncommittal smile was back. 'I'll . . . think about it.'

'Wonderful.' Alice felt anger rise again, sharp in her chest. It was clear that Vivienne never intended for her to do anything more than print neat, predictable contract terms up in her office all day long. She rose. 'Anything else?'

'No, that's fine for now.'

'Then I'll get back to work.'

Alice withheld the urge to slam the door on her way out, or stomp up the stairs like a petulant teenager, but as she stood in the middle of her office — surrounded by ordered stacks of paperwork, the pretty window box, and the threadbare rug she'd discovered in an antiques shop — she found herself shaking with an unfamiliar *frisson* in her veins. She wasn't just angry, she was frustrated too; trapped up here with the intercom waiting to sound, and her inbox constantly refilling, and those bloody 'Final Notice' bills still piling up from Ella's sprees.

Ella.

Her gaze fell on the postcard, propped up against her overflowing in-tray: a message from the woman who had never really existed. Ella had gone through the trouble of finding a convincing card, Alice noted with equal parts resentment and admiration as she reread the short, scribbled lies. The Italian scene was genuine, the elegant print along the top of the card declared it compliments of the Hotel d'Angelo, and even the postmark read 'Roma'.

Alice stopped, staring at the postmark. It was smudged, but unmistakable: *'Roma, l'Italia. Maggio 6.'*

The data never lies.

Her intercom sounded again with a fierce buzz, but instead of answering, Alice simply turned it off. She stared at the card, her mind already conjuring the vivid scene. Ella had been there, in Rome, herself. She had stayed at the hotel, found the card, perhaps on the reception desk, or tucked amongst the complimentary stationery; she had written and mailed it, before strolling off to sample the local frescos, or buy a cup of that wonderful gelato. Alice could see her, carefree and happy, as clearly as if she was there herself.

Before she could take a moment to reconsider, Alice reached for her computer keyboard. A few quick clicks later, she had the number.

'Hello, FlyMe Travel?'

'Yes.' Alice gripped the phone with fierce determination. 'I'd like to book a ticket to Rome. Leaving today.'

17

Embarking on her hastily improvised travel plans, Alice waited for her voice of reason to appear and quell the reckless spark in her veins. To her surprise, it stayed silent. She booked a last-minute ticket to Rome, leaving that evening, sped home, threw a handful of clothing and toiletries in her small case, and scribbled a vague note to Flora; arriving breathless at the airport as if she took off on spontaneous European jaunts every other weekend. It wasn't until the plane made its descent and she emerged, blinking, from the chaos of Italian customs, that it struck Alice just how irresponsible she was being. Flying all this way on a whim because of a single postcard? It was ridiculous, it was foolish.

It was thrilling.

'*Hotel d'Angelo, per favore. Via San Antonia,*' she instructed the taxi driver.

'*Si, signorina!*' The short, wiry-haired man swerved away from the kerb. 'Your first time to visit?' he asked, as Alice quickly buckled herself in.

'No, no,' she smiled tiredly at him in the rear-view mirror, 'I've been before.'

'Ah, good.' He nodded approvingly, cutting into the main flow of traffic to a hail of horns and screeching tires. 'Is such a city, you must see again!'

They sped into the dark; the neon lights of the

airport landscape soon giving way to open countryside and the gentle shadows of hills and farmland. The windows were all rolled down, and a pleasant breeze whipped around Alice as she gazed out of the car, the driver whistling along to the radio.

She'd really done it.

Alice felt a thrill of disbelief. One minute she'd been staring listlessly at the view from her office, and now, mere hours later, she was driving through the outskirts of Rome. For her whole life, travel abroad had been such a careful, lengthily planned endeavour: weeks spent searching online for reviews and bargains, then the bookings, and confirmations. Even her big backpacking adventure with Julian had required vast amounts of planning to make the most of their precious funds. But all along, it had been possible just to toss a few garments in a bag and be gone? The revelation somehow seemed startling to Alice, that people actually lived this way.

And now, she did too.

'You pick good time, the weather is *molto bene.*'

They were deep in the city now, speeding past busy open squares. Fountains and statues stood on almost every corner, spot-lit in the dark. Alice leaned further out of the window, absorbing the fleeting glimpses of store-fronts and street life as they drove, breakneck, through the jumble of streets until at last they turned down a narrow, cobbled road. The driver slowed, easing past tightly parked cars and careless pedestrians before coming to a stop in front of a tall, narrow town house.

'The hotel is here?' Alice checked the name against Ella's postcard; this was the place.

'*Sì. Grazie.*'

She paid with notes still crisp from the airport currency exchange, and paused a moment on the front steps. It was a quiet neighborhood, she could tell, a world away from the central districts of chain hotels and all-night convenience stores. Here, the buildings were flat-fronted, packed together and elegantly crumbling beneath the antique street-lamps. Further up the street, a few busy restaurants overflowed onto the pavement, spilling crisp linens and laughter out into the night. As Alice watched, a crowd of young people strolled past, their crisp shirts, glossy handbags and relaxed smiles radiating a foreign kind of ease.

Yes, this was the place. Ella wouldn't have picked somewhere self-important, dripping marble and chandelier fittings; Alice knew that much by now. She liked things luxurious, true, but with character. As she stepped inside the polished lobby, Alice looked around carefully, as if seeing through Ella's eyes. The dark green tiles on the floor, the quaint artworks and tiny curios beside plush couches, the collection of bronze owl figurines perched above the reception desk — she approved. They both did.

★   ★   ★

Her room was on the second floor: a small, but well-proportioned space decorated in deep

232

shades of red, with vintage maps framed in gold behind the enormous bed. Alice gazed around happily while Pascal, the night manager, placed her case carefully in the middle of the dark wood floor and presented her with an old-fashioned key.

'Please excuse,' he apologised, 'but you must see Carina tomorrow, to check in properly. The computer is crashing all day.'

'That's fine,' Alice nodded, making a note to become friendly with this Carina. She'd hoped for immediate information about Ella's stay, but Pascal had given her a large, leather-bound guest book to sign in, and a surreptitious peek at the previous pages revealed only sporadic entries. Clearly, the main reservation system was locked in that sleek, flat-screened system.

Pascal must have mistaken her silence for disappointment, because he quickly toured the room, proudly showing off the tiny, cobalt-blue bathroom stocked with exclusive bath products, and the small balcony, its railings twisted with fragrant flowers. Alice followed, silently applauding Ella's exquisite taste, until he exhausted the range of delights on offer and looked at her eagerly from under wire-rimmed spectacles. 'You need directions, for food? There are many trattorias nearby.'

'No, thank you.' Alice assured him, already feeling tiredness settle in her limbs. 'I'll just rest now, after the trip.'

'Very good.' The man bobbed his head slightly and retreated, closing the heavy door with the softest of clicks.

Slowly placing her bag on the dresser, Alice stepped out onto the dark balcony, inhaling the scent of blossom, and an unfamiliar city. She could hear voices from the streets nearby, and the distant hum of traffic, and as she stood there, clutching the narrow, wrought-iron railing, a wave of possibility rolled through her.

It was perfect.

Ella had been here, she could feel it. Tomorrow she would find more clues; maybe staff here had talked to Ella about her travel plans, or perhaps Ella had even checked in as Alice, and she could access 'her' room bill details. There could be a phone call charged to the room, or a fresh credit card registered for payment to lead her even deeper into Ella's trail . . .

Alice shivered with excitement at the prospect. Suddenly spinning round, she took two long steps back into the room and hurled herself onto the bed with glee. The soft bedspread rippled under her; her reflection in the mirror showed her eyes bright and full of hope.

She was getting closer.

★   ★   ★

The next morning the all-knowing Carina was still nowhere to be seen, so Alice took a list of cafés from Pascal and set out, in her goddess dress and a comfortable pair of sandals. The city was hers to discover, and for the first time, she had not a single plan in mind. Alice was free to wander as she willed, and she would relish every moment of it.

'Dessert, *signora*?'

Alice looked away from the busy midday square to find her waiter. 'Absolutely,' she beamed, taking the menu. She was full from the plate of delicious seafood and soft, warm bread, but that was no reason at all to miss out on the many delights of pastry, or chocolate, or ... 'Panna cotta,' she decided. 'And another glass of wine, *grazie*.'

Sitting back in her chair, Alice let out a sigh of contentment. She'd spent the morning strolling through the winding backstreets, taking in the washed reds and terracotta of the faded buildings, and now she was settled at a shaded table out on a small, paved square. Trailing boxes of flowers surrounded her in a pretty garden, and in the middle of the piazza a glorious fountain gushed streams into a low pool, the water glinting in the sun.

'It's the next left, I'm telling you.' A harried group of tourists came to a stop nearby, peering at their maps.

'No, that was the plaza.' A man hitched his pack higher, glancing around but not seeming to see anything at all. 'It's back the way we came.'

'Are you sure?'

There was more disagreement, and then they moved off, hurrying to make whatever tour they'd booked. A few years ago, Alice knew she'd been just the same, attempting to cram every attraction into her trip for fear of missing out. Now, she was gloriously free from such concerns. It felt almost indulgent not to make the most of her time in Rome, but she'd already seen the Pantheon, viewed plenty of old churches, even strolled the Catacombs — and felt no desire to race around the city doing it again. This was her stolen weekend, Alice decided, beaming at the waiter as he delivered her dessert. She could sit for half the afternoon in this café if she liked, soaking in the soft gold tint to the light, and the sensuous curve of the statue on the corner. And perhaps she would.

Nobody knew she was there.

★ ★ ★

When the last sweet spoonful of custard was gone, Alice left a generous tip and wandered on her way. Turning down a tree-lined boulevard, she found herself surrounded by stylish store-fronts, hung with dark awnings and boasting designer shoes and handbags behind the spotless glass. She browsed idly up the street for a while, under the watchful eyes of the polished staff, but it wasn't until she reached a small boutique on the corner that she felt the first tug of temptation.

'Antonia's', the name read in gold script on the window. Alice stepped inside and found herself surrounded by pale peach walls and gilt edgings, the wood floor set with antique cabinets displaying an occasional flash of vibrant silk, or a rich leather shoe. She looked around, enchanted. Some alchemy of the light illuminated everything in a sheen of pale gold, like the sunlight of the

236

city itself, and at the far end of the room, a wall of tiny vials glittered on glass shelves, framed by the sweep of a pair of heavy silk drapes.

'*Buon giorno.*' A middle-aged woman appeared at her side, petite and impeccably attired in a simple navy dress that Alice recognised must have cost a fortune from the way it cinched her curvaceous figure into a generous hourglass.

'I'm just looking, thank you.' Alice's eyes drifted past the expensive shoes and jewellery, drawn to the glass vials that twinkled at her from across the shop. The woman followed her gaze, a small smile settling on her glossy rose-coloured lips.

'A new perfume, perhaps?'

Without another word, she swept Alice towards the display. Up close, Alice could see long glass stems reaching inside the bottles, each topped with a curved glass stopper, and tiny labels of elegant script marking the mysterious vials.

'Oh, no, thank you,' she protested half-heartedly. 'I never wear it.' An old flatmate had been strictly intolerant of scent of any kind, and Alice still purchased perfume-free moisturisers and gels, remembering her stern lectures about invading other people's olfactory space.

The woman fixed her with a disapproving stare.

'Except rose, sometimes.' Alice gazed wistfully at the rows of delicate glass and faint amber liquids. 'Just a subtle note . . . '

Assessing Alice in one swift look, the woman gave a superior smile. '*Rosa?* No, that will not do

237

for you.' Then, before Alice could react, she moved nearer so that her face brushed the skin at Alice's throat. Closing her eyes, she inhaled deeply. 'Yes,' she said, stepping back and looking at Alice anew. 'Jasmine, perhaps, and cherry blossom.'

Alice stood fascinated as the woman set about fetching vials down, muttering quietly to herself in Italian. When the small polished table-top was covered, she took out a tiny china bowl and began to mix, adding droplets from one bottle; a silver spoonful from another, sniffing delicately at it as she went.

'You are single, no?' She glanced up questioningly. 'Alone?'

'Well, yes.' Alice felt as if she was witnessing an alchemist at work. 'But . . . ' She trailed off, watching the woman take a small box from a drawer and scoop a tiny pinch of green powder into the liquid. The dust settled for a moment on the surface of the bowl and then dissolved, turning the perfume a clear jade hue. 'But I don't see — '

'Is ready.' The woman was unconcerned with Alice's confusion. She breathed in the mixture one final time, gave a firm nod and then dipped one of the glass stems into the liquid. Rounding the table, she advanced on Alice. 'With this, you are unforgettable.' She solemnly touched the glass to Alice's wrists and neck as if she was anointing her.

Alice inhaled the deep, rich fragrance, and the woman's sweeping claim was proven right, because in an instant, Alice remembered the last time she'd smelled such a scent, as vivid as if she was reliving the moment as a child again, hovering by her mother's heavy vanity case as she dressed for another night away.

'Can I help?' Alice had stared at the array of bottles and lotions strewn on the dressing table as if surveying a foreign land. Natasha usually shooed her out, but that night, she must have been struck by a rare flush of maternal impulse, for she patted the seat next to her and invited the young Alice to stay and watch. And watch Alice did, because dressing, to her mother, was an art. First, the lingerie, with hooks and clasps and layers of silk that still bewildered a cotton-clad Alice. Then came make-up, Natasha sitting on the dressing-table stool, the extravagant lilac upholstery of which had caused a three-day war. Then, finally, came the perfume.

'Which do you think?' Her mother had asked, surveying the selection. Alice's heart rose with the importance of her task. She studied the bottles, discarding a few unattractive options, and finally reached for a small, heavy glass one. She'd picked it for the neatness of the plain, square shape, but as she unscrewed the cap and sniffed deeply, her mother made a sigh.

'Oh,' Natasha closed her eyes for a moment as she breathed the deep, luxurious scent. Alice watched a rapturous expression drift across her face, then she blinked, looking at Alice with a new softness. 'Yes,' she told her. 'This one's just right. It's for special occasions.' Natasha held the bottle almost reverently. 'For only the most important people.'

Alice had never smelled her mother wearing that perfume again, but it didn't strike her until she was older that whatever those wonderful occasions, and whoever the important people were, they did not include her. From the way the bottle sat, untouched, on the dressing table until the day Natasha packed her things for good, Alice guessed that no other day in Sussex lived up to the precious contents either. But to Alice, it didn't matter. That scent was a moment they'd shared — something she had chosen just right — and just the faint aroma made her feel the way she had in the bedroom that day: teetering on the edge of glamour and adventure, and other impossibly adult pursuits.

'*Signora*? You like?'

The woman's thickly accented voice brought Alice back to the present, and the gleaming little shop in the centre of Rome. She blinked.

'The perfume? Oh, yes.' She breathed it in again, the faint echo of jasmine and dark spices drifting around her in a cloud of luxury. 'This is perfect.'

The woman gave a satisfied smile. 'I know it.'

She poured the mixture into a fresh vial, screwing a gold cap on tightly and laying it gently with the stopper in a slim box, surrounded by wafts of tissue paper and padding. The box itself she wrapped with more paper, and fastened with a thick velvet ribbon before presenting it ceremoniously to Alice.

She didn't look at the price as she scribbled her signature on the debit slip; nor, she decided, would she gasp at it later, when it appeared on her statement. Striding out of the shop with a lightness in her gait and a contented smile on her face, Alice breathed in, and remembered.

18

The lobby was deserted when she returned to the hotel, so Alice delayed her plans for investigation, and rested instead; drifting into a light sleep with the balcony doors thrown wide, and a cool breeze slipping over her naked body. It might have been the satin-soft touch of the linens, or the intoxicating breath of perfume, but for some reason, her dreams were shockingly erotic, and when Alice woke, possibility was thick in her veins.

She felt different.

Older, somehow, but freer too. She studied her reflection in the mirror as if seeing someone else. Her body seemed lush and vivid, backlit by the burn of sunset, framed by dark, rich fabrics. And, Alice thought for the first time, perfect.

She dressed slowly, in the delicate lace lingerie that had only that month begun to fill her wardrobe — following the example of Ella's receipts. Spritzing her bare wrists and neck with another light cloud of scent, Alice carefully applied her make-up, leaning over the mirror with the windows still wide, and the curtains drawn fully back. Somebody could easily see her, from another building across the courtyard or even the street beyond, but Alice found that she didn't care. She slicked on a layer of lipstick, arching her back as she met her own gaze, deliberate in the polished glass.

Yes, she felt different.

The dress was bright red silk, another of Ella's excellent selections. As Alice skipped lightly down the hotel steps and hailed a convenient taxi, she saw an adolescent boy in the street stop to stare at her, his ice cream momentarily forgotten, dripping dangerously low. She laughed, blowing him an impulsive kiss, and slid into the car. '*Via Veneto, Per Sempre,*' she declared, naming a new bar she'd overheard two glossy-haired shoppers discuss. It was apparently the most stylish, exclusive spot in the city, and Alice felt it a crime to waste her new dress on anywhere less.

★ ★ ★

'*Martini, per favore,*' Alice decided, perusing the elegant script of the cocktail menu just a short while later. Not for tonight her usual half-hearted mixers or weak, fruity drinks. She wanted something with an edge, something that would burn going down. Snapping the menu shut, she slid it across the lacquered bar. The bartender caught it with a deft movement and nodded his head slightly.

Alice turned and made a slow sweep of the room. The designer shoppers hadn't failed her: from the marble floor to the glitter of the chandeliers, the space oozed luxury. Brown leather booths were set back along one wall, and in the far corner, a white-haired man was gliding his fingers along the keys of a grand piano, lending the night a jaunty soundtrack of classic

243

Rat Pack tunes. After too many months of flashy London bars, with ear-splitting DJs and after-work happy hours, Alice watched the scene with blissful relief. Even the people seemed more sophisticated: clustered in small groups, casually clutching wineglasses and tiny evening bags, the women all immaculately polished, and the men . . .

Well, the men.

Alice's gaze lingered on a group in the corner. They were dressed in suits, sharp and effortless; the tabletop littered with Martini glasses. Two women sashayed over, returning from somewhere, and the men immediately stood to help them shimmy back into the booth, exchanging flirtatious comments and teasing smiles. It was all so perfect, so effortless, that Alice half-expected the name of an expensive liquor brand to descend, and hover tantalisingly above their stylish heads.

One of the men looked up suddenly, and caught her eye. Alice turned away out of habit, but curious, she forced herself to look back. He was still staring at her. She gave him a hesitant smile, growing bolder even as she felt his eyes sweep over her. He was blond, with hair a touch too long, which fell in a tousled cut over the collar of his stiff white shirt and charcoal suit jacket. Rising from the booth, he began to walk towards her.

Alice felt a rush of anticipation, hot and unfamiliar. She turned back to the bar, so that when the blond man reached her side, she was coolly sipping her cocktail.

'*Scusi.*' Leaning slightly on the bar, the man smiled at her and began to speak.

'I'm sorry, I don't know Italian.' She gave him a sideways glance. Up close, he had an angelic air to him, all blue eyes, cheekbones and lightly tanned skin; younger than she was, perhaps, but not enough to matter.

'No? That's a relief.' He switched into English, tinted with an unfamiliar accent. 'My Italian is appalling,' he continued, smiling even wider. 'I offend people here without even trying.'

'Really?' Alice arched an eyebrow, as if she were a Hitchcock blonde. 'Just think what scandal you could achieve if you really meant it.'

He laughed, while she glanced away and took another sip, feeling a new power spark in her veins. Not merely flirtation, but something edged with a challenge. Risk. She had never been the most beautiful woman in the room, and by no means was she that night, but it struck Alice with a curious certainty that in this dress, this perfume, this reckless impulse of hers, she might just be someone to be reckoned with.

Slowly, deliberately, Alice angled her body towards him. 'I can't quite place your accent,' she mused, carefully crossing her bare legs.

'Me neither,' he grinned, edging just that smallest step closer to her. 'Some French, some Spanish . . . My work takes me all over.'

'Which is?'

He gave a bashful sort of shrug that nonetheless had a practised air, 'Fashion, advertising. I'm Rafael.'

Alice shook his hand slowly. 'Pleased to meet

you.' She met his eyes in a steady gaze, her hand lingering in his for a moment longer than necessary. 'I'm . . . Angelique.'

'Angelique.'

The name had left her lips unbidden, but as he repeated it, his accent almost caressing the consonants, Alice felt a sudden thrill. The brief impulse she'd pressed down weeks ago rose back up, stronger in the gleaming lamplight. This time, instead of unease, Alice saw only the possibilities unfold.

She could be anyone, anyone at all.

'So what brings you to Rome?' Rafael made a gesture to the waiter, and then turned back, fixing Alice with a fascinated expression. It was easy to tell that his was a studied charm — effortless now, but no doubt accumulated from years of rehearsal — but Alice was almost glad. He was playing his part, just as she was deciding on hers.

'The art,' she declared, as the lie began to take root in her mind. 'I'm a collector, and I advise a few clients . . . ' She gave a casual shrug that mirrored his own response. 'This is only a brief trip: I came from London last night, and tomorrow I fly on to Miami.'

Rafael looked at her with interest, the kind her usual plain response of 'lawyer' never received. 'You were here to see an artist? Or acquire a classic?'

'Mm,' Alice took another sip of her cocktail, buying time. She could see this Angelique take form, already vivid in her mind: a jet-setting woman, who drifted between continents at a moment's notice, armed only with red silk and flair.

'I deal in modern art mainly,' she decided, giving Rafael a flash of smile. 'I came to see a new work, by a friend actually, but, well . . . ' she sighed, 'it wasn't what I'd hoped.'

'No?' The barman delivered Rafael a short, amber drink, and he tipped him generously from a silver billfold.

'No,' Alice straightened her posture a little. Angelique would never slouch. 'His earlier paintings had such vibrancy, such life, but his latest series . . . They seem almost derivative.'

Rafael nodded. 'I see that a lot with the companies I work with. In the beginning, it's all innovation, you know? Then, as soon as they have the reputation, it all just gets flat and repetitive.'

'Exactly,' Alice agreed, exhilarated. He believed every word she said. Why would he not? She'd had no reason to doubt Ella's casual untruths; she'd taken her at her word.

It was almost amusing, the trust they placed in perfect strangers.

He glanced behind them, to where his friends still sat. 'I have some people with me. If you've got the time, I'd love to introduce you.'

'Of course.' Alice took the hand he offered to help her down from the stool, following him across the room with a swing in her step.

'Everybody, this is Angelique.'

The group greeted her with smiles and air kisses as Rafael presented her, moving to make space for them in the booth. There was Anton and Paolo and Lucia and several more besides: a blur of sleek hair, sparkling jewellery and infinite ease. Ordinarily, Alice knew she would have been intimidated by a collection of such glamorous foreign strangers, but this was no ordinary night. She made the introductions with light smiles and a careless air, settling beside Rafael as if it were her due.

'Jeannine works in the art world too,' Rafael helpfully pointed out, nodding to the voluptuous brunette across the table. She was exchanging hushed, intimate comments with one of the men, her head tilted close to his as she gazed up through her eyelashes. At the sound of her name, she broke off the conversation.

'*Sì*, at the Galeria Menata, in the Parioli.'

'Oh, the Menata.' Alice adopted a knowledge-able expression. 'I've heard good things about the place.'

Jeannine smiled generously. 'I like it, but not for long. I shall move soon, I think. It gets — how you put it? — monotonous for the while.'

Alice relaxed back into the space beneath Rafael's arm, slung over the back of the seating. 'I know what you mean,' she agreed, as if she really did. 'That's why I work for myself now. I couldn't stand the hierarchy, all the petty politics.'

There were murmurs of agreement.

'A toast,' Paolo declared, sweeping back his dark curls with one hand. 'To independence.'

★ ★ ★

Drinks were refreshed, the old piano player made way for a sultry singer, and all the while, Alice built on the impulsive foundations of this Angelique's imaginary life; Rafael's body pressed against her. She fed her alter ego's history with details plucked from Flora's schooling at St Martins, and Cassie's varied travels, and snippets from stories she'd heard at work, or read in passing newspapers, until she was confidently debating the merits of national arts funding with Anton, and exchanging insider beauty tips with the lovely Lucia as if she really were the other woman, feeling not a moment of fear or doubt.

'A tiny backstreet salon in Paris,' she told Lucia, describing a beauty spot she'd seen praised in last month's *Vogue*. 'It's nothing to look at from the outside, but I swear, it's better than anything in the St-Germain.'

'Really?'

'But of course, you don't need my advice.' Alice gave an approving smile, as if she had the power to judge. 'I'm sure your diary is overflowing with the best places.'

'True,' Lucia nodded, in that almost arrogant way Alice had found was second nature to these women. 'Still, I will look it out.'

Suddenly Jeannine unleashed a torrent of loud Italian. The others all looked over. Paolo protested, and the pair of them became entangled in a quick-fire exchange, hurling retorts at each other.

'They were married for a short while,' Rafael explained in a low voice, his breath light against Alice's earlobe. A shiver rippled down her spine.

She leaned closer. Rafael's hand dropped to her shoulder, softly stroking a tiny circle on her skin as he explained the fraught nature of his friends' relationship. Alice was so distracted by the delicious sensation of his touch, she had to fight to register a single word.

' . . . so we never know if they'll get back together, or not.' Rafael stopped the stroking. Alice longed for more.

'Staying friends with an ex-husband is a terrible trial,' she offered. 'I tried it for a while, but it was all too messy.'

'You were married?' Again, Rafael looked at her with interest.

Alice flickered her gaze skyward in a world-weary way. 'Twice, actually.' She felt his eyes still on her, so she decided to elaborate. 'The first time, I was too young to know better; so naïve and idealistic. And the second, well . . . ' she thought fast. What would this Angelique have done? ' . . . He was older, and I was madly in love. We tore each other apart, of course, but . . . ' she paused for an expressive sigh, ' . . . what could I do? When it comes to love, I just have to be bold, never mind the consequences.'

'So true.' Rafael gave her a slow look, full of intent. 'We are but slaves to passion.' His hand slipped to her waist, stroking through the silk of her dress, and Alice caught her breath. His charm may be practised, but their strange alchemy of attraction was real enough. As she drifted into a pleasant haze — focused only on the slow sweep of his fingertips on her hip — she wondered, how long had it been since she'd felt desire so close and real? How many months since she'd been breathless, sweating, caught up in nothing more than lust, deep in her stomach?

Too long.

Tilting her head towards him so that her lips grazed his cheek, she whispered softly, 'Shall we go?'

He drew back to look at her, and Alice held his gaze. Although her heart was pounding, and the risk was intoxicating, she stared back, bolder than she'd ever been in her life before. Alice didn't proposition men, or seduce strangers, or even be so direct about the lust that was sharp in her veins, but Angelique?

This was easy for her.

Rafael's lips curled in a slow smile; he nodded. 'Much apologies,' he told the group in a loud voice, already pulling Alice to her feet. 'My friend has an early flight.'

'It was lovely to meet you all,' she agreed, leaning over to exchange more kisses with the women. Then Rafael ran his hand down her bare back in a secret caress and Alice forgot niceties; she let him usher her out of the bar and into the dark street, barely steps from the heavy glass doors before he pulled her against him.

The kiss was hard and hot, and Alice tripped against him, dizzy as he held her upright. 'My apartment is near,' he murmured, hands tight against her waist. Alice nodded, afraid her voice would belie her truth. She didn't do this, it wasn't her, but *oh* — she let out an involuntary moan as his lips closed on her neck. As her head fell back, she caught sight of people down the street: eyes flicking curiously towards them while Rafael's hands dipped lower, brazen.

Alice didn't care.

The rest was a blur of kisses and roaming hands, Alice pressed almost horizontal in the back seat of a taxi as she lost herself to the pressure of his touch until they jerked to a sudden stop. Rafael dragged her from the car. They must have passed a lobby, and the stairs, but clutching Rafael's jacket — his hands burning against her skin as they slipped beneath the draped back of her dress — Alice barely noticed. The only surroundings she registered were the hasty rattle of keys, and a distant church bell, and then the polished floor was hard against her, cold as he dragged her down. She gasped. Pinning her arms above her head with one hand, Rafael watched her, his eyes dark with lust. Alice's blood was surging. She wanted more, before she lost her nerve and this all faded away. Pushing up, she tried to reach his lips, but he ducked back just an inch, teasing her. Alice tugged at her wrists, but his weight was too heavy, pressing them into the floor, so she made a noise of frustration, and arched up again, this time reaching far enough to capture his mouth in a ragged kiss. She bit down on his bottom lip and then he broke, releasing her arms and kissing her hungrily again, his hands tangling in her hair, her dress, her thighs. Alice was mindless. Her usual detachment was gone, and instead, the world had shrunk to nothing but the heavy press of his body on hers, and the heat of their mouths and the gorgeous pressure — *oh God, there* — as he pushed up her dress and drew his hand firm against her.

It wasn't enough.

Pulling herself from his embrace, Alice rose to her feet. Her heart was racing, and her breath was coming fast, but still, she found herself steady as she turned away from him and took a few steps towards the open bedroom door, slow and provocative. She paused for a moment, the shock of reality suddenly threatening to strip her of her bold abandon — *was she really doing this?* — but then Rafael groaned, 'Angelique,' and, cloaked in her foreign name, Alice felt a rush of power. This wasn't real; it didn't count.

She unhooked the slim straps of her dress, letting it fall to the floor in a flutter of red silk before continuing into the bedroom.

19

It was still dark when Alice climbed out of her taxi and skipped up the hotel steps. She felt almost drunk from the events of that night; dizzy, and faintly disbelieving. Vivid flashes kept flooding her mind, and without the murmur of somebody else's name to give her distance from her own actions, Alice's cheeks flushed hot with the memories.

She'd been shameless.

'*Signora Love?*'

A determined-looking woman moved across the lobby towards her. She was dressed in a red suit with crisp shirt, and despite a name-tag gleaming on her lapel, it took Alice a moment to realise this must be the elusive Carina.

'Yes?' Alice wavered by the elevator, still half-existing back in Rafael's tangled sheets. 'Is the computer back up? Because I'd rather go through check-in tomorrow. It's late,' she apologised, patting down her dishevelled hair, 'so I'd really — '

Carina turned her back on Alice and snapped her fingers. Two uniformed men appeared from beside the reception desk: young and dark-haired, with neat blue shirts and navy shorts. Police uniforms, Alice registered. She looked at them blankly.

'Is something wrong? Has something hap-pened back at home?'

They didn't reply. Instead, the men studied her curiously while Carina began to speak in rapid Italian, gesturing emphatically with every other sentence. Alice waited, confused, until she caught sight of Pascal in the background.

'Is something wrong?' she asked, taking a step towards him. Immediately, one of the policemen moved to block her path. For the first time, Alice felt a tremor of fear. 'What's happening?' she demanded, louder this time. 'What is this?'

Carina finally broke off her tirade. She glared at Alice. 'You are foolish, yes, to come back? To make fun, and scorn me?'

Alice shook her head, still trying to follow. It was too far from the gloss and glitter of her evening to this cold reception. 'No, there's some mistake. I've never been here before.'

'Ha!' Carina gave a disdainful snort. 'Not three months ago you come and stay with us, and then leave without payment.' Turning to the police, she continued, 'The cards she give us are finished. She vanishes, like *poof!*'

The men looked at Alice again, this time with clear disapproval. 'This be true?' one of them asked, his accent thick.

'I didn't!' she protested, and then suddenly understood the fuss. Ella must have absconded without paying the bill. Or rather, Alice Love had.

Her first instinct was relief. Taking a deep breath to steady her nerves, Alice began her well-practised explanation. 'I'm sorry for the confusion, but this is all a mistake,' she told them, giving what she hoped was a reassuring

255

smile. 'The woman who was here, before, she stole my passport. She's been using my identity.'

Her apology was ignored. 'You think I do not know you?' Carina's voice rang out in the lobby. She stabbed one red polished fingertip in Alice's direction. 'I remember everything: the same dress, the same hair. It is you!'

Alice took a step back. 'It isn't, I promise. She just used my name, and looks like me, and . . . ' She trailed off. Her defence sounded flimsy even to her own ears. And the dress! Of course, she would have to be wearing the same outfit as Ella this time. Carina struck her as a woman who would not forget an ensemble.

This was serious.

'I need to call someone at the embassy,' she announced, trying not to panic. Once she had someone speaking fluent English, who would understand about ongoing investigations and fraud, then all this confusion would all be settled.

'*Sì, l'ambasciata, domaini* — tomorrow. For now, you come.' One of the men, stern-faced, reached for Alice's arm. She jerked back.

'No, not tomorrow. I want to talk to them now!' Alice thought with horror of the stories she read in the newspapers: of tourists trapped abroad, facing unlikely charges from local police; of confused late-night confessions and no access to lawyers. She swallowed again, the gravity of her circumstances making its full weight felt.

Carina glared, again complaining in Italian. The men nodded and began to move towards Alice.

Alice looked around wildly. 'Pascal,' she called across, 'the embassy — how do I contact them?'

He looked uneasy. 'Is too late. In morning, perhaps . . . '

'But I've got to!' Fear rose, sharp in Alice's chest as she took in the handcuffs dangling from the policemen's belt loops. 'I have to call someone. This is all a mistake!'

Pascal shook his head. The policeman once again reached for her, but Alice folded her arms and — mustering as much icy defiance as possible while wearing a slip of red silk at 3 a.m. in foreign surroundings — declared loudly, 'I'm not moving until I speak to someone at the British Embassy.'

And so they arrested her.

★　★　★

Alice's panic, which she'd fought so desperately to control during the brief drive in the back of the police car, flared to life again as she was led through the busy station, metal cold against her wrists. She was surrounded by incomprehensible chatter as the men talked around her, but could only imagine what they were saying. Her whole life, she had never so much as received a parking ticket. Her record — until Ella — had been unblemished. And now? There was dark ink staining her fingertips, and disdainful looks all around. She shivered, chilled in her wisp of a dress. They hadn't let her go back to her room for a change of clothes, or even a cardigan, and now, under the harsh fluorescent lights and accusing stares, Alice feared her beautiful outfit looked provocative and cheap.

After an age spent wilting under the accusing gazes of passing officers she was taken to a small cold room and her questioning began in earnest. Hours passed as she trembled on a hard metal chair; a rotating parade of officers attempted to exhort a confession from her. She had defrauded the hotel of almost a thousand euros, they told her, left a cancelled credit card as security, and fled to the Amalfi coast. She was a thief, and a liar, or perhaps just mistaken, no? The fragments Alice could decipher were as contradictory as they were confusing, and soon, even their faces blurred from her tiredness and fear. But one thing was made very clear: the sooner she admitted her crimes, the sooner they could process and release her. Papers printed with dense Italian were thrust across the table to her, a pen placed in her hand.

Alice shook her head again, exhausted. 'I can't help you,' she explained. 'I need to see a lawyer.'

The officer scowled, and pushed the pages at her again.

'No,' she fumbled, wishing there had been a section in her phrasebook for emergencies like this. '*L'ambasciata. No firma . . . firma . . .* ' she trailed off, useless. The door opened and another man entered the room.

'Is nothing,' an older officer told her in broken English. He loomed over her with dark hair and a thick moustache. 'Just an explanation. What you say has happened.'

Alice quivered. 'I'm sorry,' she swallowed,

feeling utterly powerless. 'I don't understand it. I can't.'

'But you must.' The man looked down at her, softening. 'Is no importance, is just official.'

'No, please . . . ' Alice felt the sharp sting of tears prick her eyes. The fact she'd been celebrating only hours before haunted her now. Nobody knew where she was. 'I really . . . I just need to speak to . . . ' Her voice wavered, but the man didn't wait for her to finish. He scribbled his own name on the form, and pushed it again towards her.

'See? Is not so hard. You sign, and we go call the embassy for you. All straight in a minute.' He smiled, encouraging. Alice felt a wave of tiredness pull on her bones. She just wanted to be back at the hotel, warm in the soft folds of that bed. She blinked again at the dense print, her head clouded. Why would he lie? For all she knew, it was nothing more than official procedure.

Her hand reached for the pen.

'*Si*, good girl.' The man nodded approvingly.

But Alice paused, the pen inches from the paper. If there was one thing she'd learned from her years as a lawyer, it was that she never signed anything she didn't understand.

Never.

'No, thank you.' Her voice emerged calm, as if from someone else. And perhaps it did. Alice may be panicked and weepy, but she felt the memory of Angelique still lurking at the back of her consciousness, full of poise. Grasping at that new, unexpected reserve of strength, Alice gave the officer a polite smile. Angelique would not be bowed. 'I'll wait until my lawyer gets here, thanks all the same. And now, I'd like to make my phone calls.'

The man's face darkened.

'My phone calls,' Alice repeated, her confidence returning. The panic that had fluttered in her chest since the sight of those first policemen seemed to melt away. She was innocent, and that was enough. She could handle this. Straightening her posture, she stared at him evenly. 'International law is not so different, I think? I won't sign anything.'

Although she had been making that same protest for what felt like hours, there was clearly something new in her tone that made the officer incline his head slightly, and retreat. Moments later, she was led to another small room, identical to the last except for one precious fact: the table held an old plastic telephone.

Alice rushed over, not even waiting to sit down before she stumbled through the international prefixes: dialling the number she always called first, the one she knew by heart.

'Julian? It's me. I need — '

' . . . *not around right now, but if you leave a message . . .* '

Alice made a noise of frustration. Of course, it was the middle of the night. She waited impatiently for his amiable message to finish, and then gripped the phone tighter. 'Jules,' she started finally, 'it's me, Alice. I've, um, run into some trouble. I've been arrested. In Rome. Italy,' she added, in case that wasn't clear. 'I need you to call the embassy here, and find me a lawyer, and . . . I don't know. Something.' She sighed, already realising how futile it was. By the time he woke, she would have been languishing here for hours; and then the time it would take to rouse the Embassy, and muster the appropriate personnel . . .

'Just, try something, will you? I really need your help.' She hung up, and just as quickly, dialled again, repeating her message to Stefan's voicemail this time.

Then she stopped. Alice thought hard, but her list of emergency contacts was shockingly low. She couldn't call her stepsister, of course — Flora could barely navigate across London, let alone co-ordinate an international rescue effort — and besides Julian and Stefan, Alice was at a loss for who else to try. She knew a dozen or so people who would list her at the top of their call sheet, but when the task fell to her? Alice was sorely lacking.

'You come with me.' Her moustachioed policeman was back, this time beckoning her from her seat. Alice reluctantly followed him down a bleak grey corridor, until the chatter from the lobby could no longer be heard, and there were several thick doors between her and daylight.

'What will happen to me now?' she asked, looking around. They were passing holding cells: narrow spaces with cinderblock walls and tall metal grilles sliding across every compartment. People were sleeping on narrow benches, or slumped in the corner, gazing balefully at her as they passed.

The man directed her into an empty cell at the end of the row, and Alice had no choice but to follow his command. He unlocked her hand-cuffs, and then, in a swift, surprising gesture, shrugged off his navy jacket and slung it around her shoulders, warm from his stocky body. He looked at her, with what could almost be sympathy. 'Now, you wait.'

The bars screeched as he pulled the grille closed.

★ ★ ★

Hours passed. Alice soon gave up attempts to sleep on the narrow bench; instead, she lay staring at the stained grey ceiling and wondering why it was she felt so calm. The spectre of more paperwork and threatening policemen still loomed and she wasn't even sure if help was on its way. She knew she should be huddled there in a panic, but ever since her alter ego, Angelique, had infected her system with strength and an imperious tone, she hadn't felt any of her early cold fear. She had spent her life saving everybody else from their tangled messes, hadn't she? So why wouldn't she be capable of handling this one, too?

Yes, Alice decided, stretching into a new position. If there was one thing this trip to Rome had taught her, it was that she could deal with whatever events came her way — be they irate hoteliers, impatient police officers, or even seductive young men . . .

The more she thought about it, the more Alice realised that there might be another lesson too. Don't get caught.

★　★　★

By morning, she had settled into a vaguely comfortable position hanging backwards off the bench, with her bare legs stretched at a right-angle up the wall in front of her. The moustachioed policeman was replaced by a baby-faced trainee, who added a scratchy blanket to her haul, and provided a tray of coffee, yoghurt and a half-hearted fruit cup.

Alice nibbled on them without complaint, as she contemplated her next move — once she was released, of course. From what she could glean of her interview, Ella had taken recommendations for hotels around Amalfi before fleeing: 'Positano', the policeman had repeated several times. Perhaps that was a town Ella planned to visit, or a derogatory term for British criminals, but either way, following Ella's route south seemed to make the most sense now that —

'Well, isn't this a Kodak moment?'

Alice jerked her head up at the sound, losing her balance and sliding into an ungraceful heap on the floor.

Righting herself quickly, Alice stared up at the unlikely guest, looking at her from the other side of the bars with a definite smirk of amusement on his lips. She blinked, but the apparition remained. Nathan.

20

'What are you doing here?' Alice struggled to her feet.

'What a great welcome. It's lovely to see you too.' Nathan stood aside, waiting while the policeman unlocked the heavy gate. He glanced around the cell. 'Of course, I can always go, if you're enjoying the alone time.'

'No, don't!' Alice quickly pulled on her shoes, joyful. 'I'm sorry, I just . . . wasn't expecting you.'

'And I wasn't expecting a call from Stefan at five in the morning, saying you'd got yourself thrown in jail.' Nathan ushered her down the long corridor. 'You're lucky: I was in Geneva, tracking some useless embezzlement case. I figured my suit of armour could use a polish.'

Up close, she could see that Nathan wasn't quite as relaxed as he seemed. There was day-old stubble on his face, and his shirt had heavy wrinkles in it; his broad shoulders tense. At that moment he was officially Alice's favourite person in the world. If he'd brought coffee, she would have recommended him for sainthood.

'Well, I definitely appreciate it.' Alice beamed. 'I'm not usually one to play the distressed damsel, but God, if ever there was a moment I needed a white knight . . . '

Her heels tapped on the polished floor as they hurried through the main lobby. It was busier in daylight, full of people waiting, the earlier ominous atmosphere now one of cheerful chaos. 'Wait, I have to . . . ' Alice shrugged off the jacket and looked around, trying to find the moustachioed man. 'And my handbag. They took it when they booked me in.'

'Already taken care of.' Nathan turned back and then stared at what she assumed was the full force of the red dress. 'No wonder you got arrested,' he murmured.

The fact that he had just likened her to a prostitute was not lost on Alice. 'I'll take that as a compliment,' she informed him, her gratitude dimming slightly. Presenting the jacket to the desk clerk, she stumbled through some rudimentary sign language to convey her meaning. When she'd finished, Nathan was staring at her bare legs with less than a virtuous expression. Sainthood, perhaps, would wait.

He held the front door open in a gesture of exaggerated chivalry. 'After the lady.'

'And there I was just thinking you'd called me a whore,' Alice quipped as she bounded down the front steps. But it was impossible to stay annoyed: outside, it was a glorious morning, with blue skies and a fresh breeze. Ah, breeze. She closed her eyes and turned her face up towards the sun. Six hours in a gloomy cell had certainly renewed her appreciation for natural light.

When she opened her eyes, Nathan was looking at her with that same expression as before: equal parts bemusement and disapproval.

'What?'

'You shouldn't have taken off like this. Stefan

didn't even know you'd gone.'

'Says the man who invites strange women away on a whim.' Alice replied drily, following him towards a sleek, dark car. They'd avoided the subject of Paris and his proposition for so long, but she didn't see the point any more. 'You're hardly the poster boy for reliability.'

Nathan coughed. 'But you thought that was crazy,' he pointed out. 'So why this?'

Alice shrugged. 'I took a philosophy class once.'

He looked blank. 'What does that have to do with anything?'

'One of their great challenges was always this idea of certain knowledge,' Alice continued, enjoying herself. 'What we could rely on being true. And the problem is, there's nothing certain. Not gravity, not existence. Even if everything seems predictable, it doesn't mean it won't be different tomorrow.'

'So you came to Rome?'

'So I came to Rome.' She opened her door and slid into the soft leather seat, almost sighing with pleasure. Oh, the padded upholstery. And was that . . . ? Yes, a seat-warmer!

'You seem pretty upbeat, all things considered.' Nathan got in the other side, but didn't start the engine. 'Are you sure you're all right? They didn't hurt you at all, or — '

'Gosh, no!' Alice exclaimed. 'They treated me fine. Decent breakfast, actually. Continental, some hotels would call it.'

He stared at her again, but Alice was already dreaming of the delicious hot shower that awaited her, and the sumptuous fluffy robe hanging on the back of her bedroom door. Her flight wasn't booked until evening, so that left plenty of time to investigate Ella's hasty departure. Amalfi wasn't far, if she remembered correctly, and surely held the next thread in her trail; Alice hadn't travelled all this way simply to turn round and return home, content with some sightseeing and a few delicious meals. No, she was determined to discover something more.

Before she knew it, they had pulled up outside her hotel. 'Right,' she smiled at Nathan. 'Thanks for straightening everything out. I really do appreciate it.' She opened the door and made to climb out of the car.

Nathan looked confused. 'Where are you going?'

'To take a shower, of course.' Alice looked at him. 'And change into something more appropriate, since you think I'm bound to be arrested again in this.' As soon as the comment was out of her mouth, Alice softened. Ill-advised remark aside, she really did owe him. 'Thanks for everything,' she added, warmer this time. 'I hope it didn't put you out too much. I'll be sure to call Stefan and let him know I'm all right. Have a safe trip!' Giving him a grateful smile, she slammed the door behind her and hurried towards coffee, and the rest of her day.

*　*　*

Despite her hasty farewell, it occurred to Alice that Nathan probably hadn't flown all the way down from Switzerland just to act as an escort to her hotel door. Sure enough, when she returned to the lobby to check out, she found him sipping from a cardboard cup and flicking idly through back issues of *Time* and *Newsweek*.

'If I'd known you were waiting . . . ' Alice was gratified to catch another appreciative look from Nathan as she approached. She'd changed into her flowing sundress, letting her hair dry in messy curls and spritzing on a light cloud of her new perfume.

' . . . You'd have got a move on with that shower?' Nathan finished. 'I thought I was going to have to call up to get you out.'

'It was illegally good,' Alice agreed, perching on one of the leather chairs. Then she laughed. 'Maybe that's not the best choice of words, all things considered.'

'True.' Nathan's grin faded. 'I was thinking that, uh, I owe you an apology, for what I said before, about the dress. You're right: it was way out of line.'

'Thanks.' She gave him a small smile. 'It's all right.'

'Good,' Nathan exhaled, and immediately the confident expression returned. 'Then we better get moving. We're on a schedule here, you know.'

'Actually, I don't.'

'Oh, right, I should have explained in the car. I'm taking you back to England.'

'Taking me?' Alice arched an eyebrow, amused.

'We're booked on the two o'clock flight.' Nathan checked his watch. 'Which gives us time to get to the airport and check out some duty-free . . . ' he trailed off, finally catching her expression. 'What is it now?' He looked woeful. 'I didn't call you anything offensive; I tried especially.'

She laughed. 'And I appreciate the effort. But I'm sorry to disappoint you. This isn't the nineteenth century, and you're not my legal guardian.'

'I should hope not,' Nathan murmured, giving her body another long stare.

Alice snapped her fingers. 'Um, up here?'

He looked up. 'Sorry. Distracted.'

'Evidently.' Alice was enjoying their banter, despite herself, and Nathan's mistaken belief that she was cargo to be transported back to her closest male relative. With this new frisson under her skin, she found herself able to flirt and quip as playfully as she did as Angelique. None of this seemed real, it was all just a temporary escape.

'So?' Nathan prompted. 'I did mention that schedule . . . '

'Yes, see, that's the thing.' Alice bit her lip. 'Your plan doesn't really work for me. I have a flight already booked for tonight, so I'll just keep to that, and see you in England.' She shot him a bright smile and tried to manoeuvre her case towards the front desk, but Nathan was on his feet in an instant, blocking her path.

Narrowing his eyes, he looked at her for a long moment. 'You're up to something,' he said slowly. 'Where are you going?'

'Just to do some sightseeing,' she shrugged, the picture of innocence — or so she hoped.

'Now that I'm here, it seems a shame to waste the time.'

'Yes, *here*.' Nathan's eyes took on a devious gleam. 'You just happened to book the same hotel as this Ella woman?'

'She must have mentioned it in passing.' Alice shrugged. 'You know how these things work: subconscious triggers, and all that. Now, could you let me past?'

He wagged his fingers at her. 'Not so fast, missy. I want to know what you're playing at.'

'Missy?' Alice had to smirk. Nathan grinned back.

'Better than 'madam', I think.'

'Given your record, definitely,' she agreed. 'And I told you, I'm just off for some sightseeing. I thought I'd rent a car, drive down to the coast . . . ' Alice knew as soon as she'd spoken that she'd said too much. Nathan's eyes lit up.

'You're going to Positano!'

Alice paused, 'What do you know about that?'

'Plenty,' Nathan replied, smug. 'I made some calls before getting you out. That's where they say she went.' He frowned. 'Is this what you've been doing — running around trying to track her down? Because you won't find her. I told you, she's long gone by now. A professional like her, she'd cover her tracks.'

Alice gave an impatient look. 'I know that, I'm not stupid.'

'Yet still you're here, playing Nancy Drew.'

Alice bristled. 'I suppose that makes you a Hardy Boy then.' She was tempted to tell him about everything else she'd discovered: Ella's schedule, the volunteering, and every other tiny detail she'd found in her search for answers. She'd been nothing if not thorough. But Alice caught herself just in time.

'This has been fun, but I'd better leave you to that schedule of yours.' She took a step to the side.

'No, you can't.' Nathan mirrored her with a step of his own, blocking her way again.

'Come on,' Alice chided him playfully, 'even Nancy Drew managed to get around in that sports car of hers.'

He looked down at her, all humour disappearing from his brown eyes. 'I'm serious, Alice. You can't just go running down there. For all you know, she skipped out on those bills too, and you'll get arrested all over again.'

Alice hated to admit it, but the man had a point.

'You're right.'

Nathan nodded. 'I know I am.'

'Which is why you'd better come with me.'

'Me? No, Alice, I said — we have flights booked, and I need to take you — '

'Again, with the taking!' Alice sighed, before remembering that exasperation probably wasn't her best tactic — not when she wanted him to drive her a few hundred miles or so and question local hoteliers on her behalf. She beamed at him instead. 'Face it, I need you. I'm going to Positano no matter what you say, so you can either let me go and get in trouble all over again, or come along and make sure I don't.'

'I could kidnap you and force you on that plane instead,' he muttered darkly.

'I wouldn't recommend it.' Alice sidestepped him, patting him lightly on the chest as she went. 'I bite.'

The desk clerk was efficient, checking her out in a matter of minutes. They offered to comp her room, as penance for the inconvenience, but Alice insisted on paying her bill, as well as Ella's. She didn't know what panic had made the other woman leave without paying, but she knew this much by now: Ella didn't steal from small businesses if she could help it, and neither would Alice, whatever the expense. Thanking Pascal profusely for his attentions, she picked up her shoulder bag and strode happily for the exit, and the possibilities that awaited in Positano.

Nathan followed, as she knew he would.

★   ★   ★

The drive was smooth and swift, and with a soundtrack of classic Motown playing low on the stereo system, Alice found herself slipping in and out of sleep; drifting through the hours as the muted green and gold tones of the countryside slipped past. In what felt like no time at all, she was being gently shaken awake — Nathan's hand soft on her arm.

'Mmmneh.' She yawned, her voice thick with sleep. 'Are we here?'

'Almost. I thought you'd want to see this part.'

Alice opened her eyes fully, and looked out of the car. They were driving on a twisted road, set

272

into the side of rocky cliffs. Above them, a jumble of whitewashed houses rose, lodged on the hillside at a perilous incline, while to her right, the cliffs fell away to a crash of blue water; patches of golden sand nestled between the rock.

'It's beautiful,' Alice breathed, looking out at the vast stretch of ocean. The sky was powder blue, dotted with wisps of cloud, and out in the water she could see tiny white sailboats scattered across the horizon. 'No wonder Ella came here.'

Soon, the road veered inland, through the steep, winding streets of Positano town itself. It was the most charming place Alice had ever seen: red tile roofs perched tight together, tiny gleaming cafés and stores set out on the main streets, and bougainvillaea spilling from every terrace and steep, uneven wall.

'The woman at the hotel in Rome — the snooty one?'

'Carina.' Alice stared rapt at the contrast of white walls against the blue, blue ocean beyond.

'Right. She said she gave Ella a list of five hotels here, so it shouldn't be too hard to work our way through them, see what they know.' Nathan glanced over. 'If you're tired, you could just nap here. It'll probably be faster if I'm on my — '

'No. Thanks.' Alice tried to rouse herself. Never mind sleep, she had work to do. 'I'm coming with you.'

'OK, but don't get your hopes up,' Nathan warned, slowing the car as they approached what Alice assumed was the first hotel: an elegant building set back from a small square. 'This

273

town is a tourist hive in summer. It's doubtful anyone will remember her at all.'

'They will,' Alice vowed. 'We'll find *something*.'

★ ★ ★

But Ella had clearly made an art of being forgettable, because nobody could recall even laying eyes on the woman. Desk clerks consulted with managers, who consulted with security guards, but each demurred, regretfully informing them that CCTV footage and client records were strictly confidential. Unless they had a police warrant, or proof that this woman had, in fact, been a guest, well, they were sadly unable to help.

'That's it then.' Nathan returned from the last reception desk with a sigh. 'Five strikes, and we're out.'

Alice refused to be defeated. Casting her eye around the lobby, she thought hard. It was the most stylish of all the hotels, set on a cliff-top, with sprawling white terraces and uninterrupted views of the ocean, but aside from the luxury of the airy white rooms, it had the most . . . Ella-esque feel. It wasn't something she could explain to Nathan, but after the weeks she'd spent picking through Ella's every movement and purchase, Alice had developed an instinct for the other woman's taste. With lemon trees dotted around the slim pool outside, hot pink flowers spilling over the long balcony, and even vines twisting up the inside walls in an unexpected garden, of all the hotels they'd seen, this was the one she'd pick for Ella — and herself.

'So, what's our next step?' Alice asked, 'Hacking into the security system? Slipping the cleaning staff a few euros to jog their memories?'

Nathan coughed. 'Didn't you learn anything from your night behind bars? Nothing illegal, Alice, that's the number-one rule of the job.'

'Oh.' She was disappointed. 'Really? I thought — '

'You thought wrong.' Nathan fixed her with a stern look. 'Sure, there are some guys who run around breaking the rules, but they give the rest of us a bad name. I get what I'm after the legal way.'

Alice frowned. 'Then what do we do now?'

'Go back to England.' Nathan softened. 'I know you wanted to find her, but you're chasing shadows here, it's time to give it up.'

But Alice wasn't ready to do that. 'We should have some lunch first,' she suggested.

'We can eat in the car.'

'Yes, but look at the restaurant here.' Alice pointed invitingly at the sunlit terrace and sweeping ocean views. 'We could sit outside, have some drinks . . . although, you might want to . . . ' Alice reached over and straightened Nathan's shirt, smoothing down his hair.

'Thanks,' he replied, a touch sarcastic. 'Personal grooming's been kind of far down my priority list. After, you know, flying in and rescuing you from the squalor of a foreign jail cell.'

Alice wasn't so easily managed. 'Is this where you try to guilt-trip me into obedience?' She grinned, her hand still resting on his chest. She felt a flicker of excitement from the bold touch.

'Maybe.' His eyes were glinting as he looked down at her. 'Is it working?'

Alice smiled, flirtatious. 'Not yet. You'll have to try a little harder.'

'Damn.' Nathan adopted a hang-dog expression. 'What if I tell you about getting woken at 5 a.m.? Or spending hours manfully wrestling with the Roman police force for your freedom? I didn't even have time for breakfast,' he added darkly. 'I've had so much coffee and sugar, I feel like I've got the shakes.'

'Poor baby.' Alice took his hand and led him towards the terrace. 'All the more reason to get you fed.'

★ ★ ★

Nathan didn't even pretend to protest about flights and timing once he was seated, with a cool beer in his hand. Considering that he'd refused even to leave Rome only a few hours before, Alice thought her new-found powers of persuasion were doing rather well. Ella was right, she decided, gazing happily at the vivid ocean views; men did enjoy the *femme fatale* routine. Her red dress had played a part last night, true, but so had the lure of foreign travel and mysterious investigations.

276

The temptations of adventure were not to be overlooked.

'It's not the fifth *arrondissement*, but it'll do.' Alice leaned back and gave Nathan a deliberate smile.

He looked up, surprised, but quickly rearranged his features into their usual friendly expression. 'And there I was, thinking we weren't going to talk about that.'

'Sorry,' Alice laughed. 'Unspoken agreements aren't worth the words they're not spoken with.'

Nathan grinned. 'Is that your official legal advice?'

'Mm-hm.' She took another sip of wine. 'I won't even bill you for it.'

'No, it's OK, I'll just take it off my expense claim for this search and rescue.' He winked, and went back to his steak.

Alice wasn't so easily dismissed. Nonchalance had been Nathan's default setting since the day they'd met, but she wanted to know who he really was, beneath that casual smile. If she couldn't be direct now, with this restless impulse still fluttering in her veins, then when would she ever be?

'Do you do it often?' Alice took off her sunglasses to watch him. 'Invite strangers to run away on an illicit weekend?'

'You make it sound so dramatic,' Nathan chuckled, still utterly at ease. The sleeves of his shirt were rolled up, pale against his tanned skin, and he looked as if he belonged there, lounging in the sun.

'A little hotel, blazing rows over pastries . . . ?'

Alice fixed him with a sceptical look. 'No, you were the one promising the drama. I'm just curious,' she shrugged. 'It isn't often a girl gets propositioned like that.'

Nathan gulped his beer, looking less comfortable now. 'I guess that's the point. All that small talk, dancing around anything that really matters . . . Isn't it better just to cut through all the bullshit?'

'But you're so good at it,' Alice teased. 'Charm is what you do best.'

He met her eyes, frowning slightly. 'Is that really what you think?'

'Come on,' she scolded, even bolder now. Consequences be damned, she'd spent too much of her life holding back out of caution, and careful politeness. 'You say you want to get to what matters, but with you, it's been nothing but jokes and meaningless banter about Flora's ceramics. I haven't seen you break a sweat over anything.'

'You should have seen me when Stefan called,' Nathan said, looking away. 'I broke a sweat then — and the speed limit, getting to that police station.'

Alice laughed again. 'With a client list like yours? I'm sure you've had plenty of rescue calls.'

'Not like this.'

There was silence for a moment, just the light chatter of guests around them, and the steady crash of waves below. There was something sincere in his eyes, Alice realised; a directness she hadn't seen before, except . . . at the party. His

278

proposition. She hadn't dreamed of actually accepting him then, but things were different now.

She was different.

'It's nice here, don't you think?' Alice remembered Ella's urging to cut loose. She felt a thrill, anticipating the risk of her next words.

Nathan seemed thrown by the sudden change of subject. 'Sure. Gorgeous weather, amazing views. What's not to like?'

Alice swallowed, her heart already racing. 'So why don't we stay a night or two?' she said, her voice even despite the weight of what she was suggesting. 'Think of it as collecting on that Paris rain-check.'

21

Nathan's mouth dropped open, but Alice held his gaze.

He shook his head. 'You've, uh, had a crazy few days. You're not yourself.' Nathan took a swift gulp of beer, as if that was the end of the conversation. But he didn't seem quite so cavalier.

'You know me better than I know myself?' Alice challenged, still smiling.

'No, but — '

'I'm a grown woman, Nathan, I can do whatever I want.' Alice watched him, full of power. It was time to find out if there was anything solid behind the flirtation. 'So is that a yes, or a no?'

He was silent for a long moment, but just before Alice could wonder if she'd made a mistake, the edge of his lips curled upwards in an unmistakable smile.

Relief surged through her. 'I'll check about their vacancies.'

Alice walked away from the table with a swing in her hips, almost drunk with exhilaration. Rafael had been her practice run — an experiment in sheer, reckless pleasure — but this was different. She wanted Nathan for more than a foreign fling, but even she knew that this new bravery might not last, back in England. No, it had to be now, before her calm logic returned.

Nathan caught up with her in the lobby.

'You'll miss work,' he warned, placing a hand low on her back.

Alice slowed, relishing his touch. 'So will you. Whatever will we do?'

He moved even closer. 'I'm sure we'll think of something.'

Alice felt his phone vibrate before she heard it, pressed against his side. They paused, momentum suddenly interrupted. Nathan looked at her, questioning; it was her choice.

'Take it,' she decided. 'We're not in any hurry. This is a holiday, after all.'

He checked the screen. 'I won't be a second,' he promised, backing towards a quiet ante-room.

Alice forced herself to breathe. She wandered to a quiet corner of the lobby, trying to calm the tremble of anticipation that seemed to have gripped her body, but too soon, doubts began to filter through. Was she going too far? She could still remember the feel of Rafael's body against hers; Nathan wasn't a random man in an unknown bar — he was real, and decent, and what if this wrecked any chance that they could have something proper between them? Alice gulped.

'Anything good?'

Nathan's voice was sudden in her ear, and Alice startled. She'd been staring idly at the foyer exhibition of photographs, black-and-white prints in ornate frames: *Lifestyles of the Rich and Famous*. There were the Clintons, splashing by the pool, and a candid snap of a Kennedy or two, back in their day. Even Hollywood's latest superstar, Chris Carmel, was lounging on the terrace, a Martini glass in hand and —

'Wait.' Alice peered closer at the last photo. There was a woman sitting at the table behind him, her back to the camera and no more than a sliver of her body in the far right of the frame, but Alice could have sworn . . . 'Does she look familiar to you?'

'Nope.' Nathan gave a cursory glance before turning back to her, his smile full of suggestion. 'So, about that room . . . '

Alice ignored him, fixated on the flash of pale skin, and the wisp of a dress in the picture behind the heart-throb. The woman's hair was gathered up in a messy kind of knot; leaning back with a wineglass tilting from one outstretched wrist.

'Alice?' Nathan slipped his hand into hers and tugged lightly.

She stood firm. 'Give me a second.'

'There are postcards of the photos, if you want. See?'

Alice tried to decipher what it was that had caught her eye. It may only have been a fragment at the edge of the photo, but there was something about the pose that was oddly familiar: the nonchalant, almost carefree posture. She'd seen it before, Alice realised, as the memory finally surfaced; that glass tilted out just so as they relaxed in a bar after work, or met for drinks at the weekend.

Alice gasped.

'It's her!' All thoughts of seduction were suddenly forgotten as Alice stared at the photo in amazement. 'It's Ella!'

'What?' Nathan jerked his head around to the lobby, as if he expected to see their quarry strolling through to the pool for an afternoon dip.

'There, in the photograph, behind Chris Carmel.' Alice jabbed her fingertip towards it. 'Do you see?' She beamed at Nathan triumphantly.

'Alice,' his voice softened, 'it's OK. It's been a crazy few days. Let's keep the rain-check for another time and get you home.' He took her arm and tried to guide her away. 'You'll feel more like yourself after a good night's sleep.'

'I don't need sleep,' Alice protested, shaking off his hand.

He thought she was backing out, she realised: that she was looking for an excuse not to follow through with her proposition, but none of that mattered now, not when she was so close to a break-through. 'Look!' She pushed him closer to the display. 'That woman with her back to the shot: I'm telling you, it's Ella.'

Nathan glanced back at the photo. 'Alice, she's barely in the frame at all — I can't make out a thing.' He gave her a pat on the shoulder. 'I know you want to find her, but this is going too far. That could be anyone.'

Alice refused to yield so easily. She snatched a leaflet of the exhibition details from the side table and eagerly scanned through the small print until she found the titles. 'It's from May,' she announced. 'The dates match. It's her!'

'Let me see that.' Nathan reached for the

leaflet, as if her word wasn't enough. Looking from the photograph to the details and back again, he shook his head in surprise as the possibility finally dawned. 'You know, from the photos I've seen of her you could be right . . . '

'Of course I am,' Alice replied. 'The manager said we needed proof she was here, and now we have it.' She felt a thrill rush through her, better than any seductive urge. It had been the smallest clue, perhaps the only one Ella had overlooked, but Alice had found it. Nobody could erase themselves completely; you just had to look hard enough. 'Ask for access to the security footage,' she told Nathan, beginning to push him towards the gleaming marble front desk, 'and the guest logs for that week, and — '

'Hey, I've got it,' Nathan cut her off, amused. 'I have done this before, you know.'

'Right,' Alice nodded, practically vibrating with impatience. A bored, wealthy-looking family were trailing through the front entrance; if they reached the desk before him, he would have to wait hours for assistance, she was sure. 'So, can you? Now?'

He paused, no doubt to tease her.

'Nathan!'

'OK, OK, I'm going. Now, come watch the master at work.'

Alice rolled her eyes at his arrogance, but after watching him talk his way through the desk clerk, charm the manager in low, courteous tones, and secure them access to the security suite and those all-important date-stamped video files, she had to concede, he was very, very good at what he did. And after twenty minutes spent squinting at CCTV footage from the terrace on the day of the photograph, they found exactly what she was looking for.

'Which room is she going to?' Alice leaned forwards on the edge of her seat with anticipation as Nathan deftly switched between camera views, tracking Ella as she finished her drink and strolled back inside. She seemed relaxed, Alice decided, as if she didn't have a care at all, or any notion that someone might one day be watching.

'Hang on.' Nathan looked equally as transfixed as they watched her browse newspapers in the lobby, pause to chat with a passing guest, and finally — finally! — skip up the elegant staircase towards her room. 'Second floor, number . . . ' he paused as Ella swiped her card-key, expanding the image on screen until the discreet gold number on the door was visible, ' . . . two one three.' Nathan announced. He turned quickly to the guest manifest printout, but Alice was already scanning the page.

'Two one three . . . ' Her heart sped up as she looked for the name, the one piece of truth Ella might inadvertently have left behind. It might just be another alias, but that at least would give her something more to follow, something more to know.

And there it was. Ella had checked in on the twenty-fifth for four luxurious days of relaxation — registered with a passport in the name of . . . 'Kate Jackson.'

Alice looked back at the grainy black-and-white image, frozen on screen. Kate Jackson. She had her now.

★ ★ ★

Hugging the printouts to her chest, Alice was perfectly content to depart for the airport, and as they set about the airport checks, and long security lines, she marvelled at the chance discovery.

She'd done it.

Her sense of triumph was giddy and fierce, enough to make memories of that grey police cell melt away. All her intuition, all her quick-thinking, every instinct she'd had about Ella, built from weeks of tracking and poring over those statements, they'd all paid off. Alice had been right about her. What had stung most about Ella's early, shocking deceit was that Alice hadn't known her at all. But now . . .

Well, Alice thought gleefully, settling into the scratchy airplane seat, now she knew Ella better than she would ever have imagined. She had found her, when police and professionals couldn't.

She knew how Ella thought now.

★ ★ ★

'I still reckon you're taking this all too well.' They had been in the air a while when Nathan's voice broke through her thoughts. 'You didn't even pause for breath after getting locked up by foreign police.'

Alice looked over, amused. 'So, you'd have preferred to find me weeping and traumatised in that cell then?'

'Well, no,' Nathan corrected himself with a grin, 'but maybe pale and repentant, with a single tiny tear.'

She laughed. Somehow, they'd slipped back into their easy banter, but this time at least, Alice knew there was truth lurking beneath the charm. Some substance. 'Didn't Stefan tell you?' she replied. 'Crisis management is what I do best. I'm made of stronger stuff than that.'

'I'm beginning to see,' Nathan agreed. 'Man, the first night I spent in jail, I was a mess.'

'You got arrested?' Alice perked up.

'Sure. Three times so far, but that first one was the worst. I was a wreck. I mean, up until then, most of my work had been staring at the computer screen, or interviewing bankers in their nice, air-conditioned offices. And suddenly, I'm sitting in the corner of a stinking jail cell in the far corner of the world with a bunch of drug dealers, wondering if anyone even knows I'm there.'

'But let me guess, by the end of it, you were playing cards with them and doing their secret handshakes like a pro.' Alice imagined the scene.

'Uh, nope.' Nathan grinned cheerfully. 'By the end of it, I was still huddled in the corner, too scared to look anyone in the eye.'

'What about the other times?' Alice asked, digging a pastry from their bag of airport provisions. She passed it to him, the thick glaze dribbling between her fingers. 'You said it happened more than once.'

'Yeah, but those stories aren't as impressive.' He bit into the snack.

'Huddling is impressive?' Alice teased.

Nathan laughed. 'You were supposed to be awed by my strength and resilience.'

'Oh, my mistake.'

'I suppose it's a hazard of the trade, when you're poking around in people's bank accounts,' Nathan went on. 'See, some investigators, well, let's just say they operate in a legal grey area, but like I said before, your reputation is everything in this game, so I make sure to play by the rules. Or, only bend them a little.'

Alice glanced out of the window. She doubted Nathan would approve of her more reckless approach to tracking Ella, but it had worked, hadn't it? He would have told her that coming to Italy was a waste of time, and that using her name to prompt investigations when it was still tainted by Ella's crime was irresponsible, even dangerous. But without that dangerous impulse, she never would have discovered Ella's next alias. Sometimes, Alice was coming to realise, recklessness was entirely necessary. Quiet questions and careful planning would only take you so far.

Sometimes, you had to leap.

'Do you think it's her real name?' That one, all-important question had been distracting Alice ever since confirming the check-in log.

'Could be. If she thought she'd put enough

distance between herself and the Ella Nicholls identity, or even using your name . . . she might have risked it.'

'But you're not convinced.' Alice read his expression.

He sighed, his shoulders lifting and settling with the breath. 'I really don't know with this one. She's not like the other cases I've worked.' He gave Alice a rueful smile. 'It's not just about the money here. To be honest, I'm not sure how much more help I can be. I'll keep looking for your savings,' he added quickly, as if to reassure her, 'and I'll run that name through whatever checks I can, but if she's gone, there's not much good it'll do.'

Alice nodded slowly. She didn't like to think of Nathan hunting down that Safe Haven money, but after his talk about rules and regulations, now probably wasn't the time to ask him to leave it be.

'And you shouldn't be chasing after her either,' Nathan added, a warning note to his voice. 'You've seen what can happen when you get tangled up in someone else's fraud, and that's only the start of it.'

'I know.' Alice tried to sound agreeable. Yes, she did know what could happen: she could discover the information she craved. 'Still, you got to polish up that rusty armour of yours.'

Nathan grinned. 'Yeah, thanks for that.'

'My pleasure.'

* * *

289

Although it was only 2 a.m. by the time the taxi deposited her outside Flora's house, Alice felt as if she'd crossed great continents in her quest. Part of her was still disbelieving, as if the weekend had been simply an idle fantasy her mind had conjured while she sat in the garden, reading the newspapers, perhaps, before finishing up some outstanding contracts and meeting Jules for a drink. That was her usual territory, Alice knew, but even though the familiar Hampstead streets were dark and drizzling as if she'd never been away, she still felt wrapped in warm, golden light of Italy and that sense of freedom.

Nathan climbed out the other side and pulled her suitcase from the boot. He looked exhausted and unkempt now, having snatched even less sleep than Alice in the past few days. 'You got everything?'

She nodded. The excitement of her search was ebbing away, and now every part of her seemed heavy and dull. 'Thanks. And you'll tell me — '

'The minute anything about Kate turns up.' Nathan managed a smile. 'I'll start running her through some databases first thing: police records, credit agencies, all the rest.'

Alice yawned. 'OK.'

'You want me to walk you up?' Nathan nodded towards the door, hair falling into his eyes.

'No, I'm good. You go and get some sleep.'

'Oh, I will,' Nathan looked wistful. 'I have a breakfast meeting. Remind me to ruin the man who invented those.'

'Will do.' Alice mustered a tired smile.

There was a pause. She glanced up, meeting his eyes for a moment. In the light from the taxi, they were warm, and Alice felt a sudden rush of affection. He hadn't been obliged to come running from Switzerland, or help on her determined expedition to Amalfi, but he'd done it all, with grace and — mostly — good humour.

Impulsively, she reached up and hugged him, a swift, strong embrace that surprised them both. 'Thanks for everything,' Alice whispered, her cheek against his stubble. Nathan's arms closed slowly around her and they stood for a moment, pressed against each other, closer than they'd ever been.

'Any time.'

There was something intimate about standing there in the dark, and his murmured reply, that made Alice flush and quickly disentangle herself. The sun-baked terraces of Positano were an ocean away. They were home now.

'So. I'll . . . see you.' She grabbed for her case, almost tripping on the kerb in her haste. The night before, she'd been coolly stripping in a stranger's bedroom, and now she felt utterly thrown by a single embrace. Alice backed away. 'I mean, of course I will.' She exhaled, embarrassed. 'I need some sleep, clearly.'

'Take care.'

She turned and hurried towards the house, forcing herself not to look back, not until she heard the engine of the taxi again, and could watch it disappear, out of sight, around the corner.

The adventure, it seemed, was over.

22

Flora was asleep when Alice let herself in, curled on the sofa with the television on, waiting up for her, perhaps. Alice covered her in a blanket and slouched up to her room, relieved, at least, that her stepsister's wide-eyed inquisition would wait until after she'd had some sleep.

The next morning, however, her respite seemed altogether too brief.

'Ohmygod, you're back!'

Alice barely had time to struggle awake before she was smothered with Flora's panicked affection. 'Are you OK? Did they hurt you?' She bounced onto the bed, gripping Alice fiercely as she searched for signs of abuse. 'God, I can't even imagine what you've been through! What do you need — tea? Breakfast? Did you eat on the plane?'

'I'm fine,' Alice protested tiredly, as she squinted at her bedside clock: 8 a.m. Oh, too soon. 'Really, I just needed some sleep.'

'You poor thing.' Flora ignored her, producing her homeopathic medicine box. Reaching for the first bottle, she shook several tiny white balls into the cap. 'Here, open your mouth. This should soothe your nerves.'

Alice thought that perhaps she wasn't the one in need of soothing, but she stuck her tongue out obediently nonetheless.

'Take them every hour until you feel better,'

Flora pressed the bottle into her hand. 'Now tell me every — Oh! The tea!' She bounced back off the bed. 'I found your favourite camomile brand, or do you want something else? Because I could — '

'Flora!' Alice pulled herself out of bed. She felt disorientated — almost jet-lagged — though of course, there had been only a tiny time difference involved, however far the theoretical distance between those polished bedrooms in Rome and her own rumpled sheets. 'I'm all right, really.'

'But everything that happened!' Flora edged closer, staring at Alice in distress. 'I don't understand how they could do something like that.'

'It was just a mix-up,' Alice reassured her, pulling on her dressing gown. 'And the police were fine: scary, but professional. It wasn't as if I was stranded in North Korea or anything. Now, how about that tea?'

She made her way downstairs, slipping free from the hazy blanket of sleep. She could have used another eight hours of blissful rest, but the world — and the Grayson Wells Agency — was waiting regardless.

Flora followed her closely, still no doubt alert for signs of post-traumatic shock. 'Well, if you're sure . . . '

'I am,' Alice insisted. 'Really, all I needed was sleep. I'll be fine for work today . . . ' She walked into the kitchen, bright with early morning sun. There were fresh raspberries in the fruit bowl, and, mm, peaches too. Alice selected some and

293

found herself a bowl. 'Is Stefan back yet?'

Flora shook her head, perching on one of the side chairs. 'He's in Stockholm another night.'

'Oh, I wanted to thank him in person. That man really is amazing,' Alice filled the kettle. 'He sorted everything out for me. You really shouldn't have worried.'

'I didn't.' Flora's voice was small.

'What do you mean?' Alice bit into her peach. Now, plans: she could pack some of the fruit to eat at work, and was that cold chicken in the fridge for a sandwich?

'I didn't know to worry — I didn't know anything at all,' Flora replied with a petulant note. 'Stefan only told me what happened when you were on your way back.'

'Oh,' Alice looked up. 'Well, that's good, right? You didn't have to get worked up about something you couldn't control.' If Flora had been this worried after just a few hours of waiting, Alice could only imagine the weeping and wailing that would have ensued from whole days of angst.

But Flora didn't seem to be pacified. 'Why didn't you call me?' Her lower lip began to tremble. 'I shouldn't have to find out this stuff later. I'm your sister!'

Alice blinked in surprise. 'It's not like that. They hardly gave me any time with the phone, and I just thought Stefan would be able to help. You know how he is about sorting things. I didn't call Dad or Jasmine either,' she offered, hoping to mollify her.

It didn't work.

'But I could have helped!'

Alice's expression must have betrayed her thoughts because Flora shot up. 'I could have!' she cried. 'I could have even come with you to Italy! But you didn't even think of that, did you? You just left me that stupid note.' Her face crumpled. 'You all just leave me sitting around, like I'm some kind of child. 'Oh, let's not worry Flora,' ' she mimicked. ' 'She'll just get worked up over nothing. She won't be any use.' Well, I am, I can be!' Flora swiped angrily at her damp cheeks.

'Flora, calm down.' Alice was bemused. She was the one who had gone through all that peril, yet somehow, it was Flora shaking with self-indulgent sobs instead. 'It's OK. Everything worked out in the end. I'm fine, see?'

Flora sniffed loudly. 'I'm just saying . . . You could have called.'

'Fine,' Alice agreed quickly. 'I could have. And next time I get locked up in some foreign prison, you'll be the first one I contact, I promise.' She patted Flora carefully, waiting until the tears subsided. 'There, now do you want some of this tea?'

Flora nodded.

'And how about some breakfast — muesli, or something?' Alice fetched down a bowl and poured out some of her favourite brand, steering Flora back to the table and handing her a spoon before turning back to her own lunch preparations.

And Flora wondered why nobody called on her in a crisis.

Alice stifled a sigh, thinking again of those angry portraits, and Flora's insistence that everything was fine. She snuck a look at her stepsister, now carefully picking raisins out of the bowl, looking pale and delicate. Everything wasn't fine, that much was becoming clear, but they were adults now, and if Flora didn't want to confide in her . . . Alice wasn't quite sure what she should do.

'Have you got plans today?' she asked casually, sealing up a Tupperware container of salad for lunch. Somehow, she didn't think Flora should be left drifting around the house alone another day.

Flora looked up. 'Oh, yes . . . I have to go to the gallery and look over the final plans for the show. You'll be there, won't you?' She looked anxious. 'On Friday?'

'I wouldn't miss it.' Alice reassured her. 'Are Dad and Jasmine coming up?'

Flora shook her head. 'They're in France, remember? At the cottage until September.'

'Oh, right.' Alice remembered the summer holidays of her youth, complete with rickety caravans and outlandish mileage plans. 'But you must be getting excited about it, hmm?'

Flora gave a weak smile. 'Of course. It'll be fun.'

Alice wasn't entirely convinced, but she was already running late. 'Great. I have to dash now, but how about we get a takeaway tonight, and I tell you everything that happened in Rome?'

Well, almost everything.

Flora brightened. 'Like a girl's night in?'

'Sure,' Alice agreed, imagining the rom-coms and toenail polish that awaited her. 'Why not?'

★ ★ ★

It wasn't until she arrived at the office that Alice realised Flora was the least of her problems. Despite the fact her weekend had been full of adventure, so far as the rest of the world was concerned, nothing had changed in the slightest. The morning post was piled high in the entrance hall and the answer-phone blinked angrily with messages. Alice surveyed the mess with a sigh. She could make short work of the backlog, she was sure, but slogging through the same tedious organisation seemed, on this particular morning, to be a personal insult.

She felt rebellion spark in her veins.

Meandering past the front desk, Alice made her way back through the empty office rooms, passing empty work stations and forlorn desk chairs until she reached the notice board.

Kieran Bates and Julia Wendall . . . Alice ran her finger down the list until she found them. She'd plucked their names at random to throw at Vivienne the previous week, but now that she was back, they seemed full of possibility. Just as she'd remembered, their list of auditions was painfully slim. Kieran was a gangly, sharp-eyed boy in his late teens, whose strange intensity should make him a sure thing for the catalogue of damaged serial-killers-in-the-making that those gruesome crime dramas demanded, but who had been sent instead to read for an ever-thinning list of bumbling comedy roles in second-rate soap operas and (Alice did a double-take) children's shows. Julia, on the other hand, faced the opposite problem: she had been relatively successful as a child actress, but now faced the challenge of overcoming her babyish looks and finding adult work. Alice had seen her in the office a few times and had little doubt that some fresh braids and an audition wardrobe that didn't feature logo T-shirts and skin-tight jeans might go a long way to helping her career, but of course, it had never been her place to say.

It still wasn't, but that didn't stop her scribbling a few details from the other agents' charts, or accessing their client files from the database once she was settled up in her office. Alice had long kept the list of master passwords in her drawer, so it was no trouble at all to log in to the agent area, and download the lists of current casting notices and internal memos that kept everyone up to date on available jobs.

Alice stared at the data thoughtfully, jotting brief notes as the ideas came. The problem wasn't that Vivienne was a terrible agent — or any of the others there at Grayson Wells — but more the simple facts of their industry as a whole. Clients had a limited time to be the new, fresh faces on the scene, once that glow of novelty faded, and other, brighter prospects came along, it was easy to be shuffled to the bottom of the priority list and overlooked for easier commissions. Alice had little doubt that with the full force of Vivienne's talents now behind him, Nick Savage would quickly ascend the ranks, but it was what happened next, after those few early breaks had been forgotten, that really determined an actor's career.

Or hers.

Alice felt a sense of possibility grow, the longer she considered their files. If she knew Vivienne, then neither Kieran nor Julia had received more than an emailed list of appointments for months now. Surely they would leap at the chance for some personalised attention, particularly if it came under the Grayson Wells brand name? The only real challenge then, so far as she could see, was the small matter of how to become their new agent without the knowledge or support of their old one.

'Alice?' After an hour of strategic planning, her intercom buzzed to life. 'Alice, it's Tyrell. We need you down here. Vivienne's out and Saskia hasn't showed up yet.'

Of course she hadn't. 'Fine, I'll be right down.'

She pushed her notebook aside with regret. The moment she descended those stairs, her whole day would be gone, she knew. There would be phones to answer, deliveries to sort, and clients requiring coffee and small talk — and her own work would still be there, waiting, when she returned. It wasn't until Alice was halfway to the door that it struck her. Tyrell hadn't even bothered to climb two flights of stairs and ask in person, he'd just buzzed and expected her to come running. Like she always did.

She stopped.

Alice returned to her desk with a new sense of

determination. 'Hi, Tyrell? I'm afraid I can't do it. I'm buried up here.'

'But the phones are going crazy.' Tyrell sounded confused.

'Then call a temp in,' she replied, unmoved. 'The agency number is on a blue Post-it, by the copier.'

Alice rang off before he could object. Whoever it was who had talked about the power of 'no' was clearly on the right track, she decided, wondering for the first time why she hadn't simply refused their appeals before. It had always just been easier to keep things running herself, but now, it struck Alice as a rather self-defeating strategy. The more she did, the less any of them expected to do, until the sight of a missing receptionist sent them into a panicked frenzy. Well, no more. Alice set her intercom to 'silent' and swivelled back to those restricted internal files. She had some future clients to woo.

★ ★ ★

'Once more everybody, and this time, really hit it!'

Alice stifled a groan as the thumping R & B track cued up to the intro. There were still ten minutes until the end of her Wednesday class, but already, her work-out vest was sticking to her body in damp patches, and her neck ached from attempting to mimic the diva's head-tossing moves. Alice wasn't sure quite what elastic limbs enabled half the class to swing their hips so, but whatever it was, she was still sorely lacking.

'If I die, can you tell my family I went doing Pilates, and not a Beyoncé routine?' The murmur came from just behind her, where Nadia, the freckled woman from her other classes, was breathing heavily; clearly worn out.

Alice smiled with what little energy she had left. 'Come on, it's a worthy cause. Who wouldn't want to die trying to get that circular hip-thrust thing just right?'

Nadia grinned back. 'Right. Keep your eye on the prize.'

'Quiet, ladies!' Their petite instructor barked, terrifying in her lurid pink vest and Lycra hotpants. 'Less chat, more dance. And five, six, seven, eight!'

With a last burst of energy, Alice lurched into the routine. Well, less lurched than lunged — her weeks of training were providing some improvement, at least. She found herself relishing the more aggressive style of the movement, feeling a now-familiar rush of endorphins as she threw herself into the steps. She hit the last pose with considerably more precision than she'd ever mustered before.

'See, I told you it gets better.' Nadia managed to enthuse, once they'd stretched to warm down and were gulping from bottles of water en route to the changing rooms.

'I don't know about better,' Alice still felt the ache in her muscles, 'but, marginally less terrifying, sure.' She found her locker and sank down on the bench for a moment, too exhausted even to peel off her trainers. But it was a satisfied sort of exhaustion, the kind that kept her coming back here, long after it became apparent nobody had any information about Ella.

'Ella? Ella?'

Alice finally glanced up to find Nadia looking at her expectantly. 'Oh, sorry, I was spaced out there,' she hurriedly covered, beginning to hunt through her gym bag for her towel.

'No problem. I get like that too after class.' Nadia reached to scoop her hair up into a messy bun and began to undress. 'Sometimes I just kind of drift home, without even paying attention to the bus route or anything.'

'And then you wake up and wonder why you're not in Walthamstow,' Alice agreed. 'It's muscle memory, I suppose. Like with the steps.'

'Speak for yourself.' Nadia took off her thin glasses and propped them on her locker shelf. 'My muscles aren't remembering anything at the moment.' She gave a dramatic sigh. 'Oh, well, if I wanted life to be easy, I'd be doing beginner's yoga.'

Alice smiled, remembering her own ill-advised brush with the yogic arts. 'Good luck with that. Anyway, see you next week!'

'Yup!' Nadia paused by the shower area, arms full of shampoo and gel bottles. 'Hey, I'm getting together with some friends for a drink when I'm done here. Do you want to come along?'

Alice looked over in surprise. 'Um, I have plans, actually. But, maybe another time?'

'Sure,' Nadia grinned. 'Have fun.'

★ ★ ★

Alice thought that she would, but when she arrived at the busy Soho pub to find Yasmin, tight-lipped at a corner table, she couldn't help but wish she'd taken Nadia up on her offer instead.

'Hi,' Alice began brightly, sliding into a seat. 'Sorry I'm late. The class ran over, and then the Tube . . . Well, you know how it is.' She gave an apologetic smile, even though Julian's invitation had said nothing about Yasmin joining them. She had, it seemed, ascended to the ranks of automatic inclusion, a rare feat indeed. Alice scooped a handful of chips from the bowl in front of them, reminding herself to be friendly. 'So, how have you been?'

Yasmin wet her lips. 'Oh, fine.' She shrugged vaguely, glancing back towards the bar. 'Work, the usual.' There was a pause. 'And, you?'

'I've been great.' Alice dunked a chip in ketchup and savored the crisp, greasy crunch. For some reason, she always craved salt and fat after her gym workouts, even though it must cancel out all her health points. 'Things have been hectic what with — ' Alice caught herself. 'No, I better wait until Julian gets back, save you hearing everything twice.' She looked around. 'Where's he disappeared to?'

'He's just getting our drinks.' Yasmin shifted in her seat. She looked uncomfortable, more so than usual.

'So . . . ' Alice searched for non-contentious topics, 'work going well?'

Yasmin gave a tiny shrug. 'Same as usual, I

suppose. Busy,' she added, twisting her watch strap.

'Oh. Well, that's good.'

In the absence of any more small talk, Alice reached for another hot chip, smothering her disappointment with more starch and fat. She'd been looking forward to an evening with Julian of the kind they'd used to share: relaxed and easy, stretching over hours and a bottle of wine as they caught up with news and future plans. She'd wanted some time alone for a change, to tell him about her adventures in Italy, and all —

Alice paused, a chip wavering halfway to her mouth. He hadn't called, she remembered suddenly. Alice had left that message with him from her police cell in Rome, but Julian hadn't been in touch at all, except the brief text setting up drinks that night. She'd assumed that he'd called Stefan and been updated on their rescue efforts, but even so, wouldn't foreign arrest warrant some kind of follow-up enquiry?

'Hi, Aly!' Julian appeared at their table, balancing their drinks. His hair was shorter, neatly cut for a change, and he was wearing a surprisingly designer-looking navy suit. 'White OK? I thought I'd get you started.'

'Thanks.' She took it from him before everything spilled.

'So, how have you been?' Julian collapsed into a chair beside Yasmin. 'Did you go to that art fair you were talking about? I would have called about it, but we were caught up this weekend — some friends of Yasmin's visiting from the States.'

Alice stared at him curiously. An art fair?

'So, of course we did the tourist things, and I managed to get a table at Nobu.' Julian paused to take a gulp of his beer. 'But all those reviews of the service must be crazy, because our waiter was awful. Remember the mix-up with the crab?' He nudged Yasmin. She nodded faintly. 'But Yauatcha was excellent. We'll all have to go again sometime. You'll love it there,' he told Alice.

'Oh. Right.' Alice was thrown by his nonchalance. He must not have found her message at all, she realised. He certainly wouldn't be chatting on about tourists and art fairs if he knew she'd passed her weekend in a police cell. 'Actually, I didn't make that fair,' she began, suddenly relishing the prospect of seeing his reaction in person. 'I was away. In Italy.'

Julian spluttered on his drink. 'What? Italy? How the hell . . . ?'

Alice laughed at his stunned expression. 'That's not the best part. I got arrested!' The words still sounded foreign coming from her lips, but she couldn't help feeling a glow of triumph at the shock on Julian's face. Alice Love was predictable no more.

Julian blinked at her for a moment in disbelief, but then his face relaxed. 'God, for a moment there, I believed you.' He shook his head, laughing. 'Italy, huh? Did you bring me back some pasta?'

Alice was about to inform him that she really wasn't joking when Yasmin got to her feet. 'Could you just . . . ?' she gestured, interrupting. Alice moved aside to let her past, and she disappeared towards the toilets.

'So, come on, what did you really get up to?' Julian slouched back in his seat, idly picking at the label on his bottle. 'More contract work dragging on?'

Alice looked at him, a touch annoyed. 'I'm not kidding, I promise. I went to Rome for the weekend. It was a spontaneous trip.' She frowned. 'You really didn't get my message?'

'What message?'

'I called, from the police station, when they arrested me.'

Julian still looked unconvinced.

'I'm telling you the truth,' Alice protested. 'I swear, on ... on my first-edition Noel Streatfeilds,' she declared. Julian had tracked down the books for her as a birthday gift, years ago; Alice didn't tend to prize possessions, but those were sacred.

Slowly, the truth began to dawn. Julian's eyes widened. 'No! Really?'

Alice grinned. 'Really!'

She sat back and took a sip of her wine, waiting for the barrage of questions and curiosity, but instead, Julian just looked at her, frowning.

'What?' Alice finally asked. 'Don't you want to know what happened?'

'You went temporarily insane?' Julian's voice rose. 'God, Alice, what the hell were you thinking?'

Alice tensed at his disapproving tone. 'I don't know, that I'd go on a weekend city-break, like thousands of other people?'

'You got arrested!'

'Well, obviously I didn't plan that part!' She stared at him, bemused. 'But you'd know all of this if you checked your messages. Jules, I can't believe you. What if they hadn't let me make any more calls? I could still be locked up there, waiting for you to send someone from the embassy!'

'I didn't get any messages,' Julian insisted, whipping out his phone as evidence. He tapped the screen a few times. 'See, no new voicemails. You must have dialled the international code wrong.'

'I did not.' Alice folded her arms. She remembered Julian's outgoing message quite clearly. 'Maybe you deleted it by accident, or something.'

'I doubt it.' Tucking his phone away, he mustered a forgiving smile. 'The message isn't important, Aly, what matters is that you're all right. I take it they didn't press charges?'

'No . . . ' Her gaze drifted past him, to the depths of the bar where Yasmin had disappeared so swiftly. If Julian was certain he hadn't deleted it . . . She paused. But that was ridiculous. 'You said you spent the weekend with Yasmin?' Alice found herself asking none the less. 'So you were with her Saturday night?'

Julian blinked, following her gaze. 'Yes, we had her friends staying with us, I told you.' There was a beat. 'Alice!'

'What?'

'Are you accusing — ?'

'No, no.' Alice quickly back-tracked, noticing

the storm on his face. 'I didn't say a thing, did I?'

'But you implied — '

'Of course not!'

The space between them was filled with a sudden tension.

'Yauatcha,' she changed the subject brightly. 'I've heard so much about that place. Did you have the venison puffs?'

Julian shot her a look, but he didn't press the issue either. 'Ah, no. Yasmin did, though.'

'Oh?' Alice carefully sipped her drink.

'I did what, sweetie?' Yasmin reappeared from the crowd, her lipstick immaculate once more.

'I was just telling Alice about our meal,' Julian smiled at her as she slid into her seat, but Alice noticed the harsh set of his jaw.

'Right.' Yasmin seemed equally unsettled. 'It was lovely.'

'So I've heard.'

Alice stifled a sigh as another long pause dragged out. Next time, she would definitely take Nadia up on that offer.

* * *

Alice eventually made her escape with talk of early nights, and buckling down to work again, but the strange tension from the evening lingered with her over the next few days. The foundation of her and Julian's friendship was shifting, but Alice didn't know quite how she felt about it — or should feel, even. For so many years, Julian's presence had been part of the basic fabric of her life, unchanged by their slowly revolving set of relationships, but the opening of this rift was something new.

Part of Alice wondered if it was for the best. It occurred to her sometimes that perhaps the reason she found it so much an effort striking out to meet anybody new — and why Julian's affairs never seemed to last more than the early halcyon days — was the comforting intimacy they had with each other. She had a male presence she could rely on, and while that didn't provide the romance Alice quietly longed for, it had been love in one form, at least. But the more she thought about it, the less of a consolation Julian's easy companionship now seemed. Perhaps her liaison with Rafael had reminded her what passion she was capable of, or maybe even the growing chemistry with Nathan heralded new, more immediate possibilities, but either way, Alice wondered if it was time to take a step back, for both their sakes.

When he called the next morning, she didn't pick up.

23

As Alice set about surreptitiously wooing her new clients with careful phone calls and clandestine meetings, she realised that she had, perhaps, more spirit than she'd given herself credit for. On the surface, she may be going about much the same life as before her reckless jaunt to Rome, but she was starting to see her routine wasn't set in stone; there was, it seemed, scope for a little of her foreign flair on more familiar soil. From the spritz of perfume and those brightly coloured silk blouses she now selected for work in the morning, to snatched coffee breaks with her new friend, Nadia, and the more risky matter of her secret manoeuvrings at work, Alice began the strange yet exhilarating task of bringing spontaneity, daring and general hints of irresponsibility to her old, no-longer-so-predictable life.

'I just love these early watercolours. You can really see the sense of youthful naïvety in her brush-strokes.'

Alice melted back against the gallery wall as another cluster of guests strolled closer, gazing with tilted heads at Flora's collection of paintings. It was the opening of her grand retrospective, and the sleek, airy space in Notting Hill had been transformed into a haven of floral studies, garden views and — at last — assorted kittenish delights. It was still early, but already the gallery was buzzing with throngs of enthusiasts. The event, Alice was proud to see, was an unqualified success.

'The washed colour palette is very important in her early work, isn't it?' One of the women, middle-aged in flowing silk trousers and a fine-knit vest peered knowledgeably at the prints.

Helena, the gallery manager, materialised beside them.

'Absolutely,' she agreed, polished blonde hair swept back from her face in a high, tight ponytail. 'You know, not many people notice, but you can see how Flora was inspired by the pale tones, giving the paintings an almost ethereal effect.'

The group nodded, but Alice hid a smile. Those pale tones that had proven so inspirational were actually the result of her father knocking a pitcher of water over on a stack of finished paintings, the night before Flora's first-year portfolio was due. They'd dried them on radiators, and ironed the pages flat while Flora wept inconsolably, but the damage had been done; the washed effect was unavoidable.

'There you are.' Julian made his way through the sleek hair and loosely draped suits, ducking to kiss Alice on the cheek. 'I almost didn't see you, hidden away back here.'

'I'm eavesdropping,' Alice told him. Despite her decision to detach a little, she was glad to see his face in the crowd. Still, after their last meeting, she wasn't so quick to relax. She cast a careful eye around the room, before asking casually, 'Is Yasmin with you?'

'She's not coming, actually.' Julian didn't seem disappointed. In fact, he appeared affable and at ease, back in a pair of his slouchy corduroy trousers and a crisp shirt.

'Oh, shame.' Alice murmured, relieved. 'Everything all right?'

'Honestly, I didn't think it would be her thing. And I guess I haven't seen you for a while — I mean, just the two of us.' He looked at her, giving a slight double take. 'Wow. You look great tonight.'

'Thanks.' After much deliberation, Alice had decided to wear that infamous red dress again. 'Flora insisted we go dressy,' she explained, feeling the need to justify it. 'She's around here somewhere in a full-length ball gown.'

Julian laughed. 'I'll have to say hi, congratulate her on all of this. Or, should that be Stefan?'

'What do you mean?'

'Well, this is all his doing, isn't it?' He nodded at the spotless white walls, neat rows of paintings and flow of admiring fans.

Alice frowned. 'Not at all. Flora's worked really hard getting things set up. She's been planning the curation all month.'

'My mistake.' Julian held up his hands. 'I guess I didn't take her for the planning type.'

'And there's a whole set of new work,' Alice continued, feeling strangely defensive.

'The kittens?' Julian began to smirk. 'I saw those.'

Alice was just about to inform him that those kittens had taken weeks of precision and skilled study when she felt the presence of someone just behind her, and a hand light against her back. She knew from the faint drift of familiar aftershave who it was, and she felt a thrill.

'Hey, you.' Nathan leaned closer to graze her cheek with a kiss.

Alice murmured a response. She'd wondered if he would come, and whether she'd be seized with awkwardness after her outrageous behaviour in Italy. But looking at him, she just felt . . . happy. 'Are you all caught up on sleep yet?' she asked, trying to seem casual.

'Almost. I was out for fifteen hours straight on Monday, after that meeting.' He sighed at the memory. 'Good times.'

'Lucky you.' Alice smiled back. He was wearing the pale suit he'd worn at Flora's garden party, louche and cool. 'Some of us didn't have the luxury; I've had to work right through.'

'Poor baby.' He patted her head, an echo of her gesture in Positano. Then his eyes skimmed over her outfit, and a knowing grin began to tug the edge of his mouth. 'There may be trouble ahead . . . '

Alice gave him a warning look. 'Hush you. It's almost . . . nine o'clock,' she made a show of checking his watch, 'and I haven't been arrested yet.'

'A fine achievement,' Nathan responded drily. 'Did you remember to bring your Get Out of Jail Free card?'

'Sure I did,' Alice teased, growing bolder. 'You're standing right here.'

There was the sound of a cough. Alice looked over to find Julian watching them. 'Oh, sorry,'

313

she recovered. 'Nathan, this is Julian. Jules, this is Nathan. The investigator who's been helping me out, remember?'

Julian nodded slowly. 'You mentioned him. Once, I think.'

'Great to meet you,' Nathan held out his hand, and after a beat, Julian reached to shake it. 'I hope you've been keeping an eye on Trouble here.'

Julian raised an eyebrow.

'Apparently, it's my middle name.' Alice laughed. And in a way, she supposed it was. After all, it had been Angelique that had let Alice be free of herself, back in Rome. Which reminded her . . . 'You better not tell everyone about my mis-adventures,' she nudged Nathan gently. 'Investigator-client confidentiality.'

'Is that what we are now?' Nathan rested a hand against the small of her back. 'Shame.'

Alice caught her breath. The flirtation that had been so careless and bold back in Italy suddenly took on new meaning, here under the bright Notting Hill lights.

Julian chuckled, breaking the moment. 'I think the sooner we forget about that trip, the better. Temporary insanity, right, Aly?' He turned to Nathan with a knowing grin. 'In all the years we've been friends, she's never been the spontaneous type, and that's, what, going on a decade now?' Julian looked at her for confirmation.

Alice nodded, her thrill fading slightly.

'She's the one who keeps the rest of us in line,' Julian continued, giving Alice an affectionate pat on the shoulder. 'I don't know what I'd do without her.'

'Is that so?' Nathan gave her a slow look. 'You know, I'd never have guessed.'

'I'm a woman of many layers,' Alice quipped back. Julian still had his hand resting on her shoulder — a touch possessive, she thought — so she edged a step away. 'Layers and infinite mystery. Which is my cue to excuse myself for a minute.' Smiling quickly at both of them, she turned and disappeared into the crowd; her hips swaying with just a touch more sass than usual.

Alice made her way to the tiny bathroom and rinsed her wrists under the cold tap, reminding herself to stay calm. The dress, the banter, Nathan . . . If she'd had any fears at all that her brave streak might disappear now she was back in England, this week had proven them wrong. Angelique lived on, after all.

Having touched up her lipstick, Alice reached for the small vial of perfume she'd decanted into a travel atomiser, holding it beneath her nose the way they would smelling salts, a hundred years ago. Jasmine and spices; golden lights, heels tapping on polished floors. The memories were immediate and vivid, and Alice gave a happy sigh.

Of course she could do this.

★ ★ ★

The gallery was soon packed with Flora's moneyed acquaintances, and the many art world professionals wise enough to know a sound

315

investment when they saw one. As Alice circulated, she overheard more than one prospective buyer muttering about the conventional, insipid paintings — and then in the same breath, declaring their intention to buy. Part of Alice smarted that they were still sneering at Flora's beloved art, but with tiny red dots adorning almost every piece's label before the evening was halfway through, the joke was clearly on them.

'It'll definitely appreciate.' Helena was just ahead, murmuring to a dapper, bulky man in tight red trousers and an oversized navy jacket. He had a slightly uneven nose, from which he was looking down at one of the kitten paintings. 'Of course, Freddie, it's not your usual style, but in these difficult times . . . '

'Yeah, I know.' He had a blunt Cockney accent. 'This Hallmark crap is the only thing that'll shift for sure these days.' He leaned closer to Helena. 'I don't know how you do it, love.'

Her eyes flickered skywards in agreement. 'Think of them as an asset, not art,' she continued, evidently eager to make the sale. 'You can keep them in storage, or something.'

'What the fuck,' he shrugged, careless, 'I'll take it. All of them, if I can.'

'Actually, those aren't for sale.' Alice spoke up, their sneering tones too much for her. She stalked closer, giving Helena and the man an icy smile. 'We're holding those back, for now, until she completes the series.'

Helena looked confused. 'But I thought — '

'No.' Alice folded her arms and let her gaze

316

drift over Freddie. She curled her lip slightly. 'Of course, Flora may change her mind, with a different buyer.'

His eyes widened. 'And who the fuck are you?'

'Her sister,' she replied with a smile. 'Enjoy the rest of the show.'

Alice left them staring in disbelief. She'd just cost Flora a lucrative sale, but it was worth it, she was sure. Those kittens belonged with somebody who would actually appreciate them, not leave them wrapped in storage as if they were nothing more than stock certificates.

'You realise there are people out for your blood right now?' Nathan appeared, handing her a glass of wine. He nodded back across the room, to where Helena and Freddie were glaring at her.

Alice shrugged, unconcerned. 'Some people just have no taste, that's all.' She took a sip of the wine and studied him from under her lashes, torn between trying to continue their flirtation, and asking about Kate Jackson. As always, her curiosity about Ella won. 'Any news on that name yet?' She tried to sound casual.

He moved back into a slight alcove. 'I was wondering how long it would take you to ask.'

'How did I do?' Alice followed. He was tantalisingly close now, his jacket pressed against her bare arm.

'You know, pretty good.' Nathan pretended to muse. 'You didn't jump me the minute I walked through the door.'

'Tempting as it was,' Alice quipped, only partly joking.

'I'm sure.' He paused, looking out at the groups of casual guests, sipping Pimm's and nibbling the tiny cucumber sandwiches the caterer had set out on lace-adorned tables to play up the English country theme. Alice was surprised they hadn't hung bunting and served Earl Grey as well. 'It's a great showing tonight,' Nathan remarked. 'Flora must be happy.'

'Yes, wonderful.' Alice waited impatiently.

'And it was nice to meet that friend of yours, Julian, wasn't it?' he teased.

'Nathan!' Alice broke. 'I have a blunt object, and I'm not afraid to use it.' She wielded her wineglass in what she hoped was a vaguely threatening manner.

He laughed, already pulling out a folded sheet of paper. Alice forced herself to take it calmly, and not snatch it from his hand. 'She paid at the hotel in cash, so there wasn't much to go on, just the name' he began, as she glanced through the long list. 'I scanned for credit, property, driving licences . . . After I cut them down for age, I got our short list here. Those two are dead, that one has been missing five years, and *she* became a *he* last summer.'

Alice could still see at least two dozen names. 'So what next?'

Nathan had his smug look on again, a fact that Alice found remarkably reassuring. 'Next, I ruled out most of our remaining candidates with a few calls. The only one I couldn't track down was Bachelorette Number Twelve there.'

Alice followed his pointed finger to a single notation, just an address in Bath with none of the other details the rest of the possibilities had amassed. 'It's her?'

He nodded. 'Seems so. Just one record of her there, a credit card registered to that address. Which is suspicious enough, but what do you know? There was a nasty outbreak of fraud and identity theft nearby.' Alice brightened, and Nathan laughed at her obvious enthusiasm. 'Three people in apartments across the street fell victim, back at the start of January just before Ella appeared in London.'

'That can't be a coincidence,' Alice breathed.

'It seems to be her,' he agreed. 'I've started contacting the police, getting access to the reports and any investigator files, so we should get something back soon.'

'Maybe I should get in touch with the victims,' Alice suggested. It had been hard enough waiting for Nathan to provide this information — she wasn't about to sit back and let somebody else follow every clue without her. 'I mean, they might be more relaxed, chatting to someone who's been through the same thing. And I'll be able to recognise anything linking them to Ella.'

'Sure,' Nathan shrugged. 'I'll send you over the details.'

Alice beamed at him. 'Have I told you how wonderful you are?'

Nathan adjusted his jacket, falsely modest. 'Well, I don't like to brag . . . '

'Yes you do,' she laughed. 'But this time, you deserve it.' Seized by an impulse she couldn't quite control, Alice stretched up on her tiptoes and kissed him on the cheek.

As soon as she was back down on solid ground, she regretted the gesture. Nathan was looking down at her strangely, and their cosy alcove suddenly felt too small. She glanced up at him, about to make a casual quip, but her eyes caught his, dark and intent, and she quite forgot what she was planning to say.

'There you are. I've been looking for you all over.' A familiar voice cut through the intimate moment and Alice looked up to find Julian closing in. He glanced back and forth between them, frowning. 'What are you two conspiring about?'

'Oh, nothing,' Alice slipped the list into her bag. 'Having fun?'

'More now I've found you.' Julian grinned at her. 'Here, I got you some juice.'

'Already taken care of.' She held up her glass. 'But thanks.'

'I thought you didn't like to drink at these things.' Julian frowned. 'Anyway, you're almost done. I can take that.'

Alice looked at him curiously. 'I'm fine.' She took a deliberate sip of the wine and looked back at Nathan. 'So, did you guys have a chance to get to know each other? Julian is an accountant, over at Deloitte.'

'Really? How's that working out for you?' Nathan lounged back against the wall and surveyed Julian.

'Pretty well, actually. I'll be heading up my own department from next month.' Setting the glass of juice down nearby, Julian put his hands in his pockets and gazed back at Nathan evenly.

'You're in the same field, aren't you?'

'Not exactly.' Nathan seemed amused by the thought. 'I don't sit around all day, crunching numbers.'

Julian raised an eyebrow. 'My mistake. I suppose you're running around, chasing after petty thieves then.'

'That's one way of putting it, I guess.' Nathan folded his arms.

Alice blinked back and forth between the men. There was a definite sense of challenge in the air. 'Do you play any sports at all?' she asked Nathan quickly, trying to dispel the strange tension. 'You guys should get together for squash sometime. Julian's always looking for new partners.'

'Aly and I used to play together, in university,' Julian added, 'Did she say we've known each other since then?'

'No, *Aly* didn't.' Nathan just looked amused. 'It's great that you've been buddies for so long. Like brother and sister, right?'

Julian narrowed his eyes. 'Not exactly.'

Alice frowned at him. 'I think I'll try and find Flora again,' she decided, starting to manoeuvre her way between them.

'Wait a sec.' Nathan stopped her, his hand closing softly on her arm. 'I was going to ask if you're free next week at all.' He smiled down at her, ignoring Julian completely. 'I'm off working a case this weekend, but we could get together, Wednesday maybe? Reminisce about our vacation.'

Alice felt a glow at the invitation, but before she could reply, Julian spoke up again. 'We've

321

already got plans, I'm afraid.'

She turned, thrown. 'No, we haven't.'

'The Hitchcock season, remember?'

Alice blinked. 'I haven't said I can make it yet.'

'Great.' Nathan threw a smile at Julian. 'I'll call you then.'

'But, Alice — '

Feeling increasingly caught between them, Alice searched for an escape, 'Flora!' she called across the room. The slip of pink satin didn't turn, but Alice had found her exit. 'I've got to run,' she said brightly, pretending she didn't notice the careful stares being exchanged over her head. 'But yes, Nathan, call me about next week,' she smiled at him briefly. 'And you have fun at that film,' she told Julian. 'With Yasmin.'

★ ★ ★

She found Flora in the middle of a knot of people, Stefan beaming proudly at her side as the compliments flowed.

'Hi.' Alice slipped in beside her. 'Isn't this great?'

'Really great.' Flora smiled brightly. 'It's all perfect.'

'And what's next for you?' a slim, bespectacled man asked eagerly. 'Any new mediums, or product ranges planned?'

Flora shrugged prettily. 'Oh, I don't know. Whatever I feel like, I suppose!'

They all laughed, but Alice was studying Flora's face carefully. Something wasn't quite right. Flora seemed full of her usual bubbly enthusiasm, but Alice could sense an almost fierce self-control radiating beneath the angelic curls. She may be fooling everyone else, but Alice had known her too long to be deceived. Flora wasn't happy.

'Sorry, everyone, but I'm going to have to steal my sister away for a minute!' Alice announced, steering Flora out of the circle.

'But I can't,' Flora protested, 'Everybody's expecting — '

'They'll wait,' Alice told her. 'Besides, Nathan and Julian are about to start marking their territory around me, or something. Rescue me, please. I need you!'

'You do?' Flora started to smile.

'Absolutely. I need some air. We'll only be gone a little while.' Alice was already pulling her out onto the street, away from the clusters of admiring fans and whatever it was that was making her so tense.

'So what's happening with Nathan?' Flora trailed after her across the road. It was still light out, soft with dusk hues, and Alice quickly found them a low wall on which to perch, watching the trickle of passers-by heading out to restaurants and local bars.

'Nothing's happening,' Alice told her, before allowing herself a small smile. 'Yet.'

Flora lit up. 'Really?'

'Perhaps. I mean, I'd like it to, maybe . . . ' Despite the cool flirtation she'd enjoyed all evening, Alice almost felt like an adolescent again, confessing her attraction. 'But you can't say anything.'

'Lips sealed, I promise.' Flora mimed extravagantly. A passing group of rowdy teens stared at her, clearly dazzled by the pink satin ball gown, but Flora was oblivious. 'So, do you like him? Did anything happen, in Rome?' She beamed excitedly, with a genuine enthusiasm she hadn't shown in all the past hours of flattery.

'Yes, and no,' Alice confided slowly. 'But I introduced him to Julian tonight, and now they're in some kind of strange masculine showdown.'

'A duel?' Flora gasped.

'Not quite,' Alice laughed. 'I don't know . . . It's not like him to be so protective. But, I suppose it has been a while since there's been any prospects around.'

'Since James,' Flora agreed quietly.

Alice looked up, surprised she remembered the last, and only, man to break Alice's heart. 'Right, not since him.'

'Maybe Julian's realised that he's madly in love with you, and can't bear to see you with anyone else.' Flora sighed happily.

Alice laughed. 'I doubt it. These things are never that simple.'

She gave Flora a careful look. 'So . . . how are you feeling? It must be nerve-racking, having your new series up for everyone to see.'

Flora gave a small shrug. 'Not really. I'm used to it by now, I think. And everyone's said such nice things.' She swung her legs back and forth, pink kitten heels clattering against the wall.

'Yes, but you've been under lots of stress.' Alice tried again. 'Maybe now you'll get to relax a little. You could go on that holiday with Stefan you were talking about,' she said encouragingly. 'Somewhere with white beaches and little umbrellas in your drink.'

'Maybe.' Flora shrugged, and then turned to Alice with excitement again. 'So, Nathan. Tell me everything! I saw you off in that corner earlier, very private . . . '

Alice smiled. 'No, we were just talking about the investigation. We've found an old address for Ella, in Bath, so I think I'm going to go out there and ask around.' She paused, suddenly remembering Flora's hurt at being excluded from the Rome affair. 'You could come with me, if you want,' she added. 'I mean, it would be nice to have the company.'

Flora's eyes widened. 'Really?'

'Sure.' Alice was glad she'd suggested it. Time away together would, perhaps, encourage Flora to open up. Plus, her trademark innocence might be a useful tool when it came to investigating Ella's past. 'It could be fun.'

Flora hopped down from the wall. 'What are we waiting for?' she exclaimed. 'Let's get on the road straight away. I'll drive, and you book the hotel, and — s'

'Woah! Aren't you forgetting something?' Alice grabbed her arm. 'Your opening? The room full of people gushing over your life's work?'

Flora bit her lip. 'I'm sure they wouldn't miss me. I've said 'hi' to everyone there at least twice already.'

Alice frowned. 'Flora, are you sure you're all right?'

'What do you mean?'

'I mean . . . ' Alice paused, noting the defiant angle of her chin. Flora clearly wasn't in the mood for sharing now. 'No, never mind.' She linked her arm through Flora's as they began to walk back towards the gallery. 'The investigation can wait, one night at least. Let's get you back to your adoring fans.'

24

They set off the next morning, equipped with five emergency break-down numbers and what seemed to be the entire contents of Marks and Spencer's snack food section.

'So you think this Kate Jackson woman is really Ella?' Flora curled up in the passenger seat, slurping on a carton of juice. They were just emerging from the traffic of London, onto the wide swathes of motorway that would eventually take them to Bath.

Alice kept her eyes on the road. 'I'm not sure. She did everything she could to cover her tracks after she left, but I'm hoping she wasn't so careful, before.'

A person just didn't emerge from the womb a criminal mastermind: they had to learn it. And along the way, Alice hoped, they made some mistakes.

'I still can't believe you have to do all this yourself.' Flora made a face. 'Can't the police run like, DNA tests or something?'

Alice grinned. 'She's not a murderer.'

'You don't know that. She could be anything!'

'No.' Alice shook her head firmly. 'I know her, she's not that kind of person. And even what she stole from me — it was only what could be replaced. She doesn't do this to hurt people.'

There was silence, and when Alice glanced

over, she found Flora watching her with curiosity. 'What?'

'You don't even sound angry,' Flora said slowly.

'I'm not. Well, I was at first,' Alice admitted, carefully checking the rear-view mirror before moving into another lane. 'But what was the damage, after everything? The bank's refunded my money, the credit card debt is being written off. And . . . ' She'd been about to mention Safe Haven, and all the good Ella's donation was doing over there, but caught herself just in time. Instead, she said vaguely, 'And, perhaps she did something worthwhile with it, after all.'

'That's very . . . zen,' Flora said dubiously.

'Don't get me wrong, I'm sorry about all the inconvenience it caused for you and Stefan, and everyone, but,' she shrugged, 'she didn't leave me any worse off, in the end.'

'But didn't someone have to pay?' Flora asked. 'Money can't just appear, right?'

'So some multibillion banking corporations had to eat into their profits. Let's all take a moment to weep.'

Flora giggled. 'Alice!'

'What? You know it's true.'

'I know, it's just . . . where did this come from?' Flora looked at her, clearly taken aback. 'You've always been the one going on about rules, and doing the right thing.'

'You make me sound so exciting.' Alice remarked dryly.

Flora giggled again. 'No, it's good, I think. You

328

seem . . . happier now.'

'See?' Alice flashed her a grin. 'This mess hasn't done me any harm at all.'

Perhaps Ella had even planned it that way.

* * *

When they were nearing the outskirts of the city, Alice had Flora call ahead to the first victim and set up a brief chat. Illana Mayers still lived at the same address as before, and would be happy to talk with them. Soon they were turning up Elmwood Avenue: the former home of one Miss Kate Jackson.

Flora climbed out of the car, looking around eagerly, but her face quickly settled into a more bemused expression. 'It doesn't look like a hotbed of fraud and deception.'

Alice had to agree. The suburban street was quiet, leafy and entirely unremarkable. Semi-detached houses lined the road, divided by hedges and freshly painted fences, and although there wasn't anything as idyllic as children playing freely in the street, there were enough toys scattered in front gardens, and bicycles leaning against garage doors to prove the area a family-friendly zone.

'Why would Ella bother living somewhere like this?' Flora followed her up the road, 'It's miles out of the city centre.'

'I don't know.' Alice looked around, trying to put herself in Ella's mindset again. By now, it was simple. 'Maybe she wanted the peace and quiet. Or maybe she just figured people round here wouldn't be shredding all their important documents.'

'Weird.' Flora shrugged. 'I mean, what does she do — just pick a place, and show up, and start stalking people?'

'Not stalking,' Alice corrected. 'Watching.'

'Like there's a difference.'

The address from Nathan's file was near the top of the road: a large Victorian house with gravel at the front and four buzzers lined up beside the door, marking the separate flats. Alice tested the door, but it was firmly locked, no doubt an after-effect of the fraud. Sure enough, when Illana buzzed them in, there was a pile of letters jumbled on the doormat, and a simple hall table for post and other deliveries: an invitation for theft and mail tampering if ever Alice saw. No security cameras either, of course, and she would bet that the residents didn't know each other well enough to guess if that non-descript woman slipping in behind them was a friend dropping by or an imposter set on stealing their life savings.

Illana was waiting in the doorway on the second floor. A nervous-looking woman in her early thirties, she was outfitted in baggy sweatpants and a T-shirt, with her dark hair scraped back in a ponytail.

'Hi.' She greeted them with an awkward smile. 'Come on in. I can't talk long, I'm afraid, but maybe it will help.'

'Thanks so much for seeing me,' Alice quickly moved to reassure her: giving a friendly grin and whipping out her notebook and pen. They followed Illana through to the sitting room, which was strewn with magazines, dirty cups and random items of clothing.

'I'm sorry about the mess,' Illana blushed. 'I didn't have any time — '

'Oh, no, it's fine!' Alice insisted, as Flora plucked a pair of tights from the couch and took a seat. 'You should see our place; you can barely see the floor sometimes.' Flora raised an eyebrow at the obvious untruth, but the white lie worked: Illana perched on the edge of a chair, seeming to relax.

'So, you want to know about the identity theft?' she asked Alice. 'It was a while ago now, and I told the police everything I could.'

'Let me guess,' Alice said sympathetically. 'They couldn't help at all.'

'They tried,' Illana offered, 'and the banks too, but it took months to unravel everything, and get them to replace the money.'

'But you got it all back in the end?' Alice sent a meaningful look at Flora.

'Yes, eventually. I was lucky, they didn't open any credit cards or anything in my name, but Patrick — he lived downstairs — he had about seventy grand of debt by the end of it. They were calling him all the time, really hassling him.'

'And you never had any idea who did it?' Alice prompted.

Illana shook her head. 'They said it could be criminal gangs, you know, professionals, but if you say it was this woman, Kate . . . ' She sighed. 'I really don't know. CCTV showed a woman withdrawing the money at ATMs, but it was always dark, or she had a scarf around her hair or something. Sorry, I wish I could be more help.' She gave a weak smile.

'You're doing great!' Flora piped up.

'This is going to sound strange, perhaps,' Alice began, 'but did you make any new friends around that time, or even before then, any time in the last six months or so? See, that's how it happened to me,' she explained. 'Kate — this woman — she met me in a class, and struck up conversation. We became friends, that's how she was able to access my papers and things.

Illana blinked. 'No . . . no, I don't think so. I mean, I keep pretty much to myself.' She blushed. 'So, I would have noticed if there was anyone new hanging around. The police went through this all,' she added, 'when we realised it was more than one of us, in the building. They thought it might be a friend, or partner, or something, so they interviewed everyone. But . . . ' She trailed off.

'She would have been about my height,' Alice tried again. 'Brown hair, perhaps, although she could have dyed it to anything. Average features, but . . . ' Now it was her turn to trail off. Her descriptions were so vague as to be practically useless.

'Sorry,' Illana apologised again. 'I really didn't meet anyone new, or see anyone suspicious. That was the thing: we couldn't explain it.'

'That's OK.' Alice tried to smile. 'You've been really helpful.' She and Flora got up. 'Can I leave you my number, in case you think of anything?'

'Sure,' Illana took the scribbled details and

showed them to the door. 'Good luck, I guess.'

Alice waited until they were on the street again before sighing. 'Well, that was useful . . . '

'She seemed nice,' Flora noted, glancing back up at the flat.

'Nice, yes, observant, no.' Alice frowned. Clearly, Ella had infiltrated Illana's life in some way, but had been so discreet, she hadn't even noticed. She unlocked the car, wondering how Ella had blended into the background so completely — nondescript clothing, perhaps, and an average haircut. It had always been Ella's charm and vivacity that made an impact, so Alice had little doubt she could become invisible should the situation demand.

'So, who's next?' Flora slid into the passenger seat.

Alice consulted her notes. 'Randeep Karimi. He moved just after it happened; he's an assistant manager at CompuWorld, working a shift today. Let's hope he's more of a help.'

But he wasn't. In fact, out of the three people who had been thoroughly defrauded by Ella, not one could recall so much as meeting her.

'Nope,' the final victim, Patrick O'Neal, shifted restlessly on the spot. He was a laddish man with greasy red hair, whom Alice had managed to catch at his Saturday football league, taking a half-time break from what was clearly a raucous, violent match on the far corner of a muddy park. 'Never seen her.'

'You're sure?' Alice asked again, a note of desperation creeping into her tone. Illana had been useless, Randeep apologetic but blank;

Patrick was her final hope. 'You didn't meet anyone in a bar, or club, around that time?'

His face stretched into a sleazy grin. 'Darlin', I meet girls all the time. Doesn't mean I remember them.'

Alice sighed. 'This one, you would have maybe taken home? Or — '

'Look, I told the cops everything I could.' He shrugged. 'Anyway, there's no chance it was just some girl ripping me off. The fuckers took everything. It was a gang, right. Professionals.'

'Yes, but — '

'Look, I ain't got time for this.' Patrick started backing away. 'Good luck with it, yeah?' He turned and jogged back to where his team-mates were gulping sports drinks on the sidelines.

Alice began to walk back across the field, dejected. It had been a long shot, she knew, but still, she'd expected something to be revealed; a small gem of insight or information into Ella's makings.

'Well?' Flora was perched on a park bench in the sun. She was wearing a pretty, gauzy white dress, with her hair in two thin plaits. 'What's the news?'

'No news.' Alice sat down beside her with a sigh. 'He says he hasn't seen her, but he would hardly even talk to me.'

'Why not?'

She shrugged. 'Busy, with the game. Also, I doubt it's his finest moment — being defrauded like that.' Alice looked at the small figures, dashing around on the other side of the field. 'He's been telling himself it's the work of a vast

334

criminal network, I think, to take the edge off. Nobody wants to admit it's as easy as one woman and an old bank statement. It undermines their manly prowess, you know?'

Flora laughed. 'Why don't I try talking to him?'

Alice smiled over at her. 'That's sweet of you to offer, but I don't think it'll help.'

'No, really, let me try,' Flora argued. 'I can help, you know, with his manly prowess.'

Alice raised an eyebrow, but Flora made a knowing face. 'Come on, it's not like I'm exactly threatening.' She held up a braid in each hand as evidence.

Alice laughed. 'Well . . . OK. Why not?' She looked back across the field. It wasn't as if she had any better options, and if Flora could actually prompt him to reveal something . . . 'But these will have to go, I think.' She reached over and began to undo Flora's hair. 'They do make you look, um, rather young.'

'I know.' She shrugged, apparently unconcerned, and started combing out the other plait. 'Sometimes it's just easier, looking fifteen. People don't really expect anything from you.'

Before Alice could think more about that curious statement, Flora leaped up. 'Wish me luck!'

'Good luck. And remember to ask him about anyone he invited home,' Alice added, 'and if they — '

'Relax!' Flora laughed. She fluffed out her hair and quickly applied a slick of Vaseline to her lips. 'I've seen you do this all day.'

Alice watched her trot enthusiastically towards the football game. The match was underway again, with shouts and the frequent blast of the referee's whistle drifting on the breeze, but clearly, the lure of Flora's angelic visage was temptation enough for Patrick. All it took was a comment to one of the teammates, and within moments, he had been fetched from the pitch. She certainly had her skills, but as Alice waited, she wondered about that cryptic comment. Flora had been so upset at being left out of the Italy operation. She'd accused Alice of underestimating her, but on the other hand, there she was, happy to act young and helpless because it was just easier that way — to have people doting on her, and doing everything in her place.

Soon, Flora was bounding back across the field. 'Well?' Alice rose to greet her.

'What a wanker!' Flora exclaimed, screwing her face up in disdain. 'He kept giving me these sleazy looks, like I was in my underwear or something. And when he asked me out for a drink, and I said I was married, he was all, 'It's not a death sentence.' '

'Sorry,' Alice apologised, 'I should have warned you.'

'Oh, no, it was fine,' Flora beamed. 'Anyway, he seemed totally clueless, like you said, but there was one possibility. I talked Ella up like she was a dangerous spy or something — so he wouldn't feel stupid — and he said there was one night in December he took a girl back, but woke up the next morning with no memory at all, like he'd blacked out. It could just be he drank too much,' she added, 'and she bolted in the morning when she realised what she'd gone home with, but still . . . '

' . . . It could have been Ella,' Alice finished, thoughtful. 'She might have used a sleeping pill or something, to make sure she wouldn't actually have to . . . you know.'

'Ugh.' Flora shuddered. 'He really is a dick.'

They took a moment to reflect on Patrick's shining personality.

'Well, thank you.' Alice gave her a hug. 'I don't know if it'll be any use, but at least I know we tried.'

'No problem! It was kind of fun,' Flora confided, as they began to stroll towards the car. 'Like I was undercover, or something. Was that what you were doing out in Italy?' she asked, eager. 'Digging for clues, and infiltrating places?'

'Sort of,' Alice admitted. 'Only, I didn't really plan it. One minute, I was reading the postcard she sent from Rome, and the next, I'd booked the ticket and was on my way to the airport. I've never done anything like it before,' she added. 'But it was wonderful.'

'It sounds so exciting,' Flora said wistfully, 'just picking up and taking off like that.'

Alice laughed. 'You're the one who can disappear at the drop of a hat!' Out of anyone, Flora surely had the most flexible life: no mortgage, or responsibilities, and a career she could pack away in her suitcase whenever she felt like it. 'Stefan travels all the time, and nobody says you have to stay at home waiting for him,' she pointed out. 'You're young! Why not go off

337

adventuring, even just for a weekend or two? Or apply for that art residency in Florence, and really absorb a place for a while.'

Flora fell silent. 'I couldn't,' she answered eventually, throwing Alice a brief smile. 'That programme isn't my thing, I told you that. And, well, could you imagine me travelling on my own? It would be a disaster. I'd get lost before I even left baggage reclaim.' She gave a self-deprecating laugh and changed the subject. 'So, who's our next interview? Another victim?'

'No, we've talked to them all. That's it, I'm afraid.'

'Really?' Flora's face fell. 'I thought we'd find *something*.'

'Me too.' Alice almost felt foolish, thinking of the glee with which she'd greeted Nathan's latest information. She'd been so certain it would lead to Ella, or at least another facet of her trail. But, after everything, Ella was too good. Kate Jackson was just another dead end.

They reached the car, but Alice idled in the shadow of the trees for a moment, not too keen to face the traffic of the weekend motorway so soon. Flora hopped up on the hood of the car and swung her legs.

'You know, I'm kind of glad she got him in trouble with the credit card people. Patrick, I mean. He really was disgusting.'

'Now who's not playing by the rules!'

Flora giggled. 'I know! But he deserves it, more than the other two, anyway.'

'Maybe that's why she did it,' Alice said, almost to herself. She knew that it was ridiculous of her to attribute Ella with intentions and conscience, but she couldn't help wondering if that's how she too had viewed her victims. It couldn't be a coincidence that out of the three, the only one who had seen a mound of problems with false credit cards and loans had been the most unsavoury. Illana and Randeep may have seen their bank accounts temporarily emptied, but theirs was a minor upset compared to Patrick's ongoing woe.

'That would be cool,' Flora mused, thinking on it. 'Like, a Robin Hood. Only, instead of stealing from the rich, she takes it from banks, and loan companies, and complete assholes.'

There was a pause, and then Alice asked, 'So what am I?'

Flora frowned. 'Huh. OK, maybe not.'

Alice shrugged, reaching for the keys. The football players were beginning to scatter, some headed in their direction. 'Come on, we better get back before Patrick tries to win you over with his charm and chivalry.'

'Oh God, yes.' Flora hopped down, and all but threw herself back in the car. 'It's a shame, though, there weren't any clues or anything. I guess it was a wasted trip, after all.'

* ★ *

Alice thought much the same, but as she began to review her notes over the next few days, she wasn't quite so sure. On the surface, she had nothing but the meagre facts her trip to Italy and Nathan's enquiries had managed to glean: that

Ella had used a passport in the name of Kate Jackson, and that she'd lived discreetly under that name for several months before coming to London. Her victims in Bath had no idea she was targeting them, and, unlike with Alice, she hadn't struck up any friendships or false relationships in order to gain access to their personal information. Ella had taken classes under Illana's name, bought clothes and groceries, perhaps even volunteered, the way she had done at Safe Haven, but none of it had been done with the same veneer of friendship she'd used with Alice.

But that, in itself, was what puzzled Alice the most. If Ella didn't need to get close in order to steal the other victim's information, then why had she done so with Alice? All those months of their friendship, she'd been risking discovery: any one of her lies could have unravelled at any time. Had it been a challenge, to see if she could get away with it, or was it something more?

Alice couldn't help thinking of that quiet street in Bath, and the temporary life Ella must have led there. Following her victims' every move, yes, but also, making sure to stay invisible and utterly unseen. It would have been lonely, Alice decided. All that time, never confiding anything real to anyone, for fear that it would bring her down — she could only imagine how isolated Ella had felt. No wonder she wanted to reach out, perhaps even building her life in London, so that this time, she could enjoy more of a regular existence, with friendship and routine. Perhaps, this time Ella had genuinely meant it.

Alice lingered on the thought. It was tempting to believe that not only had their friendship contained a few shards of truth, but that it might have genuinely meant something to Ella as well. For weeks, Alice had been building a new picture of this woman in her mind. This latest element seemed to fit: the loneliness, the need for human contact. There was something vulnerable there. Relatable.

But despite this potentially softer side to Ella's actions, Alice couldn't quite manage to forget the truth. Ella had left, in the end — with her money, and her trust, and her good reputation. Alice just hoped that when she found her, Ella would have a good enough reason why.

25

With all her present leads on Ella now exhausted, Alice was able to turn her attentions back to the agency. Unlike her previous tactics of hard work, honesty and reasoning, her new unorthodox route to becoming an agent was reaping rich rewards. Thanks to several phone calls, detailed strategy emails and even a couple of hasty, clandestine lunch-hour meetings, Alice had secured Kieran and Julia as her very first clients. She'd been honest with them about her relative inexperience when it came to agenting, but (as she explained it) that just provided her with ample time to devote to their every need, and the enthusiasm to make an impact. Having been all but abandoned by Vivienne, they were willing to take that risk, and signed fresh contracts to that effect, adding Alice as their named representative at Grayson Wells.

Her first victories were complete; now the only real challenge was how, exactly, to break the news to Vivienne.

* * *

'So, I was thinking we meet around six tonight.' Julian called after lunch on Wednesday of the following week, when the rain was streaking her windows with a dull drizzle, and it felt like summer was simply a passing dream. 'We could grab some food before the film.'

Alice paused. 'I told you, I can't make it. I have that date with Nathan tonight, remember?'

'Oh.' Julian didn't sound wholly enthused. 'I wasn't sure if that was going to happen.'

'Yes,' Alice replied lightly, 'he called to set it up. We're having dinner at this little place in Soho.'

'Well . . . have fun then, I suppose. And check around before you order anything,' Julian added. 'Half those places should be shut down by health and safety people. You can always tell from the state of the toilets.'

'Um, thanks. You have fun too.' Alice rang off, her mood too good to be dampened. And it wasn't just her gleaming new status as an agent that made her swivel on her chair with excitement.

She'd been planning all week for the date. Not in an over-wrought way, she was quick to tell herself, more the idle musings that always preceded these sorts of things — the outfit planning, the selection of shoes, the well-timed hair-washing the night before. Alice didn't want to admit she'd put more thought into this particular dinner than any other in a long while, but the dress laid neatly on her bed at home (with the perfect necklace, purse and jacket set out nearby) spoke otherwise. She may not be the sort to spin out romantic fantasies the way Flora did, but Alice had an instinct that this might finally be . . . something real.

There was a light tap at her door.

'Yes?' Alice looked up as Saskia edged in.

'This just got faxed to the main line.' She seemed disgruntled as she manoeuvred around a stack of files and delivered the papers. 'When are you going to get the intercom fixed? I shouldn't be away from the desk,' she added, as if that were her sole worry, and not the inconvenience of two flights of stairs in her perilous heels.

Alice took the papers with a breezy smile. 'Thanks. And I'm not sure about the intercom . . . They said it was beyond repair.'

'Then why not get a new one?'

Alice shrugged. 'I'm sure I will, when I get the time.' The intercom was, in fact, in perfect working order; sitting in a box at the bottom of Alice's wardrobe at home. But since she'd apologetically announced news of its passing, her co-workers had ceased their interruptions almost entirely, as if making their helpless requests to her face was too much of an effort.

'Fine.' Saskia didn't appear pleased by the thought of navigating those stairs on a more regular basis. She turned to go, but then added, 'Oh, Vivienne said she wants to talk to you.'

Alice froze. 'Did she say why?'

'I don't know. She said to go and see her after the agent meeting.'

Of course she did. Alice had known her extra-curricular activities wouldn't go unnoticed for long, and she could just imagine what choice words her boss would have waiting to deliver. That was, unless . . .

'The meeting,' Alice stopped Saskia before she left, 'has it started yet?'

Another shrug. 'Maybe. They're all down there.'

'Thanks.'

Alice waited until she'd departed, then began to collect her notes. The weekly meetings were a tradition; gathering to exchange news of clients and possible agency opportunities, and boast about their particular successes. It wasn't that she was excluded from attending, but Alice — or Vivienne — had never seen the point. After all, she wasn't an agent.

At least, she hadn't been before.

Skipping lightly down the staircase, Alice found the agents in Vivienne's salon, distributing themselves amongst her array of antique furniture. She took a seat on one of the velvet-upholstered wing chairs, feeling every inch the interloper. A few of the other agents gave her a look of brief interest, but they were quickly distracted by Vivienne, holding court with a story involving all manner of London theatre luminaries.

' . . . And so I said to Sir Kenneth, if you expect me to put that thing in my mouth — ' She broke off, looking at Alice with confusion. 'Didn't Saskia say, darling? After the meeting, *after*.'

Alice gave a pleasant smile and braced herself. 'Oh, she did. But I thought I'd join you all. Now that I'll be moving to the agent side of things, I mean.'

That caught their attention. Even Tyrell, sharp-suited in navy pinstripes and his usual black Converse sneakers, lowered his phone to

345

look at her in surprise.

'Well, I didn't think . . . ' Vivienne looked perturbed, but Alice turned her attention to the others.

'Don't worry, I'll still be taking care of contracts, for now,' she said carefully. 'I'll just be working with a couple of clients as well, sort of testing the waters.'

Alice felt a faint wave of nausea roll through her. Never mind Rafael, and moonlit seductions, this was by far the boldest thing she'd ever done. 'Vivienne suggested I start with Kieran and Julia,' she continued, 'so I can get a feel for things.'

Vivienne, having suggested no such thing, was looking even paler than usual, but before she could speak, there was a cough.

'Ah, congratulations,' Anthony said, reaching to shake Alice's hand vigorously. 'Yes, well done indeed. Excellent news.'

At his cue, the others joined with their own warm words. 'Good luck to you.' Tyrell flashed his gleaming smile at her. 'Just make sure you don't fall behind with those contracts!' He laughed, not at all joking.

'Thanks,' Alice beamed back regardless. 'It'll take me a while to get the hang of things, I'm sure, but I'm looking forward to being a part of the team.'

There was silence.

Vivienne cleared her throat. 'Well, now that we've got the . . . big announcement out of the way, shall we get down to business?'

As the rest of the agents settled, pulling out

files and papers, Alice took the opportunity to sneak a glance at Vivienne. She was staring at her leather-bound notebook, but the tight smile on her scarlet lips betrayed her obvious displeasure. Alice forced herself not to waver. This was a calculated move, she reminded herself; the lengths that Vivienne had gone to avoid directly confronting Alice over the Rupert affair had proven, if anything, how indispensable Alice was to the agency. If Vivienne hadn't wanted to risk offending Alice over that, then neither — she hoped — would she object to this.

'So, Alice,' Vivienne finally looked up, fixing her with a dangerous smile, 'why don't you go first? Let's hear what you've achieved so far for dear Kieran and Julia.' She waited, clearly expecting mumbled apologies, but Alice simply opened her notebook.

'I haven't had much time, I know, so please bear with me.' She gave a self-deprecating smile. 'I've withdrawn Kieran from those comedy auditions, and decided to focus on pure drama. So, I've managed to set him up with some meetings next week: just informal drop-bys with commissioning editors at Juno, Pipergate, and BBC Drama, but it should give them a fresh reminder about his look, to keep in mind for future castings.'

Vivienne's smile slipped.

'Now with Julia, I think her problem has been more at the audition stage,' Alice continued, her confidence growing. 'So we've had a chat, and she's agreed to meet with me to pick out a new work wardrobe, and change her look to target older roles.'

'That's all very well,' Vivienne seized the chance to interrupt, 'but shopping trips aren't exactly jobs now, are they?'

'You're right,' Alice smiled back. 'So I also have a list of eight different auditions lined up for her next week. We'll be able to get immediate feedback on the new approach, and move on from there.' She closed her notebook and waited, heart pounding. If there were ever a moment for Vivienne to lash out, then this was it.

An eyebrow flickered in displeasure. Alice steeled herself for war. But, as if realising the delicacy of their public setting, Vivienne just pursed her lips. 'Hmm. We'll see.' Her gaze drifted to the next victim. 'Tyrell? This is no time to be checking emails. Put that thing away and tell me about what's happening with Nick Savage.'

Alice felt a great rush of celebration. She was officially the newest agent at Grayson Wells.

★ ★ ★

After such a major victory, dinner with Nathan seemed like a breeze. Alice slipped home early to get ready, even inviting Flora to help select some jewellery and fix her hair up in loose curls. By the time Nathan arrived to pick her up, she was perched calmly on a stool in the kitchen, watching Stefan stir-fry a spread of vegetables with his usual efficiency.

'Look who's here!' Flora led him in with a

348

none-too-subtle exclamation, as flushed as if she were the one going on her first date. She stood by the counter, beaming proudly.

'Why do I feel like a teenager again?' Alice joked, nodding at their audience.

'I'll have you back by curfew, I promise,' Nathan laughed, leaning over to kiss her briefly on both cheeks. He was smarter than usual: cleanly shaven, with a crisp shirt and pair of dark trousers. Alice liked that he'd thought to make the effort, and not just dashed there straight from work.

He made small talk with Stefan and Flora for a few minutes — about the restaurant selection, and some upcoming charity event — and then they were on their way; Nathan's hand light on the curve of Alice's back as he ushered her out to his car. 'I know, it's a waste in the city,' he said, as if pre-empting an argument he'd had too many times. 'What can I say? It's in my blood.'

'The open road?' Alice waited while he opened the car door for her.

'No, dependence on oil and drive-thrus.'

Alice laughed, slipping into the seat. 'As long as you don't start talking about r.p.m. and acceleration speeds,' she advised. 'I'll just glaze over if you do.'

'Car talk, off limits — duly noted.' Nathan grinned. 'Now, where are you on American football and the NFL?'

* * *

Dinner passed by in a pleasant haze of wine, delicious food, easy conversation; a miraculous change from the other, awkward dates Alice had suffered through. But with Nathan, it was simple: no stilted pauses, or searching for common interests. It was as if their time together in Italy really had broken through that early stage of carefully selected confessions and measured responses, and now they were free to laugh and chat without caution.

'I can't believe you finished that dessert.' Nathan followed her out onto the narrow street. 'On top of everything else!'

'I was hungry.' Alice gave a careless shrug, slipping her hand through the crook of his arm. The rain had stopped, leaving a crisp freshness in the air; the sound of evening drinkers drifting down from the pubs and bars nearby. 'Besides, it was clear you weren't going to let me share any of yours.'

'I would have,' Nathan argued, not entirely convincing. 'Maybe. Just a little. And I wouldn't do that for everyone,' he added, patting her hand.

Alice laughed. 'Well then, I feel special.'

'Good.' Nathan looked up and down the street. 'So . . . shall we get a drink somewhere?'

Alice smiled. She didn't want to end the night yet either, but the prospect of a noisy bar didn't appeal. 'How about we walk for a while?' she suggested. It was warm enough that she just needed a cardigan over her fluttering dress, her stacked sandals safe enough for an evening stroll.

'Sounds good to me.'

They fell into an easy pace together, meandering through Soho and across to Covent Garden. Alice had walked this route a hundred times in daylight, but somehow, the dusk light made everything seem different; emptied of the usual rushing shoppers, it was peaceful, almost pretty.

'Do you miss the States?' Alice asked him. 'You said you were from North Carolina, was it?'

Nathan nodded. 'But my mom moved to Florida, after Dad died, and I went straight to New York for college, so . . . it hasn't been home in a long time.'

'I wonder about that,' Alice said quietly. 'Whether home is somewhere you find, or just wherever you decide to make it.'

She could have been living in her neat one-bedroom in Stoke Newington by now, had it not been for Ella, and her creative approach to charity fund-raising. Would she have been happy there, Alice wondered — if everything had gone exactly to her plan: if there had been no living with Flora, or trips to Rome, or new discoveries. Or Nathan.

Somehow, she didn't think so.

'It's funny how things work out,' she murmured, almost to herself. Her feet were beginning to ache, but Alice liked the casual intimacy they had out there in the dark, so she led him to where several cobbled streets met at a junction, marked by a pillar of sundials. It was a well-lit spot, with several restaurants in sight just down the many streets, but for a moment, they were completely alone. She settled on the low, stone steps, and flexed her toes in front of her.

Nathan chuckled. 'Comfortable?'

'Enough,' Alice tilted her head up to Nathan with a smile. 'Care to join me?'

He sat down beside her, and then, as if it was a familiar gesture, and not the first concrete sign of anything more, he reached to take her hand. Alice caught her breath, carefully folding her fingers in his. It was hard to believe that this was the first real gesture they'd shared; everything else had been merely talk.

'There's actually something I've been meaning to ask . . . ' Nathan began, after they'd been sitting in comfortable silence for a moment. 'This thing, with Ella.' He gave her a cautious look. 'Why is it you want to find her so bad? And don't tell me it's about the money,' he added, 'because we both know that's not true.'

Alice began absently to trace a pattern on his palm. She wanted to be honest, but something held her back from admitting the full extent of her compulsion. Would he even understand? 'I don't know,' she began slowly. 'I just . . . it feels like I'm supposed to follow her, like she would want me to.'

'But she can't have.' Nathan looked at her with obvious concern. 'She ripped you off and fled the country. The last thing she'd want is anyone coming after her.'

Alice felt the urge to defend Ella, but carefully swallowed it back. 'I just can't help it. Don't you ever feel this way about your cases, as if . . . as if you're playing some kind of game, and it's you and them in this grand battle of wits?'

352

'Yes, but, it's a job for me. I don't know the people I'm chasing, and I don't for one minute think I ever will.' He paused, as if deciding whether or not to say something. 'I don't want to sound like I'm telling you what to do, because we both know how that turns out.' He gave her a wry smile. 'I just think, you're too attached to this woman. Or to your idea of her,' he corrected. 'I mean, that's all you've got, isn't it? She lied about everything else.'

Alice said nothing. She knew it might sound absurd to anyone else, but she really did know Ella now — more than she ever had when they were supposedly friends. The scraps of her life she'd left on the paper trail added up to something more than a blank debit outline: they were moments in her life, dozens of tiny choices.

'I just worry what's going to happen at the end of all this.' Nathan looked at her, affection clear in his eyes. 'When you don't find what you're looking for.'

Alice had a different concern: what happened when she did?

But as they sat, Nathan's body warm beside her, Alice realised what he was offering — and how much she might lose if he found out the true extent of her investigations. He followed the rules, he'd made that clear, and here she was accumulating a whole library of little white lies in pursuit of her truth.

'Maybe you're right,' she replied carefully. 'Maybe I should just let it all go. Stop looking for her, the money — everything.'

'It wouldn't be like she'd won,' Nathan

agreed. 'But you'd be saving yourself all this trouble.' He put his arm around her shoulders, drawing her closer. Alice let herself lean into him, soothed by the steady rise and fall of his chest as a group of people clattered past, their heels tapping on the cobble-stones. She felt guilty for what was about to come next, but the opportunity was too convenient not to take.

When the people were out of sight, she slipped her fingers through his free hand, closing it around her palm. 'So, should we stop?'

'Looking for Ella, you mean?'

'And the money.' Alice held her breath. It would be such a simple way out; no threat of anyone else tracking it back to Safe Haven, no messy questions tainting their good intentions or Ella's good deed. It could all just be forgotten to everyone — except her.

Nathan drew back slightly to look at her. 'You'd be OK with that?'

'I think so,' Alice lied.

'Then I reckon it's for the best.' Nathan sounded relieved. 'It can't have been easy for you, having this constant reminder that she betrayed your trust.'

'Mm-hm,' Alice murmured. He was wrong: the constant reminder was a good thing, urging her on to delve deeper, risk more. But she didn't want the chance of the police finding Ella before she did. No, Alice wanted to look Ella in the eye herself, and have her know she was the one who had found her.

Not such a dupe any more.

'We should get back,' she said brightly, pulling

her sandals on again. 'Before I get so tired you have to carry me to the car.'

'I could manage a piggyback.' Nathan got up, and offered his hands: pulling Alice to her feet, and then further, close against him.

'Thank you, for everything.' She stopped for a second. 'You've been . . . really great, helping me out with this.'

'Hey, it's been my pleasure.' He gave her a lop-sided grin, clearly flirtatious again. 'It certainly made my life more interesting for a while.'

'I think your life was interesting enough,' Alice managed to tease, beginning to walk. 'Jaunts to the Caymans, Switzerland . . . '

Nathan laughed. 'I wasn't talking about the travel.'

Alice felt herself blush, just a little.

'But you'll drop it now?' Nathan's tone became more serious. 'I know you wanted answers, but every case has a natural life-span. This one is just over.'

Alice nodded, so she wouldn't have to lie again.

'So I guess this means you won't need me to bail you out any more.' He carefully slipped his arms around Alice's waist.

'That was one time!' She relaxed against him, banishing the sense of guilt. 'You're not going to let me forget it, are you?'

'Nope.' Nathan's eyes were playful, but they were still intense enough to make Alice's breath catch. As he lowered his lips to hers, she smiled to herself.

Ella, for now, could wait.

26

And that, it seemed, should have been the end of it: Nathan wrapped up his investigation, the bank refunded her savings, and Alice's credit rating was restored to its former faultless glory. To anyone else, it appeared that Ella's brief swathe of havoc had been mended, and there was no need to spend any more time dwelling on it all.

But Alice couldn't let go.

Over the next few weeks, she found herself busier than she could remember: working hard at the agency to establish her new clients, and keep on top of the pile of regular contract tasks; dashing across the city for drinks or dates with Nathan. But through it all, Ella remained a constant presence, lingering in the back of Alice's mind. Soon, her frustration grew. The dead end that had been Kate Jackson almost seemed to taunt her; she knew there was some vital lead she'd overlooked, a piece of data that might just reveal everything, but no matter how many hours she pored over her files, she just couldn't find it.

'Earth to Alice!'

Somebody snapped red polished fingertips mere inches from her face; Alice jolted back to reality to find Cassie staring at her expectantly. They'd arranged to meet up after work for a drink, having hardly seen each other for a few weeks.

'Oh, sorry!' She slipped down from her stool and greeted her with a hug. 'Hi! How are you?'

'I'll be better with some vodka inside of me.' Rolling her black-rimmed eyes, Cassie shrugged off her leather jacket, revealing a wisp of white silk that was almost entirely transparent under the spotlights of the tiny cramped club. 'God, it was mayhem on set today. It's like they've never seen Brad in the flesh before.' She paused a moment, letting her gaze drift over Alice's figure-skimming black jersey dress, draped low to show more than a hint of cleavage. A knowing smile spread over her face. 'So, come on, what's his name?'

'Hmm?'

'The man you're fucking.' Cassie gave her a mischievous grin. 'Cause it's obvious you're getting *something*.'

Alice laughed. 'I'm not! Well, yet,' she added, with a meaningful look. 'And his name is Nathan.'

'Thank God!' Cassie exclaimed, summoning the bartender with one dramatic hair-toss. 'I was beginning to think you'd taken vows. I was going to offer Vitolio's services, for the good cause.'

'Cassie! I can't believe you,' Alice laughed. 'What are you, his pimp?'

Cassie relaxed against the bar. 'There's no need to act so scandalised, darling. We're in an open relationship, all totally above board.'

'Really? That works for you?'

'Wouldn't have it any other way.'

'But don't you get jealous when he's out with other women?'

Cassie shook her head, 'Oh, he doesn't actually see anyone else. It's just a technicality — so if I meet somebody . . . well, I won't have to choose.' She gave a nonchalant shrug, as if the prospect of fidelity was simply passé.

'How very foresighted of you,' Alice remarked drily.

Cassie grinned. 'Be prepared — wasn't that what they were always telling us in Brownies?'

She passed Alice her drink. 'So, is that the big news? You said we were celebrating.'

'We are.' Alice beamed. 'I've booked my first job — for Kieran. It's some twisted child molester in a big TV drama. They start shooting next week, and their original guy dropped out, because he didn't want to be associated with such a horrific role. Isn't that wonderful?'

'Congratulations!' Cassie toasted her. 'God, I wish I'd seen Vivienne's face. She must have hated it.'

'She did look rather . . . put out,' Alice agreed, remembering the tight-lipped congratulations. 'But she can't do anything, not as long as she's getting a cut of the commission.'

'Of course,' Cassie agreed. 'If there's one thing that woman loves, it's money. Just watch out she doesn't go taking credit for everything.'

'Oh, no,' Alice vowed, enjoying the slow burn of alcohol as it slid down her throat. 'I'm not going to sit quietly up in my attic any more. This is only the beginning.'

★　★　★

358

One drink turned into three, and soon Alice was flushed with excitement. She was usually bored at clubs like this, finding them too loud and hectic, but tonight, the brash style suited her mood. She even danced, alone and unselfconscious in the midst of the hipster throng while Cassie held court with a group of sharp-haired women dripping dark eyeliner and expensive ripped jeans, Alice's weeks of dance class giving her the confidence and rhythm she'd always lacked before.

Pausing for breath, she made her way back to the bar for water. Almost immediately, a man swooped in to make his approach. His introduction was lost under the thud of music, but Alice didn't mind; it wasn't as if she would need it.

But instead of politely turning away, something made her stop, a wicked thought taking shape. With a tattoo twisting up from under the vintage T-shirt and at least two days of stubble on his face, he certainly wasn't Alice's usual type; a different woman, however, might just have a thing for bad boys.

'I'm Juliet,' she told him, feeling a now-familiar thrill as the untruth left her lips. She smiled at him invitingly. She didn't feel quite as careless as in Rome, but that same impulse had returned: to be bold, to be somebody different, even just for a little while. 'It's a pleasure to meet you,' she said, her voice dropping a little.

'Juliet, huh . . . ' Taking her outstretched hand, the man turned it over and bent his head to kiss her palm. 'With a name like that, I don't think this is going to end well.'

'Probably not,' Alice pretended to muse, already assembling the cocktail of personal history that would make up this other woman. 'But as long as we don't go trying to fake our own deaths, we'll be fine. You can go off and write heartbroken poetry, and I'll put you in a novel one day.'

'You're a writer?' His lips curved; more at the prospect of being immortalised in prose than with admiration for her feigned profession, Alice was sure.

'Hmm? Oh, yes.' She gave a self-deprecating shrug. 'Erotica, mainly. It's a growing market, and I really like to push the boundaries . . . ' Alice trailed off, watching as his eyes widened. This was almost too easy. 'So what brings you here tonight?'

'Just some drinks with friends.' He moved closer, ostensibly in order to speak louder in her ear, but mainly, Alice noted with amusement, to glance down the front of her dress. She could hardly blame him. The pink lace balconette bra that, months ago, had been her first sure fact in Ella's tangled trail, peeped out from beneath the slashed neckline in a flash of colour.

'So, these books of yours,' he murmured, leaning even closer, 'how much research do you do?'

Alice laughed. 'Enough. I need them to be authentic, after all. It's the little details that make something arousing, don't you think?' She raised an eyebrow, teasing. He grinned back.

'Fuck, yeah.'

Alice didn't ask him about himself, she wasn't going to share more than this drink and a few lies with him. Still, she relished the bright flicker as she spun Juliet's self-deprecating story, the direct glances and careful shifts in body language that left her breathless, and this stranger hanging from her every word. This was what her clients must feel like as they recited lines from somebody else's script: the curious self-awareness that came from inhabiting another persona, yet still watching, as if from outside herself.

' . . . So I wrote a few short pieces for the *Erotic Review*, starting out, and — Oh, there's my friend.' Alice looked past him to where Cassie was lounging in the shadows, her pale skin lit up by a flash of strobe lighting. 'I should go.'

The man followed her gaze, raking over Cassie's revealing outfit. 'My boys are just in the back, we could all hang out,' he offered eagerly.

Alice gave him a polite smile, already done. 'No, thanks. She just went through a wretched break-up,' she lied, as if confiding. 'She's not really in the party mood.'

He looked back, in time to see Cassie throw her head back and laugh, posing for the snaps of a roving party photographer. 'You sure? Because we were going to head to a private party at — '

'I'd rather not.' She neatly sidestepped him. 'I'm engaged, you see. But thanks for the drink.' Alice raised her glass to him, and then just walked away, slipping into the thick crowd as

361

Juliet, and all her erotic adventures, simply evaporated, leaving only adrenalin kicking in her veins from the stories she'd spun.

'Come on.' Making a breathless detour back to the table, Alice tried to coax Cassie onto the narrow dance-floor. 'This song is incredible.'

Cassie looked up, half-hidden in the shadows. 'Just a sec, Aly. I'm in the middle of something.' There was a guilty edge to her expression, and as she leaned forwards for her drink, the reason became clear: sprawling beside her in too-tight jeans and another ridiculous cravat, one arm draped around her bare shoulders.

'Dakota.' Alice greeted him coolly, her elation suddenly fading. 'I didn't know you were in town.'

'Yeah, just scoping for some shoots.' He was playing with an unlit cigarette, tapping it nervously between thumb and index finger as if he could feel the force of her displeasure. Or, more likely, he was wired. 'How've you been?'

'Oh, just peachy,' Alice replied. She reached for Cassie's bony wrist. 'We'll be right back.'

Cassie's protest was lost under the music as Alice dragged her determinedly towards the front exit.

'What the hell are you playing at?'

Outside, it was dark and muggy, the dirty backstreet empty save the clusters of casual smokers who looked up at the sound of Alice's fierce demand.

'I don't know what you mean.' Cassie looked away. 'Will you let go of me?'

'So you can go back inside, to him?' Alice

released her, suddenly not so much angry as worn out. Over and over again, she'd watched Cassie do this, as if the outcome would be any different. Her optimism would be almost admirable, if it wasn't so tragic. 'God, Cassie, are you really going to do this again?' She couldn't help the pleading note that crept into her voice. 'Seriously?'

'He's sorry,' Cassie insisted, folding her arms defiantly. 'He . . . he just does this stuff because he's scared, because we mean so much to each other . . . ' The words were confident, but her eyes began to shine with tears. 'He can't help it, sabotaging everything, but, Alice, I know he can get it together.' Cassie looked up, carefully swiping under the lashes to preserve her eyeliner.

Alice exhaled. This was usually her cue to soften, comforting Cassie and encouraging her to move on with her life; to put those painful almosts behind her. But this time, Alice couldn't find it in her, and looking at Cassie — with that powerless expression she always wore whenever Dakota came sauntering back around — Alice knew suddenly what she had to do.

'He's a selfish, cheating piece of shit,' she said, shortly. Cassie blinked with surprise, but Alice just stared evenly at her, some long-frayed cord in her snapping cleanly apart. 'If he loved you, he wouldn't hurt you. If he loved you, he wouldn't keep you dangling like this. It's your fault, Cassie!' She was in full flow now, gathering all the harsh truths she'd bitten back for the sake of their friendship. 'Not the old stuff, in the beginning — you trusted him, and he let you down, fine. But everything since then: the past five fucking years of misery, that's all your doing. You could be happy, with Vitolio, or someone else, but you don't want it, do you? All that shit you were saying about an open relationship, it's all just so you can go running back to him!'

'But — '

'I don't want to hear it,' Alice cut her off, still cold. 'You keep telling yourself these stories, all his excuses, but at the end of the day, he's not with you because he chooses not to be! We all have a fucking choice, and you're choosing to be miserable and wretched.' She took a breath, steeling herself. 'So, I'm done.'

'What do you mean?' Cassie's lip trembled, eyes wide with confusion.

'I'm done — with you, with all of this. Go back to him, get your heart broken again, whatever you want.' Alice shrugged, sharp and final. 'But I don't want to hear a word. Cry to somebody else.' Cassie opened her mouth in protest, but Alice didn't pause. 'I mean it. Don't call me, don't even see me while you're still doing this. I can't take it any more.'

In her whole life, Alice had never fought with a friend, or walked away from somebody in tears, but as she turned the corner, she didn't feel even a pang of regret for her decision. With every step away from Cassie's forlorn figure, she half expected her resolve to slip, pulled down by guilt and sympathy, but none came. She had truly reached her limit.

★ ★ ★

It was almost midnight, but Alice found herself still restless, walking back towards the main street that was overflowing with late-night revellers. She could catch the last Tube home, if she hurried, but the prospect of a cup of tea and bed seemed weak when she still had so much energy vibrating in her system. Pulling out her phone, she quickly dialled. 'Hi, Nathan?'

'Hey you,' he sounded relaxed, but then concern crept into his tone. 'What's going on? Are you OK?'

She laughed at his panic. 'Oh God, you're going to think I'm in trouble every time I call, aren't you?'

'Only when it's this late,' Nathan chuckled. 'So you're all right? No need for bail and a lawyer?'

'None at all,' Alice reassured him. She paused by the kerb, pre-emptively raising her arm to hail a cab. 'I could go for a takeaway though. Say, at yours . . . ?'

The suggestion lingered between them, its implications clear.

'I'll order now,' he said immediately. 'Chinese? Pizza? Thai?'

'You choose.' Alice felt herself smile, already full of anticipation. The food was hardly the most important thing. 'I'll be there in twenty.'

*　*　*

The food was cold by the time they got around to eating it, but none the less Alice thought it the most delicious takeaway she'd ever tasted

— sprawled on Nathan's bedroom floor surrounded by hastily discarded clothing. Soon, however, tiredness overtook them, and they returned to bed; collapsing heavy-limbed into a satisfied sleep.

For a few hours, at least. Then, Alice woke with a start, her earlier comment in the club flaring bright enough to cut through the sleepy afterglow of her late night and Nathan's arms, warm around her. She sat up, breathing quickly as the possibility became solid: crossing over from a vague dream state to something real and full of potential.

Faking their own deaths.

The thought of Ella had woken Alice before, but this time, it wasn't just a jumbled dream — this time, it was revelation. Nathan had said that there was no recent trace of this Kate Jackson aside from the address he'd found, that it was just another alias. But what if the opposite were actually true? What if Kate Jackson was Ella's original identity? Alice considered it breathlessly. There had to be a starting point, surely, before the fake identities and lies had begun; there had to be a real person, buried beneath Ella's casual deception. Perhaps this was it. That would explain why she hadn't run up vast debts in the name, or left the sort of wreckage she'd so casually inflicted on all her other victims. Because she'd wanted to keep it clear and unblemished, a sort of back-up, for when the false names ran out.

The theory made sense. More than that, it seemed irresistible.

Nathan mumbled beside her, his arm still draped across her stomach, but Alice was suddenly too energised to sleep. Easing herself from under his embrace, she slipped out of bed and pulled a crumpled blanket around her shoulders. Tiptoeing past discarded clothing and her high-heeled shoe — tossed against the door in what had been a pleasant blur of hands and lips — she crept out of the bedroom, carefully pushing the door closed behind her.

Nathan's flat was modern and minimal, with a study area set up on the far end of the open-plan living area, complete with gleaming desktop computer system. Alice padded across the room, her feet bare on the cool wooden floor. Settling in front of the computer, she said a silent prayer; after everything Nathan had learned from his career, she was expecting a raft of passwords and security checks, but when she reached for the wireless keyboard and hit the spacebar, the computer woke from sleep mode with a low whirr.

Perfect.

The computer display showed 4 a.m., but Alice was wide awake as she grasped the mouse. She ran searches of the name, 'missing', and any other pertinent phrases she could think of, filtering to the rough time-span Nathan had mentioned. If Ella really was Kate Jackson, then this Kate would have disappeared years ago: fading into nothing so that other, false names could take her place.

Two dead; one missing — that was what Nathan had said about the original short list.

367

Working swiftly, Alice verified the deaths from online articles and local newspaper archives. A slow decline from cancer; a bloody car wreck: she skimmed over the web pages, already ruling them out. Besides, Ella wouldn't be so dramatic as to fake her own death, not when it would be simpler just to slip away one day — go out into the world as one person, and come back as quite another. No, Alice knew, that just wasn't her style.

But the missing woman . . . ? Now, she had more potential.

Alice wasn't sure how long she sat there, bathed in the pale glow from the desk light, but the longer she looked, the more the data led back to one specific suspect, the Kate Jackson from Devon, who had turned twenty-nine years old last Thursday. At least, that's what she would have done, but since she disappeared during a trip to Australasia five years ago, nobody had a clue if she was even alive to celebrate. Alice read through every mention she could find, but sadly, a solo female traveller going astray in that part of the world wasn't rare; the coverage was depressingly thin: a sidebar in a national paper, and a few stories in the local press, showing her anxious parents and older brother urging for more police support. Alice squinted at the small photo that adorned every story, snapped from an earlier, happier stage of her travels. The woman was smiling in a pale blue bikini, brown hair, brown eyes, medium height and weight. Entirely forgettable. Easily disguisable.

It could be her.

Gazing at the grainy photo, Alice tried to see Ella in the girl's features, but no matter how long she stared at it, she couldn't be completely sure if it was her or not.

What had she been running from?

There was a sudden noise from the bedroom. Alice leaped out of the chair and quickly switched the screen off, casting the room into dark again. Dashing towards the kitchen area, she flung open the fridge just as Nathan padded in, sleepy in an oversized pair of athletic shorts.

'What are you doing up?' Yawning, he wandered closer, wrapping his arms around her in a lazy bear hug.

'Just getting a drink.' Alice relaxed back against his bare chest, reaching for the water purifier. She went through the motions of pouring herself a glass and sipping the drink, sneaking a look past his shoulder to check there was no sign of her online investigations. The screen was dark, her secret safe. 'Come on,' she smiled up at him. 'Back to bed.'

'Good,' Nathan yawned again, tugging her towards the bedroom. 'I was getting lonely in there without you.'

Alice laughed. 'Uh-oh. It's too soon for you to be getting clingy.'

'Yup, that's me. In fact,' he turned, pressing her up against the doorway with a dark grin, 'I'm surprised you haven't got tired of how needy I am.'

'Right,' Alice agreed, letting her head fall to one side as he kissed his way up her neck. 'What with the constant travel, erratic schedule, stubborn streak — '

'Are we still talking about me?' Nathan reached her lips, kissing her for a long moment before pulling away. 'Because I'm hearing a lot of you in there too.'

Alice wrapped her arms around his neck, savouring the weight of his body against her, and the soft slide of fabric as her blanket slowly fell to the floor. Kate Jackson wasn't going anywhere tonight.

27

Kate Jackson's brother was named Carl: thirty-two years old, single and — as Alice's extensive online investigations had revealed — a senior market research analyst at a company in Kilburn. With a new focus, Alice quickly threw herself into the research, learning everything she could about the man, no matter how superficially trivial. The data never lies, after all, and soon she discovered that he liked sci-fi movies, Neil Gaiman books, and old episodes of *Battlestar Galactica*; he lived in a house on Bellevue Road with two other men who seemed similarly unencumbered by responsibility or female companionship.

It was almost surprising to Alice how little time or effort it took to assemble a profile of Carl's every taste; using what she had gleaned from Cassie's many stalking expeditions, and her own new research skills. Abandoned MySpace pages, little-used LinkedIn profiles — the information was all there, waiting to be found. It helped that he was clearly active in several online communities, rich with past messages and profiles just brimming with helpful information, from his preferred refreshment (Starbucks vanilla lattes), to his opinion on the latest 3-D movie technology (*Avatar* was, apparently, the mark of things to come). Soon, after some careful cross-searching of user names and email addresses, she had acquired all his contact information, including mobile phone number, and — most importantly — his address.

Which was where Alice found herself one Thursday morning, having pulled herself from bed at a painfully early hour, to cross the city and wait at a bus stop just up the road from Carl's house. She'd located three Starbucks branches on his likely route to work, but she couldn't leave it to chance; if she was going to find a way of meeting this man, then she had to be certain of his routine. Sure enough, at eight thirty-two, he emerged from the front door and hoisted a nylon backpack onto his shoulder. Alice readied herself for action, but Carl clearly wasn't as prepared: he was barely five steps down the front path when he paused, patting his pockets and checking through his bag in a familiar panic. Turning back, he lifted a pot plant beside the door, fished out the spare key, and let himself back in. A moment later, he re-emerged, setting off towards the Tube.

Alice followed, a careful twenty-metres behind.

It was easy. She'd been worried about appearing suspicious, or attracting his attention, but Carl remained entirely oblivious all the way to Kilburn, ear-buds plugged in, and his attention entirely commanded by the thick, dog-eared novel he pulled from the pocket of his jacket. Clutching a newspaper as her own disguise, Alice was able to close the distance between them to a mere fifteen feet as he swiped through the barriers and headed up the road, stopping first, she was gratified to see, at the café on the corner. Option number three it was then.

Alice pushed through the doors and took a place behind him in the busy morning queue, close enough to touch. Her heart was skipping at the prospect of perhaps being so close to the truth about Ella, but she forced herself to stay calm. Calm and casual, and faintly awkward — that was the way to work him, she'd decided. And so, as he reached for a sandwich, she did too, grazing his hand with hers in what appeared to be a completely accidental move.

They both jumped back.

'Oh, I'm sorry, you take it!' Alice gave him a nervous grin.

'No, you go ahead,' Carl replied, just as awkward. She'd thought him rather ordinary from afar, with short brown hair in a nondescript cut, and a glazed, weary look as he shuffled through his morning commute; up close, however, she could see a certain delicacy in him, a cautious, introverted aura. She searched for a resemblance to Ella, but there was nothing decisive. Alice made her smile a little warmer.

'No, I couldn't. Look, it's the last, and you were here first . . . '

He shook his head. 'See, I'd feel bad now. You take it, really.'

'Well, thanks.' Alice gave him a shy look, reaching again for the coronation chicken on white bloomer she had absolutely no intention of eating. 'That's very sweet.'

Carl looked away, seemingly embarrassed, and

there was a long pause, while the woman in front loudly ordered a startling combination of tropical tea with espresso and vanilla. Alice couldn't help but screw up her face at the thought. Noticing Carl was stifling a grin too, Alice caught his eye.

'Where do they come up with these flavours?' she murmured conspiratorially. 'Maybe I'm a purist, but if you can't even taste the coffee . . . '

'Right,' Carl agreed, louder than might otherwise be expected — if Alice hadn't read his blog treatise on the proliferation of pointless flavours just the other night. 'Next thing, it'll be orange mocha Frappuccinos!'

Alice paused, 'Wait, that's from *Zoolander*, right? I love that film.'

Carl lit up. 'It's a classic. They've, uh, been talking about a sequel,' he added, almost awkward, 'but I don't think they should risk it.'

Alice nodded. 'Right. They'll probably just ruin everything, they always do, with those franchises.' She gave another shy smile as they edged forwards, Carl now taking his turn at the register to order. He reached for his wallet, but Alice cleared her throat. 'Let me. I mean, you let me have my lunch . . . ' She held up the sandwich as evidence.

Carl began to flush. 'Oh, I don't — '

'Really,' Alice insisted, already passing coins over to the barista. 'You can pay me back another time. I just started work around here,' she added, looking down briefly in a show of nerves before meeting his eyes again. 'So, I'm sure I'll see you again.'

Carl swallowed. 'Uh, cool.' He nodded. 'I . . . I'm Carl.' He held out his hand abruptly; Alice juggled her bag and package to her other hand and shook it.

'Ella,' she said, trying to look flustered. 'Um, nice to meet you, Carl. I have to . . . ' she gestured towards the door, 'So, um, bye!'

'Bye.' Carl was still gazing after her with a faintly shell-shocked expression when Alice turned and left the café.

It wasn't much, she knew — just a passing flash of dialogue — but there would be more. You didn't just spill about your missing sister to a complete stranger. No, those sorts of confidences needed time and familiarity. Alice had no doubt they would get there, eventually. Carl and Ella were set to become very good friends.

★ ★ ★

Her new clue about Ella aside, life went on as normal for Alice. At least, 'normal' as far as her new routine was concerned. When she took a moment to reflect on her hectic schedule, she realised happily that it couldn't be more different from the life she'd had before. Instead of spending her days up in the attic, poring over fine-print legalese, Alice was meeting with casting agents and scouts, and booking her now-growing client roster a promising array of roles. Lunch was crammed with more appointments, or dance classes at the studio, meeting Flora for an occasional snatched sandwich in the park nearby. What with her developing relationship with Nathan too, she barely had time for breath — yet still, despite the hectic pace of her schedule, Alice refused to lose sight of her real prize.

Setting her alarm to wake her extra early three times a week, she continued to go to meet Carl in the Kilburn Starbucks, extending their conversations to cover books, television, and the boredom of his job in research — and hers as an executive assistant — over coffee and, soon enough, muffins too, before they had to dash to work. Carl now seemed genuinely happy to see her each time, even working up the courage to falteringly ask for her number.

Alice felt guilty over her deception, but she couldn't bring herself to stop — not when the answers about Ella were so close. All she needed was more information about Kate Jackson, and Carl was the only one who could help with that. Just a few more weeks, she told herself, then she could find the answers she craved.

★   ★   ★

'Tell me again why I don't just quit.' Nadia reached forlornly for her glass of wine one night at the end of a busy week.

Alice had met her for drinks at a bar near the gym, skipping the virtues of a hip-hop class for the more immediate pleasures of alcohol and molten chocolate cake.

Slumping back against the dark red leather banquette, Nadia sighed. 'He did it again today:

just talked right over me all the way through our client meeting. Every time I spoke up, it looked like I was being needy and, I don't know, an attention whore.'

'Dickhead,' Alice said sympathetically. An art director at one of the smaller advertising firms, Nadia was struggling with her assigned copy-writer, an arrogant arsehole who reminded Alice of her own pleasant exchanges with Tyrell. 'You could slip laxatives in his coffee next time?'

'Oh, I wish.' Nadia broke into a grin. She pushed her glasses further up her nose. 'Although, now that you say that, I'm sure the work experience kid he has running down for drinks would go in on that plan.'

'Do it,' Alice said. 'Right before a big pitch. I mean, it's not as if he contributes anything. What was that last one you told me about, for the deodorant?'

'Oh God, the caveman and his harem of slave girls.'

'Mmm, original,' Alice giggled. 'He's no Don Draper, that's for sure.'

Nadia gave a flutter of her eyelashes, and faked a swoon. 'Don't even talk about them in the same breath.' She took another sip of wine. 'What about you, how's the dragon lady?'

Alice made a face. 'Awful.'

'Oh?'

Alice tried to phrase her reply without revealing any specifics about agenting or the office. She didn't like to lie, but she couldn't risk Nadia calling Grayson Wells one day to speak to Ella Nicholls, so, to her new friend — like Carl

377

— Alice was a supremely overqualified, if underappreciated, legal assistant. 'She's gunning for one of the associates,' Alice told her instead. It was, technically, the truth. 'Trying to take credit for all her work. They both were attached to . . . this project, but Vivienne blocked her all the way. Now it's a success, of course, she's saying it's all her doing.'

'Of course,' Nadia agreed. 'And you're stuck watching it all.'

Alice nodded slowly. She'd overheard Vivienne chat with a producer, gushing about how she'd personally saved poor Kieran from a life of obscurity with her single-minded tenacity and determination. It was all very well to keep Vivienne's associations with her clients — since Alice could see her name still carried weight in important circles — but she was getting a creeping feeling that her own efforts to relaunch Kieran and Julia's careers might not yet earn her the respect she desired.

'That's the problem sometimes,' she said thoughtfully. 'You can work as hard as you want, but if someone's not willing to recognise your achievements . . . '

'You can't force them.' Nadia gave Alice a rueful grin. 'Want to go halves on those laxatives?'

★ ★ ★

They were deliberating a second slice of cake when Alice's mobile rang.

'Sorry.' She reached to switch it to silent.

378

'No, take it,' Nadia said, getting to her feet. 'I'm just nipping to the loos anyway.'

'OK. Shall I order, if the waiter comes by?'

'You're a bad influence.'

'I'll take that as a yes.'

She waited until Nadia was out of sight before hitting redial. 'Hi, Jules, what's going on?' Alice tried to catch the eye of a passing waiter.

'Alice, I've been trying to reach you for ages.' Julian sounded anxious.

'I missed your call by about two seconds,' she pointed out.

'But I tried earlier, and I've been texting.' His voice dropped, and he announced flatly, 'It's over. Yasmin's moving out.'

'Oh God, what happened?'

'It just . . . ' he sounded weary, 'I don't know, we've been fighting so long . . . Look, could you come over? All her stuff is here, and . . . I just want to get drunk. Can you come?'

'I . . . ' Alice glanced around, the waiter finally choosing that moment to materialise by her side. 'I'm kind of busy right now, but later?'

'Aly . . . ' Julian drew the word out, part-pleading, and she was reminded how many times they had played out the post-break-up ritual over the years. And not just for Julian; when James stopped returning her calls, Alice had spent three days in a pair of his old pyjamas, crying on the sofa while Julian provided a never-ending supply of sympathy, tissues, and homemade blackberry crumble.

'Sure, fine,' Alice agreed at last, looking apologetically up at the waiter. She mimed scribbling the bill. 'I'll be there soon.'

'Thanks.' Julian sounded relieved. 'And bring vodka. I'm all out.'

Nadia returned just as she was signing the credit slip. 'I'm really sorry,' Alice apologised, and explained about the call. 'Can we do a rain-check on that next slice of cake?'

'Sure.' Nadia was sympathetic. 'Here, I've got the tip.' She rummaged in her bag, coming up with a handful of pound coins. 'Is he going to be OK?'

Alice sighed. 'I think so. I mean, he usually is. But, this one lasted a while.'

'Well, usually for break-up wallowing I'd say *Dirty Dancing* and *Pretty in Pink*, but maybe he wouldn't be into that.'

'No, I don't think so. Jules is more of a Woody Allen kind of a man. He'll be sprawled out in front of *Annie Hall*, muttering about our inability to form meaningful relationships, I'll bet.'

★ ★ ★

He was. When Alice arrived on his doorstep bearing alcohol and Kettle crisps, she could hear Diane Keaton babbling in the background.

'You look terrible,' she told him affectionately, reaching up to ruffle his unkempt hair.

'Thanks.' Julian was wearing a greying pair of tracksuit bottoms and his old university T-shirt. The wallowing, clearly, was well underway. 'You brought the booze?'

Alice held up her off-licence carrier as

380

evidence, making straight for the living room. Yasmin's belongings were already stacked in neat piles at the edge of the room: gaps in the bookcase and a half-empty mantelpiece marking her imminent departure.

'So you're sure?' she asked, picking up the remote and pausing the film. 'It's really over? No chance of making everything up?'

He shook his head slowly. 'No. It's done.'

He threw himself on the sofa and gazed morosely at the screen. Woody had been caught mid-kvetch, his mouth wide and disgruntled.

'I take it Yasmin's found somewhere else to stay?' Alice took a seat beside him, kicking off her shoes.

He nodded. 'She went straight to the airport, for another bloody business trip. I guess she'll take her stuff when she gets back.' He tipped his head back and exhaled. 'Fuck. I'm too old for this, Aly.'

Alice passed him the bottle to open. '*Annie Hall*? Yes, I thought you'd grow out of it years ago.'

Julian mustered a weak smile. 'Hush you, that's Woody we're talking about.'

'Exactly.' Alice gave him a playful nudge. 'You know, for someone who isn't a Jewish, New York intellectual, you've got a rather strange attachment to the man.'

Julian took a swig, straight from the bottle. 'What can I say? He knows a thing or two about the futility of commitment, and human connection . . .'

Alice rolled her eyes. 'I'll watch the damn film

381

— again — because that's how good a friend I am,' she informed him, with a grin, 'but seriously, Jules, next time, how about we find a new break-up anthem. *Terminator*, maybe; I could live with that.'

'Next time?' Julian groaned. 'You mean I'll get to fail at this all over again?'

'Oh, at least two, three times.' Alice kept her tone light, but he looked so morose that she softened. 'Did you love her?' she asked gently. He'd never said so, but she wasn't sure if he would.

He shrugged: a slow, defeated gesture. 'I don't know. Which is a no, I suppose. But I thought . . . I thought this one would work. At least a bit longer, anyway.' He took another gulp, and passed the bottle to Alice. She sipped, wincing at the taste.

'Don't you have any mixers?'

'In the kitchen, maybe . . . ' He let out an extravagant sigh.

Alice grinned. 'God, all that way.'

'Don't mock me, woman, I'm in mourning.'

'For Yasmin, or the idea of a stable, committed relationship?' Alice challenged, shooting him a sideways glance.

He rolled his eyes. 'Wait until the film is finished, at least.'

'Fine then,' Alice tugged open the bag of crisps and offered it to him. 'But I refuse to sit through *Hannah and Her Sisters* as well. My love for you has its limits.'

★   ★   ★

By the time the film was finished, they'd worked their way through a large portion of the vodka, with the help of a carton of sugary fruit juice Alice had dug from a back cupboard. Sprawled on the sofa, Julian slumped with his head resting almost in her lap.

' . . . And she was obsessive about flossing,' he added, expounding on Yasmin's multiple flaws. Aside from her rigid work schedule, taste for Ronan Keating records, and completely unreasonable embargo on butter, oral hygiene rated highly. 'After every meal, she'd disappear off to the bathroom with that little packet of string.'

'How dare she?' Alice couldn't help but tease. 'What next: bathing daily? Washing her clothes on a regular basis?'

Julian lightly nudged her thigh. 'You're supposed to be offering me unconditional support in my time of grief, you know?'

'Sorry, forgot.' Alice yawned. 'She's a bitch, and you've made a lucky escape from a lifetime of misery and doom. Better?'

'Much.' Julian fell silent a moment, and then let out a defeated sigh. 'There was nothing wrong, really. I mean, that stuff annoyed me, but it wasn't serious. Not enough to cause the break-up, at least.'

Alice tilted her head down. 'So what really happened?'

'She was . . . pushing. Not being a nag or anything, but she kept bringing it up: where this was going, what it really meant.'

'Not exactly unreasonable,' Alice had to point

out. 'You've been seeing each other, what, six months now.'

'Seven.'

'Seven then. And she moved in; it's a big step. You can't really blame her for wanting to know if this was real, or just . . . killing time.'

Julian sighed again. 'That's just it — I know. And I know that I didn't have anything to say to her that would make her stay.'

Alice paused, surveying their near-comatose bodies and various debris; the Beach Boys' *Pet Sounds* now filling the room with its melancholy harmonies. 'So, why the wallowing?' she asked eventually. 'If you didn't love her, and you don't seem to mind so much that she's gone . . . Isn't this a good thing? At least, you'll be able to meet somebody else now. Someone better for you.'

Julian gave her a dubious look. He heaved himself up until they were side by side. 'Aren't you tired of it yet, Aly? All this running around, trying to . . . I don't know, fit yourself to someone; like some Meccano model.' His head fell back on the cushions. 'I mean, all this effort . . . And for what?'

Alice reached over to give him a comforting hug. 'Oh, I don't know; how about love, companionship, human intimacy.'

He rolled his eyes. 'But we have all that already.'

'You'll get there, eventually,' she told him. 'Think of it as one of life's enduring mysteries.'

'Oh, jeez,' Julian made a face. 'You really have been spending too much time with that American.'

'What are you talking about?' Alice made a mock innocent face. 'I've always been one to look for the meaning in the journey, not the destination, and dig deep, every day, to share my inner radiance with — Hey!' she squealed, as Julian began to tickle her. 'Not fair! You know I — ' Alice laughed, trying to push him away, but with years of experience behind him, Julian knew exactly which spots to target. 'Stop it!' she spluttered, gasping for air. 'I mean it!'

'Weakling.' Julian shifted, crushing her into the sofa while she flailed helplessly. Finally, he lifted himself up onto his elbows, grinning down at her. 'You know, that never gets old.'

'Actually, it does.' Alice laughed, but instead of letting her up, Julian gazed down at her, a peculiarly intense expression suddenly drifting into his eyes.

He gave her a smile, quiet and intimate. And then he moved to kiss her.

Alice stopped. She knew that she should break away now, make a comment about his maudlin despair and put some safe distance between their bodies, but a morbid curiosity in her made her stay.

How far would he go?

Slowly, Julian reached down to brush a stray lock of hair away from her cheek. His hand lingered there, his weight still pressing her into the sofa with his mouth just inches from hers, breath metallic with the faint smell of vodka.

Still, Alice didn't move.

The thought had crossed her mind, of course. In their ten years of friendship, it had occurred to her, occasionally, what they might be like together, as a real couple. But the prospect had faded, with time and familiarity, until only Flora's jokes about declarations of undying love reminded Alice of the possibility.

But this wasn't love, or anything like it.

Alice waited for his lips to find hers, still strangely detached from the whole situation. Was he really going to do it? After all these years, just reach for her blindly — as if she was nothing more than the nearest warm body? He was upset, and even drunk, but as Julian gazed into her eyes and edged his face closer to hers, Alice didn't find it much of an excuse. He didn't want her, he wanted reassurance that he wasn't doomed to be alone.

Her anger grew.

Julian pressed against her, his mouth already opening to deepen the kiss. He dropped a hand to her hips, slipping up beneath the fabric of her top as he began to settle back on top of her, making a slight groaning noise under his breath as his fingers found her stomach, her bra . . .

Alice pushed him away with so much force, he tumbled to the floor.

'What?' Julian protested, not even looking shameful.

'What?' Alice repeated, struggling to her feet. 'You grope at me like I'm some kind of rebound fuck, and you're the one asking what's going on?'

He blinked at her, wounded. 'That's not what this is.'

'Really?' Alice forced herself to calm down. He was upset, he didn't know what he was doing.

'So you genuinely have feelings for me?' she asked. 'Strong enough to risk our entire friendship for?'

'What if I do?' Julian picked himself up. 'You can't tell me that I'm the only one. This has been building between us for a long time.'

Alice gaped. 'No, it hasn't. And in case you forgot, I'm seeing someone!'

'Right. The American,' Julian said, with a hint of arrogance. 'Like that's going to last. He's not right for you.'

'Whereas you are?' Alice exhaled, her sympathy melting away. 'God, Jules, you break up with Yasmin and then, whoosh! Six hours later, you're happily trying to . . . I don't even know!'

She stopped, struck by a sudden chill. All these years, she'd thought him a safe part of her life, she'd believed she mattered to him. But now, he seemed ready to throw it all away on a cheap, drunken one-night stand.

Was that all she meant to him?

Alice looked at him, hoping he would realise his mistake, better late than never at all. He could apologise, and she could forgive him, and eventually, they could go back to normal again and pretend this madness never happened.

But Julian just blustered, 'I don't know why you're acting this way. I thought this was what you wanted!'

'Which makes it even worse.' Alice shook her head. She couldn't believe this. 'If I was secretly in love with you, do you really think this is what I deserve? Some hormonal fumble on the couch,

387

with your ex-lover's belongings still piled around us?'

Julian coughed. 'Look, OK, maybe my timing isn't the greatest here, but — '

'No, Julian!' Alice exploded. 'You don't get it. I'm not your stand-by; I haven't been waiting around for you to settle for me!'

'That's not what I meant. Aly, come on; you mean the world to me!'

'No, I don't,' Alice replied softly. In the background, Brian Wilson was wailing softly about wanting to go home; he had the right idea. 'If you cared at all, you wouldn't have done this.'

As if she was in some terrible dream, Alice walked away. She closed the door quietly on her way out.

28

He didn't call. Not that night, guilt-stricken; nor the morning after, sober and faintly embarrassed. The week passed without a single word, not even a half-hearted attempt to laugh the whole thing off. Julian simply disappeared, and every day that passed, Alice felt her affection for him fade a little more. Confusion and hurt soon cemented into anger. She couldn't understand. Their friendship might not have mattered enough to stop him reaching for her in one vodka-soaked impulse, but surely he cared enough to try to repair the damage?

Apparently not.

'Oh, I thought you'd be out with Nathan.' Flora appeared in the living room on Friday night, her grey cardigan drooping in soft folds around her body.

Alice looked up from the pile of contracts she was attempting to speed through. 'No, he's off in Switzerland again.'

Flora gave a pale smile. 'Chasing rogue investors through the Alps?'

'More like filing paperwork with uncooperative banking officials.' Alice pulled a face. 'Not quite so glamorous, granted. But he will bring back those Lindt truffles you like so much.'

'Great.' Flora let out a sigh. 'So, do you want to watch a film, or something? I've been in my studio so long, I'm sick of the place.'

'Maybe later.' Alice shot her a distracted smile. 'I need to get these finished.'

Flora wandered closer. 'Anything exciting?'

'Not in the least,' Alice felt a surge of resentment. 'Vivienne has decided that our entire boilerplate contract needs reconstructing. By next week.'

Flora's eyes widened. 'Will you manage in time?'

'I'll have to,' Alice replied shortly. 'Otherwise she'll start talking about how I can't manage both of my roles.'

Even the memory of Vivienne's smug look as she deposited her notes — full of red ink and illegible scribbles — made Alice want to growl with frustration. She would have thought that bringing commissions and credibility to the agency would give Vivienne some satisfaction, but it seemed Alice was still over-reaching her natural position, and needed to be frequently reminded of her true place.

'Well,' Flora drifted back towards the door, 'let me know when you're done.'

'Will do.' Alice returned to the dense page of co-representation clauses, but she couldn't focus. It felt like wasted time to her, sitting around while there were other, more pressing matters to attend to. Nathan may be gone, but that just meant that she had a convenient opportunity to be out with somebody else. Toying with her mobile, she deliberated the call she was just itching to make.

Carl.

She had played it cool so far, not wanting to

scare him off, but he had yet to ask her on a real date, and those coffee breaks and casual conversations weren't yielding anything useful about Kate Jackson. Alice even offered up a small tragedy of her own, inventing a dead brother in the hopes of eliciting some confidence, but still Carl hadn't mentioned Kate. Clearly, she needed to step up her game.

Dialling, Alice settled into what she thought of as the person Carl knew: shy, sweet, and just as awkward as he was. 'Hi . . . hello?' she asked hesitantly, when he answered on the second ring. 'Carl? It's Ella. From Starbucks,' she added, as if she wasn't sure he'd remember.

'Ella, ah, hi.' Carl sounded flustered.

'Is it OK I called? Is this a bad time?'

'No! No, it's fine,' Carl reassured her. 'Uh, how are you?'

'I'm fine.' Alice left an awkward pause. 'And you?'

'I'm fine.'

Another pause.

'I, um I was wondering if you were free this weekend at all.' Alice spoke quickly, running her words together. 'There's a *Lord of the Rings* showing at the **BFI**. If you want,' she added hurriedly. 'But it's fine, if you have plans, or you just . . . don't want to.'

'Oh, that sounds great.' Carl sounded conflicted. 'But, I'm actually down in Cornwall right now, for the weekend. A friend of mine is getting married, so, we're all here for the stag do, and . . . ' He trailed off.

'That sounds fun!' Alice tried to seem as if she

were masking disappointment. 'A whole group's there?'

'Yeah, my flatmates, and our schoolfriends . . . But, maybe when I get back . . . ?'

'Absolutely!' Alice agreed. 'You just call me and we'll set something up.'

'OK. You have a nice weekend.'

Alice hung up. Pushing aside her pile of work, she wandered restlessly through the house, her frustration growing. She was so close — at the agency, and with Carl too, but she just kept hitting this wall. What would it take to get where she needed to be?

She was staring absently into the fridge, hoping for a satisfying answer to materialise in front of her, when the doorbell went.

'Hi, sweetie!' Cassie was waiting on the doorstep, dressed in a chic tube of tight black fabric. She beamed at Alice with what must be freshly whitened teeth, such were their luminescent glow. 'I wasn't sure if you'd be in! There's a big launch thing in town; want to come with me, get drunk on free champagne?'

Alice gazed at her evenly. 'That depends,' she replied a little coolly. 'Will I be treated to three hours of moaning about the fact that Dakota has left you again?'

Cassie's smile slipped. 'No. I mean, yes, we're finished, but . . . It was my doing this time.'

Of course it was. Alice shook her head, still impatient. 'Cassie . . . I'm really not in the mood for this.'

'But I'm sorry!' A flicker of sincerity shadowed her face. 'You were right, I-I just couldn't let him go. But I needed to hear it.' Cassie gave a sharp nod, as if still trying to convince herself. 'So, what do you say?' She gave Alice a hopeful smile. 'Come out, party with me. We'll have fun, I promise!'

'Fine,' she conceded at last, shooting Cassie a warning look. 'But the minute you start sobbing into the Cava, I'm leaving, you understand?'

'And you won't have to!' Cassie insisted brightly, her vivid confidence back again. 'I'm done, cold turkey. Going on three weeks now!'

'Congratulations,' Alice murmured, still dubious. 'Now, this party of yours . . . Wags or indie wankers?'

'Go short, tight and trashy,' Cassie grinned, striking a pose to illustrate. 'Come on, it'll be fun.'

★　★　★

And it was. The slick party was crammed with feuding minor celebrities, gazing balefully from their separate corners in patent heels and designer suits, while Cassie, Flavia and the rest of the group grew louder and more raucous with every new bottle of free champagne. Soon, thanks to Petros's scuffle over the affections of a British girl-band member, they were summarily ejected from the bar, and decamped en masse to a cramped, sweaty shack of a bar in the depths of Dalston, where a trio of stern-faced Jamaicans slung drinks from a vat of potent cocktails, and Alice's scrap of bright red Lycra stood out like a flaring neon sign amongst the scruffy plaid shirts and skinny jeans in attendance.

She didn't care. Between her friends' constant theatrics and Alice's own breathless flirtations, she was having a wonderful time. Ella became Juliet became Angelique as she whipped through what felt like an avalanche of pick-ups and come-ons. Even when a drunken, desperate Dakota made a surprise appearance, begging for Cassie to give him another try, the night wasn't ruined. Cassie simply told him to fuck off, and show some self-respect — they were finished.

She was almost giddy from the power of it for the rest of the night. 'I can't believe I did that!' Cassie exclaimed, on more than one occasion. 'You just have to *do it*, Aly. You've got to say 'fuck them', and take what you want.'

★　★　★

Alice wished it were so easy. What she wanted were the deep, intimate details of Kate Jackson's life, complete with photos and fingerprints to compare with Ella so that she could know, for certain, if this was even the right track she was pursuing, but with Carl off in Cornwall for the weekend she had nothing left to do but wait. Again.

She had already spent too much of her life waiting, Alice decided the next afternoon, resisting the urge to rip up Vivienne's contract notes and feed them through her shredder. Waiting never won her anything at all; it hadn't taken her to Italy, for excitement and adventure, or helped her finally claw her way up at the agency. It certainly wouldn't yield the information about Kate Jackson that would let Alice know, once and for all, if there was more to be found on Ella's trail, or if she had disappeared for good.

She sighed, trying to quell the impatience that raced through her. The most frustrating part was, she didn't even need Carl to confirm her theory. She needed him for access to his flat, and whatever anecdotes or background he could offer to explain why his sister had decided to leave her old life behind and become the woman Alice knew as Ella; but as for the proof itself . . . ? All the photos and clippings she needed were probably stashed away in some shoebox under his bed, or framed in small prints in the flat.

His currently unoccupied flat.

Alice paused, the idea taking shape with breathtaking speed. Carl was gone for the weekend, and so were all his flatmates. Thanks to her early experiments in the subtle art of stalking, she knew where the spare key was kept, and who was to say she'd even need to stay that long? She could simply slip in, find some photos of Kate, and nip out again. Ten minutes, perhaps, to secure the firm answer she needed. Otherwise . . . Alice thought of weeks more spent gaining Carl's confidence, probing him about all the distressing details of his sister's possible death. This was surely the better, more decent option, she told herself. She would prevent so many more lies.

A small part of Alice reminded her that this

was breaking and entering she was considering. But if this were Italy, and she were Angelique, she wouldn't be hesitating for a second, so why hold back now, when answers were so close to hand? She just had to plan this properly. And she was nothing if not an excellent planner.

She reached for her notebook and a felt-tipped pen.

★   ★   ★

Just a short while later, Alice had everything she needed. Almost. Skipping downstairs, she detoured to Flora's studio.

'Hey, can I ask a favour? Well, two,' she corrected herself.

Flora looked up guiltily, from the angry slashes of red paint she was sweeping across the canvas, but Alice barely reacted to the painting.

'Wow, I love that colour,' she remarked. 'Anyway, the favours? I need to borrow your car — just for a couple of hours.'

'Sure,' Flora seemed dazed, as if she wasn't fully present, but she always got that way when she was immersed in a project, so Alice waited a few moments for the distracted look in her eyes to fade.

Flora took a few breaths. 'The car?' she repeated finally, as if only just registering the request. 'That's fine. The keys are in the hall.'

'Thanks,' Alice smiled gratefully. 'There is this one other thing . . . '

'What?' Flora crossed to the basin in the

corner, scrubbing at her paint-stained hands.

Alice bit her lip. 'I . . . um, I was here with you. All evening. If anyone asks, all right?'

Flora looked up. 'What's going on?'

'Nothing,' Alice reassured her quickly. 'It'll be fine, I promise. I just, I need you to cover for me. So if someone calls, say I'm in the shower, or something. Can you do that?' She watched Flora with a flicker of nerves.

But instead of interrogating her, Flora said simply, 'Of course. Call if you need anything.'

Her lack of curiosity was strange, but Alice had too much else on her mind for now to dwell on it. As she drove carefully towards Bellevue Road, she tried to think if she'd forgotten any vital detail. She'd been tempted to wait until the cover of dark, but instinct told her that she would appear less suspicious in daylight. A nondescript woman letting herself into a house one evening wouldn't raise alarm, in even the most well-patrolled of Neighborhood Watch zones. Similarly, for all the black catsuits that the heroines of various movies used for their attire, only a burlap sack marked 'SWAG' slung over her shoulder would be more conspicuous. A quick perusal of her wardrobe had yielded plain jeans, a summer vest top, and a pair of flip-flops: as unmemorable and ordinary as she could find.

Parking on the next street, Alice emptied her purse and pockets of identifying documents and fastened her hair up under a baseball cap to disguise its length. She caught herself in the rearview window for a moment and paused, taking in the excitement in her eyes. She should be conflicted over this, she knew. Anyone else would feel guilty, even shameful, but instead, Alice felt only a thrill at how close she was to the truth. It would be simple, swift, and give her all the answers she needed. What was there to even think about?

Still, as she locked up the car and walked quickly towards the house, Alice felt her nerves flutter to life. The streets were quiet, but she kept her head down, almost flinching as a man ambled past with his golden retriever. Calm, she told herself, forcing deep breaths. Nothing to worry about.

Number fifteen was dark, and the driveway empty. Alice strolled up the front path, forcing herself not to rush. She was painfully aware of somebody in the front garden of the house opposite, an older woman watering the flower-beds from an old-fashioned can. But this was London. She probably didn't even know Carl's name, let alone the fact that he had gone for the weekend.

Alice's breath caught, just for a moment, when she fumbled under the plant pot, but then her fingertips found the key and just like that, she was closing the door safely behind her.

She was in.

Pulling on a pair of thin cotton gloves, Alice looked around. The house was clearly a male-only domain, with greying carpets, basic metal shelving and computer magazines and gadgets strewn around, but Alice found it surprisingly neat and clean. Aside from a lone plant wilting in one corner, the living room was given over entirely to two hideous beige couches, a vast flat-screen TV and a tangle of gaming equipment lined up in strict order across the floor. There were no signs of personal mementoes, or photographs of any kind, so Alice moved swiftly upstairs, trying each bedroom in turn until she found a pile of letters addressed to Carl Jackson on the desk in the corner room. Jackpot.

Alice began searching the room: quick, but methodical, ignoring the creeping sense that she didn't belong there. Desk drawers held old issues of *Wired* and a range of office supplies arranged in careful rows according to colour and type, but nothing useful. She checked under the bed, in the wardrobe — all the usual places, with a growing sense of urgency, but it wasn't until she began rifling through the row of storage boxes in the bottom drawer of his dresser that Alice felt her certainty return. Like her, he kept his bank statements and important papers in one single file, but beneath them, buried even further, were handfuls of photographs, loose and crumpled at the edges.

Settling on the floor, Alice began slowly to flip through the strange record of another man's life. Baby pictures and blurry university graduation shots; summer tourist snaps and back garden barbecues — they were clumped together in no particular order, and peering at each in turn, Alice felt a strange sense of intrusion, as if she were a voyeur lingering on the edge of every frame. There was a fascination too. His old friends, relationships, and random passing moments were laid out for her to see, and with the documents she had stacked neatly to one side, Alice realised that she held the narrative of his life right there in front of her. It was almost like she owned him, in some strange way.

There was a sudden burst of noise.

Alice leaped to her feet, looking around frantically, until she realised it was just the sound of her phone ringtone. She pulled it out of her pocket and retrieved the new text. It was from Nathan.

'I take it back, the Swiss are even less helpful than the Germans. See you soon X.'

Alice stared at the short message, feeling her discomfort creep in again. What would he say if he could see her then? But she had work to do. Tucking her phone away again, she returned to the task of sifting through those photographs, wondering if she would ever find any hint of Kate, or if Carl had excised his sister from his life as thoroughly as she had his from hers.

And then she found them: a thick wedge of family photos, tucked into a plain black folder. Carl and his sister, Kate, together. They were there as children, in matching mud-stained romper suits, and then surlier teens, gawky and overgrown. Christmases, birthdays, family holidays; ugly jumpers and embarrassing juvenile haircuts — the years flickered by as Alice pored through every last one, her hopes sinking with every new shot.

It wasn't Ella.

The photo from the newspapers had been vague, and full of promise, but watching Kate grow before her eyes it was clear that this was somebody else entirely. The nose was longer, the jawline rounder — aspects easily corrected with surgery, it was true, but other things were not. Alice held one of the last photos, a summer snap of Kate beaming over her shoulder. She was wearing a bikini with bright orange straps, aged in her early twenties, perhaps, but Alice's gaze was fixed to the thick scar running down her left shoulder blade. It was twisted and deep, the result of some unknown surgery, and although the skin was pale again, its imprint was clear. And, Alice realised, surrendering her last hopes for good, permanent.

Ella had no such scar. Alice had seen her wearing strapless tops and low-cut dresses; her shoulders were dotted with a smattering of tiny freckles, but no pale crumple of skin.

She'd been wrong.

Alice slumped into a heap, all her fierce determination evaporating in an instant as her dreams became foolish fantasies. What was she doing there, browsing through a sweet man's belongings in search of something that didn't exist? Without the possibility of Ella's story urging her on, Alice was simply a creepy woman skulking on the floor of a stranger's bedroom. Kate Jackson was missing, probably dead, and there she was, rummaging in her brother's private memories as if she even had the right to lay eyes on them. Alice shuddered, guilty.

A blast of music from a car radio passing outside snapped her back into action. She wanted to just flee, but caution forced her to place the photos carefully back in the approximate order she'd found them, adding the other folders and magazines and sliding the box into place. She looked around the room, checking everything appeared untouched. She wished she could magic it that she'd never been at all, but this clean-up would have to do. Hurrying, Alice all but tripped back down the stairs and out of the front door.

She was bent double, sliding the key back into place, when Alice heard an imperious voice behind her ask, 'What are you doing?'

Alice stood up so fast, she felt a rush of blood fill her head. Standing at the end of the front path was the woman from across the road, watering can still in hand. She was wearing khaki trousers and a navy cardigan, her ash-blond hair cut in a feathery sort of bob. To Alice's horror, she looked the very definition of a nosy neighbour. 'Is everything all right?' the woman asked, her tone clearly implying that it wasn't.

Alice sucked in a breath, visions of police cells and angry interrogation suddenly looming. Again. Only, this time, she wasn't innocent, and her activities certainly wouldn't be so easily explained.

'Hi!' Alice exclaimed, her voice artificially bright. 'Can I help you?'

The woman glanced past her to the house. 'Are the boys back so soon? They said they'd be gone all weekend.' She narrowed her eyes at Alice, 'They asked me to keep an eye on things, you see.'

Alice forced herself not to panic. 'Everything's

fine!' she declared, dragging her voice back to more reasonable levels to trot out the excuse she'd prepared. 'Reese was just worried he'd . . . left his laptop unplugged.' she named one of Carl's housemates. 'There was a game paused, and if the power had run down, he would have lost the high score.'

The woman's frown lessened; it was a plausible excuse, at least.

'So, I really better run,' Alice forced a smile, even as her stomach gave a lurch of fear. 'I'll let him know you're keeping good watch on the place!'

Alice tried to move past the woman, but she stayed firmly in place. 'You know, I think I'll just give the boys a ring. They did leave their number.' She whipped a mobile from the pocket of her floral-print gardening apron. 'What did you say your name was?'

'Lucy,' Alice replied, perhaps fast enough to seem genuine. 'But I talked to Reese just before coming over — they're about to start the ceremony.'

The woman frowned. 'Still, I think I should ring . . . And you're a friend of Reese's?' Her haze drifted to Alice's hands. She'd left the gloves on, Alice realised.

Alice tried to edge further down the path. 'I'm his girlfriend!' she explained.

The woman stopped. 'I thought Reese was the homosexual one.' She pursed her lips — whether at Reese's sexual preference or the obvious lie, Alice wasn't sure — and began to press buttons on her phone. Alice gulped.

'Really? Ha! He can't be! We've been going out for weeks now . . . ' She attempted to manoeuvre round the woman, but a hand shot out and gripped her wrist with surprising force.

'You just wait here until I've had a chance to speak to them.'

'No, I'm sorry,' Alice tugged, her panic rising. 'I have to go.'

But the woman had already dialled, and was holding the phone to her ear. 'Yes, Carl? It's Patricia, from across the road — '

Alice yanked harder against the woman's steely grip. As soon as this interfering biddy found out that she wasn't a legitimate visitor, it would all be over. There would be police, and questioning, and formal charges, and Alice's world would fall apart all over again; only this time, there would be no sympathetic solicitors on hand to unravel the mess she'd made. She could see it now: the bewildered disappointment from Nathan, the ruin a criminal record would do to the rest of her life . . .

God, what had she risked?

Alice snapped. Pushing, instead of pulling, she sent Patricia reeling back. She let out a squawk of protest, but Alice was too close to freedom to care. She gave a final, desperate twist to free herself, lunging clear as the woman stumbled, falling heavily to the ground.

Alice didn't look back. She leaped towards the front gate and took off down the road at a sprint, Patricia's outraged cries for help echoing behind her. Breathless, she dashed around the corner and all but leaped into Flora's car, fumbling to fit the key to the ignition. The taste of fear was metallic in her mouth. But finally, the engine growled to life, and then she was gone, driving away from the quiet road with all the restraint she could muster.

29

Alice was shaking by the time she arrived back at the house. The whole drive, she'd been gripped by a desperate panic, her careful planning nothing compared to the many ways in which she could be caught. What about CCTV footage, and traffic cameras? What about her fingerprints, scattered over the plant pot, and front door? She hadn't been thorough enough — no, she shouldn't have been there at all.

'Alice?' Flora caught her, just as she burst through the front door. 'What happened? Are you OK?'

Alice nodded, then shook her head, words failing her.

'Come, sit down,' Flora led her quickly to the kitchen, pushing her gently onto a chair. 'Did something happen? Should I call someone?'

'No!' Alice cried, in a strangled voice. 'No, you can't.' She gripped Flora's hands tightly. 'Did you talk to anyone while I was gone? Does anyone know I wasn't here?'

'No, Alice, calm down.' Flora shook herself free, and went to pour a glass of wine. 'Here, drink this.'

Alice gulped obediently, her panic finally beginning to ease. Nobody knew she'd been there, she told herself again, and the neighbour would only name Lucy, a mysterious friend of Reese's. There was nothing linking her to Carl, or Ella, or her own, precious identity. Taking deep breaths, Alice forced herself to calm.

When she'd finished the wine, she found Flora perched next to her. 'So . . . ' Flora prompted. 'What did you do?'

'I . . . I don't know what I was thinking,' Alice answered, and then it came tumbling out: the Kate Jackson lead, the lies to Carl, and the lapse in her sanity that led her to believe it was a simple proposition to break into someone's house and rifle through their personal documents.

'Flora,' she wailed, as the full extent to her madness became painfully clear, 'I *groomed* him. I found out all his favourite things, and then I lay in wait, like some kind of psycho stalker.' Alice gulped. 'That's another charge, isn't it? Stalking. Oh God, what if they do manage to track me down? What happens then?'

Flora patted her shoulders. 'Stefan knows lots of lawyers. We can claim some kind of temporary insanity, brought on by your trauma from the fraud. I'll testify how you've been going mad for weeks, muttering under your breath and all that. It'll be fine.'

'Fine!' Alice repeated the word. This was not, and would never be, fine. 'But, you'll say I was here, if the police come asking questions?'

'Of course.' Flora struck Alice as being curiously calm, but that, at least, was a blessing. One of them should be.

Alice exhaled. 'I can't believe I'm even asking you to lie for me . . . God, I'm sorry.' She gave a pale smile. 'Maybe it would be better not to, so I don't drag you — '

'Don't be silly,' Flora cut her off. 'We're in this together. You're my *sister*,' she added, with extra force.

Alice nodded, closing her eyes for a moment. Her heartbeat was slowing, and the nausea in her stomach seemed to be subsiding. She was safe here.

It was over.

'I just can't believe how easy it was.' She finally looked back at Flora. 'So easy to get swept up in it all. I was so certain I'd found the truth — that Carl was the key, to tracking Ella.'

'It was a good idea,' Flora offered, before amending her statement. 'I mean, if you look at it objectively. But, don't beat yourself up.' She gave Alice's shoulders a sympathetic squeeze. 'It's not like you did anything really wrong. Nobody got hurt.'

'Well, I think that neighbour woman might have a sore bum.' Alice gave a rueful smile.

'I wish I'd seen it.'

'No, you don't,' Alice corrected her. 'Not exactly my finest moment.'

'But you got away OK. That's what matters.'

Alice nodded slowly. Yes, she'd managed to get away — just — but not through any skill or planning on her part.

There was silence in the kitchen, as Alice yet again mentally ran through her near-miss; the woman's grip tight on her wrist . . .

'I know what you need.' Flora brightened suddenly. '*Gilmore Girls*! The next box-set got delivered today. You always say that show calms you down. And it would back up your alibi,' she added, as casually as if she were discussing tea plans, and not potentially obstructing police enquiries.

'Sure,' Alice agreed, exhausted. 'Let's watch it.'

But while the sofa, blanket, and a tub of Häagen-Dazs brought some comfort for the rest of the night, it wasn't so easy for Alice to escape the seedy reality of her actions for long.

How could she have been so reckless?

It wasn't guilt or conscience that sobered her but fear. The lies she'd been telling with such ease for the last months suddenly seemed fragile and perilous, ready to tumble around her at a moment's notice. Nadia, her classes, even the casual flirtations in bars and clubs — they were a catalogue of small crimes she'd committed with enthusiasm, but now, Alice knew, they had to stop.

She flinched as the sound of a distant siren drifted by.

It was too dangerous, Alice vowed, surveying the neat pile of notebooks and files that she'd accumulated in her search for answers. How Ella herself had coped with this constant spectre of discovery she wasn't sure, but this would be the end of Alice's obsession. It had been months now since Ella had disappeared, and while Alice had scraped together what clues and insight she could, Nathan had been right. It was time to let it go, before her reckless deceptions caught up with her, and did her more damage than Ella herself had wrought.

'Alice, I need those copies down here for the delivery guy.' Saskia sounded far too pleased as she buzzed up on Monday morning. 'Like, now?'

'Fine.' Alice prodded at the hateful new intercom that Vivienne had presented as 'a little gift'. 'I'll be right down.'

With a sigh, she reached for the latest in what seemed like a never-ending stream of paperwork. Vivienne was rising to the challenge of burying Alice in contract work, and there hadn't been a night for weeks that she hadn't hauled home a stack of contracts to finish. It was almost just as well that the rest of her schedule was almost entirely empty. Just as she'd vowed, she had cut off all contact with Ella's activities, but without her dance classes, investigation, or even occasional drinks with Nadia, she had plenty of spare time — and a pang of wistful regret whenever she thought of her jazz class.

But it was for the best, Alice reminded herself, skipping down the staircase. She had managed to extricate herself from months of lies without detection, and that alone was worth the cost. So she missed the distraction of Ella's routine, or the thrill that came from spinning some elaborate story. She was just lucky she'd kept her lives so separate, and that it had been simple to detach one from the other. All it took was a new mobile number and for her to stop attending her normal classes, and it was as if Ella had never existed.

'Anything else?' she asked Saskia, a note of

irritation in her voice as she passed her the papers.

'Not right now.' Saskia sashayed off.

'Sitting this one out, huh?' Tyrell sauntered into reception, idly tapping away at his ubiquitous phone console.

'What do you mean?' Alice found a jumble of post that had yet to be sorted, and began to pick out the letters addressed to her.

'You know, Vivienne and — ' Tyrell paused. 'Oh, you don't know. Whoops.' He added, unapologetic. 'Maybe you were kept out of the loop for a reason.'

Alice felt an ominous chill. 'Tell me what's going on.'

He sighed. 'She's meeting with Kieran right now, up in her office. I'm surprised you didn't know. But hey, I guess he's not really *your* client . . . '

Alice was already hurrying away before he had time to finish. She barrelled up the stairs and pushed open Vivienne's door to find her serving Kieran macaroons from a silver platter, her head bent towards him conspiratorially.

' . . . And of course, I had no doubt you'd find your niche — '

She broke off, looking at Alice without even a hint of guilt. 'Yes? Did you want something, dear?'

Kieran brightened. 'Hi.' He waved awkwardly. 'Vi said you weren't going to be able to make it.'

Alice gaped. 'I . . . I mean, what . . . ?' It took her a moment to recover, such was the blatant underhandedness of Vivienne's secret little meeting. Then Alice realised: this was exactly what she'd done to win Kieran over herself, she just hadn't had the nerve to do it under Vivienne's nose. Pulling herself together, she forced a smile.

'I had another meeting, but I cancelled.' Alice walked over and greeted Kieran brightly. 'Is that a new haircut? I like it!' Settling into a chair, she reached for a macaroon; meeting Vivienne's gaze in a defiant stare. 'Now, what have I missed?'

★   ★   ★

The meeting was nothing more than a general chit-chat, praising Kieran for his stellar performances, and assuring him that this was only the beginning of his glittering career. Alice had heard Vivienne's routine countless times, but on this occasion every compliment felt like a personal insult. The moment Kieran had been ushered out, full of best wishes about his upcoming auditions, Alice turned to her.

'I must have missed the memo, about this little meeting.'

Vivienne arched her eyebrow. 'Now, darling, don't get all het up. I just thought it time Kieran and I caught up, it's been so long since I saw him last.'

'Yes,' Alice replied coolly. 'He did mention it had been at least five months since you'd last contacted him.'

Vivienne laughed gaily. 'You know how busy I get!'

'Exactly.' Alice fought to keep her temper.

'Which is why we agreed I'd be taking over with Kieran. And Julia,' she added, in case Vivienne had organised a little tête-à-tête with her too.

Vivienne's smile slipped. 'Not taking over, Alice,' she corrected. 'Co-agenting. I'm still representing them all. You've just been . . . handling some of the grunt work on my behalf for a little while.'

Alice froze. 'What's that supposed to mean?'

Vivienne shrugged. 'What it always meant, darling. I happen to have some time for a new project. And Kieran's showing such promise . . . '

'Because I worked with him!'

'Now, now,' she scolded Alice with a faintly parental air, 'there's no room for possessiveness in this business, darling. We're all one big family at Grayson Wells.'

Alice couldn't control the note of challenge that slipped into her tone. 'So you're taking him back?' she asked, just to be sure.

'Back? Oh, sweetie,' Vivienne laughed, 'he was never yours. At the level they're at now, Kieran and dear Julia are in need of someone with real experience.' Vivienne flashed her a smile: deadly, and full of victory.

Alice glared back.

'You didn't think I would just let you run riot with my client list, did you?' Vivienne narrowed her eyes, her vivacious act finally slipping to reveal pure steel. 'I have a responsibility to them, to protect their interests. You still work for *me*, you know. Oh, and one other thing,' she added, just as Alice was about to leave. 'I need you to co-ordinate the hiring of a new assistant.'

'Saskia's leaving?' Alice could barely even muster surprise. Now which was it, the 'breakthrough' role in an upcoming Brit-flick, or a relationship with an ageing, yet generous, producer?

'Not leaving, promoted.' Vivienne allowed a small smile to cross her scarlet lips. 'I'm making her a junior agent.'

Alice felt her mouth drop open. By the smug look on her boss's face, this was exactly the reaction she'd been after, but even that knowledge couldn't help Alice maintain some façade of self-control.

'Saskia, an agent?' she repeated slowly, remembering how the girl could barely operate the photocopier, let alone take responsibility for an actor's livelihood.

'Yes,' Vivienne beamed, the glossy black of her freshly dyed hair matching — Alice thought bleakly — the dark recesses of her heart. 'I gave you a chance to prove yourself, but I think it's clear you're best suited to the contract work, so I'll be training her up instead. I think she shows a lot of promise,' she added cruelly.

Alice could only stand there, numb.

'So, put an ad in the usual place,' Vivienne instructed briskly, 'and handle the interviews. You know the drill! Oh,' she stopped, before leaving, 'we're having a little party to celebrate. Down at the bar at five. I know you're not much of a drinker, so would you mind covering the phones?' Then she was gone to her lunch appointment, leaving Alice to slump her head to the desk in despair.

Alice seethed for the rest of the week. She'd taken a risk to become an agent — to prove she had some hustle in her, after all — but now Vivienne was never going to forgive her. It was becoming painfully clear that as long as she stayed at Grayson Wells, she wouldn't see one ounce of respect.

'So, quit.' Nathan hugged her closer, landing a supportive kiss on her forehead as the taxi wove its way through evening traffic. 'Tell the witch where to shove her broomstick, and just get out.'

'To go where?' Alice replied, already tired of a conversation she'd had two dozen times in her own head. 'In case you haven't noticed, the economy isn't exactly booming. And without references . . . ' she sighed. 'Vivienne is claiming credit for everything I did with Kieran and Julia. As far as anyone else is concerned, I don't have any experience.'

The cab drew up on the corner, and they climbed out, dashing through the rain towards the restaurant. 'Look, let's not talk about it,' Alice said, ducking into the tiny entrance. 'Any mention of Vivienne is just going to keep me stressed. I want to just relax.'

'OK.' Nathan shook water out of his hair. He looked bedraggled but sturdy, and Alice sank against him for a quick hug, glad of his arms around her. 'Whatever you want.'

'I'll hold you to that.'

★ ★ ★

Inside, it was vivid and bright, with clusters of diners crowding the small room; the delicious scent of garlic and herbs were making Alice's mouth water.

'So, I was thinking . . . ' Nathan began, once their starters had been dispatched, and Alice was feeling somewhat closer to human.

'Yes?' She looked at him across the candle-lit table; the food and intimate atmosphere all soothing her frayed nerves.

'Maybe the next time I have to skip town for work, you could come with me.' His eyes took on a hopeful edge. 'I do get to visit some interesting places.'

'Brussels?' Alice teased. 'Zurich?'

'I was thinking more the Caribbean.'

Alice's eyes widened. 'Really?'

'If you want to,' Nathan added, as if there was a possibility she wouldn't. 'You've seemed so stressed lately, I thought it could be fun.'

'Um, yes.' Alice answered faintly. 'I think white sands and palm trees could definitely qualify as fun.'

'Great,' Nathan seemed relieved, and it struck Alice that he might actually have been nervous about asking her. 'Since, you know, we had such a great time in Italy and all.'

Alice laughed. 'Ah, yes. Well, at least we know we travel well together!'

'Right, as long as I do the driving and you stay out of jail,' Nathan teased. 'Now, if you'll excuse me for a sec . . . '

He paused on his way past to kiss her. Alice exhaled happily, watching him go.

'Ella!'

Alice was lost in thoughts of turquoise water and tropical drinks when she heard a familiar voice calling. 'Ella, over here!'

She looked up, horrified, to find Nadia waving at her, peeling off her coat at the front of the restaurant. 'Oh my God, where have you been?' Nadia plunged towards her through the crowd, eyes wide with concern. 'I've been trying to get hold of you for ages. Your number says it's out of service, and nobody's seen you at the gym. I've been getting worried!'

Alice bobbed up out of her seat in shock. 'I . . . ' she stuttered, 'I'm sorry, I've been . . . busy.'

Nadia paused, her concern now making way for confusion. 'But we had plans. That lunch — remember? You didn't even let me know, to cancel.'

A rush of guilt swept through Alice. 'I know, and I'm really sorry . . . ' She turned to check Nathan was still safely out of sight. He was. 'Vivienne's been a nightmare, at work,' she tried to explain, even though she knew full well there was no excuse for the surgical precision with which she'd cut Nadia out of her life — or rather out of Ella's life. 'But I'll call you with my new number, OK, and talk properly? I don't want you keeping your date waiting.'

Nadia looked at her, puzzled. 'OK,' she said slowly. 'We'll talk later. But you're all right?'

Alice let out a long breath of relief. 'Yes, I'm fine!' Or at least, she would be once Nadia was gone. 'I'll tell you everything later. And you can tell me who that guy is,' she added, mustering a gossiping grin.

Nadia softened. 'I will,' she promised, matching Alice's smile with her own — full of excitement. 'Wish me luck!'

'Good luck,' she replied as Nathan appeared beside them.

He looked back and forth between the women. 'With what?'

'Nothing!' Alice exclaimed, her heart-rate increasing. 'Um, this is a friend of mine, Nadia. Nadia, meet Nathan.'

They exchanged polite greetings, Alice powerless to do anything except watch as the two parts of her life came crashing together.

'Great to meet you,' Nathan said, leaning on the back of his chair. 'How do you know — '

'The gym!' Alice interrupted. 'We met at dance class. Oh, look,' she exclaimed, sending a desperate look across the room, 'I think your table is ready.'

'The gym?' Nathan raised his eyebrows, amused. 'I thought you were allergic to physical activity.'

Alice gave a weak laugh. 'I am. It's an embarrassment.' She gave Nadia a nudge, 'Hon, I think your date is — '

'Don't be so hard on yourself!' Nadia laughed, turning to Nathan. 'Ella's one of the better ones; she's come on no end.'

Alice froze.

'Oh, I nearly forgot,' Nadia beamed at Alice, 'they're doing a *Dirty Dancing* workshop next week. It was booking fast, so I signed us up! It should be fun, right?'

Alice nodded weakly, flicking her gaze over to

Nathan. Perhaps he hadn't heard that. It was loud, and she'd been speaking quickly, and —

'Ella?' His voice was low, but Alice could see the tension ripple in his jaw.

'I can explain,' she said quickly. 'It was . . . just a fun little mix-up.'

He looked at her in disbelief. 'You've been using Ella's identity?'

'No!' Alice protested. 'I mean, yes, at the gym, and a couple of other classes, but . . . '

'I don't understand.' Nadia looked slowly back and forth between them, her forehead creasing in a frown. 'Ella, what's going on?'

'Her name isn't Ella,' Nathan said, his eyes not leaving her. 'It's Alice. Alice Love.'

'Nathan . . . '

Nadia frowned. 'What do you mean?'

'Yes, *Alice*, what do you mean?' Nathan folded his arms.

'I can explain,' she said again, but the note of guilt in her voice was clear.

'Excuse me,' a young waiter bobbed nervously just behind them, his arms full of plates. 'Could you maybe take this outside? You're blocking the way.'

'Of course,' Alice told him, at the same time as Nathan said, 'No need.' He pulled his wallet from his jacket pocket and pulled out several notes, tossing them on the table. 'I think this should cover it.'

'Nathan!' Alice felt something twist inside. He wasn't even getting angry, just staring at her with terrible self-control. 'This is all just a silly misunderstanding!'

'I'm sure,' he agreed, almost too affable. 'Nadia, good to meet you . . . ' With a nod, and a final glance at Alice, he turned to leave, striding quickly out of the restaurant into the dark street.

Alice grabbed her things and hurried after him, dashing out into the rain. 'Nathan, wait!'

He took three more steps and then stopped. She caught up with him, breathless. 'I can explain!' she insisted again, clutching his hand. 'Ella had signed up for gym membership, and there was time left on the card, so I thought . . . ' Alice swallowed, hearing the inadequacy of her own words. 'But then, of course, I had to go along with it as Ella because, well, I thought it would cause too many questions, and by that point I was just sick of them, so . . . '

'So you assumed her identity.' Nathan finished.

Alice nodded. The rain was soaking through her thin dress, but she didn't care. All that mattered was that Nathan listened, that he understood what she'd been trying to do.

'A wanted criminal, and you were just running around, using her alias?' Nathan shook his head in disbelief. 'And this Nadia — she doesn't know who you really are? You said she's a friend.'

'She is. But I met her in class, so I introduced myself as Ella, and after that . . . ' Alice glanced down, miserable. 'It just seemed easier.'

'God, Alice!' Pulling away, he took a couple of paces further down the street before swinging back, 'Do you realise how stupid . . . no, how *dangerous* . . . ' Nathan stopped, clearly lost for words.

'You're right!' Alice exclaimed. 'You're completely right, which is why I stopped. I haven't been back anywhere as Ella for weeks now!'

'You mean, you've been doing this all along?'

Alice realised that, perhaps, full disclosure wasn't her best tactic. But something made her keep talking, wanting to tell him everything, no matter how strange it was.

'I wanted to understand her!' she tried. 'To see who she really was, underneath it all. I tracked down the places she went, and the people she'd talked to — only, they knew her as me, as Alice, so . . . so I became Ella, instead.'

Nathan just stared at her.

'It wasn't going to hurt anyone!' she cried. 'It was just a few little lies, while I investigated.'

'She was a criminal!' Nathan yelled back. 'I've been running around, trying to separate your public records — to prove your innocence — and all this time . . . '

'I am innocent!' But Alice's voice caught in her throat. It wasn't true, she knew, not any more.

Nathan clearly thought so too. He shook his head again, final, as if dislodging all affection for her. 'I can't talk to you about this, not right now.'

'But please — '

'I mean it, Alice; I don't want to know.' He looked at her for a long moment, and the disappointment in his expression made Alice want to cry. 'You'll get home OK?'

She nodded, her eyes filling with tears.

'Right then.' He let out a sigh, and for a moment Alice hoped he might reconsider, just calm down and try to understand.

Instead, he walked away.

She turned back towards the restaurant, clutching her jacket forlornly in her hand as her dress clung to her in wet patches and water dripped down her face.

'What did he mean, your name is Alice?' Nadia was sheltering in the doorway, arms folded.

Alice stopped. 'I'm sorry.'

Nadia's eyes widened. 'You mean it's true? But why?'

'I got carried away.' Alice felt even more shameful than ever. Nadia was blinking at her from behind her thin glasses, utterly confused. It was a feeling Alice knew all too well.

'I don't understand.'

'My name isn't Ella,' Alice admitted, 'And I'm not a legal assistant either. I just . . . I made it up.'

'But . . . ' Nadia gaped at Alice for a long moment, before finally finding the words. 'What is *wrong* with you?'

Alice dropped her head.

'I thought you were my friend!'

'I'm sorry,' Alice said again, meaning it. 'I know how you feel!'

Nadia shook her head. 'I don't believe this. What are you, some kind of con woman?'

'No! I swear, I was never going to do anything. I really like you — '

'Just get away from me!' Nadia recoiled, as if Alice was some sort of freak.

'But, Nadia — '

'No, I mean it. I — I trusted you!' Nadia's voice broke. She backed away, angry. 'I don't understand . . . '

'Please, if you just listen — '

'No!' She shook her head, recovering. 'Don't you get it? I never want to see you again.' Pulling open the door, Nadia disappeared back into the restaurant. Alice could see her through the window, hurrying back to her table, no doubt to tell her date what a psycho Alice was.

Alice slumped back against the glass. Rain was still drizzling in a steady stream, but Alice found that she didn't care one bit about the damp or cold. It was over now. She couldn't just flee her lies like Ella had done, easy and quick. No, Alice's consequences were tangled around her, the wreckage clear in Nadia's hurt expression, and Nathan's angry tone.

It was over, and she'd ruined everything.

30

Alice spent the next week wallowing in regret, but the space and time she hoped would give Nathan some perspective had clearly only set him further against her. No matter how many pleading messages she left, or explanatory emails she sent, he still wouldn't so much as acknowledge her existence.

'Just, call me back, please. I know you're angry, but I think if we just talked about this . . . ' Alice trailed off, hearing herself uselessly parrot the same lines she'd been cluttering his voice-mail with ever since their fight.

She hung up. Alice hadn't thought it possible to feel more wretched than when she stood outside that restaurant in the rain, but she was wrong.

'Still no luck?' Cassie passed her a consolatory cocktail, but Alice pushed it away. She'd done enough tearful drinking: now it was time for amends. If she could even get him to pick up her calls.

'No.' She gave a defeated sigh. 'Another name on the list of people not talking to me. What is it up to now? Nadia, Julian, my supposed clients . . . ' Even Flora had disappeared to her studio all week for an intense painting session, leaving Cassie the only sympathetic ear around.

Well, somewhat sympathetic.

'Aww, screw him,' Cassie argued. She stretched her legs out on the couch, taking a long gulp of her own drink. 'It's not like you broke any laws. I checked.'

'I don't care about the law, I care that I hurt them — him and Nadia. They trusted me, and I lied.'

Cassie rolled her eyes, clearly not as concerned about the ethical nuance of human relationships, but she gave Alice a conciliatory pat none the less. 'I'm sure they'll calm down eventually.'

'No, they won't.' Alice answered grimly. 'And they shouldn't either. I deserve it all.'

★ ★ ★

Alice dragged herself through the next long, lonely days, without any of the sparkle and romance she'd so briefly tasted. Without Nathan, or her classes, or the focus of the Ella investigation, she realised that her life had reset to that quiet, grey existence she'd lived before any of this even began. Only now, she spent her days not in boredom or quiet restlessness, but a terrible guilt at having hurt people she cared about; longing to be able to put things right again. But there would be no easy fix. Because although Alice was desperately sorry for having misled Nadia, and angered Nathan with her deception, the fact was, she still wasn't sure how many of her crimes she actually regretted.

'Nathan called yet?' Stefan was in the kitchen when she got back, munching on some of those

Swedish crackers he loved so much. He pushed the plate towards her, but she demurred with a polite shake of her head. Then she looked up with horror.

'Wait, what do you know about that?' The thought of Stefan knowing the details of her illicit activities brought a new shame.

But Stefan just laughed. 'Nothing much, don't you worry. Flora just mentioned you'd had a quarrel.'

'Oh.' Alice was relieved. She crossed to the fridge and poured herself a tumbler of juice. 'Where is she, anyway? I've barely seen her all week.'

'Didn't she say? She's visiting your parents for a couple of days.' Stefan took another satisfied bite. 'Which means I get to be fishy-breathed and slovenly until then.'

'Lucky you.' Alice gave a weak smile. 'I'll remember to keep my distance.'

Stefan gave her a sympathetic look. 'I'm sure he'll come around . . . I know, it's none of my business,' he added, 'but you'll work it out. Nathan's a good guy. You suit well.'

Feigning another smile, Alice just sipped her juice. Yes, Nathan was a good man, and she'd lost him. 'Thanks. I'll, um, leave you to all your stinking glory.'

Stefan grinned. 'I'm going to meet some friends now for curry and cigars — make a real night of it.'

'Enjoy.' Alice left the room, a touch wistful. That was true devotion, surely — relegating his unsavoury habits to when Flora was gone. She

426

was halfway up the stairs when it struck her.

Their parents were still in France. Flora had to know that. She had been the one to remind Alice in the first place, and show her a postcard from them, just the other day. And now that she thought about it, since when did Flora ever travel anywhere alone? If there was ever a visit or vacation, Stefan was right there with her, to handle transport arrangements and luggage and any other need that might flit across her mind. Feeling a sudden, ominous shiver, Alice hurried back downstairs and through to Flora's studio.

It was chaos.

She'd seen the mess before, but this was something different. Alice crept inside, as if disturbing a crime scene. Papers fluttered on the floor, paints were scattered on the table, spilling dark, ominous colours over her pretty pastels, and canvases lay abandoned, etched deep with charcoal. But more than the mess, there was the sense of desperation that lingered in the air. Alice wasn't imagining it, she was sure — there was something fierce and terrible in the spill of paint and careless scatter of all Flora's precious pictures.

Something was terribly wrong.

Alice backed out of the room, trying to think what could possibly have driven Flora to such a fit. She'd been so wrapped up in her own misery, she hadn't noticed anything awry.

'I'm just heading out.' Stefan was in the hallway, pulling on a coat. Alice stepped back, instinctively closing the studio door behind her to hide the scene.

'Oh, OK.' She swallowed. 'I don't suppose . . . have you heard from Flora at all? Since she left, I mean.'

'Sure,' Stefan smiled. 'She texted just a moment ago. Your parents send their love.'

Alice nodded slowly while he flipped up his trench-coat collar and reached for an umbrella. 'Have fun tonight!'

She let him go. Whatever the reason for Flora's flight, she hadn't confided in Stefan. And so, for now, Alice wouldn't either. But that didn't mean she was just going to leave Flora to her secret despair. The moment for respecting privacy and dancing around the subject was clearly past. It was time for answers.

★ ★ ★

It was 9 p.m. before Alice arrived at the cottage, anxiously wondering if Flora had really fled to Sussex at all. It was only instinct that led her home, and as she paid the taxi driver and dashed to the dark house through torrents of cold rain, it occurred to Alice again that Flora could have been lying about everything, not just the welcoming bosom of their parents.

She could be anywhere.

Struggling to keep her raincoat over her head, Alice banged a few times on the door with the heavy antique knocker, but there was no reply. The windows were gloomy, but the spare key was gone from beneath the window box, and when she peered through the smudged windows, Alice thought she could make out a handbag on the hall table, next to a pile of newspapers and post.

Or perhaps it was just wishful thinking.

'Pick up, pick up . . . ' Alice tried calling again as she circled the house, searching for signs of life. But, like the other ten times she'd dialled that evening, Flora didn't respond. Alice felt her foot sink down into the cold of a puddle and sighed. She just hoped that her stepsister was so deep in the bliss of a massage at a luxury spa hotel that she didn't notice the calls.

She was almost ready to admit defeat and ring for another taxi when she reached the far side of the cottage, a dilapidated extension that housed Jasmine's studio. The side door was slightly ajar.

'Flora?' Alice pushed inside, blinking at the gloom. The long room seemed empty, cluttered with Jasmine's various collections and sculpture work, but then Alice caught a glimpse of pale hair in the corner, illuminated by the dim light from the large, rain-splattered windows. 'Flora, what are you doing down there?'

She was curled in a huddle on the floor, her back against an old cabinet, so deep in whatever troubles had brought her there that she didn't even notice Alice until she was standing over her. Even then, for a moment she didn't muster surprise, or embarrassment, just a blank, dazed stare that was so full of misery that it pulled deep at Alice's heart.

'Hey.' Alice sank to the ground beside Flora, careful to keep her voice soft. She felt as though she were approaching a skittish animal, and that any sudden movements would only prompt fear and a bolting escape. 'There you are.'

Flora quickly wiped her eyes. 'I was just . . . ' she swallowed. 'The storm . . . '

'It's pretty vicious out there,' Alice agreed, shrugging off her coat and draping it over Flora's bare shoulders. She was dressed only in an embroidered vest top and peasant skirt. 'Your husband had the nerve to make off with my umbrella,' Alice tried to joke, but she felt Flora flinch slightly beside her. 'Don't worry,' she added quickly, 'I didn't say anything to him. He thinks you're snuggled up with Dad and Jasmine.'

Flora exhaled. 'I'm sorry if you worried.' She turned her pale face to Alice. 'I just needed to get away.'

'I know the feeling.' Alice cautiously sat back against a cabinet and looked around. 'You picked a good hideaway. I almost missed you behind all these things.'

Flora managed a tiny nod. 'She never throws anything away.' She wiped her eyes again. 'Every time we moved, there would be more art materials than furniture in the van.'

There was a long pause, filled only by the downpour outside. Alice felt her tension finally ease. Flora may not be fine, but she was there, safe within arm's reach beside her. Alice could manage anything as long as she had that much; even her own troubles seemed insignificant beside her sister's huddled form.

After a while, Alice realised Flora was staring

430

at the far wall. She followed her gaze, to a painting of a country scene, rich with red and orange hues.

'I've never noticed that before.' Alice stared at it, propped on a far shelf against a mismatch of crockery. 'Is it one of Jasmine's?'

Flora shook her head. 'Carlos did it,' she said quietly. 'One of Jasmine's old boyfriends. We lived in Spain with him, for a year, when I was twelve.'

'Really?' Alice asked, surprised. 'Can you speak any Spanish?'

'No. Mum didn't think I should go to school. She said I'd learn more from living in the world with them. It was nice there. I had a red bicycle.' Flora sounded vaguely wistful, as if she was dreaming of whooshing down those Catalan hills. Then she sighed. 'He fell in love with the au pair next door in the end, and Mum met Terry.'

'Terry?'

'He was trying to plant a vineyard,' Flora explained, 'in Cornwall. So, we moved again. He was the last one before she met Dad. Your Dad, I mean.'

Alice was silent for a moment. It had never really occurred to her to think of Flora's life before arriving at her door; the years of trailing after Jasmine as she flitted across the European landscape — just as Alice had wandered after her own mother, from cocktail party to expensive hotel suite, until she left for good.

Both mothers had done their damage, just in different ways.

Alice reached over and took Flora's hand.

'Well, I don't know about you, but I'm starving.' She gave an encouraging smile, 'How about we go inside and see if there's something left to eat?'

'I don't think there's anything,' Flora replied, but she didn't resist when Alice tugged her gently to her feet. 'The heating's off, and I can't figure out the electricity. I didn't . . . I didn't really think it through, coming here.' She looked forlorn.

'Never mind. We'll just have to rough it,' Alice proclaimed. 'I can build us a fire, and sort out the fuse box. It'll be an adventure!'

* * *

As expected, the dusty pantry held nothing but tins of cat food and baked beans, but a rummage in the dark utility room yielded more: salt-and-vinegar crisps, a box of trifle sponges, some long-life milk and — the real prize — a half-full bottle of gin.

'Ta-da!' Alice displayed her goods. 'What have you got?'

'Some rice crackers and Marmite. And ginger beer,' Flora added, dangling the cans from their plastic casing. 'They've got another month until the use-by date.'

'Perfect.' Alice ushered Flora back to the sitting room, which they'd set up as a makeshift camp with blankets and pillows in front of the flickering hearth. The flames cast a warm glow around the room, and with the night-lights Alice had carefully set out, it was almost homey. 'Just be glad there was lighter fluid,' she said, nudging the fire with the heavy old poker. 'I don't think I could have managed from scratch.'

'I could.' Flora munched on a rice cake with surprising enthusiasm. The change of scene seemed to have fortified her; the helpless dejection in her eyes had softened to something calmer. 'I learned in Brownies. I got a badge for it, and everything.'

They fell silent again, picking at the strange assortment of food while the fire settled into low, golden flames. It felt cosy and companionable in the small room, despite the circumstances hovering over the both of them, and Alice felt the warmth of an affection that so often seemed to elude her in that house. This was her family.

'I'm sorry I wasn't around much,' she said at last, looking over at Flora. 'When you were younger, I mean.'

Flora paused nibbling on a sponge, a cautious expression on her face. 'That's OK. You were . . . busy.'

'I know, but . . . ' Alice exhaled guiltily, 'I'd spent so long looking after Dad, keeping everything in place here, after Mum left, I just wanted to get away completely.'

Flora gave a small nod, her pale hair tangled in wisps around her face. 'I know.' She looked down, toying with the ring-pull on her ginger beer. 'It's not like we were . . . sisters, or anything.'

Alice felt a pang at the wistful note in her voice. All those years she'd been so relieved to escape her father's vague chaos, she hadn't even noticed that Flora was living through it all alone

— with the added trials of her own mother's various eccentricities as well.

'No,' she agreed quietly, 'but we are now. Which is why you need to tell me what's wrong. And don't pretend that nothing is, because I know you better than that.'

Flora bit her lip, but she didn't reply.

'Flora,' Alice implored her, 'come on. Here, drink this, and then tell me everything.' She reached for the dusty gin bottle and poured a liberal dash into Flora's drink.

'I . . . can't.' Flora gazed miserably at the can.

'Yes, you can,' Alice took her hand and squeezed it. 'You can tell me anything. I promise I'm on your side, no matter what. Is it your art? Or Stefan, is something happening with him?'

The candles flickered around them as she waited, watching Flora's face for any hint of the truth.

Flora's lip began to tremble. 'No, I mean . . . I can't drink it.' She finally looked up at Alice with that expression of utter hopelessness.

'You're . . . ?' Alice drew in a sharp breath as the implications became clear. 'You're pregnant?'

31

There was silence for a moment, filled only by the distant sound of the rain. Then Flora gave a forlorn shrug. 'Maybe. I don't know.'

Alice could hardly comprehend the idea; Flora always struck her as such a child herself that the possibility of her having her own . . . 'Have you taken a test yet?' she asked eventually. Flora shook her head. Alice reached out and gently brushed hair out of her eyes. 'You should. You need to know for sure.'

Flora nodded. It was clear from the tears filling her blue eyes that whatever the outcome, this was not an event to be celebrated.

'And you haven't talked to Stefan?' Alice tried to draw out more.

'No.' Flora's voice was small. 'He . . . he's always wanted them. Children, I mean.' She let out a sniffle. 'His parents split up when he was younger too, so we were going to have one of our own. A family. Without anyone leaving, or giving up, or changing their minds.' Her voice twisted on the last part, and Alice could picture it perfectly: Flora, at twenty-one, wanting so badly to have the security she'd never known, and Stefan, sturdy and solid and adoring, wanting nothing more than to give it to her.

Alice shifted closer until she could put her arm around Flora's shoulders and rub in slow, soothing strokes. 'Even if you are pregnant, you don't have to go through with it.'

Flora curled against her. 'I . . . I couldn't.'

'I did.'

Flora drew back, staring up at her with obvious surprise. 'An abortion?' She paused for a long moment before venturing, 'Was it . . . with James?'

'No, before him. I was about your age,' she realised, remembering the panic of seeing those little blue lines, and the relief — oh, the relief she'd felt when it was over. 'It was all very straightforward, once I'd made my mind up.' She spoke quietly, staring over Flora's head at the dark centre of the fire. 'I didn't even tell anyone. I don't know why not.'

Flora pulled the blanket up around them. 'Maybe . . . ' The word came out a whisper. 'It's just, I always said I wouldn't turn out like her.'

It took Alice a moment to understand who she meant. 'Jasmine?'

Flora nodded. 'I said I wouldn't put myself first, and do what I wanted, never mind what it meant for everyone else.'

'Sounds familiar,' Alice murmured, thinking of her own mother, and the way her eyes would drift past Alice to other, better things. 'There isn't anyone else, though, not yet,' she reminded her. 'And Stefan would understand. He'd do anything for you.'

Flora swallowed. 'But we made plans. I said this was what I wanted.'

'Is it?'

The question went unanswered as the flames slowly died to glowing embers, and then began to fade out altogether. The women snuggled on the floor in the middle of a vast mound of blankets and mismatched crocheted throws. Alice found a few more logs and a twist or two of newspaper, applying a liberal splash of lighter fuel until the fire was crackling merrily again. She grew sleepy, lulled by the silence and strange sense of isolation cloaking the cottage, as if they were children, buried deep in a makeshift fort. London, and the mess of her own life, seemed blissfully far away.

'Why don't you show those paintings?' Alice asked, at last, when they were laying side by side. 'The angry ones, I mean. I think they're beautiful. Vaguely disturbing,' she added with a wry laugh, 'but beautiful.'

She felt Flora sigh next to her. 'Those were just . . . experimenting. Nobody was supposed to see.'

'But they're good!' Alice insisted. 'You can't just keep hiding them away, not when you're capable of so much more. And that artist's residency, in Florence, those paintings would win it for you, I'm sure.'

Flora's body tensed, just slightly. 'I'm not applying for that, I told you. It's not worth it.'

'Why not?' Alice probed. This wasn't just about the pregnancy, she could tell. That portfolio she'd seen stretched much further back. Years, even. 'You're too young to just settle into a routine. You can travel, try new things . . . '

Flora rolled onto her side, close enough that Alice could see the teary blue of her eyes. 'You

437

don't understand,' she whispered, her face inches from Alice. 'We made plans, I made a deal. And if I change that, everything will just . . . fall apart.'

'No, Flora.'

Flora shook her head, just once, and it seemed to Alice that there were years of disappointment in her next words.

'When you don't need them any more, they leave.'

'Is that what you think?' Alice felt her heart break, just a little, as Flora's lifetime of vague wafting suddenly shifted into focus. All this time, Alice had thought her drifting and incapable, but really, she realised, her sister had never let herself so much as try; scared of what she'd seen with her mother, and all those men who must have slipped in and out of her childhood with such ease when they found that Jasmine's charming delicacy, in fact, hid a single-minded focus that was for her art, and not them.

'Stefan's different,' Alice promised softly, trying to reassure her. 'He wants you to be happy, to have a life. He'd support whatever you wanted.'

Flora gave a weak smile. 'But would he, really? If I was the one away all the time, and he was the one left waiting for me?'

The question lay between them, full of Flora's private fears. No wonder she let Stefan guide her through the world, Alice realised. If he was holding her hand the entire time, then, of course, he couldn't walk away.

'Look, can we, can we not talk about it any

more? Not tonight,' Flora asked.

'In the morning then.' Alice got up, pulling her blanket around her shoulders as she gathered their plates and took them through to the kitchen. Flora trailed after her, barefoot on the flagstone floor.

'It's your turn now.' Flora watched as Alice began to rinse the dishes. 'What happened with Nathan? I saw him at the office, and he looked a mess.'

Alice couldn't help but feel a perverse note of hope at the news. 'Did he ask about me?'

'No,' Flora gave her a sympathetic smile. 'Sorry.'

'That's OK.' But Alice's voice betrayed the truth.

'So, it's serious?'

'It's, bad,' Alice admitted, squeezing out the dishcloth and wiping down the surfaces. 'I think it's over.'

'No!' Flora protested. 'I've seen the way he looks at you. This is just some little tiff, you'll see.'

'No,' Alice gave her a pale smile, surprised to feel her eyes well up. 'It's more than that.'

Then she told her everything.

★ ★ ★

There wasn't much Flora could offer her, beside sincere reassurance that Nathan would forgive her — eventually — but Alice was glad to have a confidante all the same. She hadn't told anyone the full, unedited version of events, and

439

unburdening herself to Flora she felt a curious release.

'Is it bad, that I don't regret everything?' she whispered, when they'd tucked themselves in for the night, clustered beneath the blankets in front of the now-fading fire.

Flora shook her head, loyal to the end. 'You meant well.'

Alice wondered if that were entirely true. The consequences may have thrown her life into disarray, but when she forced herself to look back over the past months of tracking clues and digging deeper into Ella's psyche, she had to admit there were uncomfortable truths lurking there. It would be easier to write the entire summer off as a grave lapse in sanity, but Alice knew it would be hypocritical of her to reject the lies that had hurt Nadia and exploited Carl, when those same untruths had yielded such insight, adventure and, yes, fun. Without the lies, there would have been no Italy, no seizing her independence at the agency, no new confidence and self-possession. The end may be tainting all that came before, but what had unfolded that summer had been, for a brief while, glorious.

The room fell silent again, still and black, but it wasn't long before Flora's sleepy voice drifted up again. 'Can I ask you a question?'

'Of course,' Alice yawned.

'Why haven't you looked for her? Your mum, I mean.'

Alice paused, staring up at the darkness. It hadn't even occurred to her, it had been so many years. 'Some people . . . ' she exhaled, 'if you have to go looking for them, they're not worth finding.'

Flora thought about this for a moment. 'But you were looking for Ella.'

'That's different. She's . . . I don't know . . . ' Alice was unable to describe the vivid compulsion she'd felt to discover her former friend, an urge that still lingered beneath all the guilt and recrimination. 'She has answers,' she told Flora instead. 'I want to know why she did it.'

'And not your mum?'

'No.' Alice paused, listening to their soft breath in the dark. 'It's been too long. There's nothing she can say that would make me understand.'

'Oh . . . ' Flora replied, 'OK.' This time, she was the one to reach over, softly squeezing Alice's hand. 'Thanks. For, you know, coming.'

'Always.'

★ ★ ★

Flora must have been exhausted by her troubles, because she was still fast asleep when Alice woke the next morning. Slipping out of the covers, Alice trod quietly upstairs, managing what cleanliness she could with a flannel, cold water and a spare toothbrush as she planned her day. There was nothing calling her back to London for the weekend, she decided; the change of surroundings, perhaps, would offer some clarity about her future.

Half an hour later, she returned from the village, bearing fresh groceries, milk, and a slim

441

paper bag of pregnancy tests.

'I have to?' Flora, wrapped in a hideous quilting project of Jasmine's, blinked at the haul.

'Yes.' Alice was firm. She plucked the first rectangular box from her bag and held it out. 'You can't avoid this for long, not if you want options.'

Flora nodded slowly, but still she didn't move.

'I got more than one,' Alice added, 'so, either way, we'll know. I'll be right outside the door.' She started to nudge Flora towards the yellow-tiled bathroom. 'I'll even hold your hand while you wait.'

'But, what if — ?'

'Just do it, Flora. I'm right here.'

★ ★ ★

By the time the third white stick showed only the minimal number of little blue lines, it was clear: Flora, to the deep relief of both of them, was not pregnant. Nor, however, was she convinced that she needed to talk to Stefan about her worries. Her lower lip began to tremble, and those blue eyes filled up with tears at even the mention of it, so Alice let her recover in peace. For the rest of the day, no more was said of the weighty matters in either of their lives. They feasted on a delicious fried breakfast, took a muddy walk across the nearby fields, and after Alice managed to fix the electricity, they spent the rest of the afternoon cocooned back in the sitting room, watching those dusty VHS tapes of Mr Darcy and Miss Lizzy Bennet.

442

'You're too much like Lizzy,' Flora decided, sucking on a sherbet lemon from the bagful they'd bought at the corner shop. There was colour back in her pale cheeks, Alice noticed with relief, and the sight of petticoats and breeches had clearly restored her spirits. 'You're so used to doing everything on your own, it's like there isn't room for anyone else. Any man,' she added, with a meaningful look.

'Is this a hint to swoon softly into Nathan's arms and beg forgiveness?' Alice replied drily, taking her own sweet from the sticky paper package. 'Because I'm trying that already. Sort of.'

'No! I just . . . I don't understand why he's throwing everything away.' Flora looked genuinely bewildered. 'I mean, you're wonderful.'

'That's sweet,' Alice laughed, 'but don't think you're going to turn this around on me. I may not make enough compromises, but you're the one making too many.' Flora visibly recoiled, but Alice felt she'd had time enough to face reality. 'You need to call him.'

Flora shook her head.

'You need to call him now.' Alice fixed Flora with an even gaze. 'I know you think this is all on you, that you have to deal with how you feel alone, but, sweetie, we're talking about Stefan. He'll do anything for you.'

It didn't seem as if her words had any impact, but then Alice caught sight of a flicker — just a flicker — of longing in Flora's expression.

'You miss him, don't you?' Alice asked softly. 'I can tell you do; you've checked that phone for

443

messages a dozen times in the last hour.'

Silence.

'So let me call him for you,' she offered. 'I won't say what's been going on, but I could get him down here. Then, you could talk, properly, away from everything.'

Flora was wavering, she could tell, so Alice unleashed her final weapon: guilt. 'Has he ever let you down before?' she prompted, looking right in her eyes. Flora shook her head slowly. 'So why don't you give him this chance? Hasn't he earned that much by now?'

It was a low blow, and a slow tear trickled down Flora's cheek in response, but Alice was determined. If it had been anyone else, she would have taken Flora's side unreservedly. But for all her sister's anxiety, Alice knew in her heart that Stefan was made of sterner stuff. A foreign residency, some violent paintings, even the delay of his much-wanted family — he would give it all to Flora in a heartbeat, despite what she may fear.

'OK,' Flora whispered finally. 'I'll talk to him.'

Alice summoned Stefan that evening with a vague invitation to drive down and join them all for a family weekend. Then, despite Flora's wide-eyed pleas, she left. Some things, she couldn't mediate, but they would come through this. Alice hadn't spent the last three years watching them with a wistful eye not to know the steel that ran beneath their relationship, even if Flora had been thrown into doubt by her own experience of love, and the limits it so often showed.

Catching the late train moments before it left, Alice curled up in an empty carriage and gazed absently out at the dark blur of country landscape and small towns that would take her back to London. They were more alike than Alice had imagined, she and Flora. She was old enough not to feel it so keenly, but the legacies of their parents' various carelessness had left their mark. Flora kept herself in a state of perpetual need, and Alice . . . ? Well, she realised, she'd long ago rejected the idea of needing anyone at all; spending years constructing her life to be a calm, uncomplicated, and, in the end, solitary pursuit.

But people could change. Flora had already come a long way from the needy child who first married Stefan. Now she clearly burned for some independence and autonomy, even if she hadn't yet found a way to understand those desires. And Alice too — she'd been gradually inching away from that old life of hers, whether through her hunt for Ella, or more basic restlessness, she wasn't sure. It struck her now that she might have been wrong, thinking everything had switched back to the way it had been before Ella, or before any of this drama had begun. Despite the woeful current state of her life, all was not entirely lost, Alice decided. Whatever the outcome with Nathan, or her job, she was no longer willing to sit back any more, watching everybody else's drama unfold, only edging in afterwards to restore order and calm. Those days, she realised with a quiet measure of satisfaction, were behind her for good.

32

Alice returned to London with a new sense of purpose. Her instincts to organise and to find some sort of order in chaos now applied more than ever to her own life. The hopeful messages and pleading texts were clearly not working, and however much she longed to reconcile, Alice knew that all the apologies in the world wouldn't make Nathan listen if he didn't want to. So, making one last effort to reach him, she hand-wrote a careful letter, explaining the reasons for her deception, but more importantly, the parts for which she had no regret. It would be wrong of her to apologise for everything, when she wasn't quite sure she owed it to him, but she had betrayed his trust, and for that she was sorry. She sent one to Nadia too — briefer, but heartfelt and apologetic. Alice didn't expect any reply from her, but she'd wanted to assure her that their friendship, however false when it came to surface details, had been genuine on her part.

With the letters sent, Alice's life returned to a mundane sort of normal. Flora and Stefan returned from Sussex sobered, but they seemed to have had some sort of breakthrough. Alice didn't press, but Flora, at least, was calmed by whatever had passed between them. She was still tearful at times, but Stefan cancelled his upcoming trips, and Alice found a practice application essay for the residency scrawled on the back of a kitten sketch. After such drama and emotional upheaval, it was almost a relief to return to her own regular routine.

Her urge to track Ella didn't subside. She still wondered where her friend was now, and what was the true story behind her emergence as a thief and fraud, but Alice resisted the urge to return to those thick files of data. Her compulsion would fade, she decided. It was just a question of letting go.

Not quite so easy to endure was the situation at work. With Saskia flouncing around in triumph, and Vivienne having wrested back control of her clients, Alice was left to face her contract work again, and sift through the stack of assistant applications.

'Man, no wonder Patricia hasn't booked any jobs lately; she must have put on thirty pounds!'

'Mm-hm. And that bad Botox isn't helping either.'

Alice finished her glass of champagne and shot Tyrell a disdainful glare. It was the annual agency party, hosted on the back terrace of an expensive French restaurant, and clients and co-workers alike had turned out for the chic, black-tie affair. The evening was warm and sunny, with alcohol flowing at a generous rate, but some of the guests were more concerned with sniping at their compatriots than celebrating.

'I heard she got turned down for a Febreze ad,' Saskia announced, her red curls gleaming as she leaned closer to Tyrell. 'I bet Vivienne will drop her soon. It's just an embarrassment to have clients like that hanging around.'

Alice followed her gaze. A middle-aged blonde woman — a little curvy, yes, but elegant in a cream shift and tasteful gold jewellery — was chatting to Vivienne. Alice recognised her as Patricia Houghton. Not because she was enjoying great fame or critical adulation, but because she had once featured prominently on Alice's 'most wanted' list of fading, yet prospective clients.

Alice turned back to the drinks table with a sigh. There was little point her attempting to woo anyone; Vivienne would only snatch them back. No, her agenting ambitions were securely on hold for now, the more pressing issue being whether she could find work as a contracts manager elsewhere, and perhaps escape the delightful camaraderie of Grayson Wells with her sanity intact.

Saskia let out another squeal. 'Oh my God! Do you *see* what Parker Gilford is wearing?!'

Alice swiftly left the patio, circulating with smiles and small talk for a while. There were plenty of clients who were happy to see her, and while Julia and Kieran seemed nervous — awkwardly apologising for not having been in touch — Alice couldn't hold it against them. Vivienne could be persuasive when the mood took her, and was doing excellent work on their behalf now that she had a little motivation. Maybe that was her calling, Alice mused: selecting overlooked clients to work with so that Vivienne would start paying them attention again. Who knew, perhaps if she waltzed over and handed Patricia her card, Vivienne would actually acknowledge her existence for a change.

'Alice Love!'

As if hearing her thoughts, Vivienne's voice suddenly rang out through the party. Alice looked up to find her boss charging in her direction, her black satin cocktail dress looking remarkably like armour, edged with silver cuffs and a fearsome belt. In fact, as Vivienne parted the sea of guests and stalked across the lawn towards her, Alice could see that her face was glowering angrily.

She took a step back in fear. 'What . . . What's wrong, Vi?' Alice asked, thinking in horror of the break-in, and police questions, and the swift end to her secure, if sedate, career. Nobody would hire a lawyer with a criminal conviction to her name!

'You know very well what's wrong.' Coming to a halt not two feet away, Vivienne jabbed one polished fingertip towards Alice's collarbone.

She took another step back, stalling for time. 'No, no, I'm not sure.'

Vivienne gasped theatrically. 'And to lie to my face, after everything I've done for you!'

Alice glanced around. The party was silent, all eyes on them. Saskia rushed to Vivienne's side, glaring at Alice with identical disapproval.

Oh God.

'Why don't you tell me what's happened?' Alice tried to keep her voice from trembling. It all came down to how much Vivienne knew: just her occasional impersonations, or the whole messy affair? She gulped, reaching out to guide Vivienne away from the crowd. 'In fact, let's go and talk about this inside, so we don't interrupt — '

'Hollywood!' Vivienne announced, shaking off her hand. 'You thought you could just up and leave? Taking all my clients with you!'

Alice stopped.

'That's right,' Vivienne scowled. 'Although why you think they would follow you when you have no connections or experience . . . '

So this wasn't about her crimes? Alice felt a great sweep of relief, but it was soon tempered with new confusion. 'Vivienne,' her voice dropped, as she looked helplessly around, 'I really don't know what you mean.'

'Like hell you don't! Vivienne drew herself up and glowered at her. 'I've heard all about your little plans. An agency, in Hollywood? I've never heard anything so ridiculous. Oh, don't play the fool with me,' she snapped, taking in Alice's bewildered expression. 'I know everything.'

'Rupert called,' Saskia piped up. 'He's in LA. He heard you were setting up over there, and wanted to get hold of you.' She folded her arms smugly.

'But . . . I really don't . . . He must have been mistaken,' Alice insisted.

'Ha!' Vivienne snorted. 'I've been asking around, I know everything. 'The Angelique Love Agency', indeed. Did you really think the name would keep me from finding you out?' She jabbed her finger again. 'What were you planning — to stay here long enough to steal all our information, tempt the clients away?'

'No, no!' Alice shook her head, still not grasping what on earth . . .

Ella.

It was Ella! She must be in LA, using Alice's identity to pass herself off as, what, an agent? Or had that just been a random lie, that had somehow found its way back to Rupert?

But it was Ella, after all this time.

'I just don't understand,' Vivienne was clearly through the anger phase of her tirade and into wounded indignation, playing for the rapt crowd. 'This is the thanks I get, for taking you in, and nurturing you, like my own child! And when I think of the favour I did your poor father . . . ' Vivienne held one hand to her forehead, as if she were about to swoon.

Alice rolled her eyes, 'That was years ago,' she replied, impatient. She just wanted to know what Ella was doing out there!

'So you admit it?' Vivienne gasped.

'Well, it sounds like the proof is pretty damning.' Alice was already thinking of her passport, and plane tickets. She glanced at Vivienne, standing imperiously in front of her flock, awaiting some sort of grasping, grovelling plea for forgiveness.

And just like that, the job Alice had only moments before been so scared to lose suddenly seemed insignificant compared to the real revelation of the day. She didn't need this — not when she had more important matters waiting for her across the Atlantic.

Fuck Vivienne and her theatrical power plays.

451

'I better leave then,' Alice smiled, suddenly carefree. 'Since it's clear I'm not wanted.'

Vivienne drew in a breath, her heavily kohled eyes bulging with rage.

'And yes, take this as my resignation,' Alice added, before Vivienne could think to fire her. 'Enjoy the party, everyone,' she added with a beam. Then, depositing her drink on a nearby tray, Alice happily sauntered away, leaving a hushed murmur of surprise in her wake.

★ ★ ★

Dashing straight to the office before Vivienne could change all the locks, Alice hastily called Rupert's wife to track down his international number, keeping one eye on the door in case a battalion was sent to stop her pilfering all those important client files.

'Alice!' He exclaimed happily, when she finally got through. 'You got my message?'

'Yeees.' It suddenly struck her that if she revealed Ella's part in all of this, Rupert might do something stupid, like confront her. Or, worse still, involve the police.

'Oh crap, did I land you in it with Vivienne?' He mistook her hesitance as disapproval. 'I'm so sorry. It's just, when my friend said he'd met you over here, I thought you'd left Grayson Wells for good. Or at least handed in your resignation.'

'No, it's fine,' Alice reassured him quickly, already packing away some belongings from her desk into an empty cardboard box. 'I have quit. I've just been, wrapping things up over here.'

'Congratulations!' Rupert sounded thrilled for her. 'And it's such good timing too, because I need your services. A friend of mine is working as an assistant director on a new film, and, well, he's managed to wangle me a part. It's nothing big,' he added, ever-modest, 'but it's comic, like you suggested, and it pays well. I was hoping you could look over the contract for me?'

'Of course,' Alice agreed, 'but shouldn't you find a real agent?'

'I will,' Rupert promised. 'I just don't want to rush into it. I've learned my lesson,' he added grimly.

'That's great. I'd be happy to help,' Alice said quickly. 'Now, remind me, when did I run into that friend of yours . . . ?'

'Last weekend, I think he said, at Chateau Marmont. I didn't realise he was talking about you, at first, but then he said you were an agent from England . . . ' Rupert laughed. 'I suppose you changed your mind on the Angelique thing then!'

Alice echoed his laugh. 'Yes, well . . . Did I give him a card or any contact information at all? A batch of my business cards was printed wrong,' she explained quickly, 'so he might not be able to get hold of me.'

'I'll check,' Rupert replied. 'You really should get a website running though. If I hadn't known Angelique was you, I never would have put the two names together.'

'You're right,' Alice said thoughtfully, 'You're exactly right.'

As she booked her flight for that evening and rushed home, Alice couldn't help but marvel at the ingenuity of Ella's plan. A driving licence, a credit card or two — Alice knew all too well by now how easy it was to build a wealth of identification with just a couple of original documents. And if she went by Angelique, too? Well, there would be no reason for anyone at all to link her back to Alice, not even in the entertainment industry.

The plan was flawless. At least, it would have been, had it not been for the simple matter of Rupert knowing her real name. With Alice tucked away at Grayson Wells in London, Ella could have happily paraded across Los Angeles as Angelique Love for months, if not years, with nobody any the wiser. But now, Alice had her. Now, she would finally know the truth.

★ ★ ★

Alice burst breathlessly into Flora's studio, the moment she arrived back home. 'Do you want to come to LA?'

'What?' Flora looked up from where she was curled, sketching, on the sofa.

Alice was about to launch into the grand tale of Ella's discovery when she noticed the vivid, angry paintings that now were neatly stacked along one wall. Flora followed her gaze.

'Oh, those.' She blushed. 'Stefan suggested we find somewhere to show them. Under a different name, maybe, so it doesn't confuse my brand, but . . . I can't keep hiding them away for ever.'

'That's great.' Alice smiled. 'And the residency?'

Flora beamed serenely. 'We sent my application yesterday. Stefan can come to visit at weekends. If I get it, I mean.'

'You will,' Alice declared. 'And guess what? I've found Ella, she's in LA!'

Flora gasped. 'No!'

Alice quickly explained the accidental discovery, painfully aware that she was due at the airport in a matter of hours. 'So, what do you say? Come with me?'

A thoughtful look crossed Flora's face. 'No, thanks.' She shook her head slowly. 'I think you'd better do this on your own.'

'You're sure? It could be fun. I booked the hotel Cassie's always raving about, and we could do some things together too.'

'No,' Flora smiled. 'But thank you for asking.'

'OK.' Alice took a deep breath to calm herself, full of excitement. 'I can't believe I've finally found her!'

Flora frowned slightly. 'But you'll be careful? Don't get your hopes up,' she added quickly. 'It's just . . . she might not have the answers you want. She did steal from you, remember, and run away. It's not like she wants you to find her.'

'Relax,' Alice leaned over and hugged her, 'I'll be fine!'

Although Alice's excitement swept her to the airport, Flora's words returned as she sat waiting nervously in the departure lounge with a thick stack of magazines and a makeshift dinner of sandwiches and lemonade.

Just what was she expecting from Ella?

Flora was right, of course; Alice had built a whole new picture of who Ella was now, complete with Safe Haven volunteer sessions and regular cookery classes, but in the end, Ella had still betrayed her trust and vanished, leaving debt and destruction in her wake. Alice knew some of her secrets, and the good intentions fuelling at least a little of the crime, but if she'd learned one thing, it was that she could never be certain how significant she was in somebody else's life. She may have spent the past months poring over Ella's every action with an intensity that bordered on obsession, but who was to say Ella had even given her another thought at all? To Ella, she may be just another in a long line of victims, and while Alice had been telling herself that their friendship was genuine, she couldn't know for sure.

A small part of her wondered whether Ella's new life could come crashing down as easily as her own.

Alice filed that thought away to ponder during her ample twelve-hour flight to Los Angeles. She was contemplating one last trip to the bookshop when her phone rang; the display showing an unexpected number. Nathan.

Alice caught her breath. 'Hello?' she answered gingerly, turning away from the busy waiting lounge in an attempt for some privacy. Of course, after wanting to hear from him for so long, he would choose now to call, when she was surrounded by impatient tourists and the loud call of announcements. 'Nathan?'

There was a pause, and then his voice came, steady and somehow reassuring even after everything. 'Hey.' He gave a low, rueful sort of laugh. 'I've been nearly calling you so long, I figured I should just go ahead and dial this time.'

'No, I'm glad you did,' she said quickly. 'How have you been?'

'OK, I guess.' Nathan paused again. 'I, uh, got your letter.'

'Oh. I wanted to explain,' she said uselessly. 'So you'd understand.'

'Well,' he sighed. 'I'm not sure I do.'

Alice felt an ache.

'But, I want to,' he added, and just like that, she had hope again. 'Do you maybe want to get some coffee? Or a drink. We're probably going to need alcohol for this,' he added wryly.

'I do, but . . . ' Alice tried to think of what to say, but then a loud blast of the announcement system rang out, demanding that passengers keep baggage with them at all times, otherwise risk controlled detonations and general chaos.

'Where are you right now?' Nathan asked.

'The airport,' Alice ventured reluctantly. 'I found Ella. I'm going to see her.'

'Alice!'

'I stopped looking, like I told you!' she protested. 'But a friend found out by accident.'

Nathan muttered something under his breath. 'Have you told the police yet?' he demanded.

'No. And I'm not going to,' Alice insisted. 'At least, not until I've had a chance to speak to her,

457

to talk things through. Listen,' she implored him, 'I'll be fine. She's not dangerous, just . . . '

'A liar? A thief? A two-faced, fraudulent bitch?'

Alice stopped. 'Yes, all of them, but . . . I'm doing this, Nathan. I've got to.'

There was another long pause, and then he asked quietly, 'And if I told you not to?'

Alice exhaled again, full of regret, but determined none the less. 'I don't know if you have the right to ask that, Nathan. This is just something I have to do.'

There was silence.

'Look, I have to go,' she said, feeling that ache again. It shouldn't be a choice, but if it was, she would pick Ella. She had to see this to the end. 'They're getting ready to board my flight.'

'You're really going through with this?' Nathan sounded disbelieving. 'Even if . . . '

He didn't finish, but Alice knew what he meant. Even if it meant the end for them.

'Yes,' she replied simply. 'I'm sorry.'

'Me too,' he replied slowly, 'Just . . . take care, OK?'

'I will.'

Alice hung up and sat for a moment, wondering if she'd just made a terrible mistake. But then the cabin crew announced that they'd be boarding the first rows now, and Alice felt her flutter of excitement return. Nathan mattered to her, but so did facing Ella. She may never get this chance again. She had to take it.

33

When she arrived at the hotel in LA, Alice collapsed into bed in a jet-lagged blur. The next morning dawned warm, bright and full of possibility. Scrambling out of bed, Alice threw open her window and gave a small sigh of satisfaction. Despite it being October, the weather was positively balmy; blue-skied with a faint haze hovering above the nearby Hollywood Hills. Perfect.

Cassie's hotel recommendation had turned out to be a scruffy place on Sunset Boulevard, boasting an all-night party in the mirrored lounge, but basic rooms. Alice didn't care. She leaned out on the tiny health-hazard of a balcony, Los Angeles stretching before her in a strange landscape of billboards, low buildings and busy streets. She had never visited before, but from her vantage point, it seemed to her as golden a city as Rome; not bathed in that warm glow of history, but something newer and just as alluring.

Now, where to begin? Alice grinned, realising that it was less a challenge than perhaps it ought to be. By now, her investigations had given her such a background in asking tricky questions and obtaining confidential information that she didn't even blink as she considered the challenges of the day. Navigating a foreign city, procuring Ella's address, tracking and confronting an experienced fraudster . . . She paused a moment, struck by a faint wave of regret as she remembered following the trail in Italy, with Nathan by her side, but the feeling was soon pushed aside. This was her quest, and she would finish it alone.

Dressing quickly, Alice armed herself with her trusty notebook and a felt-tipped pen, all but skipping past the sullen, hung-over bodies littering the lobby — until she stepped out of her hotel door and realised that LA, for all its many joys, was not exactly a pedestrian-friendly city. Her attempt to procure a bus timetable at the hotel reception was met with smirking amusement, while enquiries about the Metro were soon dissuaded. So, she headed straight for the rental agency, and soon took possession of a sturdy, safe, but rather nondescript car.

'Here you are, Miss Love. You have a nice day!'

Alice took the keys with no small amount of trepidation, feeling their weight in her palm. 'And I'm covered for break-down and collisions?' she checked, yet again.

The toothy young man at the counter beamed. 'Yes, ma'am. Just call our emergency hotline, twenty-four seven!'

Alice turned, looking through the window at her chosen vehicle. She'd been assured it was the safest in its class, while the plain model would make it less of a target for thieves, but still . . .

'Is it too late for that upgrade?' she swung back, fixing the man with a hopefully persuasive look. 'I was thinking, perhaps, a red convertible?'

It was cliché, she knew, but Alice couldn't help but feel that was the point: an open-topped car, wind-tousled hair, Bruce Springsteen playing on the car radio as she drove to the place where Ella had been spotted last. If this was her Californian experience, then she was going to do it properly. She strolled through the lobby of the ornate, chateau-style hotel, and took the time to relax with a tall glass of iced tea under a shaded terrace before beginning her questions.

Was this the world Ella had aspired to? Alice wondered, as she watched the sunbathers stroll from the bar to their crisply upholstered loungers. If so, she could see the appeal. Whether it was the money clearly in evidence from the ultra-casual designer details, or simply the fact of the unadulterated sunshine, Alice felt a warm glow, deep and relaxing, as she soaked in the scene.

What must it be to simply start again, anywhere you wanted?

When at last she'd had her fill of the view, Alice called Rupert's contact, briefly explaining she was an old friend looking to get in touch with Angelique.

'Sure, I've got her card here somewhere . . . ' There was a pause, and then he returned, reading off a local number and email address. 'I was going to set up a date with her. Do you want me to mention you're in town?'

'Oh, no,' Alice replied quickly. 'I definitely want to surprise her.'

Another few calls to directory assistance, and some enthusiastic Googling later, and Alice had an address. Crescent Heights. It was an older area above the main sprawl of the city, full of steep winding streets and houses buried in a lush tangle of tropical-looking trees. She slowed the car, idling by the kerb as she approached the house on what was now her third loop around the block. A large Spanish-style building, it was set a little way back from the road with two cars in the driveway and separate mailboxes on the front lawn suggesting that it housed more than one apartment — and that the residents were home.

This time Alice came to a stop just up the street and waited, eyes fixed on the green-fringed entrance. As stake-outs went, it was low-tech, she knew: a bag full of bakery goods, a cardboard cup of herbal tea, and nothing but the radio for company. But, as an hour drifted by, Alice refused to let her focus waver. She could just march up to the front door, demanding answers and a full confession, but what good would that do? She wanted to know the fabric of Ella's life now: her fake career, the new set of disposable friends, the lies she was telling this time around. So she watched, flicking between classic rock and a strangely soothing country station, until, just before 1 p.m., Ella emerged.

Alice sat forwards, her last pastry suddenly forgotten in her hand. Ella was skipping down her front steps, head bent as she rummaged in a large leather bag. Her hair was the first thing Alice noticed. It was longer now, of course, but the formerly middling brown colour had been replaced with a vibrant auburn red that fell in sleek, glossy waves. She was dressed smartly, but in a more eye-catching ensemble than she used to wear around Alice: a vivid purple ruffled top, a structured white pencil skirt, chunky gold jewellery. There were high heels and the designer purse, but more than those shiny accessories, a certain confident strut in her walk that Alice had never seen before.

She looked like a different woman.

Alice squinted, just to be certain, but Ella's face was unmistakable, even from a distance. She'd found her.

Ella climbed into her car and, a moment later, reversed out of the drive. Alice waited a few precious seconds and then started her own engine, easing after Ella as she headed off. Soon, she would know everything.

★ ★ ★

Alice kept watch for four days, until the front seats of her rental car were littered with takeaway wrappers and gossip magazines, and she'd seen for herself the new life Ella was crafting, out here in the sunshine. It was a good one. Early morning trips to a gym nearby, dressed casually in loose-fitting sweat-pants and a high, bouncing ponytail; the stop for coffee at a hippie-looking corner café on her way back. Then it was home, for a shower and change into one of her chic,

463

eye-catching outfits, before she headed out for her day. Ella didn't seem to have a normal job, and she spent her days in a mismatched pattern of leisurely pursuits: working on a laptop in another coffee place; shopping the boutiques of Santa Monica; spending an afternoon tucked in a bookshop, browsing a stack of reference books as Alice loitered in the children's section a safe twenty feet away. There were meetings too, a couple of lunches at upscale restaurants, printed pages strewn across the table, and a more casual coffee date that might well have been a social engagement — Alice observed them all, with fascination and a growing sense of resentment.

It had been seamless, she was coming to realise — Ella's transition to another city, a newer, more perfect life. While Alice had been scrambling to prove her innocence and deal with the wreckage Ella had left, she'd been here, basking in the ease and comfort that nearly a hundred thousand pounds of stolen funds could provide. Alice had allowed herself to feel warmth, even sympathy, imagining the loneliness that Ella must feel. Now, having watched her spend a lazy afternoon picking out expensive bed linens, she wondered if Ella deserved any such charity at all.

'Target has arrived. Eighteen twenty-one Melrose.'

The metallic tone of her tracker device was like a friend by now. Alice turned left, and carefully slowed the car as she approached the row of neat shops and pretty cafés. Sure enough,

Ella's car was there on the side of the road, waiting for her.

'Thanks, Greta,' Alice murmured, finding her own space and managing a quick parallel parking endeavour. Naming her GPS locator might have seemed strange at first, but after approximately thirty hours in each other's company, Alice regarded the small device with thanks and affection.

She'd lost Ella immediately, that first day out, watching with despair as she disappeared across a crowded intersection while Alice was caught by a quick change of lights. Alice had been briefly cast down, until Flora jokingly suggested she invest in some sort of tracking device. The array of discreet devices available at the nearest electronics shop was baffling to Alice, but she happily invested three hundred dollars in a sleek little pebble she affixed to Ella's back bumper that night. Now, it didn't matter if she fell behind in a traffic jam, or took a wrong turn or two, because she would always get there in the end. Wherever Ella was, she followed. Including . . .

'Purrfect Partners, pet supplies.' Alice watched, puzzled, as Ella emerged from the shop hoisting an armful of bags. She threw them in the boot, and then drove away again, picking the now-familiar side streets Alice knew would take her home.

Since when did Ella have a pet?

Alice went as far as her usual spot, just up the street from Ella's house, and watched curiously as she unloaded the bags. For some reason, an animal jarred with Alice's other information. Pets were permanent, they meant roots and commitment, not the temporary life Ella usually led.

Her phone rang, and when she reached for it, it was Flora.

'Have you talked to her yet?' she demanded immediately.

'No, I'm still gathering information.'

'Alice!'

'What?' she protested, eyes still on that front porch. 'I need all the data I can get. After all, I can't trust her to tell me anything.'

She'd always wanted a front porch. A back one too, with a rocking chair, or some kind of love-seat. Somewhere to doze in the afternoon sun, just relaxing —

'It's getting creepy,' Flora informed her bluntly. 'You need to just confront her.'

'She's wearing the prettiest dress today,' Alice replied instead, a touch wistful. 'She had lunch at a lovely restaurant too. Some kind of salad, it looked like. She sat on the front terrace, in the sun, and read a book for an hour.'

Flora made a noise of frustration. 'Alice, you've seen enough! You probably know what kind of underwear she's wearing. Just go over there and face her.'

If Alice's old debit bills were correct, then she did know the style of Ella's lingerie: imported Italian silk. She paused. Perhaps Flora was right. 'OK, I'll talk to her.'

'Today,' Flora added.

Alice glanced down. 'This evening,' she

amended. 'I need to change my clothes, I can't meet her looking like . . . Well, like a crazy stalker.'

Flora laughed. 'God forbid. But promise me you'll do it? You can't stay out there for ever, just trailing her around. It's not healthy.'

'I know,' Alice sighed. 'I'll talk to her tonight.'

It wasn't so simple. Alice tried to get some rest that afternoon and calm herself, but she could only toss, restless, as if she were facing a dreaded exam and not the very thing she'd been working towards for months now. Afternoon sunlight seeped through the curtains as she tried to play out every possible scenario in her mind, but there was just a vague outline where Ella's reaction should be. After all this time studying her every move, Alice still had no idea of the inner workings of her mind, and that, in itself, sent her nerves into a flustered tangle.

What if she didn't know the real Ella at all?

★   ★   ★

By the time she passed her keys to the valet and climbed the front steps that evening, Alice was a mess of anxious anticipation. Her device had tracked Ella to that same hotel Alice had visited before, and as she walked quickly through the polished lobby and out to the bar, she wondered whether it was a sign. In the dusk light, the terraces were almost romantic: adorned with candlelit tables, the bar open and spilling stylish patrons out into the courtyard. Alice paused a moment, searching through the crowd for Ella's

467

vivid hair. She had deliberated too long over her own outfit for the evening. After all, what was the dress code for confronting the woman who had stolen your identity? In the end, Alice found herself reaching for the one garment that would guarantee her some confidence: the ever-stunning red dress. But now, poised there on the steps, Alice was struck by a terrible thought. She'd mimicked the purchase from Ella's own wardrobe. What if Ella were wearing hers too?

Then Alice caught sight of Ella's familiar frame across the crowd, dressed in the luxuriously casual style that almost seemed mandatory in this city: a white silk tank top and tangle of delicate necklaces over black jeans. She was sitting alone at a corner table, her demeanour quiet, almost contemplative, as she waited, surrounded by noise and laughter.

Steeling herself with one final breath, Alice made her way across the floor.

This was it.

'Hi, Ella . . . or is it Angelique now?' Alice slid into the seat opposite, fixing her with an icy look. Her heart was racing, but she forced herself to breathe evenly, watching Ella's face for any reaction.

And oh, her reaction.

Ella froze. She blinked at Alice, her glossed lips dropping open slightly, and an expression of sheer panic flitting across her face.

Alice reached across and helped herself to a sip from Ella's cocktail, relaxing now. 'Don't worry,' she said, almost conversationally, revelling in the fact that, for once, she was the one in control. 'I haven't called the police. Nobody knows you're here but me.'

'But . . . ' Ella sucked in a breath, 'how . . . ?'

Alice smiled. 'You're not the only one who can keep watch, you know. I've been looking for you ever since you left England. You have excellent taste in hotels,' she added, gratified by Ella's obvious surprise. 'Although they weren't exactly . . . hospitable towards me in Rome. But Positano was lovely, of course. Thanks for that tip.'

She sat back, still playing the part of some casual observer, even as triumph surged hot in her veins. In front of her, Ella was struggling to regain some sort of composure, glancing quickly around and taking a few deep, even breaths.

'It's . . . good to see you,' she managed at last, giving Alice a hesitant smile.

'I'm sure,' Alice replied, droll.

'No, I mean it. I . . . I wondered how you were doing.'

'After you ripped me off, stole all my important documents, and left me wading through debt collectors?' Alice snorted. 'I've been just wonderful, thank you for asking.'

Ella blinked at the bitterness in Alice's tone. She took a drink from her cocktail, seeming to steady her nerves, then she reached for her bag. 'You're right. You deserve an explanation. I just have to go to the bathroom — '

'Don't,' Alice cut her off. 'Crescent Heights, isn't it? I could have the police there before you even make it back. I know you like running,' she added, 'but I'm guessing you'd rather leave with

469

a few bags, and that animal of yours.'

Ella settled back in her seat.

'So, what do you want?' She said it calmly, meeting Alice's eyes with an even stare. Whatever element of surprise Alice had enjoyed was gone, but instead of steeling herself, or seeming defensive, Ella just sat there, casual and open.

'I want answers,' Alice replied. Around them, people jostled and chatted, voices ringing out with laughter, but Alice felt completely alone with Ella. 'Why you did this?' She was unable to keep the intensity from her tone. 'Why me?'

Ella gave a rueful smile. 'Why not? You had a perfect credit record, plenty of savings . . . '

'Then why feign the friendship? You didn't bother with Illana, or Patrick, or any of your other victims.'

Ella widened her eyes. 'You have been busy.'

'See, that's what I don't understand.' Alice shook her head. 'You didn't need to pretend to be friends with me to take everything, so why even bother? I could have caught you out at any time!'

'But you didn't. At least, not then.' She gave Alice a grin, wide and too familiar. 'I should have known that once you had a project, you wouldn't give up on it.'

Alice tensed. 'Don't do that.'

'What?'

'Act like you used to, like *her*. Ella Nicholls doesn't exist.'

Ella tilted her head slightly, studying Alice. 'Is that what you think — that it was all a lie?'

'Wasn't it?' Alice glared back.

'No. Not at all.' Ella gave a slow smile. 'The details, yes, but, everything else — the day-to-day stuff? That was real.'

Alice raised an eyebrow. 'And I'm supposed to believe that?'

Ella shrugged. 'Probably not. But, it's the truth. You think I could have kept up a complete fabrication for that long? God, Alice,' she laughed, 'I'm good, but I'm not that good.'

Alice stared across at her, suddenly lost. She'd been prepared for almost everything, but she hadn't thought of this. How could she get the answers she wanted, when she didn't know whether to believe a single word Ella said?

As if reading her expression, Ella reached across the table and took hold of Alice's hands. 'No bullshit, Alice; I'm telling you the truth. Why would I even bother lying any more?' Her gaze was direct and sincere. 'You found me, it's done. The least I can do is tell you what you want to know.'

Alice looked back, still uncertain. But what alternative did she have? She'd gathered every bit of data possible, studied the patterns and dates until there was nothing left to learn, but in the end, Ella's own words were the only thing that could give her some kind of explanation.

'Everything.' Alice replied at last. 'I want to know everything.'

34

They moved to a more discreet table along one of the balconies. Alice ordered a drink but left it untouched on the heavy white linen tablecloth between them. It was unnerving, how easy it was to look at Ella and think of her simply as the same friend she used to be. Even with the superficial changes in clothes and hairstyle, the other, deeper details hadn't altered — the way her nose crinkled when she smiled; the flash of her eyes as she followed the crowd; every unconscious expression and cadence to her voice.

Despite herself, Alice began to relax.

'So, where do you want me to start?' Ella casually crossed her legs, the way she had a dozen times back in London, before.

'The beginning,' Alice replied, meaning whatever had set Ella on this path of lies.

But instead, Ella said, 'OK, the yoga class.' She took a long breath, as if bracing herself. 'The first thing you need to know is, I didn't pick you out to target, not like the others. You have to believe me.' She fixed Alice with a plaintive stare. 'That was all accidental. I mean, we got talking, and it was fun, you know? I'd only just moved to London and become Ella, and, well, it was lonely.' She was picking up speed as she spoke, gaining confidence as the story came tumbling out. 'It was just so nice to be able to relax, and be myself — or, close to myself,' she added with a knowing grin. 'I had money from the last . . . projects, and to begin with, it really was just about being friends.'

'And then?' Alice asked, trying to stay unmoved even as Ella's words gave her a small measure of relief.

Ella sighed. 'Then I realised what a good prospect you were. The flat deposit sitting there, your savings, the credit record . . . I don't target people who'll find it hard to clear their names,' she added. 'If I start with someone with a perfect record, then it's easy for them to prove their innocence. The banks just refund everything.'

'That's your justification?' Alice asked, her voice rising. 'For everything you put me through?'

Ella shook her head quickly. 'No, that's not what I'm saying, I just . . . I don't know what I'm saying really. I never thought I'd have to explain this to you.'

They fell silent for a moment, the more sedate conversations of the diners nearby drifting around them in a low murmur.

'So, you decided I would be a good 'prospect'.' Alice prompted, reaching for her cocktail at last. The drink was too bitter, but Alice barely registered it; she just kept her gaze fixed on Ella.

She nodded. 'After that, well, it was simple really. The same thing I usually do, only easier this time because I had all the personal information.'

'My important document folder.'

'Exactly.' Ella exhaled. 'And then, it didn't

matter that I meant it, because I had to go, before the first bills started arriving and you realised something was wrong.'

Alice stared at her, waiting for more. None came. Was this it? She couldn't believe that the big explanation she'd been dreaming of had come down to such an underwhelming tale. Could it have really been so simple; not the scheming and secret plans she'd imagined?

Alice felt her hopes dissolve. Yes, Ella had been practised in her various criminal arts, that didn't make Alice's theft any more significant. It wasn't so special, after all.

She wasn't so special.

'You've been doing this a long time.' It was a statement, not a question. Alice took a long gulp from her drink. She felt disorientated, Ella almost shrinking in front of her until she was just a stylish woman with a wary look in her eyes. Not a criminal mastermind, or glamorous thief. Just, Ella.

'A girl needs a skill in life,' Ella quipped, almost bitter. 'Well, this is mine.' She paused. 'You didn't get in much trouble, did you? I figured somebody like you . . . you would get things straightened out pretty quickly.'

'Stefan got me a solicitor.' Alice finished her cocktail, plucking out the wedge of fruit that adorned its sugared rim. 'And an investigator too, to try and track down the money you stole. It was Nathan,' she added. 'The man from their anniversary party?'

Immediately, Alice regretted the remark. It was confidential, the sort of thing a friend would share, and sure enough, at the mention of him, Ella brightened. 'Really? How did that turn out?'

Alice carefully collected herself again. 'Well, he was useful when it came to bailing me out in Rome. Carina doesn't send her regards,' she added.

Ella looked astonished. 'You got arrested?'

'Everyone seems to find it amusing.'

'No, it's just . . . ' Ella looked at her more closely, 'you look different. You seem different too.'

'I've had a lot of life-changing experiences this summer,' Alice replied coolly. 'Carry on.'

Ella paused, looking uncomfortable. 'Then, well, you know the rest. I went to Rome, and then down the coast for a while under a different name, to put some distance between the identities. Then I flew here. I've been in town almost two months.' She looked up, 'How did you find me, anyway?'

'You weren't as clever as you thought you were.' Alice explained briefly about Rupert, and the Angelique connection.

'That's it?' Ella gave a wry laugh. 'It's always the unexpected things, I suppose. How is Rupert anyway?'

'Fine,' Alice replied, thrown by the genuine interest in her voice. 'He's in town actually, trying to find work. The usual audition circuit.'

'And Flora, and Julian?'

'They're all right too.' Alice watched her carefully, before adding, 'At least, Flora is. I haven't heard from Julian since the night he decided to hit on me.'

'No!' Ella snorted. 'Idiot.'

'Yes, well . . . ' Alice sighed. 'I quit the agency too. Not that I had much choice; Vivienne heard I was setting up here in LA and flew into quite a rage.'

'I wish I'd seen it,' Ella grinned.

Alice smiled back without thinking. Then she caught herself. This was the risk, she knew: to be lulled back into their casual banter as if nothing had ever happened. Already, she could see how easy that would be. After all, Ella was the same as she'd always been.

'So, what now?' Ella asked, uncertain, tracing circles on the tablecloth. 'Was it true what you said, about not calling the police?'

'Would you stay, if it wasn't?'

Ella glanced down. 'Probably not,' she admitted quietly. 'By now . . . I'm looking at a lot of time in prison. I won't stick around for that. But I want to.' She gave Alice a sad sort of smile. 'I like it here. I found a great apartment, and I've started some classes, to meet people — for real, not as targets,' she added quickly. 'I've even got a kitten. His name's Marmaduke.' She gave a doting smile.

'So you're planning on staying for good?' Alice was a little thrown. She'd been expecting a flimsy pretence of a life, just another name in Ella's ongoing charade, but instead it sounded as if she was laying genuine foundations here, something permanent.

Ella nodded. 'At least, I was. It all depends — '

She stopped, interrupted by an arm snaking

around her from behind and an enthusiastic kiss landing on her cheek. 'Angelique!'

They both started, but their new guest didn't notice. He beamed across at Alice from beneath an ill-fitting baseball cap before turning back to Ella. 'Great, you haven't been waiting on your own. I'm so sorry. They've been keeping me hostage at the gates all day. I had to call in back-up just to leave the house.'

He looked back and forth between them, waiting expectantly.

'Oh, sorry,' Ella finally said in a faint voice, 'this is, an old friend from home. Alice, meet Chris.'

'H-hi.' Alice was lost for words for a moment, staring into the chiselled features that had adorned many a billboard and magazine cover.

'Great to meet you.' Chris shook her hand enthusiastically. 'Anyway, we're all over at the bar, shall I get you some drinks?'

'Thanks,' Ella replied, her eyes not leaving Alice. 'We'll be over in just a sec. Girl-talk,' she added with a grin.

'Got it.' Chris winked, and then strolled off, apparently oblivious to the whispers and wide-eyed stares he left in his wake.

'You know *Chris Carmel*?' Alice asked in a hushed voice, the moment he was gone.

Ella gave a delighted grin. 'I know!' For a moment they were united in disbelief. 'We met in Italy, just hanging out by the pool one day. He's a great guy, really down to earth. Then I bumped into him again when I arrived in town.'

'By accident, or design?' Alice asked. Of

course: the photo at the hotel, that had pulled her even further down this path. She should have known an opportunist like Ella wouldn't have let the screen god simply pass her by.

Ella gave a guilty grin. 'Maybe I checked to see which parties he would be at. But it's not like that,' she added hurriedly. 'He's, you know, *gay*.' The last word was mouthed silently, with a careful glance around. 'Anyway, we were going to hang out tonight. There's a whole group, industry mainly, but some 'normal' people too. They're really nice.' She paused, giving Alice a hopeful look. 'Do you want to? It would just be dinner and then a club or something.'

Alice was lost for words. 'You're inviting me out to . . . party?' She had to check, just to be sure of Ella's nerve.

'We'll talk more later,' Ella promised brightly, then she snapped her fingers, struck with a new idea that, of course, had nothing to do with her guilty conscience and the trail of lies she'd left in her wake. 'Call Rupert, and have him come too. There are always all sorts of producers and casting people buzzing around Chris,' she added with a sage nod, as if she were already the agent she'd apparently been claiming. 'It could be a great chance for him to meet people, start making himself known.'

'Ella!'

Only moments ago, she'd been talking fearfully about prison, and now she wanted to go lounge around with movie stars? Alice couldn't believe the nonchalance.

'What?' Ella caught Alice's expression, quickly

adjusting her own enthusiasm down to a more serious tone. 'I know, we still have lots to talk about, but it's hardly as if I'm going to bolt now. This could be a great chance for Rupert, and you too,' she added, getting to her feet.

'You stole my identity,' Alice said slowly. 'They all think you're me.'

'No, they think I'm Angelique, and you're Alice. Simple.' Ella waited, expectant.

'Rupert knows that's my name, remember?'

Ella shrugged. 'So it's a huge coincidence! Our mothers must have been reading the same pretentious novels; it's easily explained.' She bounced on the spot. 'Come on, it'll be fun!'

Alice was still trying to understand this sudden switch when she looked up, catching the briefest look of desperation skitter across Ella's face. Then she understood, Ella was still absolutely terrified: of discovery, of the police, of having her golden little world here pulled apart — everything that Alice could do so easily, with just a single phone call. No wonder she was trying so hard to drag her off to the VIP section, Alice realised. She probably hoped that if she dazzled her with A-list friends and a riot of fun, Alice could be persuaded not to give her up.

'All right,' Alice decided. It was reassuring to know that she still had some small measure of power over Ella. And it was true, a part of her was curious to see this new life of hers up close. She got to her feet and gazed at Ella carefully. 'But we talk more later.'

'Absolutely,' Ella vowed. 'It's going to be fun, I promise!'

Alice was wound too tight with caution to enjoy herself, but as she lounged in the dim VIP section of an ultra-cool club, watching as Ella laughed and joked with Chris and his surprisingly genuine group of friends, she had to admit, it wasn't entirely bad. Seeing Ella in her element like this was almost reassuring. She seemed, to Alice, to be exactly the same person she'd been back in England, albeit with a different name, and new stories to tell her accomplished acquaintances. Ella, on the other hand, wasn't quite so relaxed: her gaze flicking over to Alice every few minutes, anxious, as if she expected her to stand up, and denounce her as an imposter at any second.

'What did you say your friend's name was?' Rupert leaned over, raising his voice to be heard over the DJ's eclectic mix of hip-hop and Broadway show tunes.

'Angela,' Alice said, deliberately muddying the word with a sip from her exquisite cocktail.

'Oh, great! She seems nice!' Rupert looked around, unable to keep the joyful expression from his face. He'd hit it off with Chris almost straight away, the pair of them diving into debate over some British comedy show, and soon Chris had been suggesting to Perry, his manager, and Cleo, one of his battalion of agents, that they set Rupert up with an audition for his upcoming vampire vs. zombie apocalypse movie sequel.

Rupert pushed back his flop of fringe. 'Did I say thank you enough already?'

Alice laughed, glad of his presence in the midst of all this uncertainty — a reminder of something honest. 'It was only a drinks invite. Besides, I wanted to see you while I was in town. This time,' she added quickly.

He shook his head, 'It's not just drinks, Alice, you know that. It's . . . access, exposure, getting seen by the right people.' Rupert nodded at the casual designer suits. 'I could never pull it off on my own. It's why I never got anywhere, back in England.

'But — '

'I know,' he cut her off, before she could object, 'good actors rise to the top, eventually.' He repeated the oft-spoken mantra. 'But, come off it, we both know that's not true. The ones who stay at the top, they're the good ones, yes, but plenty who manage to grab their way up there for a while are just better at playing these games.'

Alice gave his shoulder a supportive squeeze. She'd never been too comfortable amongst these sorts of people either, thinking herself too dull or sensible to blend with their outré lifestyles. But if there was one thing she'd learned from her brief spells as Angelique — and Juliet, and even Ella — it was that perhaps she wasn't that sensible after all.

'That's why you need one of these cut-throat agents,' she grinned, nodding around at the collection of fast-talking industry types with gleaming grins and a phone console never far from their fingertips. 'They play the game, so you don't have to.'

Rupert paused, drumming his fingers briefly on the tabletop. 'Actually, I've been thinking about that. I'd like you to do it for me. Be my agent, I mean,' he explained eagerly. 'If you want me as a client, that is. It just seems like perfect timing: you coming over here, right when I need you most. What do you say?'

Alice cringed under his hopeful gaze. 'I . . . I don't have enough experience yet,' she protested. 'I couldn't do you justice.'

'Not at all,' Rupert insisted. 'You know contracts inside out, and you're already introducing me to all the right people. What more is there?'

'I can't,' Alice apologised, busying herself with a napkin. 'I really — '

'Can't what?' Ella collapsed beside her with a breathless grin.

'Alice is refusing to represent me.' Rupert adopted a woeful expression.

'Why not? That's a great idea!' Ella exclaimed. Alice gave her a look.

'You know why not,' she said, keeping her voice measured. 'I'm . . . just starting out on my own. I wouldn't be up to the responsibility.'

'Nonsense,' Ella declared. 'Don't worry,' she told Rupert, 'she'll come round. She's just a little overwhelmed by the whole Hollywood thing.'

'Um, can I have a word?' Alice practically pushed Ella out of the booth and into a back hallway.

'What are you playing at?' she hissed, the moment a leggy blonde sashayed past them into the toilets. 'Fucking with everyone else may be

482

OK with you, but this is Rupert! He's a decent guy!'

'I know he is,' Ella protested, 'which is why I think you'd be the perfect agent for him.'

Alice sighed. 'In case you've forgotten, you're the one saying you're a hot-shot LA agent, not me.'

'So why don't you?' Ella folded her arms, a note of challenge in her tone.

Alice blinked. 'What?'

'Do it. Move here, agent — for real, I mean,' Ella insisted. 'We could set up together. I've been telling everyone about the Angelique Love Agency, so why don't we make it with the real Angelique Love Agency?'

Alice's mouth dropped open for what felt like the tenth time that day. 'Are you insane?'

Ella shrugged. 'I know, it's a crazy idea, but that's what makes it genius! You have the legal experience, I've been developing all the contacts . . .'

'Ella — '

'And the best part is, I've been registering everything in your name all along, so it wouldn't even be a lie.'

'Stop!' Alice cried. 'Just stop.' She caught her breath, waiting for a trio of girls draped in skin-tight denim and leather to giggle past before asking, 'Are you even listening to yourself? This is all lies, Ella, all of it. No, wait,' she corrected herself sarcastically, 'that's not your real name either.'

'So we make it true,' Ella said, her voice rising with a peculiar intensity. 'No more running, or

483

stupid cover stories; I'm telling you, it's perfect. I'll just take another surname, or say we're cousins — that would work, wouldn't it?' She looked at Alice, as if for approval. 'And you've quit the agency now, so why not take that leap to agenting you've always wanted?'

'I've *been* agenting,' Alice shot back. 'For the last month now, until Vivienne ruined everything, but you wouldn't know that, would you? Because you left!'

Ella stopped. She looked at Alice curiously. 'Is that what this is all about? You're mad at me for leaving? Because I am sorry for that. I didn't want to go.'

She said it as if she'd had no choice in the matter. Something in Alice snapped.

'No, Ella, I'm mad at you for lying, and cheating, and stealing my entire fucking savings!' Alice yelled, her voice ringing out in the small space. 'Oh, yes, and leaving too. God, I trusted you. How you could even think I'd let you keep playing this charade, let alone go into partnership with you?'

Ella fell silent for a moment. Then she looked over at Alice, almost nervous. 'So why haven't you told the police yet, if you hate me so much?'

Alice shook her head. 'I don't hate you,' she sighed. 'You just don't understand. All this time, I've been trying to figure out who you are. Why you'd do this to me. Months, going over every bloody receipt for some clue! I even — ' She broke off, about to mention the mess with Nadia, and her own forays into the world of aliases and impersonation.

484

'You even what?' Ella looked chastened, at least.

'Nothing.' There was no use. Ella didn't see how much she'd hurt her. That was the difference between them. 'But, you understand, don't you? Why this is ridiculous. I mean, Ella, when I think about everything I went through because of you, and here you are, barely pausing for breath between your glitzy parties and shopping sprees. Funded by loans in *my* name,' she added bitterly.

'You didn't have to pay for them,' Ella replied cautiously. 'You got everything back.'

'And that makes it all right?'

Ella paused, a stubborn look lingering on her face. 'Relatively, maybe.'

'Look,' Alice stopped her with a sigh, 'I'm not going to debate the morality of what you're doing. I mean, you've probably contributed more to the world than I have with all that charity.'

Ella looked up. 'You know about that?'

'I told you,' Alice said, with a pale smile, 'I tracked everything. Hazel was pretty pissed with you for leaving, but I said you had a sick relative. In Australia.'

Ella looked truly surprised. 'Oh. Thanks.'

They were silent again, nothing but the muffled thump of the bass between them. Alice felt a heavy pull of disappointment in her chest, where once excitement had been. All that clarity and closure she'd been so determined to find seemed just as far from reach as when she'd been an ocean away. Ella had nothing for her, after all, just a mismatched handful of justifications and excuses. It was as much as anyone could offer in support of their actions, she supposed, but Alice had expected more.

She'd needed more.

'Can I show you something?' Ella asked suddenly. 'We can go in my car. It wouldn't take long.'

Alice rolled her eyes. 'You've been drinking,' she pointed out. But something in Ella's expression made her pause. What else was she here for, if not to hear what she wanted to say? 'Fine.' Alice sighed, giving Ella a familiar look of reproach. 'I'll drive.'

35

The city at night was a stream of neon and headlights, the breeze warm through their windows. Ella directed her down a series of quiet side streets, skilfully avoiding the angry rush of the main freeways.

'What's this?' she asked, turning Alice's tiny console over in her hands.

'The GPS tracking on your car,' Alice replied, with a glimmer of a smile.

'Oh.'

No more was said for the rest of the journey to Santa Monica, until Ella instructed her to pull into a deserted parking garage, tucked under a stretch of modern offices and bathed in the pale glow of security lights.

'Let me guess,' Alice remarked drily, as she descended into the concrete basement. 'You're planning on killing me, hiding my body, and assuming my identity for real?'

'Darn,' Ella grinned. 'Foiled again.'

Alice parked beside the elevator exit, unnerved by the surroundings despite her joke. She lingered in the car, safe behind central locking.

'It's creepy, I know,' Ella agreed, looking around. 'I've watched far too many horror movies set in these places. Come on.' She led Alice to the lifts and rode to the third floor. 'There's a security guard at the front desk,' she said, as if to reassure herself or Alice, she wasn't sure. 'And it's much nicer in daylight.'

They stepped into an open-plan reception area, Ella flicking on lights as they went. 'It's sort of a collective office space, for several small businesses. There's a record label, and a digital media company, and a literary agency just up the hall.' She pointed out different offices as they passed, with frosted glass windows and gleaming desktop computers at every turn. 'The plan is to share a receptionist, switchboard, mail-room: all the basic admin roles. That way, costs are low, but each individual company stays professional and competitive.'

'Um, all right.' Alice looked around, still not sure what they were doing there. She had a sneaking suspicion it related to Ella's grand partnership proposal, but surely she hadn't been serious?

She was. Ella unlocked the last door, throwing it open proudly to reveal a large, L-shaped space with white walls, bare, wooden floorboards, and wide windows.

'Is that the ocean?' Alice asked, walking over and resting her forehead, cool against the glass. It was nothing more than a stretch of black beyond the cluster of lights, but she watched it none the less.

'What do you think? We wouldn't need a waiting area because of the reception out there, of course. So, this could be our office space. Or we could split it, for privacy. A wall here, maybe.' She paced the floor in illustration.

'You actually mean it.' Alice didn't know whether to laugh or sink to the floor, worn out.

She did the latter, stretching out flat on the smooth surface, enjoying the chill where it touched her bare skin. It felt as if everything was drifting away from her, here in the dull gleam of late night and bright golden lights: the expectations, all her fierce determination.

Whatever it was she'd needed so much from Ella, Alice knew now with absolute certainty she wouldn't get it.

'It's far-fetched, I know.' Ella took a seat, cross-legged next to her. 'But that doesn't mean it couldn't work.'

Alice could think of a hundred reasons why not.

'I can't trust you,' she started quietly, but even as she said the words, she felt the strange déjà vu of familiarity. It was like they were lounging back at her flat, or on Ella's living-room floor, after one too many glasses of wine. But those days were long behind them, and even if Alice had kept them in the back of her mind during all this tracking and trailing, they were empty memories of something past. She sighed, rolling her head to the side to look at Ella. 'Even if I understand how it all got out of hand, and you never meant to hurt me, I can't trust you.'

'Not yet,' Ella agreed, a note of optimism in her voice. 'But you could, with time.'

Alice looked at her. 'Is it my friendship you want, or just the guarantee I won't turn you in?' Ella made as if to protest, but Alice gave her a weary smile. 'Don't think I don't know what you're doing here, Ella. The more tangled up I get in this agency, and all your plans, the more trouble I'd get into if I ever revealed the truth. This isn't a partnership, it's an insurance policy.'

Ella paused, rueful. 'Can't it be both?'

Alice gave a tired laugh. The strange thing was, she didn't even blame her for trying. Ella was building a life here, after what had probably been years of fleeing from one fraud to another, so it was no wonder she was so eager to cling to everything she had.

'You know me,' she said, curious. 'You know I wouldn't agree to this, so why even bother asking?'

Ella looked at her carefully. 'I don't really, not any more. The Alice I knew would have sent the police straight for me. In fact,' she said, with a glimmer of a smile, 'the Alice I knew wouldn't have wasted her time trying to track me down. Can you really blame me for trying?'

Alice was silent. She had changed, of course, and perhaps not in the most law-abiding of ways, but setting up here with Ella seemed more concrete than any white lies and minor break-in.

'You'd like it here,' Ella said, still sounding hopeful. 'The weather is wonderful, for a start, and the men all adore the accent. We'd have fun.'

Again, the collective pronouns. But for all the time they'd spent together while Ella was in London, theirs had not been an enduring friendship, with history to cling to, like Alice had with Flora or even Cassie. In fact, Alice wondered with new clarity, if the end hadn't come with so much drama and confusion, would she feel such an emotional pull towards Ella at all?

She'd been chasing somebody — something — that didn't even exist.

'Think about it, at least?' Ella's control was clearly slipping. 'You're finished at the agency, you need a new job. It could be an adventure!'

Alice sighed. 'Ella . . . '

'I want to stay,' she said stubbornly. 'This time, I want my life to be something real.'

'Without earning it?'

Ella gave a sharp laugh. 'Who earns anything these days?'

'Then what's stopping you doing this with your own name? Your real one,' Alice tried, watching for any sign of emotion.

Ella just gave Alice a look, unreadable, but tinted with some defensive shell. 'That's not going to happen,' she replied, and her tone was so final, Alice knew it to be true.

'Then, I don't know what to say.' Alice looked around the polished room, bright from the spotlights, and full of potential. It would be fun here, in the sunshine — that much was true. And with Rupert already wanting her to represent him, and all the contacts she could make . . . She shook her head. 'It's late. I need to get some sleep.'

Ella looked at her, uncertain.

'We'll talk more tomorrow,' Alice reassured her, even though she had no idea what more could be said.

'And you'll think about it?' Ella helped her to her feet.

Alice nodded. However absurd Ella's plan, Alice could sleep on it, at least until she found some other solution. 'But can I even trust you not to run? This won't work if you're just going to bolt the minute my back is turned. The police dropped their enquiries ages ago,' she added, 'and nobody knows where you are.'

Ella nodded. 'I'm staying, I promise,' she vowed. 'I told you, I'm done with that. I want something normal, for a change.'

'You call the Hollywood Hills normal?' Alice mocked with a faint grin.

'Don't knock it,' Ella laughed, switching off the lights behind them and locking the doors up tight. 'I've got a view of the whole city.'

★　★　★

Alice dropped her back at the hotel to pick up her car, idling by the kerb for a moment as the late-night crowds on Sunset streamed past: hustling towards fast-food outlets or the impatient lines snaking outside every club. Above them, the Chateau Marmont's turrets glowed in their spotlights, towering over the boulevard like a film set plucked from a different era.

'Chris is having a brunch thing tomorrow,' Ella said, collecting her things. She gave Alice a hopeful smile. 'There's some kind of sports game on TV, but I usually just hang by the pool during all of that. Want to come to my place around eleven? He's sending a car for me, isn't that ridiculous?'

'All right,' Alice agreed slowly. 'My flight back isn't until Saturday.'

'Then I have time to talk you round,' Ella

grinned. 'I have excellent powers of persuasion.'

Alice smiled softly. 'I wouldn't bet on it.'

She drove back to her hotel deep in thought. Ella's proposition was ridiculous, of course, but there was a certain neat symmetry to it that Alice couldn't help but find appealing. Right then, their lives — and identities — were tangled in all kinds of difficult ways, and the challenge facing Alice now was how to extract herself from whatever world Ella had created, without jeopardising the contacts or reputation she'd managed to achieve, in Alice's name. Or was that Angelique?

She parked and strolled into the hotel. She would have to find some way of taking her identity back that didn't do Ella any harm. Despite everything, she was still loath to report her to the police, and if she —

Alice stopped, noticing a rather familiar body slumped on one of the couches in the lobby. He was unshaven and clearly jet-lagged, but her heart leaped just the same.

'Nathan?'

He jolted awake, blinking at her. 'Hey, there you are.'

'What are you doing here?' She took a step closer, reaching out a hand to help him up. He glanced around, disorientated, before turning back to her. Then he stopped, giving her one of those half-smiles that still did curious things to her.

'Looking for you. I figured you might want my help tracking Ella down.'

Alice looked up at him. 'But you said I had to stop.'

'Which would have been the sensible thing, sure.' He tugged her closer. 'But since you seem determined to find this woman . . . '

'I did.' Her reply was muffled as she pressed herself against his shirt. God, it felt good to be near him again. Bracing herself for disapproval, Alice closed her eyes and admitted, 'I spent the evening with her.'

Nathan exhaled, but Alice felt no tension in his movement. Instead, his tone was even. 'How did that work out for you?'

'No bloody idea.' Alice drew back and gave him a rueful smile. 'I'm sorry about the lies, I really am. But none of this was about you.'

'Yeah, that was kind of hard to take.' He held her close, resting his chin on the top of her head. 'So, how about we make more things about me? You know I crave the attention.' His tone was joking, but when Alice checked the look in his eyes, she saw that he was truly sincere. He meant this.

She smiled, realising what it must have taken for him to come all this way. She mattered to him, after all. 'I can definitely manage that. How does the rest of the week sound? You can help me decide what on earth I'm going to do about Ella.'

'I take it throwing her in jail isn't an option?' Nathan hoisted his bag up onto his shoulder. Alice laughed,

'I'm afraid not. But hey, you can use your imagination.'

'Great,' Nathan drawled. 'But when this is figured out, I want to get far, far away from her. I'm thinking a hammock somewhere . . . You in a tiny bikini . . . '

Alice raised an eyebrow. 'If it's really important to you, I'm sure I'll find the strength,' she grinned. She held out her hand, and he took it. 'I have to warn you, though,' she sighed, nudging him in the direction of the elevators. 'The beds here leave something to be desired.'

'I haven't slept in days; I'll be out in a flash.'

★ ★ ★

Despite her own hectic day, Alice only drifted in and out of sleep; watching Nathan's body beside her as dawn light began to seep into the room. He lay with one arm thrown across her, rolling to unconsciously mirror her position should she turn away.

So this was it.

Alice felt a slow warmth spread through her that had nothing to do with the sun spilling through the ugly curtains, or the heat gently radiating from Nathan's bare skin. This was what she'd been watching all these years, the intimacy to which she'd only ever been a spectator. He was hers, enough to come all this way for her, at least, and stay — not because he agreed with what she was doing, but because he'd thought that she might need him. She watched him shift, stretching as he woke.

He yawned. 'Man, you were right about this mattress.'

Alice smiled as he tugged her closer. She rested her head on his chest, tracing slow circles above his heart.

'So what's the plan for today?' he asked, the words vibrating gently against her.

'I'm meeting Ella,' she ventured, but aside from a slow exhale, Nathan didn't offer any argument. Alice pulled away slightly, so that her face was on the pillow next to his, just inches away.

'And?'

This time, she was the one to sigh. 'And . . . I don't know. She doesn't have any answers for me,' Alice admitted.

'I'm sorry.' Nathan gave her a faint smile. He reached over, toying with loose strands of her hair.

'Sure you are.' Alice lightly replied.

'No, I am. I know you wanted . . . something from her.'

Alice gave a rueful shrug. 'But it doesn't work like that, does it?'

Nathan was the rare exception, but Alice knew the truth: people didn't come through with the answers or explanations that would make everything all right. She still hadn't heard a word from Julian about his drunken advances, and some painful instinct told Alice that even if he did try now, it was already too late. Just like that, a friendship could be over; and equally fast, something new could be forged.

But what of Ella now?

'I can't report her,' Alice said, still almost whispering in the stillness of the early morning.

'I can't be the one to send her to prison. It's just so extreme.'

'So what will you do? You have to end this somehow,' Nathan pointed out, serious, 'before she gets you in real trouble again.'

Still, Alice didn't have a solution. 'She has a life here,' she told him, a little wistful. 'A flat, and a kitten . . . I'm meeting her friends, for brunch.'

'Maybe there's another way,' he suggested. 'I'll look into it.'

'I thought you didn't break the rules.'

He leaned closer, kissing her softly. 'Let's just say we're bending them.'

* * *

Alice left Nathan sleeping again and drove the route to Ella's from memory, stopping at that hippie café for muffins and coffee.

'Ella?' Juggling the bakery bag and cardboard cups, Alice pushed through the open front entrance and tapped at the door to the ground-floor apartment. 'Ella, let me in, I come bearing caffeine.'

There was no reply.

Alice was just about to bang harder, when she noticed a pale blue envelope taped to the door frame, her name written on the front in Ella's familiar scrawl. It held a single sheet of paper and a set of keys. She knew in that moment what it meant, and that Ella — whatever her real name — was already long gone, but still Alice unlocked the door, set her things down, and began to read.

I'm sorry.
I know I promised not to run, but I can't risk it, not now that you've found me. I don't know where we'll go yet, but I'll be fine, I always am.

Alice stopped. She checked the apartment quickly, but the wardrobe was empty, and all Ella's personal possessions gone. There was no sign of the kitten either, and outside, the driveway was empty.

Wandering back inside, Alice stood in the middle of the polished floor, the slip of paper in her hand. She kept reading.

The apartment is yours, so is the office. The leases are in your name anyway, for the next six months. There's a bank account too, if you want it. I left a file by the fridge with all the ID and documents. If not, then there's a shelter downtown that always needs the money. Maybe you could volunteer there too. I was going to start next week.
I really am sorry it turned out like this.
I suppose I just can't help it in the end.
X

She was gone.

Alice lowered the letter, looking around her as if for the first time. The apartment was old but charming, with bare floors and large windows, a blue-tiled kitchen area, and a large bedroom with fresh linens stacked at the end of a wrought-iron bed. Outside, she could see a square of overgrown garden, dense and green with bushes and even a few fruit trees.

It was hers.

The file of documents was where the letter said: a fake driving licence sitting next to Alice's original birth certificate, bank details, and a half-finished application for citizenship. And stacked neatly beside them all was a small pile of business cards, elegant in a simple charcoal script.

Angelique Love, Agent.

Taking her coffee, Alice drifted out to the back porch and settled on the old wooden love-seat, reading the brief note again. Ella had been right about the view. The city sprawled below her in a neat grid, sun falling on Alice's bare shoulders with a warmth that was unimaginable for this time of year, back in England.

She could get used to this.

Alice stretched. Chris's car would arrive soon, and she would have to fabricate an apologetic excuse for Ella's sudden departure, but that would be no trouble. An ill relative back in England, perhaps. They would all be sympathetic, and pass on their best, and soon — all too easily — Ella would be forgotten.

There was an irony to it, Alice knew — the ease with which she could slip into this life. If she chose.

The day stretched before her, full of promise. There would be a delicious brunch with Chris and his friends, and that midday swim; then the afternoon with Nathan, lounging perhaps on the beach — or in bed. She should really start to call those casting agents too, and set up some auditions for Rupert . . .

Alice stretched out in the sun, closed her eyes, and enjoyed the possibilities.

THE END

We do hope that you have enjoyed reading this large print book.

Did you know that all of our titles are available for purchase?

We publish a wide range of high quality large print books including:
Romances, Mysteries, Classics
General Fiction
Non Fiction and Westerns

Special interest titles available in large print are:
The Little Oxford Dictionary
Music Book
Song Book
Hymn Book
Service Book

Also available from us courtesy of Oxford University Press:
Young Readers' Dictionary
(large print edition)
Young Readers' Thesaurus
(large print edition)

For further information or a free brochure, please contact us at:
Ulverscroft Large Print Books Ltd.,
The Green, Bradgate Road, Anstey,
Leicester, LE7 7FU, England.
Tel: (00 44) 0116 236 4325
Fax: (00 44) 0116 234 0205

Other titles published by
The House of Ulverscroft:

MAYA

Alastair Campbell

Maya Lowe is one of the world's biggest movie stars. Steve Watkins is her life-long friend. Both swear their relationship hasn't changed since they shared a school desk as London teenagers. But can a friendship like theirs really survive a fame as great as Maya's? Can a man like Steve, working away for a Heathrow logistics company, seriously remain part of her life? He certainly thinks so. But amid the twists and turns of Maya's public and private lives, the gulf between what Steve thinks and what is actually true gets ever wider. And in a world where the obsession with celebrity seems to make everyone want to be one, truth is hard to find.